PROMISE

OF THE

WARRIOR

Mortality – BOOK 1

Tejas Narayan
Aditya Kumaran

INDIA · SINGAPORE · MALAYSIA

Notion Press

Old No. 38, New No. 6
McNichols Road, Chetpet
Chennai - 600 031

First Published by Notion Press 2020
Copyright © Tejas Narayan & Aditya Kumaran 2020
All Rights Reserved.

ISBN 978-1-64805-909-4

Contents

For all the kids out there that still read: hopefully our world will inspire you to discover your own.

Prologue

The Flaming Crags

The full moon's rays lit up the whole pond as they struck its tranquil waters.

Half of her face hidden in shadow, a girl of nine, maybe ten, gazed across the pool in wonder at the stillness of its surface. Furrowing her brow in confusion, she knelt to take a second drink, to see if the ripples would vanish as quickly as the first time, but just before her fingers could touch the water, she jerked her hand back.

The glow. She could just barely make it out, the distant light at the bottom of the deep pond, but as she continued to watch, the deep blue of… whatever was down there became overwhelming enough that even her face was illuminated. But even though the water was perfectly tranquil, she could still easily see a dancing array of light and dark cast onto her faded brown tunic.

As though prompted this time not by thirst but by something beyond her own consciousness, she reached out again, desperate to touch whatever was creating this magical light. Whispers echoed around her, louder as her fingertips neared the glassy pool.

Then the glow became a blaze, and the light enveloped her.

The girl screamed, the sound of her voice reverberating again and again across the mountainside, and she pressed her hands to her ears as though it would drown out the world and kept screaming until her voice cracked and she couldn't find it in her to keep going any longer. Yet, even as the sound of her terror faded, the echoes persisted, becoming louder and louder until they morphed into the cry of a young man.

In an instant, the light faded, and with it, dissolved the girl's body until she was nothing more than a shadow, present but spectral. The man she had heard was breathing hard, one hand braced against the stone of the earth beside the pool, gazing up desperately at something glowing above the water so brightly that his whole face was illuminated. A rich, deep voice tinged with melancholy rang out, not around her this time, but within her very thoughts.

Aeyó veralta'an aí Inthyl, il-cindria endíya etoraí.

She tried to scream again, but her voice wouldn't work. Her voice wasn't even *there*.

The man's light-gray eyes widened, and the girl could make out his pointed ear tips, his flowing, black robes, his long, dark hair. Then, in an instant, the gray shifted to a piercing blue, the face of an armored youth taking shape in a dimly lit, stone-walled corridor.

Reitur'an verár irlo kaeryx aí aeleor.

Even though the girl couldn't move, the boy seemed to notice her, the sword in his hand lighting up the same color as the glow of his eyes as he strode with cruel purpose towards her vantage point. The blue aura surrounding the boy intensified before a shadow was cast over him, and he was standing among two others, surrounded by darkness, and the silhouette of a giant bird passed over them.

Ólo serelae'an ennara'an irvë rautalé'an aí yarívë.

The scene shifted, and she saw an ornately dressed man standing in a high-vaulted room of marble, while an old, armored dwarf watched him across the large oaken table, a scroll laid out messily before him. Again, the girl tried to maneuver her way to get a better look at the document but was once more bound in place by invisible chains.

Aëto nórya'an valera foraíya ver'an aí dímorë.

In an instant, the pair blurred together, the walls shook, and the torchlight of the room was snuffed out. A massive, jet-black wolf charged past her, leaping up and burying its claws into the throat of an impossibly large bear. Though the dark-brown beast dwarfed its assailant, it had clearly received a fatal wound.

A voice rang out in the girl's mind, not unlike the first one she had heard, but resonating with anger instead of sorrow. *Murderer! You have doomed us all!*

Snarling, the wolf stepped closer, and a third voice emerged, so spiteful and menacing that it made the girl want to collapse in terror. *Enough of your twisted lies, old one. You will pay for what you have done. You all will.* Then in a single motion, it slashed down, ripping the bear apart from head to toe, before a falcon so immense that it blotted out the sun descended over all of them. Its pitch-black eyes were narrowed in anger as it descended to face the wolf.

Irvë alatír aí tar'lenos melentó'an averár.

The falcon's eyes fixed on the girl, just before its face split into millions of facets, blazing red, as a massive crimson jewel moved away from her. Suspended in the air in a black, stone room, the crystal flared up as a man of maybe twenty knelt before it, murmuring words in a strange tongue. As he spoke, the engravings around the room began to burn the same vermilion as his robe, and suddenly, the floor was littered with corpses.

Ara aerhodion yanórwë teralí irvë íronna'an.

The man and the crystal melted into the ground, the room reforming into the slope of a mountain, and as the girl's point of view moved closer to the bodies, she could see that the corpses, each shot cleanly through one eye, had no pupils.

This time, when she screamed, her voice came out as it normally did, echoing around the mountains as she scrambled away from the pool before crumpling to the ground, lost in tears. She was so absorbed in her own shock and terror that she didn't even notice the footsteps behind her. Not until she looked up did she recognize the tall, red-robed man from the room with the strange carvings, but... younger, barely more than a boy. And in his left hand, shaking ever so slightly, he bore a dagger raised above her head.

Chapter 1

The Marshmallow Roast of Death

North Aenor

Asten

Asten's backpack was really becoming a pain.

It shouldn't even have weighed as much as it did to begin with. All Asten had packed was a week's ration of food, a roughly sewn waterskin, a small iron knife, and a coil of rope. Actually, he had taken care to avoid carrying too much. But taking turns toting Erluc's pack for four days hadn't done much for his back.

What was worse was that Erluc had packed a mountain of provisions he thought he might need to settle in Inthyl until he found a line of work. Unlike Asten, he'd decided that it would be smarter to not assume sources of food, water, or other supplies would last over the next few weeks. But as much as Asten's shoulders hurt, the relative quiet was worth the burden. He didn't mind the extra weight, and anything was better than having to listen to Erluc complain for the remainder of their journey across the barren, desolate plains of North Aenor.

Even though they hadn't come across much vegetation so far, there were patches of shrubs and occasional thickets of trees owing to the presence of the Amrast Delta. They had tried to follow these thickets; the shade provided some relief from the heat during day and shelter during the night.

He glanced up at Erluc for a moment, watching his friend's eyes fixed on the horizon. Standing almost as tall as Asten, if a little less lanky, Erluc's skin was a light olive as compared to his own frosty pale. His features were a little more filled out, less angular than Asten's, and his hair was a dark brown instead of Asten's black.

Fingering the thin steel chain around his neck, Asten kicked a stone forward a few yards, watching it tumble into the sparse grass. Suddenly, Erluc elbowed his arm, not helping to ease the pressure of the straps on his shoulder. "Check it out, a horse!"

Without looking up, for the eighth time that day, Asten rolled his eyes. *Not this again.* "Of course. And it's green and has wings, doesn't it?"

Erluc smirked, sensing an opportunity. "Green and has wings?" he echoed, a small smile appearing on his face.

Realizing a moment too late what he'd done, Asten wiped a bead of sweat off of his brow. "That was *one time*," he complained. "Besides, you almost drank as much as she did."

"Sure." Erluc laughed. Asten rolled his eyes, and Erluc threw his hands up in a show of defeat. "Alright, I'll drop it. But I still think we ought to check it out."

Raising an eyebrow, Asten finally looked up. It turned out that Erluc was, in fact, telling the truth. *Had to happen sometime.* Two horses were grazing, maybe a hundred fifty yards ahead; one glossy jet black, the other storm gray. "At least some good meat will come from those." He shrugged.

"If we get a little closer, I think I can hit them with the knives."

"Oh, please." Erluc held a hand in front of Asten, forcing him to stop. "You couldn't hit water if you were drowning in the river." And although that wasn't entirely true, Asten had nearly drowned in the River of Fire countless times. He'd eventually come to the decision to avoid jumping into large bodies of water.

With a sigh, he let the packs' straps slip through his fingers, the leather bags dropping like rocks into the dust. "Is that a challenge?"

Erluc sighed, evidently disappointed at having to forsake a rare chance for entertainment. "Maybe another time. But it'll take another two and a half weeks to reach Inthyl at the least. If we manage to tame these horses, we should be able to do it in about a week." He gestured at Asten's pack. "You're nearly out of supplies anyway."

"Alright." Asten grinned slyly, sliding away from the other boy. "I'll race you for the black one!" Dodging Erluc's extended leg, he pulled a carrot out of his meager store of food, turned to face the horse, and began to run.

His light sandals crunched in the coarse dust with each step, and the gentle breeze against his face felt stronger.

Slowing down now, Asten began to approach more cautiously, taking one tentative step after another. The stallion, now fully aware of him, began to snort and rear angrily. If Asten ran now, he would definitely be trampled within seconds.

If he died now, he was going to kill Erluc. Trying not to look scared, Asten closed the last few yards, carrot outstretched, fingers drawn back to avoid being bitten.

CRACK.

Suddenly Asten's ribs were on fire, and he was somehow flying backwards into a tree. He smashed into the wood, lightning coursing up and down his spine. Vision blurred, he vaguely heard Erluc yelling his name and saw him hurling his knife at the stallion and missing spectacularly.

Asten hoisted himself up, almost screaming in pain, and dragged himself to his pack, which lay forgotten a few yards away. Erluc, meanwhile, had retrieved his dagger and was slashing wildly at the great beast to keep it at bay, but he was clearly fighting a losing battle.

As his shaking fingers closed on the strap of his pack, Asten tried desperately to untie the knot holding it shut. But it was no use—the agony had rendered his coordination hopeless. After a few more frustrated attempts, he pulled out his dagger and severed the leather cord after two or three sloppy strokes. The pain had almost become bearable now.

Some distance away, Erluc had been forced to the ground and was now rolling to avoid being crushed. He wasn't going to last long.

With all the strength he could muster, Asten croaked, "Over here!" and flung a rock at the horse, giving Erluc time to scramble to his feet. Even though the stone was disappointingly off-target, his yell had apparently gotten the beast's attention. As the stallion turned, Asten pulled the coil of rope out of his pack.

When the horse charged, he was ready. Ribs flaring up in pain, he grabbed the stallion's neck and swung up onto its back. A lifetime of experience served him well as he swung the rope around so he was holding either side, with the middle wrapped around the horse's jaw. After knotting the rope deftly, Asten was able to tie it around twice more for safety before he was thrown off by the wild beast. As he struck the ground, his ribs screamed in protest.

But this time, adrenaline pushed him to his feet. The pain dulled, and his mind set with an unnatural determination. Drawing his knife once more, he stepped forward and prepared to hurl the blade at the majestic stallion. He had failed, and the beast's defiance left him no choice but to kill it for meat. He aimed the knife carefully, then swung his arm over and released. Perfect. The horse wouldn't feel a thing.

Suddenly, the stallion sank to its knees, reaching for the carrot Asten had dropped when it had kicked him. The dagger whizzed harmlessly overhead.

Unable to grasp the carrot through the makeshift muzzle, the horse bowed its head in defeat. Once the immediate danger was gone, Asten's vision blurred, and he slumped, exhausted. He vaguely saw Erluc rushing towards him, yelling, rummaging in his pack as he ran before everything turned to darkness.

He woke to the sight of the sun low in the sky, groaning. "How long was I out?" he asked, sitting up.

Erluc turned to face him and grinned. "Two hours or so. Here, eat something." He ripped an uneven hunk of bread from the loaf in his hands and tossed it to Asten, who bit into it gratefully.

Asten gestured to the black stallion that was trying to wear out the rope by rubbing its muzzle against a nearby tree. "You didn't untie the horse?"

"Not yet." Erluc shrugged unapologetically. "I was a bit busy making sure you hadn't gotten a concussion."

Rolling his eyes, Asten took another bite from the loaf. "Where's my knife?"

"Here." Erluc slid it over the grass, and Asten hastily picked it up. He rose unsteadily to his feet, wincing as his ribs objected. "Easy." Erluc quickly lent him a hand for balance. "Don't exert yourself too much."

"Everything hurts," grumbled Asten.

Erluc grimaced. "You might have fractured a rib, and most of the others are quite badly bruised," he said, ripping off a piece of bread for himself. "Maybe let me do the taming next time." Asten snorted, almost choking on his last bite. As usual, his friend was completely unharmed. He seemed to have tamed the gray horse without so much as a scratch. Maybe Erluc wasn't exactly brawny, but he had considerable strength for his frame, and it had certainly proved an advantage on this occasion.

Asten staggered to the horse and cut the muzzle. The beast promptly picked up the carrot off of the grass next to it and swallowed it. Shaking his head, he leaned toward the stallion, whose loathing for him seemed to have faded somewhat. "You aren't so bad, are you, you little nightmare?" Turning to his friend, he continued. "What do you think, Erluc? Ought we to name them?"

"I think… that's a colossal waste of time."

"So what?" Asten shrugged. "It's not like we have anything better to do." Patting his stallion's neck, he declared, "Isn't that right, Nightmare?"

The horse simply huffed, uninterested, and the corner of Erluc's mouth twitched. "Sounds about right."

"You sure you're not going to name yours?"

Erluc shook his head, relaxing back onto a patch of grass. "You can do the honors if you like," he yawned.

Brightening up, Asten turned to the gray horse, frozen in thought. "Lightning? Mistfoot? Cyclone?" he proposed, looking to Erluc for approval. He spouted a few more names before Erluc held up a hand to silence him, rubbing his forehead in annoyance.

"You know what, I think I'll just name the horse myself," he sighed, and Asten threw a fistful of grass at his friend, who chuckled, brushing the thin blades out of his hair. Turning to the stallion, he narrowed his eyes. "What do you think?"

The stallion neighed suddenly, and both Asten and Erluc jumped backwards, howling with laughter. Putting a hand on the trunk of a tree, Erluc steadied himself as he recovered, and a name finally occurred to him.

"Skyblaze," he decided. "I'll call him Skyblaze."

"Not bad." Asten nodded in appreciation, crossing his legs as he settled on the ground. "I still prefer Nightmare, though," he added with a shrug. "Skyblaze is a bit too grandiose."

Erluc shrugged. Looking out at the pair of stallions, he grimaced. "For wild horses, they were surprisingly easy to tame. Well, *mine* was, anyway."

"I suppose," mused Asten, lapsing into silent thought as he cleaned his knife. "Maybe they escaped from somewhere."

Erluc retrieved the odds and ends that had spilled out of Asten's satchel when he had cut the strap. After dumping them in a pile at his feet, he sat down in the dirt and started rearranging his belongings. "Could have."

They continued their preparations for the rest of the trip, talking the whole time. Erluc had included a few skins of leather in his immense pack, so Asten fished them out, cut them carefully with a practiced hand, and was ready with a rudimentary saddle for Erluc half an hour later.

Uncertain about what to do with the saddle, Erluc picked it up and turned it over in his hands repeatedly. Sighing, Asten showed him how to fit it on his gray horse as well as he could without further aggravating his ribs.

Looking around, Asten stopped, pointing ahead of them. "Do you see that?"

Erluc squinted at the horizon. "I see *something*. What is it?"

"Looks like a village," guessed Asten tentatively. The dusk light was as beautiful as it was feckless, and they could barely even make out the shape of the settlement. "If we leave now, we should be able to make it there before nightfall."

Erluc gestured towards Nightmare. "You aren't going to make yourself a saddle?"

"We don't have enough leather. It's fine. I can manage. For once, it's good that you overpacked, I suppose." Erluc snorted and mounted Skyblaze. Asten clambered up carefully and got a purchase with the reins around Nightmare's neck as quickly as possible without aggravating his damaged ribs.

They resumed their conversation as they set off once again, wondering about the unforeseen glories of their new life in Inthyl. "I've heard that Inthyl's royal stables can house up to a hundred horses," said Asten, doing his best not to slip off. Thankfully, Nightmare's walking was nearly as smooth as a trained horse's, aside from the occasional twitch or jerk. *If I didn't know better, I'd have thought these horses came straight from a stable.*

Erluc smirked. "I'd hate to be the one that has to clean them." Behind them, the Diamond River roared through a deadly rapid, the mist forming a rainbow in the setting sun. Suddenly, Erluc jerked forward as Skyblaze slipped over an uneven surface. Asten did his best to hold back a laugh.

Erluc had ridden a horse only on a handful of occasions, all passing without any explicit indication of progress. Asten, on the other hand, had years of equestrian experience to aid him. "Hunting was always more your thing, wasn't it?" he teased, knotting his hands in Nightmare's dark mane.

Erluc ignored him. "So what? You want to be a stable boy again?"

Asten shrugged. "I'm not sure yet. We have roughly enough savings for a week's lodging, and by then, one of us should've found a job."

Sighing, Erluc looked up at the first stars shimmering to life. "We'll cross that bridge when we get there." They continued their journey in relative silence, both of them exhausted from the past few days of travel.

As they rode on, Asten watched the lengthening shadows of Nightmare and Skyblaze on the ground, the last rays of sunlight highlighting the lingering dust in the air. That's all this place is, he almost said aloud. Dust and smoke. If North Aenor had ever been any more than hell to anything that didn't appreciate starving to death, those days were long gone. That was why he and Erluc had even decided to travel to the southern city of Inthyl: a life free from famine, raiders, and more famine had been an attractive package for both of them.

He squinted up at the village again; by this time, it was in clear view, close enough for him to just barely make out the thin spiral of smoke rising up into the evening sky. Erluc seemed to have noticed it as well, and the sight was clearly unsettling him. Shifting in his saddle anxiously, he looked up to meet Asten's eyes. "You know what, I've changed my mind. Let's camp outside the village tonight."

Asten frowned in surprise. "The place is right there. We need provisions, water, and shelter for the night."

"*You* need provisions. *I* packed everything I need."

"Oh, okay." He grimaced. "Guess I'll just starve then."

Erluc rolled his eyes. "You can share some of my stuff."

"Gee, thanks." Fighting a smile, Asten refocused on the problem at hand. "But we still need shelter. We can't just make camp in the middle of nowhere and expect to wake up unscathed. North Aenor is a dangerous place to be at night, with all the dark elven raids and whatnot."

Erluc sighed. "We *live* in North Aenor. But as long as we stay out of sight, we'll be fine. The village, on the other hand, is a target."

"A target for what?"

"You just said it—raiders. With that smoke, the village is a beacon for miles around."

"The smoke isn't visible in the night—"

"Or the village could be calling for help. In which case there might already be dark elves nearby," he said with finality. Asten nearly sighed aloud at his friend's stubbornness. There was no way that Erluc was going anywhere near those creatures. Each of the tales about them was more terrifying than the last.

The dark elves lived far to the North, in the Grônalz Mountains. A fearsome community of merciless raiders, they answered to no one, plundering villages and towns across North Aenor and leaving little but ashes. For hundreds of years, at least, they had been a constant threat to the villagers, most of whom lived in an endless struggle for survival. It was no surprise, then, that the northern half of the kingdom saw few immigrants.

And although Erluc wasn't one to be scared by far-fetched, fantastic tales of monsters, he wasn't about to ignore what was in front of his eyes either. Seven years earlier, the dark elves had attacked Jarcuth, a town that once lay on the banks of the River of Fire, some ways southeast of his and Asten's home village of Sering. After completely ransacking the town, the raiders had burned it to the ground.

They left behind no survivors.

Erluc had lost two cousins, as well as his aunt and uncle. And though he'd been too young to remember, Asten could've sworn that he had seen flames rising up from the remains of Jarcuth.

"I don't think I have to remind you about the ruthlessness of the dark elves," finished Erluc. Grimacing, Asten clutched the blood-red crystal that hung at the base of his neck.

About a division—seventy-three days—after Jarcuth burned down, they'd gone to explore its ruins. Obviously, they weren't trying to find anything substantial, but it was there that they'd stumbled upon the fiery jewel. Erluc hadn't thought much of it, but Asten had held on to the gem ever since that day, never letting it out of his sight.

"The smoke doesn't necessarily mean anything important," maintained Asten. "I mean, it's probably just a marshmallow roast." Erluc yawned drowsily, clearly fighting to stay awake. Arguing was always the most time-consuming thing that they did, and it was getting very old very fast.

"Fine," he finally conceded. "Let's sleep outside, behind these rocks. That's fairly sheltered. Go in and get what you need, then meet me back here in an hour." He stared off into the distance, wiping the sweat from his brow. "I don't know… there's something off about this." The persistent breeze they had experienced all day was rapidly growing into a strong wind, howling into the night. As if in response, the smoke too was thickening, making it nearly impossible to see the twinkling stars over the village.

Asten shrugged, adjusting himself on his horse.

"Watch the ribs," added Erluc, with a reluctant smile. Nodding, Asten lightly slapped Nightmare's flank and rode towards the collection of low-roofed buildings.

By the time he arrived at the village, the sun had set completely, and the smoke had thickened. He could see a curl of fire now, and he heard faint shouting in the distance.

What's happening?

He clutched the reins tightly, tentatively urging Nightmare forward. *It's okay. They're just having a celebration.* His attempts at self-reassurance weren't nearly as convincing as he'd hoped, and even the horse was starting to feel something eerie about the place.

Above him, the smoke curled around the moonlight, and Asten took a deep breath. Maybe Erluc was right. Besides, he wasn't even that hungry anyway.

Just as he began to turn around, Nightmare collapsed, a black shaft protruding from his flank. Undaunted, Asten clumsily leaped off and started to run, when an inferno seemed to burst out in his bicep, just above the elbow, and he crashed to the ground. The impact knocked the wind out of him, and his damaged ribs screamed in protest. With a supreme effort of will, he braced his arms underneath him in an attempt to force himself to his feet, but he crumpled again, feeling the rough surface of burlap against his cheek. He watched the flame cover his eyes, covering everything.

Chapter 2

Terrors of the Night

North Aenor
Erluc

What is taking you so long?

As far as Erluc could tell, Asten had been gone for almost two hours now. Frustrated, he looked to the skies, but the stars were veiled by shadow that moonless night, and he could see nothing. On any other day, he'd have gladly accepted a clouded, barren sky. But at the moment, he needed the stars to keep him company, and if they were gone, then he really was alone.

What could be taking Asten so long? Over the past hour, the smoke had steadily thickened from a faint wisp to a black, billowing pall that almost completely obscured the sky.

He shook his head. It took a special kind of idiot to ride into something like that. Nothing, not even marshmallows, was worth risking an encounter with dark elves.

And it wasn't like Asten to keep him waiting. Erluc himself was somewhat cloudier when it came to staying on time—especially if there were girls involved—but Asten didn't even have that problem. No, his best friend had a strict moral code. Unless he was occupied in a rousing discussion about the history of the Mortal Realms, there really was nothing that could have kept him engaged this long.

Sighing, he reluctantly kicked the ground, throwing the dust scattered across the wasteland onto the dwindling fire he had set up between the rocks. Almost longingly holding his hands over the dying embers one last time, he shook his head and slung his pack over his shoulder. Never once taking his eyes off the smoke rising from the collection of huts, he clambered up on Skyblaze, spurring him toward the village, pleasantly surprised at the fluidity of the wild horse's response.

Following the coal-black mass of smog downwards, he squinted and was just able to make out a rich orange glow between the houses. As he approached, he could hear the faint echoes of screams, and finally, the telltale crackle of an insatiable fire.

Asten!

In the background, the blast of a horn startled Skyblaze, forcing Erluc to lean and shift wildly to avoid being thrown off. A second, richer horn roared in response. Erluc frowned in confusion and then gritted his teeth. Drawing his dagger, he coaxed his horse into the flames.

"Asten?" he called, turning into another street. "Asten!" With his knife, he cut a strip of cloth from his tunic and tied it around his nose and mouth. His eyes stung from the ash and the searing heat. Despite the loud shouting, Erluc couldn't see anyone, not even terrified villagers trying to escape the burning wrecks.

There! Nightmare lay wounded at the end of the filthy alley. But, as Erluc spurred his own steed toward it, a burning hut collapsed into the road, sealing it off.

Swearing, Erluc doubled back, hunting for another path into the secluded lane. The horn blew again, more loudly this time, and an armored rider swerved into his path, wielding a vicious spear with a twisted, black head.

Through his makeshift mask, Erluc grimaced. Despite his own respectable strength, he was no match for an armed warrior. He urged his horse back into the blocked road, then doubled back again, trying to dart past the raider, but he was a second too slow. The man swept his spear around even as Erluc turned back, knocking him off of Skyblaze. And for the first time, Erluc got a good view of his face.

Although the man was, for the most part, humanoid, the skin was deathly pale, and his lips drawn back in a snarl, revealed his pointed teeth. But most unnervingly, when Erluc looked in his eyes, he saw no pupils—only dark-green irises. Even though he had never seen one before, he knew he was looking at a dark elf.

A second horn blasted, and green-cloaked riders swarmed into the street where Erluc lay still, not daring to move for fear of being skewered by the spear. Gleaming lances in hand, the riders rode past the scene, and one broke out of formation to impale the elf threatening Erluc.

As the elf's body fell to the ground, Erluc scrambled to his feet, searching for Skyblaze. Still winded, it took him a minute before he mounted his horse and rode back into the street where he had seen Asten's steed. The horse itself was dead, an arrow sticking through its ribs, while Asten's pack lay forgotten on the ground. Erluc kicked the roughly sewn bag of leather in frustration.

Asten wasn't here. *Either he'd made a break for it, or…*

In the corner of his eye, a small flash caught his attention, and he saw a small, red gemstone gleaming near the burning remains of a house. Scrambling forward, he grabbed the gem, paling as it confirmed his feeling of dread. Asten would never leave this behind.

In the distance, he saw the dark elven band fleeing from the village's mysterious rescuers.

…or they've taken him.

Tucking the gem into his own pack, he turned Skyblaze towards the dark elves, intending to pursue them as far as they were prepared to go, before he regained mastery over his wits and brought the stormy-gray stallion to a halt.

If he caught up to the raiders, what would he do then?

He couldn't exactly sneak up on them and snatch Asten out from right under their nose, and maybe charging in and threatening them with a worn iron knife wasn't going to go quite as he hoped, either. He needed help—preferably from steel-clad mounted warriors who had just effortlessly routed the dark elven raiding party.

Maybe.

Instead of continuing to tail the elves, Erluc instead tugged the reins to the right, guiding Skyblaze in the direction of the steadily rising moon, after the riders who were making astonishingly good pace towards the Howling Wood. That's what the people of Lindrannon called the expanse of trees, anyway.

Contrary to popular belief—and Erluc's, until Asten had set the record straight—the name arose not from the sound of the wind through the trees, but from the vicious packs of wolves that haunted them at night. Why didn't more people know that? Usually, because if there were any wolves close enough to be seen or heard, they were also close enough to tear you apart in seconds.

Generally, it was a good idea to stay away from there.

Erluc shot a quick glance up at the moonless sky, then nervously coaxed Skyblaze after the riders, urging him first into a cautious trot, then a light canter as he regretfully watched the dark elves disappear over the horizon, swallowed up by the night. *Hang on, Asten.*

Once he was sure that the riders were out of view, he urged Skyblaze towards the wood, marveling at how smoothly the stallion responded to his commands. It was almost like he was speaking to the horse. Skyblaze could even have been trained previously, except that Erluc hadn't noticed any spur marks, trims, sores, or anything else that indicated an escaped animal while combing out his hair earlier. Unless his last master had been a bareback rider who somehow trained him without any sort of spur or lash, Skyblaze was almost certainly a feral horse, if not a wild one.

He was just beginning to think he was lost before he caught a glimpse of firelight flickering against the trunk of an old beech. Furrowing his brow, he silently dismounted Skyblaze and, step by agonizing step, made his way carefully to the tree. He could hear a faint chatter gradually getting louder with every inch closer to the light.

His hand rested on the hilt of his dagger, and he gritted his teeth. *Calm down. Don't do anything stupid.* It was all he could do to prevent himself from drawing the short blade and brandishing it ahead of him.

Peering past the thick trunk, his eyes glinted. A row of tents in the distance formed a semi-circle around a brightly lit bonfire, where about two dozen warriors were gathered. Erluc watched and waited for the better part of an hour before one of the cloaked men threw a handful of sand at the fire, and the others reluctantly dispersed.

Finally. Once the others were finally out of sight, he emerged into the clearing. Deftly tying Skyblaze around a wide juniper, he sheathed the dagger.

From the corner of his eye, he spotted an abandoned bowl beside the withering fire, and he cautiously approached it. Cupping his hands above the soupy concoction, he sighed gratefully, the smell of the broth reminding him just how hungry he was.

As he grabbed the underside of the bowl, he cried out, pulling his hands back in pain.

"Careful," came a voice. "It's still hot."

Turning rapidly, Erluc pulled his dagger out from his sheath, pointing it fiercely at one of the cloaked warriors. "Stay back," he warned. "Come any closer, and I'll—"

"Yes?" prompted the man, slightly amused. He didn't have his lance, but there was a sword strapped to his belt.

Erluc grimaced. "I'll call for help," he decided.

"That might not be the best idea, either," advised the man. "This lot gets quite crabby when their sleep is disturbed. And I'd hate to have to explain to the commander how a boy of sixteen managed to sneak into our camp to eat our leftovers."

"I'm seventeen," corrected Erluc. He wasn't, not yet at least, but he wasn't about to let the man have the satisfaction of correctly guessing his age. "And I didn't mean to steal your food." He slowly lowered the dagger, and the man nodded.

"That's better." The man raised an eyebrow. "Now, what are you doing here?"

"Your troop saved my life back there at that village," began Erluc, taking a seat on the dry grass. "But those raiders got away and took my friend back with them. I need your help to rescue him."

Shaking his head, the man frowned. "You must be mistaken. Dark elves never take hostages, no matter what." Erluc grimaced. He remembered Asten saying something along those lines. But if he wasn't taken hostage... no, he had to have been.

"And they always fight to the death, do they not?" interrupted another voice. Erluc whipped around, and another man slipped out of the shadow of a tree from behind them.

"Commander," acknowledged the man who he'd been talking to first, and Erluc felt the urge to bow to the older man. *He's not a king.* But he definitely looked regal enough to be one.

"Care to introduce your friend, Kovu?" continued the other man.

Taking this as his cue, Erluc stepped forward. "Erluc, son of Neran."

Nodding, the Captain extended his hand. "Invardui, son of Arvaniar," he finished, and they shook hands. "I admire your courage, Erluc. Not many Aenorians dare to ask the Guardians for help."

"Wait, did you just say Guardians?" he questioned. He didn't know much of the tale of the Guardians, but he vaguely recalled something about a traitor to Aenor being banished, taking a clan of men with her to fight, and those that remained faithful staying back to defend North Aenor. "I didn't think that you were real."

Invardui suppressed a smile, while Kovu allowed himself a short chuckle. "It is as it should be. In the eyes of the South Aenorians, we are no more than traitors."

Erluc's brow creased. These people seemed extremely kind, rather the opposite of what he'd heard about South Aenorians. They couldn't be traitors, could they? Either way, the leader of the Guardians had piqued his interest. "Why is that?"

His face darkened. "It is unpleasant for me to speak of," he spoke firmly. "Besides, it is quite a lengthy tale, and it seems you are in a hurry."

Gritting his teeth, Erluc nodded. He needed to get Asten safe. "Before you decide if you'll help me, would you mind me giving you some advice?" he asked. Invardui extended his hand, signaling for him to continue, and Erluc nodded. "You seem like good people, and I find it hard to believe that you can be traitors of any kind. But there are many who have only heard of you in song and legend, as I had until today. If you don't make an effort to prove to them that you are, in fact, true of heart, then your reputation will forever remain tarnished."

There was a short silence before Invardui settled into a wry smile. "Remarkable." Turning to Kovu, he asked softly, "Tell me, how many days remain?"

The younger warrior took a moment before finally responding. "I believe it is the twenty-fifth today, which means exactly thirty days till the prophecy is fulfilled."

Erluc raised an eyebrow. "Thirty days? Till what?"

Invardui sighed, turning back to him. "Have you heard of the Prophecy of Alydris?" "I can barely read. I know a bit about Alydris, though. Asten's mentioned him once or twice. Wasn't he the high elven king from the Archanios that helped King Eldrath defeat the dark elves?" "One of his many triumphs," confirmed Kovu. "He also left behind a mysterious prophecy before he vanished, nearly a thousand years ago."

"And it's going to be fulfilled in thirty days?" inquired Erluc sarcastically. Prophecies weren't meant to be taken seriously. They were just mildly exciting poetry and should be treated as such. Alydris might have been a great commander, but that didn't mean he could tell the future. "So even assuming that this prophecy isn't just another couplet, what does this have to do with me?"

Invardui and Kovu looked at each other before the leader of the Guardians sighed. "You say you want our help to rescue your friend? You have it."

Erluc's brow furrowed in confusion. "That easily?"

"As long as you promise to hear me out," finished Invardui. Nodding, Erluc allowed the Guardian to continue. "Listen carefully and listen well, for this knowledge is not to be bandied about," he warned and then started to recite.

"In the Temple of Inthyl, one thousand years hence.

The Trinity shall rise to the Council's defense."

Erluc paused, trying to digest his words. "Just two lines?"

"These are the only two that we know of." Invardui shrugged. "Since these two rhyme, it's safe to say that there are at least two others. Maybe even more."

"Why are you telling me this?" Erluc demanded. "What does all of it mean?"

Kovu put out a hand to calm him down. "We do not know as of yet. The rest of the prophecy still remains a mystery to us. Yet, the combined knowledge of the Guardians is great, and we can at least understand the first two lines. The first regards a temple," he revealed. "We believe the line refers to Heaven's Citadel."

Erluc ran a hand through his hair. "Let me guess—it's in Inthyl?"

Kovu rolled his eyes. "The second line," cut in Invardui, "likely refers to the Twilight Council."

"The what?"

"It was a formidable alliance in ages long past, but now it consists only of High King Elandas and Horgenn, king of the dwarves."

Nodding, Erluc began to fiddle with his knife. "And this 'Trinity'?"

"The Trinity," repeated Invardui with a distant expression. "As to what that means, I can only guess. But if I had to, I would say that they are three heroes destined to fight for Adúnareth against the servants of Atanûkhor."

Erluc took a deep breath before exhaling loudly. *This is too much.* He shook his head. "Alright, I heard you out," he reminded them. "Are you going to help me?"

"Very well." Kovu paused a moment in thought before starting. "The raiders headed north from the village, didn't they?"

Invardui's face fell, and he turned to Kovu. "It's possible that an Ancient could have foreseen their arrival. If Uldarz could keep them apart until the destined date, then he'd prevent the prophecy from occurring."

Kovu raised an eyebrow. "You're saying his friend is also—"

"He could be," confirmed Invardui.

Erluc raised his arms in surprise. "You know I'm still here, right?" he blurted, and they turned to face him. "What in the world is an Ancient?"

Sighing, Kovu turned to face Erluc. "Ancients are dark elves who are born with the ability to use magic." He looked away. "But more importantly, we know where they could have taken him."

Erluc inhaled sharply.

"Where?"

"A fortress… in the Vale of Shadows." As he said the words, the fire seemed to dim slightly, the light on his face tinting red.

"Where in the world is that?"

Invardui nodded, and Kovu quickly produced a small wooden box from within the folds of his cloak, handing it to Erluc. Inside was a scrap of slightly charred parchment. "See for yourself," proposed Invardui. Erluc nodded, carefully unfolding the parchment, which turned out to be a map.

Erluc pored over it in amazement. "I had no idea the world could be so huge." His whole universe, everything he had ever known, could have been covered easily on the map by a silver coin.

"As far as I know, this represents only half of the continent." Invardui smiled. "The entire western region seems to have been burned."

"But what are all these places?" pressed Erluc. "I have only seen maps of Aenor before." Invardui shrugged. "I seldom travel beyond North Aenor myself—I know little more than you."

Erluc spread out the map, squinting at each letter, trying to make out the names. He managed to find Sering, tracing his path across the Diamond River, but he didn't recognize much else. "So, where are we going?"

"Here." Invardui tapped a dark patch west of a mountain range Erluc recognized as the Flaming Crags. "Now this…" he traced a line from the Diamond River to the area, "…is the fastest route. But it is heavily guarded by dark elves, and we can't risk being ambushed."

"What other choices do we have?" queried Erluc.

"If we head directly north from here, following the edge of the Manos Desert, and pass through the East Archanios, we should be able to avoid the elves."

Erluc closed his eyes briefly, imagining the course. "That looks like it will take us much longer."

Invardui bowed his head. "Assuming we can even find the fortress. It is cloaked in eternal twilight, and the night will not shield us from the elves that walk the Vale of Shadows. They see as well in darkness as we do in daylight."

Kovu lifted a bundle next to the woodpile and handed it to Erluc. "You will need this."

Erluc unwrapped the bundle to reveal a simple wooden scabbard, drawing out the hilt in one smooth motion. A thin, elegant sword flashed in the rising sun, and as Erluc examined it more closely, he could see that the blade was covered in minuscule ripple-like patterns—the mark of the near-lost forging technique of the clans. It seemed that while the clans themselves were on the verge of extinction, their legacy lived on in their descendants, the Guardians. After admiring the sword a while longer, Erluc returned it awkwardly to the sheath. "Thank you," he acknowledged with a nod. Kovu inclined his head. "Nothing of it."

"I still don't understand," tried Erluc once more. "Why would this *Uldarz* want to capture anyone? Especially Asten of all people?"

Both Kovu and Invardui looked briefly at one another before the leader of the troop finally responded. "That's more than enough for one night. You'd best get some sleep," declared Invardui. "We leave at first light."

Chapter 3

ERLUC ATTACKS AN OLD LADY

MANOS DESERT

Erluc

Water. Under the scorching sun, Erluc ducked his head underneath his sleeve to block his face from the basking rays. *Water.* Even his sweat felt dry and saltier than he cared to taste. *Water.* As Skyblaze trudged through the burning sands of the Manos, his vision shook violently, fading away in pulses, before gradually returning to him.

The thing with deserts was that they provided ample time to think. Too much, usually. And Erluc had nothing to think of, except for the sun threatening to set his thick dark hair on fire. And the continuous itching in his throat. The uncomfortable jolting of Skyblaze's steps. And Asten.

The Guardians rode ahead of him, sitting tall atop their well-groomed steeds. If there was one thing that Erluc hated the most, it was people doing things better than he did them. And compared to them, he probably looked like he was trying to *swim* through the sand using Skyblaze as a drowning man would a log.

At the head of their troop, Invardui rode with his centurion, discussing some obscure topic in hushed tones. With a finger, Erluc traced out a map of his route in Skyblaze's mane, doing his best to visualize the path he would take. As best as he could figure, he needed to pass through some forested land to the northeast and enter the Vale of Shadows just west of the mountains.

The name itself sounded evil—the perfect home to a dark elven fortress.

His horse's mane burned his hands under the intense sun. Reaching for his waterskin, he squeezed the last drops into his mouth, then crumpled the skin and tucked it back into his saddlebags. In front of him, Invardui looked back, as he had every fifteen minutes for the past three days, to check on Erluc.

Yes, I'm still here. Sure, maybe he had agreed to accompany Erluc on the journey, but that didn't mean that they were brothers. The leader of the Guardians had offered him almost no help so far, unless one was counting company.

Erluc wasn't.

Still, it would've inevitably killed him, making the journey to the Vale of Shadows alone. This was what Asten was best at—providing companionship. He might not have been the most interesting person, but he was familiar, and he could keep up a discussion.

Asten was the one person that Erluc didn't have to be different around. He didn't have to go out of his way to be ridiculous things like *respectful* or *courteous*. He could tell Asten the cold truth—most of the time, anyways—and he'd give his own genuine response to it.

Most people just pretended to agree with whatever Erluc said, rather than actually having personalities and thoughts. These were some of the people that he hated most—the ones with the hollow skulls and the permanent smiles, second only to bullies and oppressors.

Shaking his head, Erluc looked forward, shielding his eyes from a bright light ahead of him. Despite the blinding light, he could faintly make out a faint shimmer on the horizon. As he moved closer, a crystal-clear pool of water became apparent. A patch of lush grass grew around it.

An oasis! Elated, he snapped the reins, and Skyblaze dashed over the undulating dunes, leaving his rather stunned companions behind him. The grove was too near for his eyes to be deceiving him—two hundred yards at the most.

As Skyblaze advanced another bound, the cruelty of the desert dawned upon him, and the oasis slowly vanished in front of his eyes, gone with the wind. Grains of sand whipped across his face, and he winced slightly in pain, covering his eyes with one arm.

The harsh sunlight bled through the thin material, but his vision was still dominated by darkness, and his entire body was screaming in protest as the small particles showered at him. Surrendering himself to the darkness, he closed his eyes, the fatigue in his heart almost slowing his pulse, and he blacked out.

He woke up suddenly when his head painfully struck the root of a tree. The ridges and contours of the muddy, rocky ground scraped across his back. A constant pull at his ankles kept him moving. Stunned, his survival instincts kicked in. With fumbling fingers, he nervously twisted and unhitched his leg straps, bumping his head several times, before his feet finally dropped from Skyblaze's back.

Heaving himself up, Erluc scanned his surroundings for potential threats. The moon, high in the sky, was obscured by thick leafy boughs draping long vines. When he moved, the ground squelched beneath his feet. Skyblaze had come to a stop under a broad tree, exhausted after what must have been a journey of several hours without rest.

"You okay?" asked a Guardian, who Erluc eventually recognized as Kovu, sitting tall upon his horse. Nodding absently, Erluc turned to Skyblaze, whom the Guardian had been leading, and noticed the stallion was just about ready to drop.

I bet it didn't even know that I passed out. One way or another, it must've dragged me across the desert, all the way into this… swamp. Where am I? Looking around, he found Invardui conversing with a few other troops, nodding in acknowledgment when their eyes met.

Brushing himself off, he again retrieved the map. It took Erluc several minutes to decipher, his limited literacy hindering his pace, before he finally managed to read 'East Archanios'.

They had made it to the land of the dark elves.

He swallowed, his dry throat burning as the saliva passed down. He hobbled to the grand stallion and retrieved his crumpled waterskin from its saddlebags but was dismayed by its lack of contents. Smoothing it out, he shook the last few drops into his mouth. As soon as the water trickled down, his throat screamed for more. He wiped away the droplets of sweat rapidly forming on his face, internally cursing the humid air. Already, his legs were starting to itch. *Blasted mosquitoes!* He closed his eyes and listened, closing out the putrid stench of unfamiliarity. *There!* The faint cry of the crane was distant but unmistakable.

Following the sound, its dynamic steadily increasing, he came across a small brook, muddy water splashing over rocks. He leaped straight into the water, the sweat and dirt on his limbs washed away with the weak current. Though the water was far from cool, it provided a refreshing comfort to Erluc after his weary travel through the desert. Once he was clean, or at least no longer rancid, he carefully climbed out of the brook. Taking one last look at the murky stream, he headed back to rouse Skyblaze.

Once the great beast was on its feet, Erluc re-tied the rope to the stallion's bridle. Then, grasping the rope, he followed it to the stream, leading Skyblaze behind him. The horse leaped for joy and buried its muzzle in the water as soon as it saw the stream.

"Erluc," called Invardui, lightly tapping him on the shoulder. "I trust you enjoyed your nap."

"Not exactly the word I would use." He grimaced. "I don't suppose your troops have any water left?"

Invardui nodded, calling one of his men over, who handed Erluc a waterskin. Gratefully accepting the container, Erluc drained whatever was left of it.

Water really was the best. There was nothing like it. It was cold when you needed it to be and warm too. And unlike other things, it never let you down—water was always going to taste the same, no matter what Asten said about the water they'd been served in Tarrach.

Sighing, he handed the waterskin back to the Guardian with a nod of thanks, before turning to Invardui. The chieftain was sipping from his own waterskin, and Erluc raised an eyebrow. "How is it that you still have so much water left? Did you not drink any while we were crossing the Manos?"

Invardui smiled, beckoning for Erluc to follow him. "If you live out here for long enough, you learn to use your surroundings to your advantage," he explained. He led them to where several other Guardians were resting, around a weakly burning fire with a bowl of murky water boiling above it. Some kind of skin was covering the bonfire like a tarpaulin, and Erluc watched the contraption with great interest. Steam rose from the bowl and began to condense on the skin, rolling down to a point where one Guardian held his waterskin ready.

"And that's safe to drink?" questioned Erluc, and Invardui gave him a nod of assurance. *Not a bad trick.* He was impressed and there was no denying it. These men may not have been the most respected or influential, but at least they were resourceful. "Are we making camp here?" he asked Invardui once more.

"Only until dawn," assured the Guardian. "Crossing the desert does warrant a little rest, especially considering that there's still a lot of riding to do between here and the Vale of Shadows."

Grimacing, Erluc turned to where a group of men was standing in a disorganized circle, watching two warriors spar. He surveyed the fight intently, his gaze flickering from one man to the other and back as they shifted fluidly from one intricate maneuver into the next. He'd occasionally sparred with Asten, usually with pieces of bark or bamboo sticks, when they were younger. Of course, he'd had experience with a sword in hand as well, but he could never have matched up to this kind of skill. Before he knew it, he was standing with the rest of the troops, cheering on the champion, as dozens of challengers stepped up to claim his title. Only twice did the challengers succeed, after which they had to defend their newfound status.

"What about you, boy?" questioned the reigning champion as his latest challenger grimaced, picking his sword up out of the mud. "You up for a little spar?"

Erluc's eyes widened, and he didn't even have the opportunity to protest before he was ushered to the front, accompanied by a huge cheer from the Guardians around him. In the back, Invardui smirked as Erluc warily drew his blade from the scabbard that hung at his waist. The Guardian facing him twirled his own weapon lazily, and Erluc squared his feet, tensing up by force of instinct.

After a moment's hesitation, he charged with a yell, swinging his sword overhead, but the Guardian easily blocked the strike and returned with a stab. Taken aback by his speed, Erluc scrambled away, waving the sword wildly as though to swat his assailant away. *This is nothing like fighting Asten.* He hastily assumed his stance again, his heart pounding. All around them, the circle of Guardians continued to yell in delight.

This time his opponent moved first, jabbing at his knee. Erluc was forced to use all his strength to parry the blade downward, before following up with a slash to the face. The Guardian sidestepped so smoothly it seemed effortless, twisting his sword in one hand. "Go on," he taunted. "At least make it a challenge." Off to the side, Invardui watched him with a faint smile, while his comrade switched his blade to his left hand, tucking his right behind his back.

He's toying with me, Erluc thought, and the realization alone was enough to cause anger to well up within him. Clenching his jaw, he stood up straight and pointed his sword at the Guardian. "See if you can keep up, old man," he retorted. It was all he could do to force a grin onto his face, but he couldn't let them think he'd lost just yet. The Guardians surrounding them seemed to take the bluff, though, and the roars of excitement intensified.

He attacked again, with three sharp strikes to the arm, then the stomach, then the head, but the Guardian blocked all of them with an elaborate spinning maneuver. It was all too obvious that Erluc's skill was hopelessly eclipsed by that of the champion, but still, he refused to give in. Shouting, he lashed out once more, this time holding nothing back as he fought to stay on the offensive.

After a heated exchange of blows, Erluc suddenly lunged forward in an attempt to put some distance between himself and his opponent. Though his attack was reckless, and they both knew it, he seemed to have taken the Guardian off guard enough to prevent a counterattack. Even as the man recovered from the surprise, preparing to charge back in, Erluc planted the tip of his sword in the mud and pulled back the hilt, flinging a clod of dirt into the Guardian's face. Without hesitation, he leaped forward, putting all his strength into a single swing at his adversary's guard. As the blades met, the Guardian's sword was wrenched out of his hand, landing heavily in the marshy ground.

After an appropriately enthusiastic round of cheers, another challenger entered the circle. This Guardian seemed to have had the good sense not to go easy on Erluc, and after just two swings of the sword, Erluc found himself on his back, his own weapon a foot out of reach.

Although it was painfully obvious that the Guardians were refraining from using any advanced techniques, Erluc rarely managed to match up to his adversaries, but what he lacked in skill, he made up in ferocity and determination. Ducking under several of the blows that his opponent threw towards him, he managed to get the Guardian off balance, just in time to kick his feet out from underneath him.

He sparred late into the night, fighting a range of opponents until he collapsed in exhaustion.

"Not bad," declared Kovu, after he had climbed out of the mud and rejoined the circle. Invardui, who had been overseeing the session, looked over with a proud smile at his comment. "We'll make a Guardian of you yet." Unable to muster the energy to acknowledge the compliment, Erluc simply leaned against a tree, breathing heavily. He watched the next few fights, barely able to appreciate the unique fighting style of the Guardians through his own exhaustion. When the men had finally dispersed, he collapsed onto a relatively dry patch of land, drifting asleep almost instantly by the fire.

He was roused early the next day, and within a matter of hours, they were all back in the saddle, riding north to their ultimate destination with renewed determination. The horses' hooves squelched in the mud, and those Guardians on foot had trouble finding a path through the bog without ending up knee-deep in the dirty water. This East Archanios was a hellish place, Erluc noted, and while it was a step up from the desert, he would never have considered living there.

Finally, a burst of light pierced the leaden expanse above the weary travelers, and he knew he was almost out of the East Archanios. Kovu was just turning around, most likely to tell him something to that effect, Skyblaze stopped abruptly, almost throwing Erluc off of his saddle. As he looked around, he realized that the entire contingent had paused. He directed his steed around to the front to see what the issue was.

Invardui's white stallion was left without a rider, and Erluc saw the chieftain hastily approaching a thicket of trees in front of him.

What are you doing?

Erluc ushered Skyblaze forward, hoping to get a better look at what was happening. Squinting, he noticed a figure garbed in dark robes, propped up against a tree, nursing a broken leg.

In front of him, Invardui stopped to talk to the figure, who Erluc could only just make out to be an impossibly pale, old woman. "Are you hurt?" he asked.

In his short time with them, Erluc had observed a sense of honor that he would never have expected from any of the king's men. There was no chance that the local patrolmen or any provincial troops would have helped rescue Asten, and the issue would certainly never have warranted the attention of the great Twilight Legion. All said and done, the Guardians were truly the helpers of the people of Aenor—the peacekeepers. Just because their aid wasn't widely appreciated, it didn't make them any less noble. Then again, Invardui's motivation for helping him wasn't exactly clear, either. But as long as he was willing to help, Erluc wasn't going to question him.

A cold wind blew past him, and he watched hesitantly as Invardui took another step towards the crone. The woman smiled, shaking her head. Ignoring the Guardian, she looked straight past him. Straight at Erluc.

The atmosphere grew chilled, almost evil. The trees bent and strained in rage, and Erluc felt his grip on the reins tighten.

Just then, Invardui was sent flying backwards, into his own horse. The entire troop drew their weapons immediately, and Erluc swiftly pulled the knife out of his belt—the closest weapon he could reach—snapping the reins on Skyblaze.

The fierce gray stallion leaped straight at the old woman and was met with a jet of dark-purple light. Thrown backwards, it crashed into the damp mud, giving Erluc barely enough time to roll off of the falling beast.

The woman flung out her arm, and Erluc ducked to avoid another colossal blast of energy. Unfortunately, the others weren't so lucky. A pair of Guardians who were riding at her was shot at point-blank range and vaporized instantly.

Eyes widened in shock, Erluc hurled the knife at her shoulder, aiming to disable her arm; the woman flicked her wrist, stopping the dagger midair. She released, and the knife dropped to the dirt.

Invardui rose back up on his feet, drawing his fearsome blade. He called out an order, and the remnant of his troop cried out, charging towards the woman. Erluc was only just about to join them, when he saw the woman's smile broaden as she finally rose to full height.

Something's wrong. And then he saw it. All around them, skeletal hands broke the surface of the ground, clawing, fighting for freedom. First, their arms emerged and then their skulls, before finally, the entire skeleton pulled free of the earth.

Erluc stood rooted to a spot. *Skeletons? How are we supposed to fight skeletons?*

Invardui paled for a moment, before barking another order in a foreign tongue, slashing at one of the creatures to ward it off. The remaining Guardians gathered with their backs to one another, all taking up defensive stances as the last of the skeletons had extricated itself from the mud. As they turned to the huddled circle, Erluc dashed to Skyblaze, taking a moment to retrieve his own sword before finding himself cornered by three of the undead.

Raising his sword just as the skeletons closed in on him, Erluc swung it in a wide arc, just as he had the previous day, in an attempt to give himself room to fight. With each attack, he put all his strength behind the swing, hoping that a powerful enough impact would be enough to crack bone.

"What are you doing, boy?" yelled Invardui from the circle of Guardians, knocking aside a swipe from one of the skeletons. "You're holding a sword, not a stick of wood. Use it like one!"

Use a sword like a sword? Erluc shook his head in confusion, willing Invardui to explain himself, but the Guardian had already returned his attention to his own fight. Two of the skeletons charged, ducking under his wild swipe, and latched onto his sword arm, rendering him unable to do much more than flick his wrist. The third tried yanking the weapon out of his hand, but luckily Erluc's grip was strong enough to keep the hilt from slipping away. Despite its seeming lack of a brain, the skeleton seemed to realize that, and quickly changed track, raising both fists in hopes of breaking his arm.

Erluc's response wasn't planned, wasn't calculated, but was rather the offspring of pure instinct. Within his limited range of motion, he twirled his sword in his right hand, severing a rib from one of the skeletons, and snatched it up in his left. Before any of the three could respond, he smashed the bone down on the wrist of one of the skeletons holding him, wresting his arm free from the other. He marveled at the sheer cutting ability of the blade to slice through solid bone like it was water, and he realized that this must have been what made clan-forged swords so special: to be able to hold the finest edge for years without dulling.

With his newfound weapon along with his sword, Erluc began to swing at the skeletons viciously, with every stroke of the blade inflicting a new gash onto one of his assailants. Before long, though, it became clear that he was no match for his foes. His sheer ferocity gave the skeletons pause, but for each one he scythed down, another took its place. And if that wasn't bad enough, no skeleton, however mutilated, stayed down for long.

Where do these things even come from? They could be the victims of the swamp, or maybe even the woman herself: her own private army of the vanquished. It dawned on him that if he died here, his skeleton might be among them, fighting forever as a part of her undead militia. That was an unsettling image, if he'd ever seen one.

Luckily, the skeletons were both unskilled and unarmed. However, the sheer number of them made it nearly impossible to even move, let alone reach the rapidly dwindling group of Guardians just yards away.

The woman fired a deadly blast of purple energy towards him, and he was only just able to dive out of the way. Out of the corner of his eye, he saw another Guardian fall, leaving just Invardui and two others fending off a veritable army.

As he lashed out towards the nearest fiend, a jet of purple light streaked over his shoulder and caught him in the arm, causing pain to erupt across his body, so intense that he barely noticed letting his sword drop. It was instantly seized by a skeleton, and though he tried valiantly amid the agony to keep it from splitting his makeshift club, he didn't last long before the bone was sliced in half, and he was left defenseless.

The skeleton lashed out with Erluc's sword, and he leaped backward, his feet squelching in some sludge as he landed. Looking down, he groaned. *I hate quicksand.* And he was already sinking.

Chapter 4

MISSION: COMPLETELY HOPELESS

EAST ARCHANIOS

Erluc

Add that to the list of things that made him regret leaving his occasionally cozy home for this deranged journey. Heck, he'd had more luck committing suicide than rescuing Asten. And as he stood facing an armed skeleton, a sense of impending doom settled upon him. Its drastically ugly face sneered down at him, its teeth clattering dangerously. Even without eyes, the skeleton's gaze was more menacing than anything he'd ever faced.

Just then, to make matters as rotten as possible, a vine hit him in the face.

He looked around, stunned. All around him, ever since they had entered the swamp, the trees had been laden with olive-green, thorny vines.

Resisting the urge to squirm, Erluc grasped the vine in one hand as the quicksand completely covered his feet, making its way up his legs. In an effort to free his feet, he slowly leaned back, using the vine to keep from falling over completely, and sure enough, his toes emerged from the sludge. As he tried to pull his feet clear, though, the vine snapped, leaving him on his back in the quicksand.

He swore under his breath, expecting to sink, but surprisingly, his feet had come free, and he didn't seem to be in any immediate danger. Though he couldn't move his head or legs, he wasn't sinking anymore, and his arms were relatively mobile. He waved both arms behind him until one struck a second vine. After a few tries, he managed to gain a decent purchase on it, and one hand over another, he was able to slowly pull himself to solid ground, rolling to the side and knocking over the skeleton wielding his sword. He scrambled to his feet, snatching up his weapon, and the steel flashed blood-red in the morning sun, mirroring the fury in his eyes. The spell that he'd been hit with before was still affecting him, sapping the strength from his limbs as if it was eating him alive.

Instantly, the pain transformed into burning energy, driving him forward as he spun it in his hand, yelling. His intense, albeit short-lived, sparring run the day before had proved critical, and he found himself able to hold his own against multiple undead assailants, kicking their skeletal remains into the quicksand.

"Erluc!" called Kovu, beckoning over him to rejoin them.

Regrouping with the remaining two Guardians—one more had perished—he tossed another rib into the pit.

"What's going on?" questioned Erluc, still in shock. "Who is she?"

"We do not know," confided Invardui with a grimace. "Perhaps an alchemist or even an Ancient."

Fabulous. We're going to die here. He shook his head, turning to face the woman.

Although the effects of her agonizing curse had faded, his adrenaline rush was long gone as well, and he felt just about ready to drop. The witch opened her hand, and three violet orbs materialized before her, racing for the three of them. One of the balls of energy collided with Kovu and his whole body was suffused with a lavender glow before he dropped to the ground, senseless. Invardui reacted faster, diving to the side and tackling Erluc to the ground before he too was rendered unconscious by another blast.

Nevertheless, Erluc clambered to his feet, eyes smoldering. He was able to dodge exactly one energy blast before being knocked to the ground once more. The woman slowly walked up to Erluc's frail figure and scoffed. As she neared, he could finally make out her solid-gray eyes in the dim light. Invardui had been right, he realized—it was a dark elf. An Ancient.

The Ancient summoned a cloud of noxious-looking gas, which would almost certainly have knocked Erluc out, had he breathed it. Before he could, though, a huge noise erupted from the thicket of trees.

Instinctively, both Erluc and the dark elf turned. The deadly fumes dissolved into thin air.

A streak of silver rushed directly into the action and collided with the old hag, her body crumpling under its massive frame.

Shocked, Erluc sprung to his feet. His eyes met… *Skyblaze*. Never had he been so glad to see the stallion's stormy hide. He jumped up, balancing against its wide flank and then turned to face the Ancient, who was gravely injured. He briefly checked on Invardui and Kovu, who were hastily recovering, before returning his gaze to the dark elf.

As she rose to her feet, Erluc noticed that her satchel had dropped from her shoulder and had been thrown backwards several feet, near the patch of quicksand. "Treacherous boy," she croaked forcefully. "Spit on what Uldarz wants with you. I am going to make you suffer."

Uldarz? He remembered the Guardians talking about him two nights past. *They were right.*

The Ancient raised a hand and fired a badly aimed blast, which collided with a seedling a few yards to Erluc's left. It took a moment, but the pale-green quickly darkened as the plant grew to a giant mangrove. Erluc dodged the next spell by ducking behind the newly formed tree, but moments later, it shriveled up and died, reduced to dust in the wind. The Ancient gave a rather surprised look, as if she was no longer in control of her abilities, before hissing in fury.

It's some sort of time spell. Erluc's eyes widened in realization. The plant had aged and died, all in a matter of seconds. Erluc's hand closed around the blade's hilt. "What do you want with me?" His voice carried a confidence that was at odds with the fear threatening to paralyze him.

"It is quite simple, insolent child." The Ancient spread her hands, bathed in an emerald light, and an unnatural wind swirled in a vortex around her. "I want you to die."

Skyblaze snorted, his dark eyes smoldering. Erluc tried to brandish his sword, but his hand wouldn't move. The spellcaster flicked her wrist, sending a green bolt of energy at Erluc's chest and causing the gray stallion to rear in panic. Erluc didn't know if it was an effect of the incantation, but time seemed to slow down as he tried to dodge, knowing fully well that it would be in vain.

What happened next caught him entirely off guard. Skyblaze's flailing hoof struck the back of his neck, and he crumpled into the mud. And a split second later, the jet of light collided with the horse's chest, launching it backwards.

Outraged and shaking, Erluc rose. Raising the sword above his head, he charged at the evil enchantress for a final time with a roar. He was met with a volley of ice shards, which he deftly slid under, refusing to let anything stand in his way. The dark elf's expression became considerably less smug, a hint of fear creeping its way onto her shadowy face.

She twisted around in a futile attempt to find a weapon, and Erluc seized the advantage, charging with energy redoubled. He extended his sword below her chin, a scarlet streak staining her otherwise pale, grayish skin.

"Who are you?" Erluc roared. "Why did you attack us?" Intimidation radiated from his voice, but the Ancient remained unaffected. Her fingertips glowed, and Erluc pressed the sword harder against her throat until the light died down.

"You will never ascend," her raspy voice croaked, an unidentifiable accent flowing beneath her words. "Atanûkhor will prevail."

Her body shook, light emanating from the skin, and in Erluc's hand, the sword's leather grip grew uncomfortably warm. Erluc covered his eyes with his arm in just enough time, and he was sent flying backwards as a harsh light erupted in front of him. His ears rang, and his sight wavered before he was finally given the relief of losing consciousness.

Erluc woke suddenly the next morning, the horrors of the previous day still haunting his memory. He hadn't slept very well that night. After the Ancient had committed suicide, the exhaustion had finally hit him.

Luckily for him, both Invardui and Kovu had woken up and had already prepared a meal by the time he'd come to. They'd listened very intently as he'd alternated between eating and reciting the story of the previous day, asking dozens of questions in between.

"I'm terribly sorry that you had to experience that," said Invardui reassuringly. "And we are in your debt. If it hadn't been for you, we probably would've died too." Kovu nodded, looking to his leader. It was as if the both of them knew something that he didn't, and it was starting to trigger his curiosity. But he didn't push the matter further.

Instead, Erluc bit into a loaf of bread from a fallen Guardian's pack. "Are there other troops of Guardians here that can help us?" To think that almost all of them had died fighting a single dark elf… the very idea was a brutal reminder of the gravity of the situation in which he had become hopelessly entangled. How many would they need to survive once they had actually reached the Vale of Shadows?

"There is a troop in the Vale," confirmed Invardui. "But I wouldn't count on their help."

Kovu grimaced. "It's a shame, too. They are said to be one of the fiercest units of Guardians that ever lived."

Raising an eyebrow, Erluc shoved the rest of the loaf into his mouth. "And why can't they help us?"

"The answer to that question may be longer than you'd expect." Erluc nodded, and Invardui indicated for Kovu to continue. "Seven years ago," began Kovu, "a traitor—we speak not her name—was banished from Aenor. But she struck a pact with the leaders of the clan from which we came: the Inro Forthel of the woods, the most powerful of the northern clans."

Erluc nodded. The clans had resided in Aenor long before it was united and colonized by Andaerians, the first king Eltar and his followers. They had been the only humans in Eärnendor before the coming of the Andaerians from the south.

"When most of our clan left to join the Traitor, some of us remained faithful to Aenor and became the Guardians," continued Kovu. "The only leader of Inro Forthel who stayed, became the leader of the Vale troop, fighting against both the Traitor's treacherous hordes and the dark elves ever since."

"So basically, they have their hands full," interpreted Erluc.

"As I said," Invardui inclined his head, "I wouldn't count on their help."

We're definitely not going to make it out of there alive. Shaking his head, Erluc went to check on Skyblaze. The blast that the stallion had endured from the Ancient had visibly taken its toll, his beautiful dark-gray hair fading, and his eyes shot through with indigo. Erluc grimaced. He'd seen how powerful the Ancient's curses were. He could still feel the mild sting of the pain curse from time to time, and he'd seen the time spell at work himself.

If it could have aged that a single tree several centuries in mere moments, the time the horse must have aged overnight would be unbelievable. According to Asten, a healthy stallion rarely grew beyond thirty years, but Skyblaze had survived thousands, assuming the spell's effects had slowed after the Ancient's death.

Apart from the corpses on the ground and Skyblaze's condition, the only legacy of the Ancient was her satchel. As Erluc's eyes met its dark hue, foul energy emitted from it almost as identical to the Ancient's stench. Curiosity got the better of him, though. As he made contact with the rough substance of the pack, the dark elf's raspy voice echoed through his mind, a haunting reminder of its previous owner.

"Get out of my head," he snapped suddenly, and both the Guardians turned to look at him. Taking a deep breath, he lifted the satchel open. Instantly, a bright light erupted out of the bag, illuminating the surroundings, as if a captive spirit was escaping. Averting his eyes, Erluc finally looked into the pack.

Straight away, he saw two empty vials and a faceted sapphire—or at least something that resembled one—as well as a pouch of flat, smooth rocks. However, the most interesting possession of the sorceress was a scroll. Reaching in and unfurling the ancient-looking sheepskin, Erluc saw what appeared to be a map; the script of the markings was alien to him. "At least this can help us get to the Vale of Shadows."

Suddenly, the scroll blurred, and the image reappeared, the writing replaced with familiar Andaeric script.

Gasping, Erluc dropped the scroll and hastily backed away from it.

"What happened?" inquired Invardui. "Is something wrong?"

After regaining his senses, he beckoned for them to examine the map. He carefully inched back, making sure not to touch the strange parchment. With considerable effort, he managed to decipher '*Vale of Shadows*'. It was a layout of a broad valley, complete with its surroundings and the position of the sun. Amazed, he shook his head.

Invardui and Kovu took turns examining the map until they too arrived at the same conclusion as he had. "If this truly did belong to the Ancient, the dark magic that controls it must be terribly dangerous," decided Kovu. "We must get rid of it."

Erluc snorted. *A scroll that leads you wherever you want to go?* As if he would throw that away. But he assured Kovu that he'd dispose of it, quickly tossing the scroll into Skyblaze's saddlebags, maintaining minimum contact. He returned his attention to the rest of the satchel. He lifted the stones out of the bag; aside from the finely marked red scratches on the sides, they seemed rather ordinary.

"These," Invardui remarked, a glint in his eyes, "are unbelievably rare. A full set of runestones—there must be but a dozen in all of Aenor. Most, in the possession of alchemists, I'd wager." He shook his head. "You mustn't lose any of these and must keep them away from harm. In the wrong hands, these could…" he trailed off.

Taken aback, Erluc handed the pouch to the Guardian. "This is a complete set? All of them?"

"Almost," noted Invardui, looking them over. "A few of the rarer ones are missing, but who knows? Maybe one day you'll be the one to find them and add them to the collection." He returned the runestones to the pouch and held it back out to Erluc.

Erluc shrugged, accepting the bag from Invardui. He didn't know much about runestones, but apparently, Invardui did. A thought occurred to him. "Why don't you take them, then?"

Invardui and Kovu exchanged another glance. *I hate it when they do that.* Kovu smiled. "Call it a hunch, but I think you will have more need of these stones than we ever could."

The Captain nodded in agreement. "That, and treasures such as this aren't safe with nomads like us. No, better that they go with you to Inthyl."

Erluc frowned, sure that Invardui was hiding something, but he decided to let it go. Under the Guardian's watchful gaze, he transported the rest of the runestones, the gemstone, and the vials extremely carefully into Skyblaze's saddlebags.

Finally, his mind returned to the task at hand: rescuing Asten. When he'd left his home, he realized he had not seen a single soul die. Now, his best friend was a captive of the dark elves, he'd survived an encounter with an Ancient and he'd fought undead soldiers made of bones. He didn't want to know what came next.

With renewed determination, the considerably thinned group continued northwards. Although Skyblaze's condition considerably reduced their daily coverage, their mere effort and advancement gave Erluc the hope he required to continue. After all, Asten would be able to diagnose the problem once he was rescued. And Erluc couldn't blame the horse. He doubted even he would be able to travel across Eärnendor again after the way the last few days had gone.

Within two days and the night betwixt, the mountains broke the horizon of Erluc's view. After the swamp, the majority of his journey had been through the plains, and as the hills appeared in the dusk, Erluc found himself intimidated by their monstrous size, even several leagues away. Even the foothills, which they were rapidly approaching, were taller than anything he'd ever seen. And between some of the nearer of the hills lay what they had journeyed thus far to reach. Jumping off of Skyblaze's swollen back, he stared in awe. The broad valley, although shrouded by darkness, was truly breathtaking. The base of the mountain was littered with several diversely colored bushes that glowed a bright neon in the silver moonlight. A stream crawled into the valley's mouth, where two cloaked sentries stood watch, pointed spears in their hands.

Dark elves. Erluc gritted his teeth.

Scanning his surroundings, he saw two towers devoid of guards. "We'll distract the sentries," offered Kovu. "You get inside as soon as possible, undetected."

Invardui nodded. "We can cover your entry, and then we can look for the dungeons together, assuming your friend is alive."

"He's alive," declared Erluc firmly. Donning his cloak, he tucked his sword deep into its folds and concealed a dagger in his sleeve. Lifting Skyblaze's reins, Erluc advanced towards the Vale of Shadows, tailed by both the Guardians.

He hadn't made it more than two or three hundred yards before Skyblaze began acting up. He whinnied and bucked sharply, knocking an unsuspecting Erluc straight into the damp mud. Looking up, Erluc saw Skyblaze race away, saddlebags and all, into a clearing of shrubs and disappear behind the thick trees. *What's the matter with that horse?*

Suddenly, he froze as an ice-cold point just barely brushed the small of his back. Hardly daring to move, he slowly twisted his head around. A group of three elves stood behind him, spears at the ready. The nearest had his weapon at Erluc's back, and the jet-black spearheads did little to reassure him either. He immediately recognized the hue of bloodsteel, the metal from which dark elves forged their weapons, and knew that a single prick from the spear against his skin would prove poisonous, perhaps even fatal. He definitely had more things to worry about than a rebellious horse with the pox.

Of course! Erluc scowled at his feet. *How stupid did I have to be to think that the elves would leave their fortress unguarded?* Both Invardui and Kovu were brought in from behind him, spears at their backs.

One elf, the groomed hide of a black bear tossed over his shoulders, emerged from the middle of the group and gestured for Erluc to turn around fully.

Turning to face the leader, he pondered on what to say. After all, elven mercenaries wouldn't be caught up about Inthyl's latest gossip. Then again, neither was he. He simply spread his arms in annoyance. The elf sneered, and two of the guards ushered Erluc back into the plains, under the shade of two grand oak trees.

Why aren't they taking me into the fortress?

The group didn't look like outcasts, and captives were usually sent to the dungeons, were they not? Unless they had specific orders to quietly kill him *outside* the fort, however unlikely, something strange was going on.

"Psst!" whispered Erluc to a nearby guard as they walked. "I don't suppose you're taking me to the dungeons?"

Aggravated, the elf slashed his spear before Erluc's face threateningly. *Worth a shot.* The leader was engrossed in the affairs of two other guards, who were arguing about something. The elf closest to Erluc poked at a squirrel with his spear, clearly bored.

Both Invardui and Kovu were looking to him for a signal and, sensing his opportunity, he ran towards the fort, distracting the guard adjacent to him. While the guards panicked, rushing to follow Erluc, both Invardui and Kovu reached for their weapons, charging behind them.

Planting a foot, Invardui sprang at the guard, slamming his sword into the dark elf's wrist. The bloodsteel-tipped spear clattered against the ground, and the elf howled in pain, the noise echoing throughout the valley. The other two dark elves turned to face the swordsmen, rage twisting their angular features. Together they charged towards them, imposing blades in hand.

Invardui twirled around, slicing at their shins, breaking their arms and battering their noses. Though many dark elves were seasoned warriors, these clearly were no more than mercenaries—no match for Guardians. Soon, he was standing above the writhing band, wiping his blade against the dry bark of the grand trees. He tossed Erluc his sword, who accepted it with a nod.

Unfortunately, the ruckus that the brawl had caused had attracted attention, and a patrol of about a dozen dark elven soldiers had arrived, probably not to just watch the fun. The fallen leader of the troop groaned out a command, and even though Erluc didn't understand it, he was sure that it wasn't a call for peace.

The entire group ferociously charged in unison, and he felt a wave of inferno build up inside him as he roared and lashed out with his sword, his confidence reignited.

In no time, the three of them made short work of several more dark elves, but his power drained quickly, leaving him gasping on his knees as the next band charged, brandishing their weapons threateningly.

Both Kovu and Invardui were just as tired, barely able to hold their own against so many skilled opponents. Just as the dark elves were about to overcome Erluc, a dark shape swooped in from above the trees and recklessly collided with several rows of dark elves, crushing them under its sheer mass.

The remaining raiders, as well as Erluc himself, stopped in their tracks to identify the creature.

Skyblaze!

Erluc smiled, a rush of triumph flooding through him. *Better late than never.* But the great stallion looked… different. Skyblaze's fading hide had finally been reduced to a brilliant white, all traces of the clouded slate hue now extinguished. Feathery wings sprouted from his back, spreading across a span of at least two yards. A pegasus!

That was why Skyblaze had survived the curse, Erluc realized. According to Asten, pegasi were virtually immortal until they were killed, but they looked like ordinary horses until they reached full maturity, which could take millennia. The Ancient must have unintentionally aged Skyblaze to his adult form!

His confidence restored, Erluc brought his fingers to his lips and loosed a piercing whistle. The shrill noise caused the great beast to turn in his direction, and the familiar sight of his steed provided Erluc with a sense of security.

A month ago, the sight of a horse sprouting wings would have been too much for him, but the past few days had desensitized him somewhat to that sort of thing.

Invardui screamed a battle cry, and Erluc joined in enthusiastically, raising his sword high above his head as he charged towards the swarm of foes with renewed energy. The air rang shrilly with the sound of steel on steel, and even those dark elves that tried to flee were mowed down by Skyblaze's flailing hooves. Erluc jabbed and blocked and parried like a madman, the adrenaline coursing keeping him only just alert enough to avoid being cut down. A bloodsteel sword stabbed at him from the right, and instinctively Erluc flinched, but a Guardian's blade knocked it aside, twisting it in a wide arc before tearing it out of its owner's hand and flinging it several dozen feet away. Erluc scrambled back hastily, desperate for breathing room, and Kovu glanced over at him with a brief smirk.

Anxious not to lose their momentum, Erluc sprinted back into the fray, slashing at the nearest dark elf. His adversary saw the attack coming, though, and blocked easily, shoving Erluc back into a lock. They both struggled for a moment, neither giving up any ground, before Erluc twisted his blade around, just as Kovu had, wrenching the sword out of the elf's hand. Gradually, the ranks of dark elves thinned to an increasingly ragged state, until a lone enemy stood in front of Skyblaze.

A single lash of the pegasus' front leg brought it to the ground, and Kovu ran his blade through the elf's shoulder, eliciting a howl from the fallen warrior. The sword gently rested along the elf's chin, a crimson beard flowing down from its lip. Violently spitting blood into the soil, the creature glared directly into Erluc's eyes, defiance radiating from him even in defeat.

Calmly, Erluc whispered, "Why did you bring us here?"

The dark elf continued staring at him, not a breath escaping his nightmarish face. Exasperated, Skyblaze landed another kick upon the creature's disfigured hide. Grunting, the fallen soldier hissed back at the pegasus.

"The Blade's orders" were the only words that escaped his mouth, in an accent unmistakably similar to that of the Ancient.

The Blade? Was that a title?

It must have been. As titles went, it wasn't so bad. It did make this person sound like something of a tool, though. Still, the way that the dark elf had spoken of his master… he wasn't someone to be taken lightly. The dark elf looked down, and it seemed like he wasn't about to reveal anything else, even if he knew it.

The flat of Invardui's blade slammed into the elf's skull, a satisfying crunch knocking him out cold. Sighing, Erluc looked up at the pegasus. It was going to be much more troublesome to mount his steed now, the great wings blocking his usual spot on its back. And he was going to need a new saddle.

But that was an errand for another day. Patting Skyblaze's snout, they faced the hidden valley. *Skyblaze the pegasus.* He snorted at the irony.

Together with the Guardians, they strolled off towards the fortress where Asten was being held, as the final rays of light commemorated the beginning of night. *We're going to need a plan.* Above them, the first stars twinkled into existence as the silver land basked in the silent glory of a full moon.

Chapter 5

A Less than Heroic Rescue

Dark Elven Fortress, Vale of Shadows

Asten

As far as Asten was concerned, his luck had reached an all-time low.

He hoped Erluc had some sort of plan to find him because he doubted he could take this prison food much longer. That and he didn't bet very heavily on his chances. He knew his captors were dark elves, but that information raised more questions than it answered.

Asten knew enough to be sure that they never captured anyone who wasn't absolutely vital to them—for information or for a rich ransom in dire need.

So why kidnap a traveler? And why him?

Just then, the cell door creaked open. A dark elf walked in toting a steel plate and a pitcher. He flung the jar at Asten, who rolled away to avoid being hit, then dropped the plate filled with rice that looked unappealing, with a clatter. His steel-toed boot pressed on the edge of the dish, which flipped, lightly hitting the side of his waist before spilling all the rice onto the dirty stone floor.

Never mind. It was probably stale anyway.

The elf snickered to himself, causing Asten to scowl in distaste, then walked out, slamming the steel door shut. At the very least, Asten felt glad that he was at least being fed and had been unbound.

He stared dismally at the pitcher, which was overturned and leaking water. Leaning over, he pulled it upright and took a sip. The liquid was oily and bitter, and Asten gagged and spat it out. Sighing, he turned to the spilled rice. Reaching down, he winced, the pain of the slash in his shoulder flaring up. Slowly, he overturned the dish and sighed.

What am I doing? He gritted his teeth, clutching the dish with both hands. Whatever little rice was still on it tumbled to the ground. But Asten didn't care—it wasn't as if it would make a big difference if he lived for a couple more days. In the end, he was just going to die.

He turned to face the decaying skeleton, adorned with a frayed necklace of rope, propped up against the other wall. "How long did you make it in here?" he murmured. *A week? A month?* Asten shook his head, lifting a small stone and flinging it at the skull in frustration.

Whatever had been holding the skeleton together gave way at the impact, and it collapsed into a shapeless pile of bones. Now he really *was* alone. A sudden burst of anger welling up inside him, he picked up the dish and hurled it at the cell door and was met by the crash of metal on metal, and a loud *snap.*

Furrowing his brow, Asten braced his leg against the door and gave it a light push. Though it didn't open, every time he applied pressure to it, he could hear an unmistakable rattling. He got to his feet unsteadily, making his way over to the skeleton and picked up one of the finger bones. Stepping back to the door, he felt around inside the lock with it, probing insistently until a tiny, thin metal cylinder fell out.

When he examined it more closely, he could clearly see the signs of corrosion eating away at it, and sure enough, the lock seemed to be rusting as well. A smile touched his lips, and looking around, he began to form the beginnings of a plan.

Returning to the rope buried in the pile of bones, he quickly selected four or five long, sturdy fibers and twisted them into a six-inch-long string, which he held together at the ends to create a small but strong loop.

Please let this work.

He knelt, inserting the loop into the keyhole, and felt around with it until it caught—presumably on one of the lock's pins. Crossing his fingers, he quickly jerked the string back, but it broke in his fingers.

Undaunted, he fashioned another length of string and poked it into the keyhole, and when it caught this time, he pulled at it sharply. A *snap* like the first one he had heard met his ears, and when he felt in the keyhole with the small bone, another metal cylinder fell out, landing with a *clink* on the stone floor.

He repeated the process one, two, three more times, until each of the pins had been broken, and when he inserted the bone and turned it around like a key, the lock clicked open. Asten grinned to himself. Though he wasn't sure how to pick a lock, he had done a fair job of breaking one. Pushing the door open, he turned right—the way he'd seen the dark elf go, through the bars. He knew, if nothing else, that the exit from the dungeons would be a staircase. Breaking into a run, he scanned his surroundings for stairs.

There! A staircase, dead ahead. Asten flew up the steps to find himself in a large room filled with weapons and spoils of war. An armory.

Asten sprinted to the mound of trophies, digging for *something* that might help him. He flung aside skulls, battered helmets, and swords corroded beyond recognition until his fingers closed around a smooth scabbard. Yanking it out of the pile, he examined it quickly. The jet-black hilt was evidently crafted by the moon elves, while the sheath was decorated with stars on a dark-blue background. He drew the sword just as a tall, burly dark elf sprinted up the steps, scowling. In one hand he wielded a spiked warhammer.

The elven blade glittering coldly white seemed to hold his assailant back for a moment, but only that. With a yell, the dark elf rushed at Asten, swinging the massive hammer. Asten held his slim sword ready—although he couldn't yet beat Erluc in their sparring matches back home, he did have enough skill and technique to challenge his friend's innate talent and surprising strength.

Narrowing his eyes, he dove, striking at the elf's legs. The razor-sharp blade severed the straps of its leggings, leaving its shins exposed. Asten smiled slightly. With each stroke, the blade whistled through the air, weightless, with blinding speed.

He rolled to the side as the hammer came down, cracking the stone to dust. The spike left a distinct hole in the floor, fractures emanating from it. Coming up on one knee, Asten feinted at the dark elf's open legs, then sprang up, slashing at his neck.

But in a single instant, he realized that he had miscalculated the jump. The hammer, which the elf had thrust forward to counter Asten's feint, knocked him off balance even as he swung. The sword's flat hit the side of the dark elf's helmet and was wrenched out of Asten's hands as he fell. The impact against the hard stone floor winded him, but he scrambled to his feet and threw himself toward the weapon racks. He selected a hand-and-a-half leaf-bladed sword with a smooth edge, at odds with the usual jagged blade preferred by dark elves. It was as though they had tried to replicate a design of their forest-dwelling brethren and had managed to produce a gruesome, twisted facsimile.

The elf was too big and too strong for Asten to fight. They both knew that. He considered making a break for it, but the door was barriered. The dark elf snarled and raised the spiked mace, radiating nothing but menace from his blue, pupilless eyes.

Then Erluc yelled and charged up from behind, impaling the elf in the gut.

Or at least, he meant to.

The dark elf, alerted by Erluc's shout, wheeled around and swept him off his feet with one deadly strike, knocking the gleaming sword and shield from his hands. The next swing of the hammer would either crush his ribs or impale his heart.

Shaking off his incredulity and swearing, Asten dove for Erluc's fallen shield, then snatched it up and leaped to cover himself and his friend with it, even as the hammer descended.

BONG.

The warhammer rebounded, denting the dark elf's chestplate where it smashed into his shoulder blade. The elf stumbled, and Erluc pounced, kicking him in the chest. The dark elf snarled as he flew backwards into the rough wall, his skull making a gruesome crunch as it crashed into the rugged surface.

Asten tossed the shield aside. The silver plating had been crumpled and forced aside where the spike had crashed into it.

"Good one," gasped Erluc, wiping his sword on his leggings. "You all right?"

"Well enough. But we need to go fast."

"The guy who got himself captured is giving me advice?"

Asten knew that bickering would only waste time, but he forced the thought aside. "I made it out of the cell myself, didn't I?"

"Oh, great job," remarked Erluc sardonically. "What was the plan after that? Fight your way out of here alone?"

Just then, two cloaked men emerged from the staircase, their swords bloody and their faces grim. "Gates are jammed. Ready to go?"

Erluc nodded. "Let's get out of here."

"Now, who are *you* guys?" asked Asten, grabbing his new sword and following Erluc back down the stairs.

They didn't make it far.

Three dark elves turned a corner to face them, and Asten leaped forward to engage them, hoping to get the element of surprise, but he was stopped dead in his tracks by one of the men. "Wait!"

The other man parried a stab and retreated hastily just before the first charged forward, slashing two elves across the chest. Erluc drew his own sword, kicking another opponent away. Backed into a corner, the second man drove his sword through an elf's sternum, watching it fall to the ground. Asten winced at the sight. "That is disgusti—"

"Run!" Erluc sprinted ahead, and Asten followed close behind, only stopping himself in time to hear the approaching danger. On instinct, he whirled around to face the others.

"There! Into that cell! *Go!*" he hissed, gesturing fervently.

Erluc obliged, ducking to the left, and both men followed moments later. Asten slipped into the cell last, softly shutting the cell door behind him. "What are you—" Erluc faltered as he heard a dark elven patrol thunder past.

"This was my cell," he explained, indicating the water pitcher and the dented steel platter of rice. "Now explain. How did you get here? And who the devil are these guys?"

In a few terse words, Erluc narrated the story of how he'd reached the fortress, starting from his meeting with the Guardians.

"Oh," was all Asten could say. "I'm sorry I was so rude earlier."

"That's alright," assured the taller of the newcomers, Invardui.

Kovu, the other, grimaced. "This place isn't for men," he muttered. "We can explain the rest later. Let's just get as far away from here as possible."

Asten nodded, millions of unanswered questions bouncing around in his mind. They would have to wait.

"By the way, you dropped this," added Erluc. Holding out a hand, he opened his fingers to reveal Asten's red gemstone, still secure on its fine steel chain. Surprised, Asten snatched back the crystal, fastening it around his neck once more. "Thanks," he acknowledged quickly, pulling the knot tight. He stood, glancing out the cell door, before managing to unlock it a second time. Holding the door wide open, he turned back to the group. "I think we're clear, everyone."

Invardui nodded in agreement, and Erluc and Kovu followed him out of the cell. Asten lagged behind a moment to close the door quietly, sprinting to catch up with the others, who had already made a mad dash for the nearest corner. By now, he was sure someone would have noticed the remains of whoever's blood was on the Guardians' swords, and the sooner they found a way to escape, the better. "Do you know which way to the gate?" he panted, racing up a staircase. "The gate? Oh, it's at this left here." Erluc turned right at the intersection they had just reached and hilt-slammed a guard, knocking him out almost instantly.

"You said left!" protested Asten.

Erluc nodded. "The *gate* was left."

"The gate was our exit!" Erluc shook his head and motioned for Asten to follow him up a spiral staircase. "The wall? You want us to jump off the *wall?*" he exclaimed. "No. No way. Absolu—"

Kovu grimaced. "Does he always talk this much?"

They emerged on the top of a tower with two dark elves wielding bows. Invardui stabbed one through the chest as Kovu cut the bowstring of the other and pierced it through its neck with one of its own arrows. Just as Erluc sprinted out of the tower onto the rampart, a deep horn blew, and Kovu finally threw caution to the winds, yelling, "They know we're here! Hurry!" Erluc seemed to understand, crouching lower as he ran, and Asten could make out the *twangs* of elven bows as the guards shot at his friend.

Dashing after Erluc, Asten ducked and swerved to dodge the deadly arrows. One of them just missed his cheek, clattering onto the stone beside him as he took cover behind part of the wall. From its obsidian hue, he realized after a few moments that it was made of bloodsteel, forged such that it would poison whatever it cut.

Then he saw Erluc's escape plan, and his brain imploded. Erluc was coaxing a snow-white pegasus to show itself. "Get on!" he roared. "Now!" Groaning, Asten ran the last few meters and leaped onto its back.

Kovu slashed a dark elf across the chest, kicking it off of the wall. Turning back, Erluc saw Invardui dispatch the last enemy on their side of the wall before tossing Kovu his abandoned bow. Asten quickly handed him a stray arrow, and the Guardian aimed briefly before shooting back at the final dark elf on the opposite rampart. The bloodsteel arrow caught him in the chest, and he fell backwards off of the wall.

Just before they could celebrate their narrow escape, though, the sound of the horn rang once again, and this time about a dozen more dark elves swarmed onto their rampart. Asten swore, sliding off of the pegasus, and raised his sword.

"What are you doing!" yelled Erluc. "We need to go. Now!"

"Not without them!" Asten called back, pointing with his weapon. About fifteen yards from the pegasus, Invardui had already taken on the advancing tide of dark elves, barely able to keep up with the onslaught. Erluc spat a curse as well and snatched the bow and three fallen arrows from Kovu. Taking aim, he released all of them in quick succession, and three of Invardui's assailants fell, neatly shot through the eye.

As the Guardian turned to flee the charging dark elves, Kovu turned to Erluc, surprised. "You never told us you could shoot."

"I shoot." Erluc took another arrow from Asten and fired it at the nearest dark elf, who crashed to the ground with the shaft sticking out of his throat. Asten watched him with a mixture of pride and envy. Though he had gone out hunting with Erluc before, he couldn't match his friend's skill.

Just as Erluc released the last of the arrows, Invardui sprinted past them, clambering onto the winged horse. "Let's go!"

Asten mounted in front of him, seizing the reins, but even as Erluc turned to follow, the first of the remaining two dark elven soldiers reached him, not even pausing before swinging his sword at his neck. Luckily, Erluc's reflexes were fast enough for him to deflect the blade with his bow, drawing his sword. Without hesitating, Kovu rushed to his aid, taking on the second dark elf with a yell. Asten was about to slide off of the pegasus as well, but he was stopped by Invardui's hand on his shoulder. "If either of us endangers ourselves," the Guardian explained gently, "Kovu and Erluc could be killed trying to help us. Do you want that on your conscience?" Asten bit his lip, watching his friend fight for his life, but he knew that Invardui was right. If he entered the fray, he could well make matters worse.

Erluc's swordsmanship had certainly improved in his time with the Guardians, Asten noted, but it wouldn't be enough to take on a seasoned warrior like this and hope for victory. It was evident, just watching him give up one foot after, that he would soon be overwhelmed. Kovu seemed to realize it too, as he was attacking his own foe with redoubled vigor in an attempt to come to Erluc's rescue as soon as possible.

The nearer of the dark elves parried a stab from Erluc and shoved, and the younger fighter was sent sprawling, his sword slipping from his hand and tumbling over the rampart. Kovu, who had just dispatched his opponent, yelled "No!" and sprinted back towards them, impaling Erluc's attacker through the back. The horn blew once more, and this time, an even larger swarm of dark elves emerged from the tower. Wave after wave continued to pour onto the wall, until Erluc and Kovu were facing down a small army.

Asten looked back at Invardui anxiously, but the Guardian seemed to have forgotten he was there. Instead, he was watching the wall intently, his eyes steeled. Kovu had handed Erluc his own sword, saying something to him in a low, urgent voice, and Erluc had accepted it with a solemn nod and a short response: 'I promise', Asten thought he had said. Then he sprinted back to the pegasus, and Kovu lifted the sword of one of the vanquished dark elves.

For the briefest of moments, the Guardian looked back at them, watching Erluc climb onto the pegasus behind Invardui. Then he screamed a fearsome battle cry, turning again to the tide of foes, and charged towards them.

It took Asten a moment to register what was going on, but when he did, his heart dropped into his stomach. "We can't leave him here," he insisted, twisting around to face the others. Invardui's expression was still inscrutable, but Erluc met Asten's gaze, looking utterly defeated. Everything he could ever have said was right there in his eyes. *I don't like this any more than you do. We can't waste what he's doing for us. If you don't leave now, we're all going to die.*

That last realization brought Asten back into the moment. Erluc's and Invardui's lives were in his hands now. He couldn't let them down. "Take the leg straps," he called back, kicking the leather loops over to Erluc. "It might be a rough ride." Nodding, Erluc roped himself into one and helped the Guardian into the other. Then Asten snapped the reins, sending the pegasus off the wall.

The ground immediately dropped out from under them, and he swallowed, his hands tightening around the reins that he recognized from only days before. *If this is that same saddle..*

"Wait a minute," yelled Asten. "This pegasus is Skyblaze?" Arrows whizzed past them, and he jerked the reins to the side, only narrowly missing them.

"I'll explain later!" Erluc called back. "Land here!"

Are you crazy? But Asten didn't question him. Biting his lip, he guided Skyblaze into a sharp nosedive. After managing to set the beast down under the shade of some trees, he noticed two horses tied around one of them.

Invardui promptly slid off of the pegasus, turning back to Erluc. "Listen carefully now," he spoke hurriedly. "You must reach Inthyl before the fifty-fifth day of this division." The request was oddly specific, but Erluc wasn't going to waste any more time.

"Alright," replied Erluc with a nod. "Vor té dryln." *Walk in peace.*

"Vor té carast." *Walk with fortune.* The traditional farewell greeting had originated from the archaic language of Telmírin and was one of the lasting influences that elvish culture had had on Aenor.

Asten dismounted as well as they watched Invardui ride off away from the fortress. "What was that? Isn't he coming with us?"

"Don't worry. It's all a part of the plan." Erluc looked behind him and grimaced. Infuriated yells echoed from the dark elves on the walls, who immediately disappeared into the fortress to ram the gate open. "Now go!" Nodding, Asten climbed onto the other horse, which must have been Kovu's, and snapped the reins.

BOOM.

Asten gritted his teeth as the sound echoed through the Vale as they rode at full pace, away from the fortress. He silently thanked the Guardians for thinking of jamming the gate. Even if they were still in danger, at least it had bought them a few precious seconds to escape. Sensing movement in the tower, Erluc ducked, narrowly avoiding the crossbow bolt whistling over his head.

BOOM.

Blood was easily visible on Skyblaze's left wing, which had been grazed by the bolt. Swearing, Asten urged his own beast to run faster. Arrows struck the earth near them, but even with a cut wing and poison bubbling in its veins, the pegasus' agility couldn't be matched. Yet, Asten knew that Skyblaze couldn't continue on forever—he was tired and wounded and would soon be run down.

BOOM.

The gate finally came crashing down, a regiment of mounted dark elves charging out in pursuit. With a final rush of energy, Asten pushed Kovu's horse to his limits and beyond. The blast of the horn behind Skyblaze's thundering hooves beside him echoed in his ears.

Asten guided the stallion deftly, desperately trying to throw off their pursuers. But Erluc's steed was wounded and poisoned—he wouldn't last much longer. And the dark elves, rested as they were, didn't look like they were stopping any time soon. Their own armored mounts were clearly still ripe with energy.

He silently prayed for the speed of Erluc's pegasus and that they would be able to reach the cover of trees before they were overrun. The only benefit was that the horses of the elves were, no doubt, weighed down by their heavy plating.

An arrow whistled past Erluc's ear, and he exhaled, looking forward. "There!" he called. "That's the place!" Asten gritted his teeth and swung the reins to the left, swerving into an expanse of tall, flowing reeds alongside the bank of the River of Fire.

The dark elves fanned out behind them, prepared to close in, even as Skyblaze disappeared into a large group of trees on the other side. Although no horse was suited to the thick shrubbery, the vegetation provided adequate cover for them to lose their pursuers.

Before their pursuers caught up, Erluc urged Skyblaze to a halt and slid off to shimmy up a tree. Asten followed suit, but there was no getting the wounded pegasus off the ground. Intelligent as he was, he simply flattened himself against the ground, where the dappled shadows hid his brilliant white hair reasonably well. After a moment of internal debate, Asten slapped the flank of Kovu's horse, sending it crashing through the trees. Though he hated to send away a good stallion, he was sure that keeping it around would have endangered them even further.

Asten could hear a soft rustling from below them, growing louder and louder by the second, and three dark elves burst through the undergrowth, on foot now. They were without protection and lightly armed; Asten assumed they were trackers.

Turning to Erluc, he widened his eyes. "What are we going to do?" he whispered harshly.

Erluc shook his head, indicating for him to quiet down. "Any second now," he assured. "Invardui said—"

His words were cut off by the rich, resonant call of a horn and the sound of scores of horses thundering towards them from the opposite direction. Asten turned to Erluc, who nodded, and in a flash, he understood what had happened.

The plan had worked. They had survived.

Chapter 6

WITH GREAT POWER

INTHYL, AENOR

Asten

No way. I can't believe it. Asten shook his head and blinked a few times, but the image before him resolutely refused to change. Even rubbing his eyes once or twice failed to dispel the gargantuan stone rampart towering over Skyblaze. *We finally made it.*

He turned back to Erluc. "Wow."

Erluc seemed to be having a similar reaction. With the exception of the elven fortress, neither of them had ever seen a building taller than fifteen feet. And if this was only the border of Inthyl, what would the city look like?

Skyblaze whinnied in discomfort as Asten guided him through the forty-foot-high iron gates, straining his wings against the blanket tied around his torso to hide them. Erluc patted him soothingly. "It won't be much longer, big guy. I promise, once we find somewhere to settle down, you'll be able to stretch."

Though the pegasus didn't understand the words, Erluc's light, comforting tone conveyed the message well enough to the intelligent beast. Urging Skyblaze into a light canter, Asten squinted at the inner wall with a gasp.

The fortification was built of pure marble and stretched well over two hundred feet high, the immense gate wrought of silver bars in intricate patterns.

Absently tugging at the reins, he tried to picture what the Heaven's Citadel would look like from up close. From what they had seen from afar before approaching the wall, it seemed to have been constructed with marble with a glass pinnacle and accents. It was taking all of his willpower to not head there immediately. Of course, they were going there anyway to pay their respects to Adúnareth, the Falcon Lord, and to thank him for their safe arrival. *Relatively* safe, anyway. Either way, he'd get his chance to see the Citadel.

Compared to something like that, the rampart would be mere building blocks. Erluc stretched over his shoulder to get a look as Skyblaze raced across the green fields between the walls where the food for the city was grown. With a practiced hand, Asten guided the pegasus along the dusty road to the inner gateway, occasionally turning so Erluc could see clearly.

As they passed through, Asten slowed Skyblaze down to a trot while gazing around in wonder. All his life, he had dreamed of coming to the great city of Inthyl. The opportunities here were boundless. Once he managed to settle down and find some work, his life would be so much better than it had been in Sering. He wouldn't have to sleep in a barn anymore or work until the sweat was pouring off his body for a mere morsel of food. He would put the events of the past thirty days behind him until they were reduced to nothing but an exciting tale that he could tell in his old age.

An hour later, they had found a respectable inn, The Broken Fang, and reserved a room for a week by combining all but the very last of their shared savings.

They'd also managed to stable Skyblaze and finally gave him a chance to stretch his wings, but it hadn't been long before they'd been forced to cover them again when the stablemaster walked in. Now strolling through the markets, they quickly forgot about their troubles, awed by the beautiful city with its high arches and lofty spires. Even the poor didn't live far from some architectural marvel or the other.

Erluc didn't say anything, and though Asten felt that he should start a conversation, he instead continued to look around. The smithy, in particular, caught his attention, and sure enough, when Erluc turned to try and sell the crystal he'd found in the Ancient's satchel, Asten wandered over to have a look.

The building, unsurprisingly, was built entirely of marble but was lined on the inside with a darker stone Asten didn't recognize. The forge blazed in a mesmerizing pattern that he felt he could watch all day, and to the left, a burly-armed man with fair hair was hammering out a glowing bar of metal that looked more like a sword with every stroke. A broad-shouldered youth, presumably his son, appeared to be assembling a row of arrows.

Asten took a deep breath and stepped up to the counter. "Broadheads?" he asked quietly.

The young man turned to face him. "Sorry?"

"Are those arrows broadheads?" Not the best of conversation starters, he knew, but he couldn't think of another way to get his attention. The blacksmith, too, looked up momentarily, then returned to his work, pulling on some leather gloves as he held the hilt of the blade steady.

A smile spread across the youth's face. He didn't look much older than Asten. "Aye, they are. Bloody expensive to make, too. But the king's weaponmaster has offered us two hundred gold daerals for twice that many arrows, twenty-five flamberges, sixty longswords, and ten battleaxes."

Asten had no idea what that was worth. Back in Sering, a single daeral could pay for enough wheat to last a large family several weeks. But then again, new currency never reached Sering unless one was willing to walk the thirty leagues and cross the Diamond River to reach the town of Tarrach to sell their goods. Asten and Erluc had once trapped and killed a stag and brought it to Tarrach, and despite the eleven queltras they'd gotten from the transaction, they had both vowed never to make the three-day voyage again, especially not while dragging a deer carcass behind them. Besides, the water tasted terrible there.

"Is that a lot?" Asten shook his head. "Sorry, I'm new in Inthyl."

"Not a problem," laughed the young man. "For that much, we'd normally have to work for years. So, whatever we spend on flamberges or broadheads will be paid back at a tremendous profit. Assuming we can finish them in a division, of course."

"It sounds fascinating," acknowledged Asten. He meant it—smithcraft had always captivated him. Though he had never had the time to try it for himself, given the choice, he would have taken up work in a forge.

Hmm. There's an idea. "Uh, could I speak to your father?" he inquired.

"Sure," responded the youth. "Father? Someone—" he paused, turning back to Asten. "What's your name?"

"Asten."

"Nice to meet you. I'm Lannet." He turned back to the burly man. "Asten would like to talk to you."

The smith quenched the blade of his sword, laid it aside, and stepped over to the counter. Lannet retreated to temper it before it cooled down too much.

Asten repositioned himself and began to speak. "Is it just your son helping you here?"

The man nodded. "He and my daughter Lyra. Don't know what I would do without them." He offered a hand. "My name is Galimin. Is there something you wanted to speak to me about?"

Asten shook his hand firmly, using all his willpower not to wince. Saying that Galimin had a strong grip would be a tremendous understatement.

"I'm new to Inthyl, and I'm looking for work," explained Asten. "Would there be some opportunity for me to help out here?"

Galimin's smile broadened. "Praise to Adúnareth! I'll be needing extra hands now more than ever, what with the king's rush delivery and all."

"Lannet told me about that."

"Did he? Well, I'm very short-handed right now, and I could use all the help I can get," he concluded. "How often can you come here?"

Asten thought about it quickly. "Starting tomorrow, every day, for seven hours."

Galimin's smile widened before he raised an eyebrow. "There isn't a catch, I hope?"

"Only that I'm going to need an advance on my first day to find lodging. Two daerals should be enough to tide me over at The Broken Fang until I can find something a bit more permanent."

"I can afford that." He eyed Asten suspiciously. "You sure you'll be up to the work? It's not easy, you know. And you're going to need a fair bit of stamina, too." His gaze traveled up and down Asten's lanky frame.

Asten laughed. "I used to work with horses all day. I think I'll be fine."

Galimin seemed to accept that. "Very well, then. Any past experience?"

"I can make a decent hunting arrow. But I'm a fast learner." Asten stood up straighter.

Scratching his scraggly beard, Galimin nodded. "I'll take you on for a week, and if you do well, then I think I'll keep you for longer. As for your advance, you'll get a daeral now and one more if I decide to keep you on full-time."

"Fair enough. I agree," decided Asten. "I'll arrive tomorrow at eight in the morning. Pleasure meeting you."

"You too. And I hope this works out for the benefit of the both of us." Galimin turned around and bellowed, "Lyra! Bring a daeral downstairs, would you?"

"I'll be right down, Father!" a bright, melodious voice called back.

"My daughter will bring you your advance. I look forward to working with you, Asten," said Galimin, smiling broadly. "Now, if you'll excuse me, I must tend to my flamberge." Turning his back, he began to use a hammer and a pair of pliers to give the blade its traditional rippled edge.

Erluc walked up from behind, tapping Asten's shoulder. "Did you hear that? I'm pretty sure I heard a girl." Luckily for Asten, Galimin hadn't heard his friend's comment. Turning around, he shushed Erluc, to which the other boy shrugged. This was Erluc's real talent—if there were a girl within fifty yards of him, he'd know it.

The door at the back of the forge flew open, and a golden-haired girl of about seventeen ran lightly across the room, holding a gold daeral.

As she walked across the room, Erluc sighed in disappointment, fingering the hilt of Kovu's sword—*Telaris*, he'd said it was called. "Blonde," he whispered between closed lips. "All yours. Don't be too creepy," he added, giving Asten a thump on his back as he walked back to the trader he'd been conversing with earlier.

Shut up, Asten wanted to say, but he needed to make a good impression in front of the blacksmith. He'd never understood Erluc's dislike for blonde girls, but if that meant that he had a greater chance with them, Asten wasn't going to complain.

"Is this for you?" The girl stepped up to the counter and lightly slid the coin over with two fingers.

"Hmm? I hope it is." Asten grinned, snapping out of his trance. "Lyra, I assume?" He flipped the daeral, catching it with a single hand and pocketing the coin.

"That's quite a lucky guess," she jested with a smile. "So why the daeral—are you working for my father now?"

"Starting tomorrow, actually." He fiddled with his cloak, pulling it closer around his neck. Asten had never been too good at flirting per se, but he'd certainly picked up some pointers from Erluc. "He says you're very helpful."

Lyra blushed slightly. "I don't know about that. I just carry the water around, stoke the fire, talk to the customers, that sort of thing. My brother Lannet, *he* does all the hard work."

"Work doesn't need to be hard to be helpful," Asten offered with a grin. Lyra faintly returned the smile in embarrassment.

"So, what are you going to be doing?" she continued.

"Your father didn't really say. I suppose I'll be helping Lannet out crafting arrows."

"Lannet doesn't need any help. He makes those things faster than both of us put together." Lyra laughed. "Father might have you shoveling coal. We might have more time to talk then."

Internally, Asten took a deep breath. *Now or never.* "Or, if you want, we could talk now. How about we meet later for lunch?" He cursed himself internally for his half-hearted delivery, but hopefully, the message was discernible.

Lyra tilted her head, considering, her wavy yellow hair falling to the side. "I don't have anything to do today. So, why not?" she decided. "Where do you want to go?"

Asten coughed lightly, patting his chest. *Wow, I can't believe that actually worked.* He turned back to Lyra, confidence renewed. "The Winestone is supposed to be quite good," he suggested. He'd heard a trader talk about the place a few years ago, and it was the only one he knew. "Unless you have any preferences."

"The Winestone sounds great. Does two o'clock work for you?"

"It does." Even if it hadn't, he still wouldn't have risen saying anything that could ruin this. Besides, it wasn't as if he had anything to do today. "Anyway," he said, glancing back at Erluc, who was arguing furiously with an old trader, "I should probably go now. Talk to you later."

Lyra waved lightly. "See you."

With a nod of acknowledgment, Asten turned and met up with Erluc, who was walking away from the traders' huts with a frustrated expression. "Nobody wants to buy this stupid thing," remarked Erluc, tucking the crystal back into his pack. "How'd it go at the smithy?"

Asten gestured back to the smithy. "Got a job, and the smith even agreed to give me a daeral in advance."

He gave Erluc a superior look. "Oh, and I have a date later today."

Erluc snorted. "With the blacksmith?"

"With his *daughter*, you dolt," Asten responded, punching his friend lightly on the shoulder.

Erluc raised an eyebrow. "You landed the blonde?" he asked, evidently surprised. "Wow, my training has finally paid off." Shoving Erluc with one hand, Asten snickered. "How're you going to pay for it? Don't forget, we've got to pay for the inn too." He frowned at the daeral sparkling in Asten's palm. "You're definitely not borrowing from me."

Asten smiled to himself. "Oh, don't worry. I have it all worked out."

Erluc snorted. "Anyway, we should head up to the Citadel. We've waited long enough as it is." They both briskly walked the rest of the way to the city center, by which time it was almost noon. They found themselves walking in the opposite direction to a stampede of Andaerians, all rushing past them in a hurry. Asten managed to catch the words "late" and "palace" from a conversation between a passing couple.

The Citadel was easily visible now, its twisting glass pinnacle seeming to scrape the clouds themselves. They managed to struggle past the crowd, finally making it to the comparatively empty entrance arch of the temple. Asten flew up what seemed like hundreds of steep stairs two at a time, Erluc sprinting just behind him. They cautiously stepped over the threshold. The inside of the temple was virtually devoid of people, which was probably because of the ruckus far below them.

As Erluc stepped into the main atrium, his eyes widened in awe. The high-domed roof seemed like it had no beginning, finally spreading over a hexagonal room. The floor had writing etched into it in a strange, flowing, spiraling script. In the center stood a single altar engraved with three circles surrounded by intricate designs. At its base was a large opening, maybe an arm's length wide, immediately catching Asten's attention.

He turned to Erluc. "You got anything to sacrifice?"

"I'm empty." He turned out his pockets, revealing his two maps and a carrot stick, which Asten quickly snatched and bit into hungrily. Asten's eyes traveled down to his scabbard, but Erluc warned, "Don't even think about it."

"Worth a shot," he shrugged. "What about those vials? The ones you got from the Ancient?"

Erluc reached back into his pack, pulling out the empty vials. "We don't really need these, I suppose."

"So, I'm taking that as a yes?"

"Why not?" Erluc replied with a shrug, tentatively dropping them into the hole. The torches along the walls seemed to brighten, and Asten felt a wave of heat before a cool breeze entered the chamber. "Are you going to offer something too," questioned Erluc, "or can we get out of here?"

Asten snorted. "Like what? I have practically nothing."

"You think you'd fit inside the opening?" Erluc offered sincerely before a quick glare from Asten caused him to shrug and let it slide.

"Can I borrow some queltras?"

Erluc laughed. "You really want to sacrifice money?"

He had a point. *Hmm…* Asten absently scratched his head as he thought but to no avail. *Honestly, it won't kill anyone if I don't offer anything.* After all, he couldn't stand the thought of giving up something that he actually valued for an entity that had given him nothing but suffering. Before he could speak another word, a voice rang in from outside, and both Erluc and himself turned to face the entrance.

A girl of about fourteen stepped into the room, smiling at them as she moved forward to make her offering of three queltras. Asten managed a quick, awkward wave that looked more like a salute, while Erluc nodded curtly. The girl turned back to gaze down the steps. "Come on, Renidos!" she called. "Hurry up!"

"Would you slow down?" demanded the voice of a boy. Within seconds, its owner, roughly the same age, but a few inches shorter than they were, hopped up the last step and into the temple. His skin, along with his short, slightly choppy hair, wasn't as pale as was expected of South Aenorians—he looked like he had quite a bit of northern blood. His eyes were constantly moving as though he expected to be ambushed at every corner.

"About time," gloated the girl in a singsong voice.

Renidos placed both of his palms on his knees, bending forward to catch his breath. He looked up and gave Erluc a nod of acknowledgment.

The girl turned to Asten. "He's not usually like this," she confessed. "Last year, he won a medal at the Academy for running." She grinned, turning back to the boy. "I don't know what happened to you."

"You know *exactly* what happened," he shot back. "That last course at the Winestone nearly floored me." Walking forward to Erluc, he extended a hand. "I'm Renidos of House Wayron, son of Elias," he introduced. "I don't think I've seen you around here before. And I don't mean to be rude, but your clothes kind of stand out."

Meeting the younger boy's hand, Erluc smiled. "Erluc, son of Neran," he responded. "That's Asten. We got here from Lindrannon just yesterday."

"Welcome to Inthyl, then." Nodding, Renidos turned to the girl, who was waiting impatiently with a smug expression on her face. "You've already met Natalie of House Stanton."

Erluc raised an eyebrow. "As in Queen Natalie?"

The girl grinned. "Actually, I did meet her once, when I was four," she informed. "You know, back before…"

Asten grimaced, and the four of them shared a moment of silence for the late queen. It had taken a rather dark toll on the whole of Aenor when she had passed, but even eight years later, her legacy lived on.

"So, the Winestone," started Asten, trying his best to change the tone of the conversation. "Any recommendations?"

At this, Renidos brightened up. "I always have the krill—it's *divine*."

"It's terrible," countered Natalie.

The boy ignored her. "But otherwise, the flatbread is supposed to be their specialty." Asten nodded, and Renidos slipped past him, placing two silver queltras into the opening in the altar. The torches flared up once more, and Asten felt the heat intensify even further.

"Check it out," remarked Natalie, looking down from the top of the Citadel, over the city. Renidos glanced up, just about to make a small prayer. "You can see the palace from here."

Asten raised an eyebrow. "Is there some kind of celebration going on down there?"

She nodded. "The High King turns fifty-one today." Turning to Renidos, she gave him an irritated look. "We were just about to go check out the celebrations at the Gardens of Inthyl."

Shrugging, Renidos bent down to tie the laces of his boots. "So, where are you guys staying?"

Asten fiddled with his scabbard. "It's a small inn called The Broken Fang," he recalled. "Not too far from the city center."

"Right, I've been there once or twice," offered Renidos, standing up and preparing to leave. "They serve the *best* coffee."

Erluc smirked. "I knew I liked that place."

With a nod of acknowledgment, Renidos approached Asten. "Well, it was nice meeting you two," he proclaimed. "If you ever need someone to show you around the city, I'd be glad to help you out." He extended a hand, which Asten reluctantly mirrored, but both of them were caught unawares by a shock when hands met.

"Oh," blurted Asten. "Sorry."

As he said the words, he noticed something shining under Renidos' tunic and raised an eyebrow. "Uh… does that happen a lot?" questioned Erluc.

"Does what—" The younger boy looked up at him, confused at his expression before he too noticed the glow. Standing up, he produced a smooth amethyst from underneath his tunic, its piercing violet hue radiating their surroundings. Renidos shook his head, speechless. "Actually, it's never happened before," he admitted. Erluc could sense a touch of suppressed fear in his words, but the boy seemed to have held things together.

"He's right," concurred Asten. Erluc turned to his friend, only to see that the red gem that hung down to his collarbone was also emitting a strange glow. Asten unclasped the thin chain from behind his neck, holding the stone in his hand. He'd almost considered sacrificing it, but he'd dismissed that idea without a thought. The crystal was his last piece of home—it was almost a piece of himself. And while he didn't mind losing something material for a god, his recent experiences seemed to have convinced him that it was not going to be worth it. If he was going to suffer anyway, he might as well be happy about it.

As soon as the crystal was exposed, the crimson light colliding with purple rays, Erluc felt a small, steady surge of energy from the gems. "Something's definitely not right," he agreed.

Asten leaned over to see what was in Renidos' palm: a dark crystal, almost like obsidian, with the steel likeness of a serpent coiling around it. "I must be losing my mind," he muttered. Curiosity got the better of him, and as he brought the gems closer together, his observation seemed all the more accurate.

"There's no way—" began Natalie, who had been too bewildered to speak earlier.

"They look exactly the same," stated Asten, equally confused. There was a moment of silence; all of them seemed startled at the apparent resemblance between the two gemstones. The size, the cut—in every aspect except for the color, the two jewels were exactly identical.

"Where did you get that?" questioned Asten.

Renidos seemed uncomfortable with the answer to that particular question, but he managed to reply. "My father left it for me before I was born," he explained. "Now, it's all I have to remember him by."

Asten and Erluc looked at each other, slightly guilty that they'd made him recall such a painful memory, before Erluc frowned. "Wait a minute..." He turned around and crouched down beside his pack. The others watched intently as he pulled it open, and ultramarine light flooded the chamber. Blinking his eyes open, Erluc reached into the pack, retrieving the Ancient's blue gemstone. "I knew this looked familiar, but I never expected *this*."

The glow of the room was now a blend of all three colors, the three gemstones shining with blinding intensity beside each other.

Asten covered his eyes with one hand, the other held in front as though to ward off some sort of attack. By now, the glow had grown into a blazing corona, and the gem itself was almost too hot to hold. Thunder boomed despite the azure sky, and Natalie shivered. "What was that?" He opened his mouth to respond, to tell the girl that it was just a coincidence, but the first sound never escaped his mouth.

In a single instant, the pulsing of the three crystals swelled into an unnatural wave of power, finally erupting in a brilliant flash of light, surrounding, consuming Asten. He heard Renidos cry out, but the light around them was slowly fading into darkness. The sky adopted a violet hue, and the air around them grew suddenly cold.

He was dead, wasn't he? This must be what it is to die.

To his right, Asten saw Natalie, frozen in place, a fearful expression on her face. She was deadly still, and he didn't know if she was breathing or not.

"Natalie?" called Renidos softly, brushing her arm. The girl remained frozen, ignoring him entirely.

"*Fear not, your friend is in no danger.*" Erluc met Asten's gaze, completely confused as to what was happening. And although Asten saw nothing, he heard a voice, deep, resonant, and tinged with sorrow, clear as day, in his very thoughts. "*Welcome, Erluc, son of Neran. Asten, son of Varandel. Renidos, son of Elias.*"

Son of Varandel? Twisting his neck around to locate the voice, Asten cried out in shock. "Who's there?" demanded Erluc.

"*I am the firstborn of the Immortals, the keeper of life in the Void and Mortal Realms,*" continued the voice. Asten's eyes widened, and he felt his throat close up before he coughed air back into his system.

"A-Adúnareth?" Asten's tone was that of complete disbelief. "I don't understand... I didn't think you were real." It was true, he'd been brought up in Sering, where—like everywhere else in Aenor—people worshiped the Immortals. But secretly, both he and Erluc had never truly believed that such beings existed. After all, there had never been any real reason to place their faith behind such a legend... until now.

The voice seemed amused. "*It is as it is destined to be.*"

Renidos furrowed his brow. "Where are we?"

"*This is a place beyond time—the only place where I can speak with you without placing you in danger.*"

He shook his head. "Danger? From what? And what do you mean beyond—"

"*Focus not on where you are, but why you are here,*" guided the voice, and Asten sighed. As if he knew what he was doing in a pit of infinite darkness.

Still, the Great Falcon remained silent, so it must have been his turn to speak. Taking a moment to consider, Asten shook his head. "I don't..." he started, but he trailed off as a memory flashed in his mind. "Does this regard the prophecy of Alydris?"

"*Alydris' prophecy was not of his own creation. It was merely a vision granted to him by me.*" The voice paused briefly before continuing, "*The day I foresaw is upon us... it is time.*"

"Prophecy?" inquired Renidos, thoroughly lost. The poor kid must have been losing his mind.

Asten's brow furrowed, and he took a moment to digest the words of the Falcon. "Time for what?" he asked. "I don't understand."

"*You will*," declared Adúnareth.

Exhaling, Asten shook his head. One step at a time and he would understand. "What's that supposed to mean?" challenged Erluc incredulously.

Adúnareth's voice was absent for a moment, and the three of them waited patiently before the Falcon spoke out again. "*A choice*," declared the Immortal. "*And a promise*."

Then even though his feet were still on the ground, Asten felt like he was falling through an infinite emptiness, and in the rush of wind in his ears, he could hear voices just barely too faint to make out. All around him, light from an unknown source illuminated a room mirroring Heaven's Citadel, but larger, and constructed entirely of black stone in contrast to the gleaming marble of its counterpart.

At the center of the room, a high-vaulted archway with intricate carvings running up and down its length stood solemnly alone. Even as Asten turned to look at it, a wisp of crimson energy escaped the gateway, followed by another, and another after that.

Looking around, he noticed that neither Renidos nor Erluc were present anywhere around him. "Where are they?" he wondered aloud.

"*You must make your choice alone, just as they are*."

He shook his head. "Of course, I do," he muttered to himself.

Slowly, the fragments of power began to coalesce into a single burning form, but before he could get a good look at it, it rushed past him.

"Wait!" Asten called before he could stop himself. He spun on his heel, trying to make out where the mass of energy had gone, but it had vanished among the stars. The stars? Confused, he looked around at the walls of the room, but the entire structure seemed to have vanished. "Where am I?" he demanded.

"Asten." Behind him, a stern but familiar voice caused him to flinch. He slowly turned to face the speaker: the man who had given him everything, only one step shy of a father.

"Neran," he responded, his voice overcome with emotion. Neran nodded, wrapping Asten in a hug, for a moment, all the fear, the pain of the last few weeks fell away, and it was as though he had never left home. When they separated, Asten instantly blurted, "How are you here?"

"He's not," revealed Neran, stepping back. He extended his arms, and for a moment, Asten could see the golden eyes of the Falcon glimmer alive in his father's. "I thought you would be more at ease surrounded by those places and people you knew well."

He pointed, and in the distance, Asten could faintly see the flickering light of the bonfire—the bonfire they used to light every new moon back home in Sering. "How..." he whispered, taking a few steps towards the village.

"You could go back," Neran told him. "You could have this life again."

"Stop this!" Asten met Neran's gaze, frustration welling up within him. "Tell me what you want!"

Wordlessly, Neran pointed again, this time in the other direction, and now Asten could see the wisps of energy racing away from the village and into the dark. He twisted back to face what was left of his past, pain and longing tearing at his heart, but steeling himself, he turned and began to run in the direction of the fiery current.

Then without warning, he was once again indoors, in an abandoned barn he knew all too well. "You are no stranger to hardship," noted the voice of a girl.

Asten looked up to see a tall, slender young woman sitting on a hay bale a few yards away from him. "Celia," he observed, forcing himself to mask a hint of shock.

"To abandon all you ever knew for this," murmured Celia, standing. As she began to tie her long, raven hair into a ponytail, Asten swallowed. This was Adúnareth, he had to remind himself, not the girl he had fallen for several years ago. "You have a strength to you, young Asten."

"Get out of my head," growled Asten, and the corner of Celia's mouth curved into a smile.

"I was never in your head," she said, stepping closer to him. "I've been watching you for a long time, son of Varandel."

There was that name again. Brushing the thought aside, Asten pressed, "Why?"

Celia took another step towards him; their faces were inches apart. "Your future here was one of happiness," she told him. "A good life. Haven't you ever wondered what could have been, had you only followed it?"

"Every day," breathed Asten. "But I can't keep living in the past." He leaned in towards Celia, but he pulled away sharply as a flash of red illuminated the dark barn. He whirled around, and the energy was there, mere yards away.

He started to walk towards the swirling power before him, and with each step, the shadows in the barn grew darker, the light from outside becoming watery and weak, until he was just inches away and there was nothing but him and the burning energy. "What do you want from me?" he yelled at the writhing mass.

"I need you to let go," said Erluc, and Asten's breath hitched in his chest. This time, when he turned around, it was almost painful to meet the eyes of his friend. Erluc watched him impassively, and it was all he could do to remind himself that this was the Falcon, not the person he knew. "Let go of this life, so you may take upon yourself a new one."

Asten frowned. "What new life?"

Erluc looked around, and the darkness reformed into a vast, shadowed clearing with a massive crater at the center. "Only time holds the answer," he said. "But it is a dark path. Filled with pain and despair."

As he spoke, the world flickered, and suddenly, the ground was littered with bones. "Why would I ever choose that?" Asten knelt, and his eyes were met with those of a hollow, gaping skull. *"Who* would choose that?"

"A hero," said Erluc simply. "With the strength to make the ultimate sacrifice. One life for another. For thousands. Millions."

All around them, people began to appear—nameless, faceless, but *people.* And in that moment, the full weight of what Adúnareth was telling him hit him like a hammer blow. All these people, all these lives, hinged on the next few moments.

"You can save *all* of them," whispered Erluc.

Asten swallowed, wishing more than anything that this burden had fallen on shoulders other than his. There must have been someone out there, worthier, more qualified for the responsibility Adúnareth seemed to be entrusting to him.

You must make your choice alone, just as they are, the Falcon had said. What, Asten wondered, was Erluc seeing—what choice was he being faced with?

Almost without his willing it, he quietly said, "What do I have to do?"

Moments later, he felt an intense warmth against the back of his neck, like he did on a hot summer day when he stood in the sun. Once more, he turned around, and this time he was standing at the edge of a pool, clear and still as glass. Though the world around him was pitch-black, the rocky terrain was illuminated by a blinding blue-white glow from somewhere beneath the water.

And across the pool, there was the energy, once again. Slowly but purposefully, it moved towards Asten across the water. As it drew closer, it seemed to take on a form, the shape of a person. Who was it this time? Which of Asten's loved ones did Adúnareth have left to use against him?

The figure kept walking, each step just barely landing on the surface of the water, but none of them disturbed its surface. The fiery glow from before seemed to be fading, transforming the blazing form from before into a dark silhouette, and as it approached, Asten was overcome with a surge of recognition.

"Wait!" called Asten before he could stop himself. "I know you!" The figure didn't halt, didn't so much as acknowledge his words as it stepped onto dry land as it turned to face him. Though the blue light from under the surface of the water should have illuminated its features, Asten could see nothing, almost as though it were cloaked with darkness itself.

Then the shadows dissolved, and Asten was met with the visage of a fair, dark-haired girl, one he had never seen before. "Do you?" she asked him, and he had no response. She smiled, the glow from the pool casting an eerie, rippling web of light and darkness on her face. "The power is yours to claim," she said, holding out her hand, and Asten was forced to shield his eyes from the blinding light coming from it. When finally, his vision adjusted, he saw that the girl was somehow holding the red energy from the gateway, condensed into a single point. "All you have to do is accept it."

Asten met her piercing gaze warily. "Accept?"

"Surrender," she said. "If you choose it, your life as you know it ends here, today. Surrender to the world, to the power of the Mage, and there will be no going back."

The Mage? Taken aback, Asten furrowed his brow, trying to process what was happening. "Why me?" he asked again, and for a moment, the girl's smile wavered, but a split second later, it was back.

"Have faith, Asten," she assured him. "Have faith in my choice, just as I place my faith in you." She offered the swirling energy to him again, and instinctively, he took a step away.

"There's so much I still don't understand," he whispered, looking towards the pool. Deep below the surface, the blue light had shifted to a fiery red, the same as the energy.

"All will be revealed in time," the girl promised. "This is your final test, Asten. Prove to me that you are ready, that you are worthy, that you can abandon your fear and step into the future in the name of the greater good."

Nodding, Asten reached forward, but he quickly jerked his hand back. The girl tilted her head curiously. "What about Erluc?" he blurted out.

The girl's expression was inscrutable. "The path he takes is his burden alone. As is yours."

Asten took a deep breath. Though he didn't know what exactly, some hidden will within him had awakened, urging him to give himself up to something greater. And if he didn't have the strength to make that choice now, he was sure he never would. "One," he whispered to himself, closing his eyes. "Two." He reached out with his right hand. He could feel himself shaking, and for a moment, he hesitated. In that instant, a flicker of doubt crossed his mind—what was he about to do?

Almost against his own will, he whispered, "Three," and before he could talk himself out of it, he opened his eyes, placing his hand over the energy in the girl's. "What's supposed to happen?" he asked.

"There is one final test," she declared, and the world dissolved into shadow. The burning energy flowed out from under his hand, blossoming into a glorious, terrifying mass of power.

"A promise," Asten recalled, and the energy flared in response.

"*Yes*," agreed Adúnareth, his voice once more his own. Now Asten was standing back in Heaven's Citadel, but he was still alone, the sky still its unnatural purple hue. "*So, you do understand.*"

"I do," said Asten. He turned around, and the energy was there, awaiting him.

"*Then promise me this*," implored Adúnareth. "*Swear to rise as one of the Chosen in my name, to protect those who need you the most, and the force of the Mage will accept you as its vessel.*" He paused. "*The oath will bind you, and the consequences will be dire should you disregard it. Once taken, there is no going back.*"

Asten hesitated, taking a moment to consider. "What are you asking of me?"

"*When the time comes, you will know.*" Adúnareth's voice was different now, a little strained. "*Promise me, Asten.*"

No going back. The Falcon's words seemed to be echoing across his mind, whispering to him. *No going back.*

But it didn't matter, Asten remembered. This wasn't a question of his life and what would become of it. It was of the whole of Aenor, of the Mortal Realms. Whatever the price he had to pay, it would be well worth this opportunity to change the world for the better.

His breath hitched as he said the words, barely above a whisper. "I promise." The energy flared, surrounding him, infusing him with its power, and he felt a jolt in his chest, like cold fire.

Then the world erupted in a blazing light, ripping through the eerie darkness, and instinctively, Asten covered his face with both hands, squeezing his sensitive eyes shut. And for a moment, there was only him, heart pounding, the energy running hot through his veins like blood itself, and then the power was gone, and he was left in darkness once again.

Slowly, uncertainly, he opened his eyes, blinking to dispel the reddish afterimage that burned into his vision. Nothing felt especially different, except that his hands were shaking uncontrollably. He stuffed them into the pockets of his trousers, taking a moment to look around him. Though the world still hadn't returned to normal, the energy was gone, along with the voice of Adúnareth.

"This is insane," muttered someone from behind him, and he saw that both Renidos and Erluc had returned and that the air around them was tinted slightly—Erluc radiated a faint-blue aura, while Renidos glowed violet.

"*It is done*," declared the voice suddenly. "*You have survived the process and now bear my power within yourselves.*" Asten tilted his head. Did that mean that he could have died? "*Reitur'an averár irlo kaeryx aí aeleor.*" Adúnareth's tone became pensive. "*These were my words, pronounced by Alydris, one thousand years ago. 'The Trinity shall rise to the Council's defense.'*"

"I remember," agreed Erluc cautiously.

"*Asten—you will face innumerable hardships in your journeys across the Mortal Realms. Yet, through all, you will be the guiding voice in the dark, the beacon in the mists, the light when all others seem to have gone out."* Skeptically, Asten shot Erluc a glance, but his friend didn't seem to be paying him any attention.

"Renidos, you have the potential to be the force of change that emerges from the cursed eclipse of millennia of war, my war. But as you grow, and your power with you, the darkness within will threaten to overwhelm the light. You will skirt the edge of the abyss, and you must master the call of the dark before it masters you." The young boy blinked once, and Erluc gritted his teeth. Clearly, this dream was starting to get too strange for both of them.

Adúnareth paused for a moment. *"The greatest gift that I have to give, Erluc, is the power of the Warrior—the balance between the Mage's light and the shadow of the Spectre. If you are to be successful in leading the Trinity, you will have to learn to regulate your abilities. Your judgment and composure are your greatest strengths."*

Ordinarily, Erluc would have flashed a smirk or said something incredibly self-serving. But instead, he asked, "Lead them to what?"

"Have patience, and all will become clear," assured Adúnareth. *"For now, you must adjust to your new life, discover your abilities and master them. When the time comes, you will face the banished one, and your powers will be vital in your conquest against Atanûkhor's servants."*

"What?" questioned Asten. "Atanûkhor?" His voice wavered uncertainly was he said the name, and he felt the darkness around him start to stir.

The Falcon ignored him, continuing his instruction. *"Go forth, defend the Council, and defeat the power of Atanûkhor here before he succeeds. Honor your promise. Rise, as the Trinity of Eärnendor ."*

Grimacing, Asten jerked upwards and cried out, "Wait—" The color faded from the sky, the heinous violet morphing into a familiar aqua. They were back. The auras around his friends—if they had ever existed—had withered away as well.

Natalie's expression finally broke, and color returned to her frightened visage. She flinched, smiling in relief as she looked outside at the clear sky. "It was probably just a passing cloud, but I'll admit I was worried for a second," she admitted with a hesitant grin. Turning to Renidos, she frowned. "Everything alright, Ren? You look like you've seen a ghost."

"Yeah, no, I'm okay. I just had the weirdest dream," remarked the younger boy. He glanced at Asten once, who nodded. "Listen, you should probably get down to the Gardens. You don't want to miss the ceremony." The girl seemed confused, but Renidos cut her off with a wave of his hand. "I'll be right behind you." Natalie shrugged and made her way outside, uneasily bounding down the steps. Looking down to his scabbard, Erluc's brow furrowed. What was once an ordinary wooden casing, was now an ornate sheath, and a pommel molded into the likeness of a falcon capped the hilt. He pulled the blade out, and he gasped. Telaris had been reborn.

The blade shimmered a faint blue, its original rippling patterns animated like a flowing river, but even as he watched, the color seemed to fade to the normal gray of steel. Erluc flipped the sword in his hand, examining the base, before showing it to Asten and Renidos. Almost so finely that he could not make them out, Asten saw a series of runic symbols he recognized as being Andaeric. He held out both palms, and reluctantly, Erluc handed him the sword.

Asten accepted it gingerly, holding the blade up to the light to throw the letters into sharper relief. "Telaris," he read aloud.

Erluc nodded. "I don't know if it is anymore."

"Hold on," interjected Renidos, taking the sword from Asten. "I know that word. *Tel'ar.*"

"What does it mean?" questioned Asten and Erluc at the same time.

"*Eclipse*," said Renidos softly. Carefully, he passed the weapon back to Erluc, hilt up. Its blade seemed to have been shaped of a metal that he couldn't recognize—darker than steel and holding a finer edge than he had ever seen on an ordinary blade.

As Erluc gripped the hilt, a shadow crossed his right hand, solidifying almost instantly into a jet-black gauntlet. Shocked, Erluc cried out, backing away, before evidently realizing that his arm was indeed a part of his body. Renidos raised an eyebrow. "Wh… How did you do that?"

Calming down, Erluc turned to the other boy. "I don't know," he admitted. By the time he'd turned back to his arm, the gauntlet had faded. He carefully returned his new blade to its sheath, before Asten started looking at his hands.

"Check this out," he told them, and the other two gathered around him. A golden ring had appeared around his fourth finger. "Where do you think this came from?"

Renidos raised an eyebrow. "You weren't wearing it before?"

Asten shook his head, and pulled the ring off his finger, examining the unblemished gold surface. "This is just too strange."

"Well, I seem to be fine," remarked Renidos. "But the voice told me that I was… the Spectre or something."

Erluc nodded. "And we're supposed to defend this Council—"

"Maybe the Council of Nine," offered Renidos.

"No." Erluc shook his head. "The Twilight Council."

"And combat… *someone's* servants," finished Asten.

Renidos nodded. "Atanûkhor—the Emperor of the Night." He gestured to the murals on the walls of the chamber. "I know more than enough about him." Erluc glanced at the walls and grimaced. He saw the Falcon battling a great, ferocious creature over a dark canvas. The Wolf.

"That's right," remembered Erluc. "He showed me my future self and said that the world would end if we didn't succeed or something like that."

"There's a big chance that the Wolf will be the cause of that," concluded Renidos.

"Wait a second," interrupted Asten. "You *both* saw your future selves?"

Erluc and Renidos nodded simultaneously, before the younger boy asked, "Why, who did you see?"

Asten's brow furrowed. "I saw a girl."

Immediately, Erluc seemed interested. "What girl?"

"I've never seen her before," admitted Asten innocently. "I don't know who she is, but she looked important."

"Important as in *attractive* important or—"

Asten threw his arms into the air. "Great Falcon, Erluc," he said exasperatedly, rolling his eyes. "Seriously?" Now that he thought about it, she hadn't looked all that terrible. He shoved the thought out of his mind; there were more pressing matters at hand.

"Sorry," muttered Erluc, clearly unapologetic. "Anyway, you never know; you could always become a girl in the future."

Asten snorted, and Renidos let out a short chuckle before continuing. "What was all that about a prophecy?" The older boys turned to look at each other before Erluc nodded.

"Um, I think it sounds something like this…" He closed his eyes, trying his best to remember the lines. It took him a minute, but he finally managed to recall the first two phrases of the augury.

Renidos seemed confused. "Are you sure that's all there is?"

Asten grimaced. "There's more—we just don't know it." He shifted uncomfortably. "So, what do we do now?"

"There's only one thing *to* do," declared Erluc. "And I don't know about you, but I'm famished."

Chapter 7

SAVED BY THE STALKER

INTHYL, AENOR

Erluc

Erluc rolled over in his bed, reluctant to open his eyes. His neck ached from the awkward angle caused by the stiff pillow under his head. Reluctantly, he sat up, rubbing his eyes. Asten was on a stool next to him, reading a letter by the light of a candle with visible difficulty.

He turned to face Erluc. "And I thought *I* slept lightly."

Erluc sighed and clambered out of the cot. "I didn't wake you?"

"No, I was already awake. He paused, presumably taking a moment to phrase his next words. "You had some sort of nightmare?"

"I'll live." He straightened his tunic and went to fetch water, only to find that Asten had already filled the small wooden pail in the corner of the room. "Just a few memories that won't leave well enough alone," he explained, fumbling around with the blue gem that rested in his pocket. He generally didn't have nightmares, but this was totally understandable. If Invardui hadn't been able to summon the other troop of Guardians to come to their aid, who knew what would have happened to them?

"Mhmm." Asten squinted at the parchment in his hands; he seemed to be struggling to read the letter.

As he splashed icy water on his face, Erluc asked in a transparent attempt to make conversation, "So, what do we do today? Explore the city?"

Asten rolled up his letter and stood. "Erluc."

"Yeah?"

He went to the window and drew back the tiny curtain. "It's still night. You should sleep." A light drizzle peppered the glass, contorting the crescent moon high in the dark sky.

"What… oh, blast it. What's the time?"

"Two, I think. I'll check the clock downstairs." He got up, setting his parchment on the table. As he made his way to the door, he stepped on Erluc's scabbard, and his ankle twisted, pulling him downwards. Throwing a hand up for balance, he reached for the table, pulling it down with him. The end result was a loud commotion, and Erluc jumped up from his bed to see what had happened.

"You actually just get clumsier as time goes on, don't you?" he chastised with a smile, lending Asten a hand.

"Ouch," agreed Asten, standing up. "We should probably clean all of this up."

Erluc groaned, bending down to look at everything that Asten had knocked over. The runestones from the Ancient's pouch had spilled over, and Telaris had been pulled free of its sheath.

"Wait, are these runestones?" questioned Asten.

Erluc nodded, and the older boy's eyes widened, looking through them in awe. The script was alien to him— definitely not Andaeric, and the letters seemed more like symbols.

"This one stands for fire, I think," declared Erluc, twirling it around, between his fingers.

Asten lifted one of the runestones, which displayed a jagged line. "What do you think this is? Lightning?"

"Not sure, but I'd say that's a safe guess," replied Erluc, taking the stone. He dropped it and picked up another one. "This one looks interesting."

Asten peered over for a closer look. "I wonder what it means." He gathered up the runestones and dropped them back into the pouch, one by one. As Erluc moved to return his stone, he gasped in pain, dropping it. The rock landed on the blade of his sword, which had gained a faint glow. Asten leaned over instinctively. "Are you alright?"

Erluc rubbed his palms together. "I think that stood for ice. I'm fine. Just a bit startled is all." His sword started to give off a blue-white light, and the temperature in the room dropped significantly.

"How did you do that?" asked Asten, grabbing the Fire runestone from Erluc's hand.

"Careful!" called Erluc. "We can't afford to burn the entire inn down."

Asten grinned, ignoring him. He touched the rune to the edge of Telaris' blade, and it evaporated into the air, just as the Ice runestone had. Within a few moments, the temperature in the room had returned to normal, and Asten threw his hands up into the air. "See? Nothing to worry about," he assured. "I have it all figured out."

"If you say so," commented Erluc, gathering the last of the runestones and dropping them into the pouch. He pulled the drawstring and placed the pouch on the table again, before deciding to return it to its place in his pack.

Drawing his cloak more tightly around himself, Asten hastily rose to his feet. "I still have to go check the time."

"Forget that. I'll take your word for it." Erluc nodded at the parchment in his hand. "Who's the letter from?"

Asten's pale cheeks reddened slightly in the candlelight. "No one important." Erluc raised an eyebrow. "The smith's daughter," conceded Asten finally.

Erluc grinned cheekily, whistling a high note. "I take it the date went well."

Judging by Asten's face, if he could have kicked Erluc and come out alive, he probably would have. "It's just a *letter*, don't be an ass."

"If you say so. But most people don't read *letters* at two in the morning." Erluc closed the curtain, dried his face and collapsed in bed. "You should sleep too."

"So that's it then?" asked Asten. "We're not going to talk about what happened back at the temple?" He clutched his gemstone with one hand, and Erluc fought the urge to look down at his blue crystal.

Erluc groaned. "No," he replied flatly. "I don't know why you two can't just let it go."

"I don't see how we can," admitted Asten. "We talked to Adúnareth. *The* Adúnareth. I don't see how you're not at least curious to figure out what it all means." He stopped suddenly, raising an eyebrow. "You met Renidos?"

"He came to see me while you were out. I'm going over to his house today," confirmed Erluc. "I'm sure you won't be missing anything."

"Hmm." Asten exhaled, rising up to arrange his two stools beside one another. He stretched out between them, which couldn't have been comfortable, but as long as Erluc got the bed, there weren't going to be any complaints. "Night."

"Night." Erluc blew out the candle and rolled over. He was asleep in an instant.

That time he slept better. When he woke, he saw a message hastily scribbled on the floor with a charcoal stick in Asten's distinctive, untidy scrawl. It took him a few tries, but eventually, despite the terrible handwriting and his own limited literacy, he managed to decipher:

"Left to work at the forge. Back by afternoon. Try and find a job as well, but meet here at four. Something you need to see."

How long had it taken Asten to write that? His reading was far better than Erluc's, but it wasn't this good, was it? Erluc shrugged and rubbed out the message.

After freshening up, he pocketed his money, buckled Telaris to his belt, and left the room, locking the door with the large, rusted iron key and made his way down to the foyer to get some breakfast. Distracted, he called for a light coffee and some bread and cheese. As he chewed, he considered what Asten could possibly want to show him.

Absently, he dipped a finger in his drink and started drawing lines on the table. It wasn't until he had finished his bread that he realized he'd been sketching a map of the city. He noticed a door at the far end of the inn creak open, revealing a girl with a flustered expression. She turned to look at Erluc before turning away sharply. Raising an eyebrow, Erluc returned to his coffee. *Could this city get any weirder?*

Luckily, he glanced up as two girls entered the inn, heading straight for the counter. One of them glanced his way, and their gazes met for a moment. The girl flashed a grin at him, and Erluc smirked back. Walking past him, she sat at the bar.

Finally, something familiar. Sighing, he ran a hand through his hair, picking up his half-empty mug of coffee.

"Four whiskeys, Thea," the girl called over. The barmaid looked up momentarily, before nodding. It obviously wasn't their first time here.

Approaching the counter, he set his mug down softly onto the counter. "I would ask to buy you a drink," he started, "but you seem to have it covered." He took another sip, and the girls turned to look at him. Thea passed them their drinks, and Erluc slid two queltras over the counter.

The girl turned to him, tucking a strand of hair behind her ear. "Thanks, but you didn't have to do that. We're fine by ourselves."

Smirking, Erluc nodded. "So was I, but then you walked into this bar," he muttered, almost so softly that it could have been to himself. Her friend whispered something in her ear, and they both giggled. He took a sip from his coffee, turning towards them. "Yeah, I'm sorry, that was too much, wasn't it?" He flashed a guilty—completely fake—smile at her, and he could see the corners of her lips curve upwards too. "I could have come up with something better if I were thinking straight. That's on you though, I'm afraid."

The girl raised an eyebrow, unable to resist a grin, "Well, I'm sorry, I guess."

"And I'm Erluc."

"Sabrina," replied the girl with a smile. "You're not from around here, are you?"

"What gave me away?"

Sabrina grinned. "Well, apart from your accent and clothes?" she tried. "I think I'd remember seeing you around here." She took a mug herself, passed one to a friend and one to Erluc.

"You want me to help you guys finish?" he questioned.

She shrugged, a lopsided smile on her face. "I thought I'd give you a chance, you know, to come up with something better."

"I'll take that chance," he concurred, and she let out a small laugh. They lifted their glasses simultaneously, and Erluc's eyes widened as the cold liquid passed down his throat.

He heard the girls exclaim in delight, and Sabrina turned to him. "Not bad, you seem like you can handle some more." Her friend giggled, pointing at his hand, and Erluc looked down, realizing that he had unconsciously started to fiddle with his blue gemstone while talking. "Where'd you get that?" she asked.

Erluc blinked. "Oh, uh… family heirloom," he lied, using Renidos' explanation. They seemed to buy the excuse well enough, but Sabrina couldn't manage to tear her eyes away from it. Sighing, Erluc lifted the crystal to give her a closer look.

"It's beautiful," she breathed, and Erluc managed a smile. Sabrina tentatively reached out a hand before pulling it back slightly. "May I?"

Nodding, Erluc handed her the gem, watching her admire it for a minute or so, then held out his hand to accept it back. Almost reluctantly, Sabrina tilted her own hand, letting the mesmerizingly blue stone roll out of her palm and back into Erluc's.

"You like it?" he asked, and she nodded slowly. "Tell you what," he started again, his eyes twinkling. "If you can finish the next glass faster than I can, it's yours." He wouldn't usually have been so lax with his wagers, but he hadn't even felt that last glass. Besides, if it would get rid of that gemstone, he was more than happy to try his hand.

She raised an eyebrow. "And if I can't?"

Shrugging, Erluc put on a slight smirk and dropped the crystal onto the counter. "I'm sure we can think of something."

Her eyes glinting with determination, she nodded. "I'll take that chance," she declared. "Hit us again."

Thea rolled her eyes from behind the counter, and just then, Erluc felt a hand clasp his shoulder.

Turning around, he saw a tall boy, probably about nineteen, standing above him. His teeth glistened unnaturally, and Erluc could automatically tell that the boy was the type of guy that he wouldn't get along with.

"Hey, Sabrina," called the boy. "This guy isn't bothering you, is he?"

"Not at all, Robin," acknowledged the girl, rather uncomfortably. Erluc almost let out a laugh. *Robin? Seriously?*

The boy turned to glance at him, his smile fading completely. "Something funny, farm rat?"

For the first time, Erluc noticed three young men standing behind him, all in their mid-twenties. He could probably have held his own against them, but he didn't want to get kicked out of the inn on the second day of their arrival.

Robin whistled a low tone, grabbing the gemstone that lay on the table. "What's a beauty like you doing in a dump like this?"

Sabrina answered for Erluc. "It's a family heirloom."

"Is that right?" he challenged. "I don't think they find these on farms, do they?"

Erluc shrugged. "Got lucky, I guess."

"Lucky," he echoed with a snort. "I have a different, much simpler, theory: I think you stole it."

Sabrina rolled her eyes. "Robin—"

"And you know what that means?" he continued, ignoring her. "It doesn't belong to you."

Though he was tempted to scowl, Erluc forced a smirk and turned to face him. "Interesting theory."

Robin bent down to look at Erluc, narrowing his eyes. "You think I'm joking?" he mocked. "I'm fully serious here. I think I'm going to have to confiscate this."

Finally, standing up to face the other boy, Erluc's smirk faded from his face. "I'll only say this once," he stated firmly.

"I think you should give it back." He wasn't all too fond of the gemstone, but he'd die before he let someone like Robin have their way.

Robin stood up straighter, only just taller than Erluc. "You think?"

Erluc nodded. "That's right. You should try it sometime." Sabrina suppressed a smile, and even one of Robin's friends snickered.

Shaking his head, Robin gripped Erluc's jacket at the shoulders. "How about I give you something to think about?"

His jaw clenched, Erluc glared at the other boy. "You're going to want to let go of that."

"Or what?"

Erluc gripped the boy's wrists, effortlessly lifting Robin's hands away from his shoulders. "Or your boys are going to have to carry you back to your castle." As he released, he could see red pressure marks on Robin's skin.

The boy grimaced, surprised at Erluc's apparent strength. Erluc gritted his teeth, feeling an unnatural sense of aggression, and took a step forward.

After that, everything seemed to happen at once. All of Robin's henchmen pounced towards him, just as a cloaked man leaped out of the shadows. Erluc hadn't even noticed he was there, but the man seemed real enough.

He seemed to be everywhere, and though he looked at least sixty, his agility was not diminished in the least. He pushed the fumbling boys around, fending off one foe after another. His technique seemed both ancient and unconventional, shifting from a dodge to a feint to dropping onto his hand and kicking the legs of his opponents out from under them.

By the time Erluc knew what was going on, all four boys were sprawled across the floor, and his cloak was pulled back.

"Who… who the hell are you?" questioned Robin, still scrambling to raise himself off of the floor. The man pulled his hood back over his head, before sliding the gemstone across the counter to Erluc, who quickly pocketed it. Now that he was closer, Erluc could make out the old man's gray eyes, slim figure, and narrow features.

Before Erluc could take another breath, the man was swiftly on his way out of the inn, and Erluc darted after him, somehow only just managing to keep up. "Wait!" he called after the man. "What was that about?" He hadn't noticed before, but the man had led him into a side alley, far away from the crowded streets near the inn.

The man stopped, glancing back at Erluc. "You were being reckless. If I'd waited any longer, you could've killed that boy." His voice carried a slight trace of a foreign accent. No, Andaeric was not his first language, though he spoke it as fluently as Erluc would.

"Killed him?" repeated Erluc, caught off guard. "Listen—" Before he could take a step, his feet were knocked out from under him, and Telaris was somehow in the man's hand. "What the—" Erluc scrambled to his feet, scowling and trying to reach for his sword, but the man was faster.

Spinning the weapon, he slashed at Erluc's face, a blow that could easily cut his cheek open, and instinctively, Erluc threw up both arms to protect his face in an X, bracing himself for the pain, but instead of the sword cutting into his flesh, his forearms were met with a dull pressure as the blade collided with two gauntlets, black as night, that had miraculously formed around them. *What the hell?*

Before the old man could strike again, Erluc leaped forward, punching him in the gut, and snatched Telaris back. "What just happened?" he demanded, holding Kovu's sword at the ready. Now that the immediate danger was gone, he was able to think clearly enough to recognize the gauntlets from his encounter at the Citadel—they were from the armor that the future version of himself had been wearing. He concentrated, imagining himself surrounded in that same armor, and a moment later, he was.

As the man stepped back, a smug expression appeared on his face. He only seemed slightly winded by the blow from the gloved fist. "As I said," he said softly, "you are reckless." He shook his head. "You can't control your own strength, and until you learn, you will remain a threat to everyone around you."

Erluc willed his armor to melt away and sheathed Telaris. It unsettled him that even an old man could catch him off guard so easily. "Who are you?" he demanded. "And what do you want with me?"

"My name is Alisthír." He made no indication of the name of his house or father, customary though it was.

"The Exile," Erluc translated immediately, before pausing, thoroughly confused. "Wait—what language is that?"

Alisthír raised an eyebrow, intrigued. "Telmírin. The language of the Immortals, as well as the moon elves. Your blessing must have granted you the ability to comprehend it." He paused for a moment, lost in thought, before his focus returned to the conversation at hand. "Few Andaerians speak Telmírin. You must be wary to not give yourself away."

Erluc raised an eyebrow. "My blessing?"

"Let us not play games anymore, Erluc." Alisthír's eyes narrowed. "You are one of Adúnareth's chosen. The Warrior, I'd wager. Beside the Mage and the Spectre, you shall take your place as protectors of the Mortal Realms—the Trinity."

The Mage and the Spectre? Back after the incident at Heaven's Citadel, Asten had revealed that he was the Mage, and Renidos was the Spectre. *How could this guy know about that?*

Gritting his teeth, Erluc sighed. He'd had enough of this man. "I don't know who you are or if Asten put you up to this, but I'm not going to waste my time believing in this fantastical tale of *Immortals* and some nonsensical prophecy."

"What about that gauntlet?" challenged Alisthír. "Or even your newfound strength? How nonsensical is the fact that you can no longer experience the same intoxication from drink?"

Erluc flinched, and Alisthír's smile confirmed that even he knew that he'd finally gotten through. That last glass at the bar had barely tickled him. A week ago, he'd have been unbearably dizzy after drinking something as strong as whiskey, much less fit enough to fight. He clenched his fists. "Alright, even if all of this is true—and I'm not saying that it is, but let's just pretend that you're right—what does it mean? Why is this happening?"

Suddenly Alisthír's proud stance seemed to fade away, and he appeared only a bent, careworn old man. "I'm afraid I don't have all the answers that you're looking for. Only time will tell why you've been chosen. But I *do* know enough to keep you alive until the right moment arrives. It would be best for the both of us that you have faith in me to do so."

"Keep me alive?" mused Erluc. "I'm not in any danger."

"Maybe not at the moment, but I suspect that there was a reason that the prophecy was fulfilled on the destined date. Atanûkhor's forces are stirring, and you must be prepared to fight against them. All of you."

Erluc wasn't convinced. "And how do you know all of this? How do you know *any* of this, in fact?"

The man's expression became amused, as though he was enjoying a joke no one else could hear. "I'm afraid you're going to just trust me," he said coolly, pulling the hood back over his head. "Meet me at the gate of the arena at two hours past dawn tomorrow."

"For what?" called Erluc, but the man was already at the end of the alley. Sighing, Erluc tried his best to piece together whatever he could of their conversation, before giving up entirely. *What a creep.*

He wandered around the city aimlessly for about an hour before making his way to the upper-class sections of the city, behind the hill upon which Heaven's Citadel was built. A few people looked as though they wanted to reprimand him for loitering near the territory of the aristocracy, but the sword at his hip seemed to deter them well enough.

He spent about half an hour asking around before he reached the right house. When he finally arrived, he rapped sharply on the door. A fair-skinned woman, probably in her forties, answered, though she looked surprised to see a commoner wearing a sword on her front porch. Erluc asked for Renidos, who was at the door within a minute.

"Hey, Erluc," he acknowledged with a nod, before turning to who must have been his mother. "This is the guy I mentioned, the one I had lunch with yesterday."

"Oh?" The woman smiled warmly. "Good afternoon, Erluc."

"Good afternoon," replied Erluc, trying his best to sound friendly.

Renidos put on his most innocent face. "Could I head out for a while, Mother?"

Though she was clearly trying to stay polite, Renidos' mother obviously didn't want him leaving the house with an armed stranger she knew next to nothing about. "I think you'd better not. I can't keep an eye on all the servants by myself."

Erluc smiled. "Don't worry, he'll back in an hour at the most. We just need to talk." It took a bit more persuasion, but eventually, Erluc was walking with Renidos down the cobblestones. "You didn't tell her about the whole business about the Citadel, did you?" he asked quietly.

Renidos snorted. "Of course not. It's not even as if she would have believed me anyway—I hardly believe it myself." Erluc nodded; although it must have been difficult to keep the secret from his mother, he'd done the right thing. "Speaking of which, I discovered something interesting."

"Oh?" Erluc was intrigued. "What's that?"

With a grin, Renidos crouched, then sprang into the air. Instead of ending up on the road, he sailed at least fifteen feet into the air, landing like a cat on the nearest roof. He quickly dropped down onto the cobblestones before anyone saw him, and amazingly seeming totally unhurt.

What in the world? Erluc's eyes widened. "How are you doing that?"

"I think it has something to do with being… the Spectre, was it?" he speculated, fiddling with something in his pocket. "I can also run faster than normal, but I don't think I should try that in the open."

"How fast?" inquired Erluc, clearly intrigued.

Renidos jabbed his thumb back to his house. "If I were to race you to the door, I could probably make it there and back before you reached the first house." Erluc snorted in disbelief, but before Erluc could do more than blink, the younger boy slipped past him, unlatched Telaris from his belt, and had it at his throat within a split second.

Erluc stepped aside and snatched his sword back, slightly annoyed at being caught off guard so easily. "Impressive. Anything else?"

"Nothing so grand," replied Renidos with a shrug. "I have better eyesight, I suppose. What happened to you?"

"Just the armor." Erluc willed his inky protection to form around his fist, then had it melt away just as fast. "I think I'm a bit stronger, and the eyesight, like you said." He argued silently with himself for a second, before he started to speak again. There was no point in denying it anymore. "Actually, I've had the strangest day so far."

Raising an eyebrow, Renidos indicated for him to continue. It took him all of ten minutes, but Erluc finally managed to explain what had happened at the Fang, as well as his ensuing encounter with Alisthír. "This guy sounds interesting."

"I got a really peculiar feeling from him," admitted Erluc. "And he seemed to know everything about this... blessing."

"Maybe that's not such a bad thing."

Erluc tilted his head, not sure if he'd heard Renidos correctly. "What do you mean? Don't you think it's weird that he's the only one who knows anything about this?"

Renidos waved a hand. "Well, if he knows about things that we don't, then we can benefit from his help. This way, we can probably understand our abilities better too." He shrugged. "And from what you've told me, it sounds like he was looking out for you."

Wow, this kid is much smarter than I'd thought. Nodding, Erluc clapped the younger boy's shoulder. "He asked me to meet him tomorrow morning. If you want, you can come see for yourself."

Giving an affirmative nod, Renidos casually jumped atop a railing on the side of the street that they were walking across. "What about your friend?"

"Who? Asten?" clarified Erluc.

"Yeah." Renidos jumped back to the ground just as someone crossed their path, smiling warmly as they passed. "Shouldn't we take him too?"

Making a face, Erluc considered this. "I don't think he's got any powers so far. If we tell him about all this now, it'll just distract him from everything else that's been going on. I think it's best if we wait until he discovers his own abilities."

Renidos frowned, but he understood what Erluc was trying to say. "His ring does look pretty cool." A flash of bronze on his arm caught Erluc's eye.

He pointed. "What is that?" Renidos lowered his hand and deftly removed a leather band around his wrist.

"It's called a watch," he explained, handing it to Erluc. The device consisted of a thick bronze circle shaped like a clock face on a strap. A hinged gnomon shaped like a flat rod could be flipped up and down, and Erluc soon found that the entire face could be opened to reveal a compass.

"Is it for telling time?" he guessed.

Renidos nodded. "You know those huge pendulum clocks that you can find in most public places? There's one in my house."

"I think I saw one at the inn I'm staying at." He passed the watch back.

"Well, those things are accurate, but they can't be moved around, or it upsets the pendulum, and you have to recalibrate the whole contraption. So, if you want to tell time on the go, you'll have to use something a bit more primitive. This," he flipped up the gnomon, "is a miniature sundial. You can even change the angle of the gnomon to make it accurate for wherever you are," Renidos went on. "I'm not sure how exactly that works, though."

"So, you can tell the time wherever you go?" Erluc queried. Back home, the only way to know the time was to guess it from the sun or off of the huge wooden sundial in the middle of the village. His mind failed to grasp the concept of such a device.

"Anywhere in the city," confirmed Renidos. "Not the most accurate of ways, and definitely not the cheapest, but it is quite helpful."

"I can imagine." It was more or less all Erluc could do to keep the envy out of his voice. He'd had to struggle to put food on the table for his whole life, and here was a boy who sported a time-telling wristband the way he would a tunic. "Can I try?"

Handing the contraption to Erluc, Renidos slowly explained how to align the watch with his compass, and the shadow of the rod fell on the clock face between three and four.

"Blast, I'm meant to meet Asten at four," remembered Erluc.

Renidos laughed, gesturing for him to run. "It's alright. I know the way back," he assured. "I'll see you at the arena tomorrow."

Erluc nodded. "Two hours after sunrise," he reminded with a nod before turning to make his way back to The Broken Fang. By the time he got there, it was almost four. He was late.

He was always late.

Chapter 8

BLACK EYE OF THE BEHOLDER

INTHYL, AENOR
Erluc

By the time Erluc reached his room, Asten was drawing on a scrap of parchment with a stick of charcoal, using a block of wood as a straight edge. He looked up expectantly. "Well, that was earlier than I expected."

Erluc snorted and snatched his weapon back. "You said *around* four."

"I said three."

Is my reading really that bad? He gave an apologetic half-smile. "Sorry."

"Kidding." Asten stood with a grin, brushing the parchment to the side, where it joined a rapidly growing pile. "I said four." He gestured for Erluc to follow him and left the room. When they reached the bottom of the stairs, he turned and opened a door at the opposite side of the inn.

Erluc frowned. "Am I missing something? That's a brick wall." He remembered seeing that girl walk into this door during breakfast—it was no wonder that she was confused.

"Blind as always, my friend." Asten's smile widened. He felt around in his pocket, dislodging a small runestone and a key. A panicked expression crossing his face, he stuffed the stone back into his tunic, letting the cast iron key drop with a *clang*.

Raising an eyebrow in confusion, Erluc stooped down and picked up the key, handing it back to Asten. "Where does this go?"

Asten scrabbled at the wall with it, and Erluc suppressed a laugh. It looked like the guy was trying to *scratch* the wall open. Finally, he managed to insert the cast iron key into a crack slightly wider than the others and turned to Erluc with a grin. "Now… the magic begins." With some difficulty, he turned the key with a grating sound.

"Well, magic is a bit of a stretch, but I'm glad that the Mage can do *something*." Erluc allowed himself a smile, which faded quickly as Asten shoved the wall, probably intentionally ignoring him. Cracks that he hadn't noticed suddenly became prominent in a rectangular section, and a hidden door turned inward on a hinge that had been invisible before.

Asten coolly stepped through the opening, and Erluc, still trying to keep his jaw from dropping, shuffled through after him. "How…how did you…" He trailed off once he saw what was inside. "Great Falcon."

Suddenly Erluc was standing in a large, walled courtyard with a single oak tree at the center. Lush grass filled the area, with a single paved circle about twenty yards in diameter around the tree. The stone wall rose up at least twenty feet, high enough that he was amazed that no one had noticed it from the outside.

"I don't understand… how is there space for a courtyard this big?" In this part of the city, the houses were crammed so tightly together that there was barely room between them to squeeze through, let alone for a fifty-meter-wide square.

"I wondered that too." Asten sat down on the grass, gesturing for Erluc to do the same. "I looked around a bit, and I think I understand now. It's because—"

"Never mind," dismissed Erluc, lowering himself onto the ground. "How did you find this place?"

"I saw a girl coming in the back door when I was going upstairs to the room last night," explained Asten. "Obviously, that confused me, seeing as the door went nowhere, but then I accidentally bumped into her." Erluc raised an eyebrow in disbelief, and Asten sighed. "Anyway, she dropped this and left in a hurry," he continued, holding up the key. "So, I put two and two together."

"And the door?" asked Erluc. "How did you figure that out?"

Asten frowned, probably not too glad to be reliving that particular memory, but continued, nevertheless. "After spending half an hour trying to find out where the key went this morning, I nearly gave up. Then my customary dismal luck kicked in, and I tripped on a rock just as I was turning around." He gestured to the ground outside. "The key somehow got lodged in between these bricks, and when I tried pulling it out, the door opened."

"I'm not sure whether to call that lucky or unlucky." Erluc smiled.

Asten nodded. "I thought this could be a quiet place where I could relax after work, but then I decided that we could both spend time here in the evenings."

"What about that girl?" Erluc reminded him. "I think I saw her trying to get in here this morning, and she didn't look too happy."

"If she's that upset about it, then she'll come back." Asten started humming a tune to himself. "How was Renidos' house? Anything important?"

Smirking, Erluc began tracing the patterns on Telaris' blade with a fingertip. "We mostly just talked about what happened back at the Citadel—nothing too interesting." After a long silence, he pointed at Asten's ring. "Have you found out what that does yet?"

Asten raised his hands helplessly. "Nothing. I spent half an hour trying to make a pebble fly, then tried to set the tree on fire. Just as well that I couldn't, it's a nice tree." He rested his hand against the rough bark of the oak.

Erluc snorted. Asten swatted at his arm and pointed at him with the hand with his ring, presumably trying to blast him, but there seemed to be no reaction. He just shrugged, as though he were thoroughly used to similar things happening, then collapsed backwards into the grass in frustration.

"So, how was your first day at work?" Erluc unsheathed Telaris and started lazily spinning it around.

"Not bad." Asten dusted himself and sat up. "Lannet, the smith's son, accidentally dropped a block of steel on my foot, but otherwise the day went well."

Erluc let out a laugh as he relaxed on the uncut grass. "He probably didn't like you flirting with his twin sister."

Asten frowned in confusion, then grinned. "About that…"

They lost track of time as Asten narrated his day, Erluc often cutting in with criticism or a sarcastic remark, until the sun had passed the top of the stone wall. Closing his eyes, Erluc folded his hands under his head and stretched his legs out on the grass. He thought about his conversation with Renidos and even his previous encounter with Alisthír. He didn't want to believe that all of this—any of this—was true, and he should have been right. But he'd seen impossible things, things he couldn't explain any other way. Part of him wished that he could open his eyes and all of it would just go away.

He shook his head to clear it. *Stupid Immortals.*

A sharp *thwack* interrupted his thoughts, followed by a shout of pain and indignation. Erluc glanced up quickly to see Asten step back, one hand to his cheek, stumbling away from a girl who looked about two or three inches shorter than he was.

"—the hell was that?" Asten snapped, clenching his fists. "What's wrong with you?" Without wasting a moment, Erluc got to his feet and ran to his friend's side.

"You're the one that stole my key," shot back the girl. *Clearly,* Erluc thought, *this is the same girl Asten had bumped into earlier—she probably thinks he'd picked her pocket.* She leered at Asten, brown eyes stabbing through his.

Asten glanced over as though seeing Erluc for the first time. He still hadn't recovered from the encounter, and although he didn't seem hurt at all, the shock was evident in his face. His eyes narrowed.

"I didn't steal it. You dropped it." He produced the cast iron key, waving it in front of her face. The girl made a grab for it, but he tossed it into the air and caught it in the other hand. Asten laughed harshly and moved to throw it again, but Erluc gripped his wrist so tightly that he gasped, involuntarily letting his clenched fist fall open, and Erluc snatched up the key with his free hand.

"What's the matter with you?" scolded Erluc, handing the key to the girl. "Here."

"Thank you," acknowledged the girl, immediately calming down. "At least one of you has some sense."

Erluc sighed, sitting back down next to the tree. "Just for the record, I told you this would happen."

The girl rolled her eyes. "Feel free to apologize whenever you want."

"Don't hold your breath," mumbled Erluc, before he was cut off.

"For the last time, I didn't steal your key." Asten didn't seem happy about the situation. "If anything, you owe me for finding it." A small smirk crept onto Erluc's face. *I guess that's one way of looking at it.*

"I owe you?" clarified the girl. "What do you want, a medal?"

Asten's eyes lit up. "I have an idea, actually," he stated tentatively. "If you give me the key for today, I can get a couple copies recast tomorrow so that we each have one. Then we can all come in whenever we want."

She raised an eyebrow, the setting sun making her auburn hair shine like a flame. "And why would I ever agree to that?"

"Well, we *did* find the key, and we're already here," postulated Asten innocently. "And you owe me."

The girl pressed a hand to her forehead as though she had a massive headache. "Even if I were okay with this, shouldn't I be the one to duplicate the key?"

"I'd be faster. I work for a blacksmith," Asten pointed out.

She paused, turning her head. "Roy or Galimin?"

"Galimin," confirmed Asten. "You know him?"

"He's one of the best in Inthyl. My father has had several trade deals with him."

Asten smiled weakly. "He's not exactly sitting idle, but I think he'll be able to help me out."

She crossed her arms, a conflicted expression on her face. "I don't trust you," she decided, turning away from Asten. "I don't even know your names."

"I'm Asten," he volunteered. "That's Erluc." Although he'd nearly fallen asleep by then, Erluc nodded in acknowledgment of his name. "And you are?"

The girl eyed both of them warily. "Rose," she revealed. Shaking her head, she turned away from them and pocketed the key. "No, this is ridiculous. If you're not out of here in five minutes, I'm locking you both in."

"Wait!" Asten called, and Rose turned back skeptically. "I-If you don't agree to let us back in here, I'll… I'll…"

"You'll what?" Rose raised an eyebrow. "Stutter?"

As Erluc fought the urge to laugh, Asten glared venomously at her. "I'll tell the whole inn about this place."

The girl blanked for a moment before quickly regaining her composure. "You wouldn't dare."

"Damn right, he wouldn't," agreed Erluc, finally deciding to step in. He clapped his friend on the shoulder. "Sorry, but empty threats are *boring*, Asten."

Asten's expression grew even sourer, and now Rose was the one fighting a smile. Erluc turned to her, grinning. "Don't worry about him. He just gets defensive easily." Silencing Asten with a glance, he went on, "But regardless, the fact that we aren't telling anyone gives you a good reason to trust us, doesn't it?"

Eyeing the key once more, she tossed the key to Erluc, who caught it just before it scratched his nose. "If I don't get it back by tomorrow, I will find you and—"

"We get the picture," interrupted Asten, beyond through with the conversation. "I'm going to get something to eat. I'll leave the door open." He quickly collected the key from Erluc, before jogging out.

"This whole situation came up because he left the door open," wagered Erluc as Asten went out of earshot.

"Just as well that he did," muttered Rose, eliciting a laugh from Erluc.

"I take it you're not leaving?" he assumed.

Rose shook her head. "Not for a while." She sat down next to Erluc against the tree. "So, I've been meaning to ask—where are you from? Your clothes aren't from here. Most southerners don't wear leather." She twisted a blade of grass around her finger.

Erluc scratched the back of his head. "You know where Lindrannon is?" She nodded. "Asten and I come from a village there named Sering."

"That's quite far east," commented Rose. "I suppose you have a bit of an accent, too."

Grinning, Erluc added a strong southern affectation to his voice and queried, "Well? Is this better?"

"Not bad, not bad at all." Despite herself, Rose smiled. "So how long have you been in Inthyl?"

"Two days." Erluc ran a hand through his hair. "I feel like a southerner already."

Rose snorted, then stopped in mock horror. "Two days? And you're still wearing leather clothes?" She wrinkled her nose. "So, you've been wearing the same—"

Erluc grinned, cutting her off with a wave of his hand. He took off his jacket, the dark leather beaming in the evening sunlight, and handed it to her. "It's clean, I promise. You can keep it if you want." Just as she opened her mouth to protest, he continued. "At least until you get your key back," he smiled. He was glad that Asten had insisted on washing their clothes after their arrival here—it had probably saved him some embarrassment.

She started, then trailed off. "Fair enough," she conceded, looking it over, before putting it on herself. The jacket's sleeves were clearly too long for her, which made for an amusing sight, but she didn't seem to mind. Her eyes suddenly glinted, and she pointed at his chest. "Is that what you were fighting about this morning?" she asked. Erluc frowned, before realizing that the Ancient's crystal had been exposed, and he quickly tucked it back under his tunic.

"It's nothing," stated Erluc with finality. "So, do you live around here?"

Rose's expression became guarded, almost as if she disliked the question. She twisted a blade of grass tightly around her forefinger, causing it to break off. "Just on the other side of the Citadel."

Erluc thought it smarter not to pursue the matter. "And your family?"

"They're, well... family, I suppose." Rose shrugged again. "Actually, I just have a father."

"Any siblings?"

She shot him a warning glance, the blade of grass around her finger tightening so much that it turned the fingertip white. "No. None." Erluc frowned in confusion at the sudden show of stress but decided not to think much of it.

"Your father, then." Erluc wiped his brow. "He's a merchant, I suppose?"

"Hmm?" Rose looked up. "Why do you say that?"

"You said he had a deal with Galimin, didn't you?"

Rose's shoulders dropped slightly and smiled. "Not bad, for a village guy."

Erluc managed a laugh, playfully nudging her shoulder. "Thanks. For what it's worth, I didn't expect a rich girl to be anything like you." She nudged him back, and they both broke into light, nervous laughter. For the first time, he noticed two innocent, round dimples appear in the center of her cheeks as she smiled.

They both rested against the tree for a minute, trying to think of something to say next. Finally, Rose broke the silence. "Speaking of my father, he won't be pleased if I'm not back for dinner."

Erluc glanced at the sky with a frown. "This soon? It's what, six-thirty?"

"We eat early." Rose fidgeted slightly, clearly anxious to get back home.

"Well…" Erluc spread his arms. "Don't let me hold you up."

"Mhmm." She stood, then turned back, hesitating. "You know, I'll most likely be here tomorrow, just in case… you know, in case you want to talk."

Erluc held back a smile. "And how exactly do you plan to get in?"

Rose raised an eyebrow as though this were the most simple-minded question possible. "With the ke—" She grinned, slightly annoyed. "Right."

"You can come to Galimin's smithy and get it from Asten tomorrow. Here, I'll even pay for it." Erluc reached into his pocket, holding out four copper coins.

Shaking her head, Rose pushed his hand away. "I can pay for myself." She closed his fingers around the coins. "Use it to buy yourself a new tunic."

Erluc snorted. "No promises."

Rose laughed, turning around halfway to the door. "Asten knows about this plan, I assume?"

"I'll tell him," assured Erluc. She nodded, then quickly said goodbye and dashed out of the courtyard. A minute later, Erluc walked out as well, closing the door quietly behind him, then stepped into the inn and headed upstairs to his room.

Asten was stretched out across his makeshift chair-bed, tearing viciously into a piece of bread. Looking up, he tossed the remainder of the loaf to Erluc. "You hungry?"

"Always."

Chapter 9

ALL WORK AND NO PLAY

INTHYL, AENOR

Erluc

I should have thought this through.

With a sigh, Erluc pushed his still-wet hair away from his face, spraying droplets into the air behind him. *I mean, whose idea was it to train this early?* Rolling his eyes, he passed into the arena, one hand resting on Telaris' hilt. *This better be worth it.*

Looking around, Erluc scanned his surroundings for anything interesting. The arena was almost completely empty, except for a drunkard passed out in the stands. Erluc flinched, turning around sharply, and Renidos was standing behind him.

"I'm not late, am I?" he asked hastily.

Erluc shook his head. "It's okay," he admitted. "We were supposed to be here twenty minutes ago, anyway."

"That's right," spoke a voice, and Erluc turned to see Alisthír approaching them from the stands. "You're going to have to take this seriously if you want to learn."

"Take what seriously?" challenged Erluc. "You still haven't told us why we're here."

Now that he'd reached them, Alisthír extended a hand. Looking Renidos up and down, he smirked. "Pleasure to meet you. The Spectre, I assume."

The younger boy's eyes widened, and he turned to Erluc for guidance, who simply nodded. Hesitantly, Renidos met Alisthír's hand. "Renidos of House Wayron, son of Elias." If the old combatant was impressed by the boy's introduction, he didn't show it.

"How do you know about that?"

Alisthír allowed himself a smile, but he ignored the question. "Will the Mage be joining us as well?"

With a grimace, Erluc shook his head. "Asten hasn't discovered his powers yet, and I don't want to drag him into this until I have to."

The old warrior seemed slightly confused. "Asten?"

"That's his name," continued Erluc. "Why?"

Alisthír took a moment to think, but his face revealed nothing that was happening in his mind. "Very well. Your friend can stay oblivious for now, but eventually, he's going to need training." Talking now to both of them, he continued. "You're going to have to ensure his safety until he discovers his powers, and then you can bring him here."

Despite his nod, Renidos seemed slightly unsure. "How exactly are we supposed to protect him when we don't even know how to control our own abilities?"

"That's what you're here for," declared Alisthír, leading them further into the arena, towards the battleground. "If nothing else, you need experience being in situations that require decisive thinking. But for today, if you're able to pick up anything halfway useful, that should justify that this wasn't a great waste of time."

Erluc rolled his eyes. "It's not like we're completely helpless," he offered. "Asten and I fought through the

Vale of Shadows and made it out alive." Renidos raised an eyebrow but didn't ask any questions.

"So, you did," conceded Alisthír. "I suppose you wouldn't mind me testing your form, would you?"

As they reached the grounds, Erluc shrugged, and Renidos stepped to the side, watching in anticipation as the others began to ready themselves. Alisthír crouched down into a stance, and Erluc drew Telaris from its sheath, brandishing it in his hands.

The last time they'd met, Alisthír had caught him off guard, and Erluc was determined not to be taken by surprise again. However, it looked like Alisthír was allowing to make Erluc the first move on this occasion. *So much for spontaneity.* Experimentally, Erluc aimed a strike at the man's right shoulder, striking ferociously and without reservation. But Alisthír was more than prepared for such an attack. Ducking under the blow, he pushed back on Erluc's sword, knocking the Warrior off balance. Stumbling backwards, Erluc scowled, and the old man laced his fingers.

"You've fought mostly against unskilled opponents, relying largely on brute strength to win your battles. And while this has served you well so far, there are much more efficient and elegant styles of combat."

"I wouldn't call those dark elves unski—" Before Erluc could finish his sentence, Alisthír stepped forward diagonally with a feint at his shins. Caught off guard, Erluc swiped downward with Telaris before realizing his mistake, and Alisthír immediately followed up his motion with a sharp rap at Erluc's guard. The sword tumbled out of Erluc's hand, leaving him defenseless. He quickly retrieved it, settling into a crouch once more. After promising himself that he wouldn't go down to a surprise attack, this was a humiliating path for his first spar to follow.

He remembered what Invardui had told him about using his sword, and the efficient, elegant style of the Guardians. Over the course of his journey to the Vale, he'd learned that pure force wasn't enough to overcome more skilled opponents, but it seemed that since then, he'd regressed to old habits he'd picked up with Asten. Breathing deeply, he began to focus on his fight with the Guardian, with the dark elves, with the skeletons, and to recall how he had prevailed each time. It wasn't the strength of his blows that had availed him—it was the little things, like the positioning of his blade, his footwork, his control over the weapon in his hand.

Dimly, he realized that this was his first time wielding Telaris in combat, but Kovu's sword didn't feel at all foreign to him; the balance, the grip, everything seemed perfectly molded to Erluc. Maybe it was something Adúnareth had done to it, or maybe when the Guardian had entrusted it to him, he had known more than he had let on. Why else would he have insisted so fervently that Erluc keep the sword, that he not surrender it to anything less than the Falcon himself? Returning his attention to Alisthír, he relaxed his grip on Telaris' hilt.

This time, Alisthír approached first, attacking Erluc's forearm. More defensive now, Erluc parried the attack, spinning backwards, before charging into an assault of his own. Alisthír had no trouble knocking his blade aside, but this time, Erluc had his time with the Guardians to guide him, with their unique, fluid take on swordsmanship as a model for him. Instead of the

strength of his own arms, he began to rely on the momentum of his sword for power, instead directing his attention towards finding openings in the old man's iron defense. This time, he lasted considerably longer, but it had still been hardly five minutes when Alisthír casually flicked his wrist, sending Telaris flying once more out of Erluc's hand. Scowling, Erluc picked the sword up again, even more agitated than before.

"Not bad," commented Alisthír. "Your form is acceptable, though I haven't seen a fighting style like yours in decades. Clearly, you can be a competent warrior when you want to be," evaluated Alisthír. "You could benefit from a little practice, but otherwise, the only advice I can give you is this: channel your feelings to the point where they strengthen you, not control you."

Erluc remembered what Adúnareth had told him at Heaven's Citadel only a few days earlier—*judgment and composure will be your greatest strengths.* Nodding again, he sheathed Telaris, doing his best to let his anger and frustration from the duel drain away.

Scoffing, Renidos shook his head. "I'm going to need a little more than just practice to get that good." He looked completely hopeless. "I haven't had any training—I don't even have a weapon."

Alisthír smiled. "Good."

Renidos seemed as perplexed as Erluc. "I'm sorry, did you say *good*?" asked the younger boy.

"You won't have any bad habits, and we can work on directly incorporating your powers into your fighting style," explained the old combatant. "Obviously, I didn't expect all of you to have training, and it's much easier to train someone from scratch than it is to reform their technique."

Impressed, Erluc wiped his sweaty hands on his tunic. *This guy sounds like he knows what he's doing.*

"We're going to have to choose an appropriate weapon for you," started Alisthír, "but first, you'll have to tell me about your powers."

Renidos looked to Erluc before turning back to the man. "Well, Erluc and I—and Asten, probably—have enhanced reflexes and senses. The most noticeable is probably my eyesight, but they have all definitely been heightened."

Nodding, Alisthír indicated for Renidos to continue. "What about you specifically?"

The younger boy paused, looking around to make sure nobody else was watching. When he was sure that they were alone, he dashed forward, appearing at the opposite end of the arena only a moment later.

"Not bad," remarked Alisthír softly. When Renidos returned, Alisthír gestured for them to follow him to the edge of the grounds, passing into the pavilion between the stands. After navigating the narrow corridors for a few minutes, he finally stopped before a dusty wooden door. Before Erluc had the time to read the word written on it, Alisthír had huddled over the lock, doing something that caused it to click, and pushed the door open.

Barely any natural lighting reached the room through the singular grilled window, but they could all see that there were dozens of weapons stacked along the walls. The collection ranged from rusted axes to what looked like brand-new broadswords, distributed entirely randomly.

"Uh," began Renidos sheepishly. "Are you sure we're allowed to be here?"

"I won't tell if you won't," dismissed Alisthír immediately.

Erluc picked up what looked like a rapier, fiercely thrusting the point into the air in front of him. "What are all these things even doing here?"

"The majority are excess Twilight Legion supplies gathered over the years, along with scores of lost or abandoned weapons here at the arena," explained the old warrior. "These are the weapons that you'd have to use if you were fighting at a tournament, except for the Steel Trial, of course."

That didn't mean anything to Erluc, but Renidos' face lit up instantly. "The Steel Trial! It's this year, isn't it?"

Alisthír nodded. "You're welcome to come watch."

"We can participate too, can't we?"

"You're going to have to be at least seventeen by the forty-seventh day of the second division." Renidos' energy faded slightly, but Erluc raised an eyebrow.

"I guess I could participate," he suggested. "How's the competition?"

Alisthír sighed. "Formidable to any ordinary fighter, but they wouldn't be able to handle your abilities—especially not after you have control over them. Besides, the combatants are hand-picked by the provincial lords." He gazed across the selection of weapons as one would the night sky. "Now, let's focus—your greatest strength is your mobility, which I think rules out any heavier weapons, like a broadsword or battleaxe." He knelt, picking up two identical, sheathed knives, but Renidos was already apprehensive.

"I don't think so," he declared immediately. "I'd prefer something a little more defensive, and, um, less lethal, if you could."

Nodding, Alisthír proceeded to the next choice: a longsword. He passed it to Renidos, who weighed it in his hands, making a dissatisfied face. "I don't know, it doesn't feel right." He set it aside, grabbing a staff from the wall. Spinning it in one hand, he swiped at an invisible foe. "What do you think?"

Erluc snorted. "You're going to fight swords with a stick?"

The younger boy set it down, an embarrassed expression on his face. However, he seemed to like the idea of a longer weapon, picking out a spear next. It seemed to be surprisingly in condition, and he waved it around in front of him. "How about this?"

"I mean, it's better," admitted Erluc, only partly convinced.

Renidos looked to Alisthír, who shrugged. "I can teach you to fight with any one of these, but it's your weapon in the end, so it's going to have to be your decision."

The Spectre regarded the spear once more before nodding. "Alright, I think I'll give this a try," he decided. They quickly exited the room, making their way back into the fighting grounds.

"Out of curiosity," began Alisthír, "what are the differences in your abilities?"

Erluc took a moment to think, finding himself happier than he should have been. *At least he doesn't know everything.* "I'm mainly just a lot stronger, and I can summon armor."

"*That's it?*" questioned Alisthír.

"*Yes, I think so.*"

Suddenly, Renidos interrupted them. "Guys? I'd appreciate it if we could just speak in Andaeric if you don't mind."

"We were speaking in Andaeric," replied Erluc, confused. Looking to Alisthír and then to Renidos, he raised an eyebrow. "Weren't we?"

Alisthír grimaced. "*I'm afraid not.*"

Focusing on the words, Erluc's eyes widened. "That's Telmírin again, isn't it?" He shook his head. "I still don't understand how I can speak a language I've never come across before."

"It's pretty clear how," declared the old warrior. "I'd be more concerned with why. After all, if you're going to be speaking Telmírin in the future, you'll have to recognize when you're actually speaking it."

Renidos frowned. "How come Erluc gets to speak Telmírin? It's not exactly related to the abilities of the Warrior."

"Your guess is as good as mine," admitted Alisthír. "But Telmírin is Adúnareth's language, so it makes sense that at least one of you can speak it."

Erluc seemed to catch on. "Maybe it's got to do with me being the leader."

"I suppose we'll find out eventually." They finally exited the pavilion, and Erluc noticed that more people had started to appear around the arena. "Nevertheless, you need to practice speaking the language so that you can distinguish it from Andaeric when you are speaking. Adúnareth help you if you lapse into Telmírin here in Inthyl."

Renidos smirked, twirling his new spear around in his hands. "Now what? More training?"

Looking around, Alisthír considered his options. "Don't you want to try out your new weapon?" he asked, and Renidos shrugged, ultimately walking onto the grounds and crouching down into a defensive stance.

"Try not to kill me if you can help it," requested Renidos earnestly. "Seeing that it's my first practice and all."

Alisthír nodded. "Granted." He changed his stance to a wider, more vulnerable position, and moved his sword to his left hand. "Approach as you wish."

It was almost amusing to Erluc, but he made sure to keep quiet throughout the ordeal. After all, his own first practice had been considerably worse than this; then again, Alisthír was a much better teacher than Neran.

Although this was his first time in any sort of fight, Renidos' speed gave him a few moments to consider his every move before acting. Unfortunately, that was about all that he had going for him. His enhanced reflexes made it much easier for him to deflect blows from Alisthír, but he was finding it much more challenging to transition to the offensive. "Come on," encouraged Alisthír. "Attack!"

Renidos was still hesitant. "What if I hurt you?" Erluc rolled his eyes. *It's a fight, what do you expect to happen?*

"Don't worry about me," assured Alisthír. "Do your worst."

"You're sure?"

The old man tapped his foot, clearly agitated. "I'm waiting."

The Spectre's eyes narrowed, and he pounced forward. Erluc could only see a series of flashes before Renidos was pushed backwards a moment later. If anything, Alisthír's capabilities impressed him even more than Renidos'. *This guy can handle anything.* Obviously, it raised dozens of questions in Erluc's mind, but he wasn't about to interrupt the battle.

Charging once more, Renidos brought his spear around from his side, aiming for Alisthír's feet, but the blow was deflected with ease. The old warrior counter-attacked almost as quickly, aiming a strike at Renidos' abdomen. Seeing the attack too late, Renidos panicked, falling backwards.

The spear rolled out of his hands, and he was only just able to brace his fall with his hands. "Sorry," he groaned, sitting up as he wiped the dirt from his hands.

"You shouldn't be," directed Alisthír. "You evidently know what you're doing, and your speed itself should allow you to easily best any average fighter." He shook his head. "But you're scared. I don't know why or of what, but this is something that you'll have to face eventually—the sooner you do, the sooner you'll be able to unleash your full potential." Renidos nodded, but he didn't meet the man's eyes.

Erluc helped him to his feet, turning to Alisthír. "That should be enough for now."

The older warrior nodded. "It's around breakfast time, I think—you can both go and get something to eat." Turning back to them, he lowered his tone. "We won't be able to train your powers with so many people around, anyway. But if you want some more combat training, I'll be here throughout the day."

"That doesn't sound bad, actually," concluded the younger boy, regarding his spear tentatively. "I'll see you later today, then."

Erluc smirked. "I think I'm done for today."

Alisthír bowed his head. "You know where to find me if you change your mind." With that, they bid each other farewell, and Erluc and Renidos hurriedly exited the arena. The boys split ways near the main square, Renidos explaining that his mother would be waiting to eat breakfast.

By the time Erluc got back to The Broken Fang, it was already lunchtime—and sure enough, he ate two meals' worth of food. After all, he wasn't about to miss out on a chance to eat more.

When he was finally done, he went back up to the room, tossing his belt onto the bed. Tired, Erluc collapsed on it too, looking up at the ceiling. *I should be asleep right now.* But even he couldn't go back to sleep after eating that much. He could see that Asten had left for the forge earlier that morning, his old tunic still lying on his chair. *What am I supposed to do now?* He decided to head to the baths, where he managed to kill a significant amount of time before his fingertips started to shrivel up, and he was forced to leave. Changing into fresh tunic and slacks, he settled on the bed in their room once more.

He spotted the letter that Asten had been reading—presumably from the blacksmith's daughter—and he shrugged, unfolding the parchment. It took him a while, but he was able to read the first few sentences, and he smirked. Erluc wasn't going to say that this wasn't a cute thing to do. None of the girls that he'd ever been with would have written him something like this—granted, most of them couldn't even write at all. Either way, he understood why Asten wasn't complaining about his new job. Unfortunately, with his only friend otherwise occupied, Erluc had nothing to do.

Placing the parchment back on Asten's stool, he left the room once more, wandering back down to the bar. At the very least, he might find a girl or two to pass the time. Unfortunately, there was no such luck. The Fang was all but empty, save for a few men chatting around a corner table, untouched beers in their hands. For Erluc, they didn't look like exceptional company.

Rolling his eyes, he was about to exit the inn when he noticed the side door was open. Now curious, he approached more cautiously, closing it behind him without any sound. The stone wall had already been unlocked, and the courtyard was revealed.

Making his way in and shutting the door behind him, he recognized the girl lying across the grass, a folded parchment in her hand.

"I would say I'm surprised to see you, but you did tell me that you'd be here," he called out, and she looked up, her initial panic slowly settling into recognition. "Don't you ever have school or anything?"

"I could ask you the same thing," countered Rose, sitting up. Her hair was done up in a messy bun, and she was wearing dark boots that matched her leggings. She set the parchment aside, relaxing her back against the tree.

"Fair enough," conceded Erluc. "But that doesn't answer the question."

Rose made a face, eventually deciding to reply. "I'm homeschooled," she revealed. "I know what you're going to say, but it makes it easier for me to learn whatever I want at my own pace."

"No, I totally understand," agreed Erluc, much to her surprise. He shrugged, squatting beside her. "But I guess that's because I never went to school either."

"Seriously?"

"Why would I need to?" he questioned. "Until half a division ago, I thought I'd live my entire life in Sering. I can hunt, talk, and farm as well as anyone else—it seemed pointless to have to learn about anything past that."

Rose considered this, finally deciding to ask him, "But if you had the chance to learn about something new, would you take it?"

"Like what?"

She hesitated, looking around, before her eyes lit up. Quickly getting up, she walked almost all the way to the entrance of the courtyard, stopping in front of a small group of bushes. Taking a moment to search, she bent down and retrieved a long, wooden instrument, much to Erluc's surprise.

"Where did you get that?" he inquired, completely taken off guard. As she walked closer, he got a better look at the contraption—one side had a hollow round head, a narrower section extending away to the other side. Five strings were attached to the instrument, running almost all the way across the head, tied to the end of the narrow wooden extension.

Rose grinned, sitting down next to him once more. "My father tried to get me to learn it for years," she revealed. "I finally gave up when I realized that I didn't have the patience to put up with my teacher. I knew he wouldn't let me quit so easily, so I brought this here and told him that I'd lost it." She wiped the dirt off of the instrument, plucking one of the strings to make sure it still worked. "Honestly, I'd almost forgotten that it was still here."

Taking it into his hands, Erluc smiled. It hadn't been too long since he'd last played an instrument, but with everything that had happened recently, he certainly hadn't thought of it. He closed his eyes, and all the sound in his ears faded away. As he touched the strings, he realized that he'd probably break them without noticing if he didn't concentrate and made sure to apply minimal force.

He played one of the few songs that he knew, and years of repetition and practice served him well. Most people were so surprised when they learned that he could play *the strings*, since barely anyone in Sering cared enough about learning it to buy one for themselves. Erluc couldn't afford one either, but he'd won a game of chance against a musician that lived at the far end of town, who then agreed to teach him to play a few songs. Eventually, the lessons forged a friendship between them, and the man even allowed him to borrow his instruments from time to time.

When he was finally finished, he exhaled deeply, opening his eyes. There was a small pause, and Erluc waited for her to say something. Looking over, he just saw her smile, her brown eyes full of wonder.

"What?"

"Nothing," she shook her head, tucking a lock of hair behind her ear. "It's just that... I wasn't expecting that from you."

"Yeah, well, don't tell anyone," he requested. "I don't usually play in front of people." It was true—aside from the musician who had taught him to play, only Asten and their friend Hayden had ever heard him play.

"Are you kidding?" She raised an eyebrow. "Why not?"

Erluc shrugged. "Well, I used to love music when I was growing up, and my mother was a great singer. She used to perform at town fairs all the time. I guess that's part of the reason that I even tried learning to play." He shook his head. "After she died, my father couldn't really bring himself to listen to music without being reminded of her, which meant that I barely had the chance to practice at home." Setting the instrument aside, he sighed, resting his head on the tree trunk. "I don't know... I guess this is just something personal for me."

Nodding, Rose took a moment to dissolve the tension before continuing. "You should keep this," she proposed, indicating the instrument. Erluc was about to protest, but she shook her head, and he noticed her dimples appear briefly as she smiled. "I'd be happy if *someone* is using it, and it would be a crime to abandon a talent like yours."

"Thanks," replied Erluc immediately, "but you quite literally just met me yesterday. It'd be wrong for me to accept this."

With a sigh, Rose tried another angle. "Tell you what," she decided. "I'll leave it here in the courtyard, and you can use it whenever you want." He made a face, but she dismissed it with a wave of her hand. "I still have that jacket of yours, don't I? This is the least I can do."

Erluc smirked in recognition. "Fair enough," he conceded. He looked over her shoulder, and a yellowed parchment caught his eye. "What were you reading?" She hesitated before producing the scroll and placing it on his lap. Erluc squinted, trying his hardest to read the title. "A Light Between the Stars." He looked up, meeting her eyes once more. "Something tells me that this isn't just some light reading."

"I actually enjoy reading this kind of stuff," revealed Rose. "It may not be the most entertaining at times, but it helps me see things from many different perspectives."

Tracing a line with his finger, Erluc read it over in his mind, unable to form the words. "Jayon knelt in front of the," he frowned, "*day-is?*"

Rose started laughing, resting her head on the tree behind them. Placing a hand on his shoulder, she grinned, trying her best to contain her laughter. "Dais," she corrected. "I guess school isn't completely useless after all."

Smirking, Erluc nudged her arm, lazily rising to full height. "Dais," he muttered, shaking his head. Stretching his arms, he took a few steps forward. "Alright, let's go."

"Go where?" she inquired, completely confused.

"I don't know, but I'm going to go crazy sitting around all day," confided Erluc. "What do you do for fun around here?"

Rose indicated the parchment. "Read."

Covering both eyes with his hands, Erluc sighed. "Wow, that's pretty depressing." Running a hand through his hair, he indicated the inn. "You want to get a drink or something?"

"It's the middle of the day."

He shrugged. "And?"

Rose cracked a smile despite herself. "I'm still going to have to say no. I'm not allowed to drink yet."

Well, this day really can't get worse, can it? Erluc cracked his knuckles, extending his hand to her. "Fine," he accepted. "Just come on."

Taking his hand tentatively, Rose hastily got up, brushing her clothes. "So, we're just going to walk around until we find something fun to do?"

He shrugged, indicating the door. "After you." Rose made sure to lock the courtyard this time around, much to Erluc's amusement, and they exited the Fang, wandering around the streets of Inthyl.

"You probably don't have the best impression of Inthyl so far, do you?" she questioned, and Erluc smirked, shaking his head.

"I wasn't sure what to expect, honestly," he admitted. "But I guess it could have been worse."

"Ouch." Rose tried her best to hide her smile, mocking injury. "What did you do for fun in Sering, then?"

Erluc didn't meet her eyes, but he couldn't hold back a smile. "A lot," was all he said. "But you probably won't be allowed to do most of it." He looked to his left as they passed a series of shops, smirking as he recognized the florist's hut. Discreetly grabbing the stem of a long, red flower, he plucked it from the bunch as they passed, hiding it beside his sleeve. "Here," he handed it to her.

She seemed to be caught completely off guard, hesitantly accepting it with both hands. "That's sweet," she commented with a smile. "But, you know you're meant to pay for these, right?"

Shrugging, Erluc tried his best not to look behind him. "If anyone asks, I tried to tell you that stealing is wrong."

Rose grinned, raising an eyebrow. "Really?"

"Oh, totally." He nodded earnestly. "You should listen to me if you want to stay out of trouble, you know." Behind them, he heard a voice call out, and both of them turned to see the florist waving angrily from the stall.

"You were saying?" she asked him, a challenging grin on her face. They were starting to create a scene, and the florist had started to chase after them.

Erluc grimaced. *This is going to end well.* Grabbing her hand, he charged into the nearest alley, climbing a flight of steps before hopping onto the base of the adjacent roof.

Rose took a moment to react, hurriedly jumping on after him. Her boots weren't exactly fitting for so much movement, and she slipped, falling backwards. If for nothing else, the reflexes of the Warrior served Erluc well at that moment. He reached back, his fingers only just able to tighten around her wrist, pulling with the least amount of force that he could. Rose gasped, pulling herself closer to him and further from the edge of the roof, taking deep breaths. Erluc saw the florist pass into the alley underneath them, and he smirked, waiting till they were out of earshot. "You're okay," he whispered, slowly letting her out of his embrace.

Wiping a strand of hair away from her face, she looked up at him, her brown eyes still clouded from shock. "Thank you," she replied softly. Erluc felt the air around him get warmer, and he gently released her wrist, stepping back to give her more room. He cracked a small smile, and she eventually couldn't stop herself from breaking into a laugh. "Don't ever make me do anything like that again!" Pushing him back lightly, her face reddened, her dimples refusing to fade away.

Now laughing himself, Erluc nodded. "Hey, at least we aren't bored anymore."

Shaking her head, she walked past him to the opposite end of the roof, trying to determine where they had ended up. "If anyone asks what we're doing here, I'm blaming you."

Erluc waved a hand in the air, indicating the next roof over. "The jump isn't that far—if you're up for it, that is."

"You're crazy," she remarked incredulously, but she couldn't hold back another smile.

"It'll grow on you," he ensured, glancing up at the sky. The time had passed fairly quickly, at least in comparison to what Erluc had expected.

Rose raised an eyebrow. "So, do you usually take girls you barely know to places you're not meant to be?"

Shrugging, he sat on the edge of the rooftop, letting his legs dangle over the side. "Sometimes, not always," he responded. "It really depends on the day."

Sitting beside him, Rose shook her head, unable to believe his audacity. "I honestly can't tell if you're joking or not," she confided. "But for some reason, as frustrating as you are, I don't feel like pushing you off this rooftop."

"Strange." Erluc smirked, much to her annoyance. "I'm not complaining, though."

Cupping the flower in her hands, she marveled at the way the orange sunlight blended with the crimson petals. "It's such a pity that something so beautiful has to die," she commented softly. Her eyes shone auburn in the light, only just lighter than the flower itself.

Erluc looked up, moving his hair from his face. "Isn't that what makes it special?" He sighed, keeping his gaze fixed on the clouds in the distance. "You just have to enjoy it while it lasts."

She allowed herself a gentle smile, slowly rocking her legs back and forth off the rooftop. "You know, anyone else in this situation would have given me a rose."

His eyes widened. "That isn't a rose?"

"Not even close, farm boy." The calm evening breeze blew through the air, and Rose snapped off the flower from its stem, carefully putting it into her hair. "Although, I guess I wouldn't mind going by Tulip." She looked up, and Erluc smirked.

"Looks great to me, Tulip," declared Erluc. "But then again, I don't have a clue about southern fashion." He made a face. "Or flowers, apparently."

Rose blushed slightly, using his shoulder to get to her feet. "You're not all bad," she conceded. "I still think you need to buy a new tunic, though."

With a sigh, Erluc shook his head. "Maybe I'll just take one of Asten's."

"Speaking of Asten," remembered Rose, "thank him again for copying the key."

"The exchange went well?"

She nodded, smiling as she remembered the interaction. "For the most part," she confirmed. "But he seemed to be quite awkward around the blacksmith's daughter, especially when I arrived."

Erluc waved a hand in the air. "That's normal, don't worry about it."

Grinning, she stepped back, accepting the explanation. "I didn't think I'd say this today—or ever, actually—but I had fun being bored with you."

"Imagine how much fun it'd be if we actually did something," proposed Erluc half-heartedly, eliciting a smile from Rose.

"Maybe next time," she offered, walking towards a series of steps that probably led down to the alley below. "I'll see you in the courtyard soon?"

"Nothing better for me to do," confirmed Erluc, raising his legs back onto the platform. "I hope you know the way back home from here."

She nodded. "Don't worry, I'll find it," she assured. "As long as I don't have to jump across any rooftops, I should be fine."

"And I thought we were having fun," he called.

Even from the stairs, he could hear her laugh. "Goodnight, Erluc."

Shaking his head, he allowed himself a smirk, lying down on the rooftop, waiting for the sky to darken. "Goodnight, Rose," he said softly.

Chapter 10

BROKE HEROES

INTHYL, AENOR

Erluc

*H*mm? Erluc scratched the back of his head, slowly opening his eyes to the grass, the sun, and the cool morning breeze. He drowsily raised an eyebrow, yawning silently. *What am I doing here?*

He looked to his shoulder and found his answer. *Oh.* They must have fallen asleep while talking the previous night. She frowned, nudging his cheek with her head.

Adúnareth help me. This probably looks extremely *bad.*

The urge to rub his aching back gripped him, but he resisted it for fear of waking her.

It'd been nearly a full division since they'd met, and their fleeting attraction had developed into something that came dangerously close to a relationship. Of course, other insignificant things had happened in his life over that time, but they were just that—insignificant.

If Asten walked in right now, he would definitely pass out. Erluc could picture it in his head—Asten rooted to a spot, stunned. He was always dramatic in that sense. A small smirk played at the corner of Erluc's lips.

"What is it?" she asked, nudging him once more before sitting up. Her hair was still tied, a few pieces of bark camouflaged in the sea of brown.

"Nothing," replied Erluc. "But next time we do this, I'm bringing a pillow."

She grinned, leaning in, and Erluc mirrored her. He closed his eyes, and just as he could feel her breath on his skin, she stopped. She stayed for a moment, slowly moving away. He leaned in closer, and she laughed, standing up. "Bring me a pillow too, and we'll see."

He made a face. "So, that's how it is?"

She grinned, her twin dimples appearing once more. "How'd you sleep?"

"Honestly, I didn't even want to wake up," he muttered, shaking his hair clean as he stood up. "How're you going to explain this to your father?" There wasn't anything much to cover up, really, but the fact that she'd stayed out the whole night was bound to raise some flags with her parents.

His own parents would have been equally startled, now that he thought about it, but what they didn't know couldn't hurt them.

"I have it planned out." She smiled. "I went out with a friend, and I spent the night at her place."

"That should work," he admitted. She bowed, pulling his leather jacket around her shoulders. "And that?" he asked.

"Oh, it's the latest fashion." She grinned. "I wasn't sure at first, but I think it suits me."

Erluc smirked in realization and rose lazily to his feet. "I don't have anything to do today… you think you can come by?"

"Maybe." She smiled. "No promises."

"I'm taking that as a yes," he declared hopefully. "Meet back here at around four?"

She grinned, shaking her head, and made her way out of the courtyard. "Don't be late." As soon as she was out of view, he retrieved Telaris from behind the tree, stretching his arms into the air.

Great Falcon, I'm hungry. He tucked his jewel back under his tunic, making his way into the inn and spotted Asten at the bar.

"How about some soup?" Asten was inquiring. "I could go for some chilled tomato soup right now." The barmaid nodded, completely uninterested with what he was saying.

"Come on, make a decision. You're holding up the line," whispered Erluc sharply, joining him. It sounded like a few men behind them agreed.

"Soup it is," he declared, tapping lightly on the wooden counter. "With cucumbers. And garlic. And maybe some lemon and vinegar." Erluc quickly took a coffee off the counter, raising an eyebrow at him, part disgust and part intrigue. Asten grinned and turned back to the barmaid. "And spices. I mean, as many spices as you're able to put in there before you can't taste the tomato." The woman nodded briefly, wearing a strange expression before starting to prepare the soup. Erluc rolled his eyes, before deciding to head back to the table, where Renidos was tearing off a piece of fried prawn—the closest thing to smoked krill available at the Fang.

"Who orders soup?" Erluc wondered aloud. "If you want flavored water, then drop a plant in your glass." Renidos smiled weakly while Asten shook his head in disbelief. "Worst thing since salad." Erluc shivered.

"Please. You haven't eaten a bite of good food since we reached here. You can't live on coffee, you know," pointed out Asten smugly as he rose to go pick up his soup from the bar.

"Watch me." To emphasize his point, Erluc took another deep sip from his tumbler. Even if Asten *could* drink the coffee, Erluc was sure that he would despise it just because Erluc liked it. His all-time favorite beverage, and his best friend was allergic to it.

As Asten made his way back, he took a quick sip of his soup and sat down next to the others. "This isn't bad. I'm going to have to come up with a name for this."

Rolling his eyes, Renidos kicked Erluc from under the table, who didn't appreciate the gesture. "What?" he whispered harshly.

"Don't look now," forewarned Renidos so softly that he was almost whispering, "but the girl sitting behind you has been staring at you for the past five minutes, and it's freaking me out."

"That's pretty weird," agreed Asten. He pretended to adjust his stool and stole a glance towards the table behind them. Renidos was right—there was a group of girls seated behind them, and one of them was gazing with wide eyes at Erluc. *Creep.* The girl noticed him, and he quickly looked away. "Yeah, one of them's looking at you all right. Or was. I think she saw me."

"I don't blame her," admitted Erluc. "After all, it's me." Renidos allowed himself a little grin, and Erluc tapped absently on the table with his fingernails, drumming out a tune. "Safe to look yet?"

Asten shook his head. "Don't bother. She's not your type."

"In what way?" questioned Renidos, more amused than surprised. Erluc and Asten had gone over this routine hundreds of times, but this was the first time that Renidos was present.

"Blonde," clarified Asten, and Erluc nodded, already having guessed as much.

Raising an eyebrow, Renidos scanned the table again. "I actually meant the short one at the end, but I guess you're not wrong about the blonde too."

"There's another one?" Smirking, Erluc pushed a lock of hair away from his eyes, and Asten scowled. "Would you stop, already?"

"Jealousy isn't an attractive trait," preached Erluc, shaking his head in mock pity.

Unwilling to let it go, Asten countered, "And arrogance is?"

Erluc was about to reply, when a dusty scrap of parchment pinned to the corkboard behind Asten caught his eye. "Hey, Ren?"

Renidos looked up, swallowing his mouthful of prawn. "Hmm?"

"What's that about?" he asked, and both Renidos and Asten reluctantly turned around to glance at it. Nodding, Renidos turned back to his plate.

"That's an old flyer," he explained. "High King Elandas has been calling for recruits for the new Twilight Legion."

Asten's eyes widened. "New Legion? Since when?" He seemed completely awed by the news. "Imagine that— fighting for the greatest army in history. It sounds amazing."

"An amazing death, for sure," muttered Erluc.

A man from another table snickered. "As it is, you're too late. Recruitment is over. They march for the Kre'nags around the forty-eighth." Looking Asten up and down, the man made an amused face. "It's not as if they would take a boy, anyway." Feigning disappointment, Asten took another sip of his soup. It wasn't even as though he would actually join an army, given the chance.

He raised an eyebrow at the man. "And what's in the Kre'nags?"

The man turned to Renidos. "Is he for real?"

Renidos shrugged and stuffed another prawn into his mouth. "They're northerners," he clarified through his mouthful.

"Ah." The man nodded. "Should've realized from the accent. I thought you talked strange." Erluc ignored the man, taking another sip of his coffee. *What an idiot.*

Not to be deterred, Asten pressed, "Why would Elandas march to the Kre'nags?"

"Dwarves," explained the man. "Some war they're fighting, in which they're being blown to bits." He chuckled. "So Elandas has rebuilt the Twilight Legion to help them out. But that's old news, kid. I could barely walk when those flyers started going up some thirty years back."

Renidos wiped his mouth clean with a napkin as Asten carefully spooned his way through his soup. "Speaking of signing up for things, have you decided yet?" asked Renidos between bites. Erluc didn't look up, while Asten looked at Renidos in surprise.

"Decided what?" he inquired. "What are you talking about?" Erluc raised an eyebrow at Renidos, who was scraping away the last of his food. Sighing, he dug around in his cloak for the rest of his money. Asten turned to him, furrowing his brow in confusion.

"There's going to be a championship in a couple of weeks, at Inthyl's arena," explained Erluc with a sigh. Renidos sat back on his stool, wiping his mouth clean with a cloth.

"And Erluc's too scared to enter because an old man told him not to."

Asten rolled his eyes, clearly amused. "What has become of the legendary Warrior?" he taunted. Erluc sighed, draining the remainder of his vapid coffee. "Anyway, we've got bigger problems than your little tournament," asserted Asten. "Thea wants our rent by the fiftieth, which means we have to gather four daerals in around a fortnight."

Erluc nodded, turning to look at the stout woman behind the bar. She smiled back at him, and he returned to his coffee. *Bloody rent's going to be the death of me.* "So how much do we have?" he asked as he put the two coppers onto the table.

Asten squinted in concentration, before concluding, "Once you pay for the food, we will have exactly… zero."

"Zero what?"

"Zero anything." Asten drummed his fingers against the table, bringing a queltra out of his pocket and dropping it next to Erluc's change.

Erluc pressed a hand to his forehead. "Seriously?"

"Still think getting a job is a bad idea?"

Amid the conversation, Renidos had been silent. Now that he had finished eating his meal, he looked up. "Guys? I don't mean to interrupt, but if you need some money, I'm sure my mother wouldn't mind lending you a couple of daerals," he offered.

Erluc shook his head, making an excuse as they made their way to the back exit of the inn. He jammed his now slightly worn-out key into the crack, and the door to the courtyard pushed open.

"You know," began Asten, admiring his ring. "This looks like it's good quality. I could polish it a bit at the forge, and it should buy us another week or so." As he turned to push the door shut, Erluc exchanged a quick, meaningful glance with Renidos before sighing and making his way to the middle of the courtyard.

"Don't get rid of it just yet." Renidos flashed a grin at Asten. "You never know what it might be able to do."

Raising an eyebrow, Asten seemed to be trying to make sense of what Renidos had said. "What do you mean?" Renidos smirked, and the next second, he was at the other end of the courtyard. Asten's eyes widened with shock. "What…"

Erluc collapsed in a hammock he'd tied from the oak tree to a wooden pole planted in the soft dirt. It was about time that Asten got to know. "That day at the Citadel, when we had that weird dream… it turns out that we got… powers."

Renidos leaped onto a sturdy-looking branch of the tree, his feet dangling a few feet above Erluc. "Now, I can run home and back in less than a minute."

Asten leered Erluc. "Both of you?"

"Not exactly." Renidos chuckled with excitement, turning to Erluc, who sighed and reluctantly clenched his fist. He focused hard for a brief moment before something changed. His image shimmered, the blue crystal growing warm in his pocket, and he was suddenly covered in plate armor—the same color as his dark hair. Asten remembered the instance at Adúnareth's temple when they had received their powers—Erluc's hand had been covered with a dark gauntlet for a second. He hadn't expected it to be a part of a full suit of armor.

Renidos flashed a huge grin and jumped off of his tree branch, flipping forward to land near Asten. With a wink, he sprang back again, spinning through the air to rest on the oak.

Asten spread his arms wide in the universal gesture for '*seriously?*'. "I can't believe this. Typical." He spoke so softly that he could have been talking to himself. "You get super athleticism and magical armor, and here I am with jewelry." The ring gleamed uselessly on his hand. Erluc's armor slowly faded, and he sleepily collapsed back into the hammock.

"Are you sure that you haven't got *any* powers?" inquired Renidos innocently.

Asten glowered at him. He just kicked a pebble into the mud, weakly querying, "You didn't get anything else, did you?

"No," admitted Renidos. "I've been experimenting, hoping something else will come up, but I don't think I have any other abilities."

"Actually…" Erluc started, trailing off quickly. "You're going to enjoy this."

"Oh?" Renidos raised an eyebrow.

He unsheathed Telaris, telling both of them to stand behind him. Renidos raised an eyebrow, but Asten waited silently in anticipation. Erluc rested the tip of his sword on the tree trunk, focusing, and a moment later, frost began to spread from that point, leaving the bark blackened and withered. When he lifted the sword, the blade began to glow red hot, and flames appeared along its length. With a smile, he swung Telaris in an arc, decapitating an invisible foe.

"That is awesome!" exclaimed Renidos. He high-fived Erluc, who had extinguished Telaris, grinning.

"Alisthír helped me try and control it, but I still haven't mastered it fully." He smirked. "Oh, by the way, Asten," he added hastily, "I may have torched one of your tunics last week. Sorry about that."

"How does that even work?" questioned Asten, ignoring Erluc's confession. "The Guardians don't use magic, and that's Kovu's sword."

Erluc nodded. "My guess is that Telaris was affected by the blessing too." He indicated the hilt, which had two runes on either side. "When we touched those runestones to the sword, I think they bonded together."

Grinning, Renidos stretched his wrist. "Imagine if your sword started shooting fire at the arena. Those guys would lose their minds."

Asten grunted, uneasily putting his hands into his pockets. "What were you doing at the arena?"

"Training." Erluc turned around, facing the tree. Cracking his knuckles, he made a fist and threw it at the trunk. When he relaxed, there was a fist-sized imprint in the bark, and he was unharmed.

Asten frowned in disbelief. "Who exactly is this... Alisthír?" Erluc ran a hand through his hair in discomfort.

"Alisthír is a man I met at the arena last division—my trainer—and he knows that we were chosen. He knows that we're the Trinity." Asten's eyes widened, but he didn't interrupt. "He offered to train me but advised us not to reveal our powers to anyone else. He was the one who told me about the tournament." He looked at Renidos accusingly. "As for why I'm not competing, what kind of heroes use their powers to win money?"

"Broke heroes?" postulated Renidos innocently.

Asten spat into the grass. "And why didn't you tell me about these powers earlier? I'm a part of the Trinity too."

Erluc snorted, "I'm not stupid. Knowing you, if I'd shown you these powers when we'd discovered them, you would've gone crazy trying to find your own."

Asten sighed. *If I even have any.*

"Come on, Erluc! It's four hundred daerals! You could even buy your own house with that money," exclaimed Renidos. "And you'd be famous. I mean, the last guy to win this tournament became the General of the Twilight Legion and won himself a place on the Council of Nine."

"Four hundred!" repeated Asten. Renidos nodded, his eyes widened in enthusiasm. "Wait, this isn't the Steel Trial, is it?"

Erluc groaned. "Why am I not surprised that you know about this?"

Asten raised his eyebrows. "How do you *not* know about this?" He shook his head incredulously. "The tournament is held every ten years to honor the Twilight Council, and the victor becomes the Steel Champion. Imagine—"

"If you're going to narrate the entire history of the tournament, please let me know now so I can drop a tree on you," cut in Erluc. Asten hurled a fistful of grass at Erluc, who blew it off his chest.

"Well, the old man didn't say anything to me. I'm registering," announced Asten. Erluc covered his eyes with his hand in frustration. "Ren? Why aren't you entering?"

"I can't. According to Alisthír, you have to be at least seventeen to participate," he explained uncertainly. "And even if I *was* allowed, I don't imagine my mother would be too enthusiastic about it."

Erluc smiled. Although he missed his parents, he couldn't help but feel a sense of freedom once they had left Sering. Admittedly, their lives had become much more complicated since then, as well. "You do realize that you need to be chosen by a lord to represent their province, right?"

"Oh." Asten looked down, slightly deflated. "I remember that."

"Don't worry about it," encouraged Erluc, gripping his shoulder. "The competition would be seriously elite, and you still don't have any sort of magical advantage." A moment later, it occurred to him what he had said, and he hastily amended, "I mean—"

"I'll take you to meet Alisthír if you want," offered Renidos, cutting him off. "We can go after lunch."

Erluc nodded. "I'll come with you." He made his way upstairs to change to wash up and change into a cleaner tunic.

After a quick lunch at the Winestone, they set off for the arena. Their pace across the city was leisurely at best, and it was almost three by the time they reached. Luckily, Asten's timing couldn't have been better.

Together, they made it inside and walked into the arena.

"There. That's him." Renidos pointed across the arena at a group of warriors circling a man. Alisthír was having another practice session. Asten watched in awe as he swiftly routed the others, without showing any signs of fatigue.

"I know, right?" agreed Renidos, still smiling. "He's amazing."

Asten raised an eyebrow, clearly intrigued. Erluc didn't blame him; after all, they didn't know of anyone else who could handle this many opponents with such ease. That sort of fighting ability seemed almost inhuman. Once all of his assailants were on the ground, Alisthír helped them up and proceeded to walk into the stands to meet a boy who rushed to give him a tumbler. The three of them caught up with him just as he had removed his helm and was taking a hearty gulp of water as they approached.

"Renidos, Erluc, how can I help you?" offered Alisthír without looking.

Asten regarded the man coldly. Erluc glanced over at him, trying to make out what he was thinking. Clearly, his friend found something odd about Alisthír; it wasn't like him to be this hostile at a first meeting. Now that he was closer, he recognized several subtle oddities in the man's appearance. Who stands fully erect after a brawl like that? He wasn't even breathing heavily. His accent was Andaeric enough, but Asten still felt uneasy.

"This is Asten. He's…" Renidos lowered his voice. "He's the third one."

Alisthír turned immediately, extending a hand. Asten took it, and they traded looks. As Erluc watched them, he could almost see them reading each other's expressions, trying to get the measure of one another. "Alisthír," said the man. "I've heard that you're quite the erudite, Asten."

"My friends exaggerate," decided Asten after some consideration. "You must have had a lot of practice to fight so well." Renidos had zoned out and was eagerly watching another battle that had begun, and Erluc had taken a seat on a nearby ledge.

Alisthír bowed slightly in recognition. His eye caught on Asten's ring, and the Mage was quick to notice.

"It was a gift," he slipped in hurriedly.

"A gift indeed." Alisthír's smile was unsettling. "You need not keep anything from me, Mage. Whatever it is, I'm sure Erluc has informed you that I already know." At that, Asten seemed even less comfortable with the situation. Maybe that was what was bothering him—that Erluc had chosen to trust this man so quickly.

Luckily for him, Renidos returned to the conversation and sat on a nearby bench that was a part of the stands.

"Asten here wants to enter the Steel Trial," he summarized. "Erluc and I were wondering if you could… explain."

"He means they want you to talk me out of it," offered Asten. "For whatever reason." He was eager to see what this man's reaction would be.

"I *told* you the reason," reminded Erluc sharply from where he was sitting.

Alisthír nodded, taking a seat next to Renidos, while Asten stubbornly remained standing. The old man surveyed him once more. "Can you use it yet?"

Erluc took a moment to grasp the question, but Asten immediately shook his head. The ring gleamed golden as it met the sunlight.

Alisthír nodded. "Your powers are greater than you realize. All of you." He looked at Renidos, who still seemed confused about the previous exchange. "But without training, I'm afraid they lie between useless and a threat. In a tournament as prestigious as the Trial, it would be wise not to test ourselves against the murky waters of fate."

The Mage's expression soured—this was essentially what Erluc had told him.

"The prophecy is also largely a secret," continued Alisthír. "And it would be wise to keep it that way. There is still much that we don't know about it, and until you're prepared to fend off the evils of the land, you must continue your training."

"Well…"

"I see that you are one who does not budge easily, my friend," observed Alisthír. "An honorable characteristic, but a dangerous one for a hero such as yourself."

Asten shrugged. He had grown up hearing the same words from Erluc's father, Neran, but he stood by his attitude. "Fine," he finally conceded. After all, the man made a convincing case. "I'll let it be." Erluc smiled and patted Alisthír's shoulder.

Just as they were about to bid him farewell, Asten turned to the old swordsman. "Since you're already training Erluc, you wouldn't mind me coming down here once in a while to train, too, would you?" Both Renidos and Erluc had zoned out, watching intently as two women were dueling somewhere to the side. The man nodded casually.

"And what about the ring?" At that, Erluc was jolted back to attention to their discussion—Renidos still seemed distracted. "You know how to use it, don't you?"

Alisthír held his gaze, before sedately whispering back, "I'm afraid that's something that you're going to have to figure out on your own."

Asten appeared disappointed, but he had likely expected as much—it was as Adúnareth had told them. If they wanted to grow stronger, they had to do it by their own merit. As Alisthír rose to full height, and their hands met halfway.

Erluc and Asten struggled to drag Renidos from the arena, but once the two combatants in front of them had finished their brawl, Renidos reached the door before they did. They split ways near the city center, Renidos deciding to spend the afternoon at home for once. Since they'd met, they had spent most of their time together, including most meals. Sometimes Renidos would even crash with them at the Fang, to the great dismay of his mother.

They bade him farewell and crossed to the city square. "Actually, now that I think of it," Erluc started, "I actually have some work." He nodded his head solemnly. "But I'll meet you at the Fang in a couple of hours."

Asten studied him curiously, trying to read his expression, but eventually, he gave up with a shrug. "I guess I could pay the library a visit. Meet back at home for dinner?" "Sure." Erluc nodded before running off. He hid behind the butcher's shop from a moment, just in case Asten had been watching. Then, he made his way back to the inn.

He sprinted up to his room to retrieve his key, then returned downstairs and opened the back door. Closing it quietly, he waited a few moments to make sure he hadn't been noticed. After he was certain it was safe, he unlocked the hidden door to the courtyard, and as he pushed it shut behind him, he smirked.

In the corner, Rose was curled up against the oak reading from a thin codex-style book. She had worn her coffee-brown hair back in a ponytail and was outfitted in a plain skirt, a long woolen sweater covering her top. Her extra-long sleeves went past her hands, but she hadn't bothered to fold them back. In the afternoon sun, her hazel eyes seemed to physically light up as she saw him. "Well, this is progress," she admitted, setting the book down. "I only got here a couple of minutes ago."

Erluc flashed a lopsided smile. He was usually late whenever they decided to meet. It was almost worth it; Rose's face was just that much more endearing when she scolded him, her dimples appearing whenever she couldn't hold back a smile. "What're you reading?"

She shrugged. "Nothing interesting, just a collection of old poetry my father is obsessed with." At the sound of her voice, Erluc unwound considerably, letting the day's happenings slip out of his mind. "I was also thinking of getting a job, but I couldn't find anything worthwhile." She relaxed against the lush grass, looking up at the sky.

"You're not alone there," Erluc assured. "I'm in pretty dire need of one myself." He shook his head, lying down next to her.

"Really?" She smiled, rolling onto her front. "What do you have in mind?"

"Well," Erluc paused, considering it. "Nothing," he admitted. "I have no idea what I'll do." He turned to face her, and she let out a small giggle. "Hey, I'm serious!" he appealed with a faint smirk.

She did her best to suppress the laugh, but it was obvious that she was amused. Erluc rolled his eyes, stretching back out onto the grass. "Hey," she consoled him once she'd managed to contain her laughter. "Hey, that's completely fine. It's just… sometimes it takes a while to find what you're looking for, and you feel that much better when you finally do." He sat back up, taking her hand. She smelled of mint and gasped as she felt his cold touch on her skin.

"What about you?" he asked softly.

Rose raised an eyebrow. "Me?"

Erluc nodded. "Have you found what you've been looking for?" She looked deep into his dark irises with her gorgeous hazel eyes. Most of the time, he found that looking into someone's eyes was an easy way to find out what they were about. The intimacy had a way of… simplifying things in a way that nothing else could really compare. It was something about her eyes—everything around them could have exploded, and they wouldn't have noticed.

"You know," The corners of her mouth curved up, "I just might have."

A strong wind blew around them, and they could hear the leaves rustling high in the trees. Erluc flashed his uneven smirk, leaning in towards her.

Without his prompting it, his fingers interlaced with hers, and they both closed their eyes. His heart pounded in a way it never had before, even though he'd already gone through this whole routine what felt like hundreds of times. This wasn't any different. It shouldn't have felt different. *Why isn't this the same?* He brought up his free hand, lightly caressing her cheek as he tried to calm his fervent thoughts. Then his lips met hers, and everything else evaporated. All he could be sure was real was the rapid beating of his own heart, her soft, warm breath on his face, the gentle sensation of her lips just barely brushing against his.

"I'm… sorry," breathed Erluc, breaking away. As the contact ended, Rose sucked in her breath, and he smiled, savoring the taste of mint on his lips. "Probably should've given you a heads up."

"I…" She wore a subtle smile, flashing her irresistible dimples at him once more. "I wouldn't mind it if you were sorry again." She paused. "Only if you want to, that is," she added hesitantly.

"Seriously?" he asked, unable to keep the grin off his face. They kissed again, this time shorter. Once they parted again, Erluc sighed contently, rolling over on the grass.

Sitting up onto her knees, Rose indicated the tree. "Also, I was meaning to ask—what's with all these burn marks on the trunk?"

Erluc sat up, allowing himself a small smile. "Bonfire got a bit out of control today."

"What a hazard." Rose's cheerful expression melted away when she turned to look at the sun. "I have to go. I promised my father I'd be home for dinner," she admitted, and he could hear genuine regret in her melodious voice. She looked at him fondly, before brushing his arm with hers. "Give me around an hour and a half."

Rose scurried out of the courtyard, and Erluc watched her until she was out of his view.

Reluctantly, he made his way back inside. As he made his way up to their room, he saw Asten studying the cover of a large, leather-bound book. He took a few more steps, raising an eyebrow, when one of the floorboards creaked under his boot. Startled by the sound, Asten looked up quickly, a grin spreading across his face when he saw his friend. "So?"

"So?" Erluc raised an eyebrow. "So what?"

"I happened to catch you 'working' in the courtyard," Asten smirked, turning the book over in his hands. "Who was she?"

Erluc gritted his teeth. After all, he was going to have found out eventually. "You may need to sit down for this," he warned.

"Umm… okay." Turning the book over in his hands, Asten kicked off his shoes and hopped onto the low bed in their room.

"Well, she's the daughter of some local trader," Erluc started. "And she's sixteen right now."

Asten nodded absently as he traced lines between the symbols on the book's cover with a finger. "And what's her name?"

Erluc sighed, bracing himself for the coming onslaught. "Rose."

The book fell to the floor with a thud, Asten's features contorting with horror as he remembered their previous encounter. "Her! I knew I'd seen her before!" He stopped. "Of all the girls in Inthyl, you choose to go out with *her*?"

His brow furrowing, Erluc nodded slowly, as if he didn't understand Asten's stance. "What are you talking about? I'm not the one who stole her key." His voice was slightly provoking but playful.

Asten shook his head in disbelief. His first and only encounter with her had been a division ago, and that hadn't exactly gone smoothly. "How—" he started before the words failed him. "How did this even happen?"

"For starters, she slapped you," he offered. "The rest, as they say, is history."

Asten let loose a laugh in spite of himself. "You know what?" he decided. "It doesn't even matter. It's you—the very next time you see another girl, you'll forget all about her." Erluc shrugged, his head in the clouds. Reaching down to pick up the book, Asten went on, "How long has it been?"

Erluc pondered the question for a moment before replying with, "Well, we met that day in the courtyard, and we generally just ran into each other after that. Until a few weeks ago, it wasn't planned—we just happened to visit at the courtyard at the same time."

"That's almost a whole division! I can't believe I didn't notice… and you actually stayed with just one girl for all this time." Asten paused, his brow furrowing. "Are you okay?"

Erluc scowled. "Aside from a gaping deficit in money, hunger—"

"You ate four courses less than three hours ago."

"—homesickness, lack of a job and the fact that I quite literally just met an Immortal, I'm doing pretty good."

Asten's expression hardened at the mention of Adúnareth. "You haven't told her, right?"

"Of course not," stated Erluc flatly. "And Asten?" His friend looked up, raising an eyebrow. "Next time, don't watch."

They both shivered at the thought.

"I left before anything happened, don't worry," returned Asten hastily, reassuring himself more than Erluc. "Besides, I think that Lyra and I may be getting serious. I'm meeting her again tomorrow evening." The longing in his voice was palpable, and Erluc was forced to snap his fingers in front of Asten's face to jolt him out of his daydream.

Dating for more than a division now, Asten hadn't kissed Lyra once. Erluc wasn't a love expert, but he knew that most girls weren't going to wait that long, and he'd seen Lyra. He knew that many Inthyl boys would jump at a chance to go out with her.

"So, how was the library?" Erluc asked instead. He thought that would spare his friend's feelings. "Find anything useful?"

Asten sighed, "Nothing great." His eyes brightening, he shook the book in his left hand. "On the other hand, I did read a particularly interesting text about the Far Lands."

Erluc raised an eyebrow but said nothing. These were the conversations in which he was just there to pretend to listen just so Asten could feel good about himself. For the next fifteen minutes, he knew, he would have to put up with Asten pacing the room, talking about the history of men and the lineage of Eltar. With luck, he would be able to get to sleep before his friend finished.

About halfway through his discourse, Asten jumped, and Erluc got up. "What happened?"

The Mage bent down, picking up a small stone from the ground. "This fell out of my cloak just now—gave me a fright."

Gave me a fright? Erluc smirked. *Never thought I'd hear that from you.* The southerners were really influencing them—he'd only heard Rose and Renidos say such things in the past. Either way, he let it go. "Is that a runestone?" He opened his pack and retrieved the pouch that served as the store for the runestones. After counting them, he looked up at Asten, eyes narrowed. There were three missing, including the two bonded to Telaris. "Which one was it?"

"Lightning," was the curt reply. Erluc recalled that as the runestone that Asten had examined in their room. He must have slipped it into his pocket without asking. Erluc flicked Asten's hair before returning the runestones to his pack.

"Honestly, I completely forgot this was in there," admitted Asten, spinning it around in his hand. Suddenly, the runestone seemed to dissolve into the metal of his ring, and electricity sparked between his fingers. Swearing as the current swept through him, he tore off the ring and flung it away from him. It clattered onto the wooden floor, spinning before gently landing on its side. Lines of smoke escaped from the metal as if it had just been reforged and cooled. Asten carefully lifted it and returned it to his hand.

It was surprisingly cold. He straightened it, about to mourn the loss of the runestone, when he noticed the lightning rune was now engraved on the ring.

Erluc gasped, "What the hell was that?"

"I-I'm not sure." Asten stared at the ring. "But I think that my ring just bonded with it." He turned it around so that the rune was facing upwards.

"Like Telaris?" Erluc's mind flashed back to when he'd dropped the ice rune onto Telaris, and Asten had done the same with the fire rune. The runes had merged with the sword.

Asten nodded. "Adúnareth gave me this ring… I-I think this was meant to happen." He looked on the verge of crying in happiness.

Erluc whistled and patted his shoulder. "Looks like someone got their powers after all."

"I still don't know how to use it," he reminded half-heartedly.

"Well, I do," assured Erluc. "Just do the same thing that I do with Telaris." He paused, trying to phrase his explanation. "Really, the only advice I can give is to focus. I try to picture whatever I'm trying to do, and the sword just does it on its own."

"That's probably easier said than done," Asten grunted. "And Telaris was *given* to you. Whatever power I have probably comes from within—it likely doesn't work the same way."

"You're probably right," agreed Erluc. "Just try."

"Even if this works, I can't shoot lightning inside here, can I?" He considered firing the bolts at Erluc, but he doubted that his friend would appreciate the gesture.

Instead, Erluc spotted a shed outside the bedroom window. Pushing the window open, he scanned the area to make sure that no one was around. "Here," he told Asten. "Aim for that shed."

Asten nodded, closing his eyes as he pointed at the shelf with his left hand. As Erluc watched, the golden ring began to spark, and the air was briefly tainted with the overpowering smell of ozone before energy sparked around Asten's hand. He flinched, just as the energy shot forward, flying straight outside as a blinding white streak. It flashed brilliantly as it collided with the wood below, and when the spots had cleared from his eyes, the shed was ablaze.

Erluc shoved Asten back into the room, tightly bolting the window down. He laughed the same way that he had when they had released all the horses from the stables back in Sering.

"Whoa!" was all he could say. Asten broke into a smile, and they bumped fists.

"Just wait till Ren sees this. He's going to freak out!" declared Erluc, unbuckling Telaris and propping it against the wall. Asten acknowledged the comment, but he was already half asleep; the effort had completely drained him. With a grin, Erluc splashed some water on his face, making his way out of the room.

"Where are you going?" muttered Asten drowsily.

"Just for a walk. I won't be long." Easing the door shut, Erluc slipped out of the room and made his way downstairs, outside, to the courtyard. He took a few cautious steps around the old oak, where Rose was sitting on a low branch. "Even for you, this is pretty late."

"Got held up talking to Asten," he explained. "I hope I didn't miss anything important."

She shook her head, a small smile on her lips. "No, just wanted to talk."

Hoisting himself onto the branch beside her, he nodded. "Anything in particular?"

"Not really," she admitted. "But now that you mention it…" She looked down. "You know what it's like to have a secret?"

He smirked, making sure to not look her in the eyes. "I have a bit of an idea."

Taking off a hairpin and stashing it in her dress, she squeezed his hand. "It hurts having to keep it from someone, especially if you care about them."

Believe me, I know. Erluc's brow furrowed. "Who do you have to lie to?"

Gathering back her hair, Rose leaned into his shoulder. "My father, mostly. But everyone at home, I think. Everyone I know."

"About us?" guessed Erluc. She nodded, and he wrapped an arm around her. "Why, would they not take it well?"

"Oh, you have no idea." They both smiled weakly, and for a while, they just sat there on the branch, Erluc running his fingers through his hair. She shifted slightly. "I sincerely hope Asten isn't watching us again."

Heat crept up Erluc's face in a flush even he knew was obvious. "You saw him?" Grinning broadly, he shook his head. "No, he's passed out upstairs. And besides—according to him—he left before anything happened."

Rose made a face. "Do you believe him?"

"I can always tell when he's lying. Sure, there are times when I doubt him, but I believe him. Don't you?"

"I believe *you*," she said.

A thought occurred to Erluc. "Wait, so you haven't told anyone about this? About us?"

She shook her head. "Have you?"

"Well, Asten and Renidos know…" He frowned, counting them on his fingers. "Oh, and Thea."

Her face at that was a picture of horror. "*Thea?*" Clearly, the barwoman didn't have the greatest reputation for keeping secrets.

Very obviously holding back a laugh, Erluc shook his head. Rose's eyes widened, and she shoved him out of the tree. He landed flat on his back with a *thud,* and he cracked up, shaking with mirth as she slid off the branch to crouch next to him. "This isn't funny!"

"I'm sorry." Erluc couldn't take his eyes off of her exasperated face. "It's just that... you're really cute when you're flustered." Her cheeks flooded red once more, and he let his head fall back as he laughed.

Rose punched his leg lightly, looking off in the direction of the inn. "How are you like this all the time?"

He raised an eyebrow, finally recovered. "Like what?"

"Carefree," she clarified. "Confident. It's like you know that everything is going to work out the way you want it to."

"Maybe I do," he countered with a smirk. "Or maybe I'm just that charming."

"Is that right?" She raised an eyebrow, but she couldn't resist a smile. "You know, sometimes I think you're going to ruin my life."

"Well that's a first," Erluc allowed himself a slight grin. "I usually only hear that *after* I break up with someone."

"See?" she replied immediately, rising to her knees. "You always have an answer for everything, and I can't stand it."

"Give it time." Erluc smirked. "It'll grow on you."

She made a face, pushing him back down. "I hate you."

He sat up slowly, rubbing his neck. "Really?"

Rose nodded mischievously, her eyes glinting. "More than anything."

He brought one hand to her face, slowly caressing the side all the way to her eyebrow and tucked a lock behind her ear. "Prove it," he said softly. He let out another breath and slowly lowered his hand as he stared into her deep, brown eyes. Just like it had earlier that day, the whole world drew to a stop, and there was nothing but Rose, her face inches away from his. The only thing he could hear was the beating of his own heart and the release of his breath. Erluc moved closer and felt his lips crush against hers, the taste of mint flooding across his mouth.

She gasped, finally breaking for air before they sank back into each other, and in that moment, there was nothing else. No worries, no responsibilities… no secrets. They were free.

Chapter 11

The Calm Before the Storm

Inthyl, Aenor

Asten

"Apparently an old woman had brought me to Sering in her arms, begging for someone to take me in." Asten began. "Erluc's parents did, and I was raised as their son. And then, of course, he was born a division after. After his mother died when I was nine, I learned that I wasn't really her son, but up until that, I'd more or less believed I was a part of the family." He shook his head.

Lyra's affectionate expression turned to shock as she rested her hand on top of his at the center of the table. After all of their restaurant dates, the pair had run out of establishments to visit. Asten had tried bringing her back to the Fang that day. "You were *nine?* What did you do after you found out?"

Asten shrugged. "I lived with Erluc and his father for another year and a half, then insisted on leaving so I could carry my own weight. I started work on a farm, tending to the horses, and I slept in the corner of an abandoned barn. But either way, whenever times got tough, I could always count on them to keep me going. Even after I left their house, they made sure I always *felt* like a part of their family.

They gave me everything—everything except my name. That old woman told them that before she left." He took a deep breath and continued, "When I turned seventeen, Erluc and I decided that we would come to Inthyl to try to make it on our own—it was like losing my family all over again."

"That must have been a hard time for you." Lyra's voice was as sweet as honey. "You must have been really brave to make that decision."

She was right, except it had been Erluc who'd made that decision in the end. Asten just smiled. "What about your family? Apart from your father and brother, I don't think you've told me about anyone else."

Lyra's face brightened. "My mother is a physician at the Royal Infirmary, so we spend painfully little time with her," she explained. "Apart from my cousin in Lendrach, and her parents, that's my entire family."

Asten nodded, continuing the story. "When I was younger, I used to dream that I had a sister, and my parents were secretly emperors from the Far Lands. They would always apologize for abandoning me, saying that they did it to protect me. Together, we'd sail off into the east, and I'd finally be home." He stopped, a distant expression in his eyes. Lyra caressed the top of his hand, carefully sipping her steaming tea. Asten knew he didn't have much storytelling prowess, but still, he had finally begun to open up to her.

After they were done eating, and Asten had tried his best to recall all of Erluc's usual jokes, they both rose, strolling over to the door, and she turned back to him. "Thanks for lunch," she said gratefully. "And I know how hard it is to talk about your past."

"I didn't put you to sleep?" asked Asten with a smirk, and Lyra shook her head.

"No, of course not," she assured him, turning to glance at the sun just outside the window. "Anyway, I guess I'll see you tomorrow at the forge."

"Um, sure," agreed Asten, maybe a little too quickly. He hesitated, a rapid storm of thoughts taking place in his head, before he added, "Though if you want, you could always, you know, stay here a little while."

Flipping her hair over her shoulder, Lyra grinned. "Really?" she asked.

"Here, follow me." Beckoning lightly, Asten stepped over to the door leading to the back area. They slipped behind the inn, Asten leading the way, and he pushed the key into the wall. As he gave it a shove, the large brick door slowly opened, revealing the garden. They walked in together, and Lyra's eyes widened at the sheer size of the hidden courtyard.

Unfortunately, it just so happened that someone else had reached there before them.

Erluc was sprawled out on the grass near the end of the courtyard, fiddling with an instrument in his hands, and a girl was sitting up in the hammock. She had a bowl of blueberries in her hands, and she quickly put one in her mouth while thinking of something. Rose was dressed similarly to the last time Asten had seen her, but today, her hair flowed down to her shoulders, and her pin was in her dress. Asten hadn't noticed before, but she was much more attractive than she usually looked.

"Tea or coffee?" she asked suddenly.

Without hesitation, Erluc answered from below, "Coffee."

"Coffee or food?"

"Coffee."

"Coffee or sleep?"

"C—" Erluc stopped himself, suddenly unsure of himself. "Sleep."

With a grin, Rose took a moment to consider her next question. "Sleep or happiness?"

"Sleep *is* happiness," argued Erluc, with a smirk. He played a chord, letting the sound reverberate through the air for a moment.

Rose rolled her eyes, throwing a blueberry at him, the fruit harmlessly glancing off his cheek and rolling into the grass. "Come on, you have to answer."

Asten considered leaving for a moment, but before he could take a step, Erluc looked up. Rose seemed to notice them at the same time, and Lyra stepped forward, probably tired of standing around in silence.

Asten flashed an apologetic look at Erluc, who quickly shook his head as if they had other things to worry about. He set the strings down, approaching the gate where Asten was waiting.

"Lyra," acknowledged Erluc with a smile, as they reached the gate. "Pleasure to finally meet you. I've heard a lot." Both Asten and Rose flushed as the words left his mouth, but probably for different reasons.

The girl smiled back at him, responding with, "You must be Erluc."

Rose and Asten awkwardly waved, with Asten tersely mumbling something along the lines of, "Good to see you." Erluc broke the tension, excusing both Asten and himself for a moment. He dragged his friend to the other side of the courtyard while the girls discreetly started a conversation about them.

"What happened to *don't watch*?" Erluc clearly wasn't a fan of the new habit he'd developed.

Grinning apologetically, Asten just responded with a nonchalant shrug. "Bad timing, I guess. But where were you? Renidos and I were looking for you all morning." He scratched his head before raising an eyebrow. "And why do you smell like mint?"

Erluc tried his best not to meet his friend's eyes, and his face flooded red. "I have no idea what you're talking about," he put in hastily. "And we had a deal—don't reveal the courtyard to anyone unless it's necessary."

Asten shrugged. "I was bored, and I couldn't find you anywhere."

Erluc rolled his eyes. "And you didn't think to check here, of all places?"

"Truth be told, I haven't been here in a while," admitted Asten. "By the way, when did you manage to get the strings? And how did you afford to buy it?"

"I didn't," clarified Erluc. "It is Rose's, but she leaves it here for me to use whenever I want." A wave of Rose's hand cut him off, and he jogged back up to the girls, Asten hastily following from behind.

"I should probably get going. My father is probably wondering where I've been," she told him softly.

Erluc wanted to protest, but from her own description, her parents were excessively strict, and he didn't want her to get in any trouble on his account. "Alright, I'll see you," he wished, and she balanced on her toes to give him a kiss on the cheek.

Seriously? Asten grimaced, looking away, before realizing that Lyra was still there. *Thanks a lot, Erluc.*

His best friend's willingness to… publicly display his affection was not entirely unheard of. And while Neran had tried to talk with them about it last year, Erluc would benefit from a soft reminder.

Or several loud ones.

They finally broke away, and Rose smiled. "You too," she replied, just as she hurried away from the courtyard. Her auburn hair swung to her side as she passed the gate.

Erluc turned to Asten, "I'm going to go get some lunch." He paused, turning to Lyra. "It was nice meeting you." She gave Erluc a lasting look as he passed her to exit the courtyard.

Just as he passed the door, he winked at Asten, who sneered. Lyra grinned, turning back to him. "So, he was really nice."

"You have no idea," muttered Asten under his breath.

"And what about Erluc's friend?" she questioned. "I get the sense that she really likes him."

Shaking his head, Asten snorted. *Shocker.* He might have sounded a little resentful, and maybe he was. But he'd grown up watching Erluc's popularity with girls rise to the point at which he didn't even have to make an effort. "No kidding," was all Asten managed to say.

Lyra traced the bark of the tree as she sat on top of Erluc's hammock. "And I feel like I've seen her before."

Asten shrugged. "You might've crossed paths in the city," he offered. "Erluc mentioned that her father is a trader."

"That must be it," agreed Lyra. "Do you know which school she goes to?"

He shook his head. "Probably somewhere around here, but she doesn't seem the type to come out of Inthyl Academy." Suddenly, he heard a loud crash and turned to see Erluc and a sweaty Renidos urgently burst through the courtyard gate.

Renidos' grin faded from his face as he saw the couple, and he froze. "Whoa." Asten glared at him, while Lyra raised an eyebrow. "I hate to interrupt, but this is urgent," he put in hastily. "It's Alisthír. We need to go. *Now*." Renidos pointed at the door, before hastily sprinting outside.

"Who—" asked Lyra.

Asten turned to her, incredibly conflicted. "I'm so sorry, but I really have to go." They all exited the courtyard, Asten locking it behind him. The Trinity raced off, leaving a stunned Lyra in front of the inn with only the birds and afternoon sun to keep her company.

"I genuinely hate you guys," he groaned as they turned a corner. "If she dumps me because of that, I'm going to kill you." Renidos shrugged, while Erluc wore an amused expression—Adúnareth was clearly plotting against Asten's life at this point. They swerved through the streets, Renidos slowing to their pace, towards the palace. "Well? What was so important?"

"Hey, it's not my fault; Alisthír said to bring *both* of you." Renidos' voice was unstable. Asten had wondered why his friend was so sweaty, but a day at the arena seemed as fair an explanation as any.

"Is everything alright? Is he hurt?" Erluc questioned, slightly worried now. Renidos shook his head violently.

"No, of course not, just—" Renidos abandoned the sentence. "I hope you two washed up today." They raced past the arena, and the palace's domes were finally in sight. They continued running the rest of the way without words, and Renidos was the only one that wasn't panting after they crossed into the gates. A huge banner hung between two poles, advertising the tournament registration. Asten raised an eyebrow.

Alisthír was waiting for them in the Gardens of Inthyl, which was bursting with children and their concerned parents. The compound was inside the palace grounds but served as a park for the public. A small booth was set up in the corner, where a small line of people waited eagerly.

The old warrior rose to meet the Trinity, his conventional calm expression resting on his face. "You'd think that enhanced speed would be enough to get you here before sundown, but it seems that nothing can overcome your lethal tardiness."

"Sorry." Asten raised his arms, panting. "We're listening."

He looked mainly at Erluc and Asten when he spoke his next words. "You need to enter the Steel Trial." Both of them paused for a second, waiting for Alisthír to explain his change of mind, but he never did.

Asten scoffed. "I thought that using our powers without training would signal the end of the world or something." Just when he thought he'd had this man somewhat figured out, fate had gone and pulled the rug out from under him. "Care to explain?"

Erluc shot him a glare, but Alisthír seemed not to notice Asten's attitude as he pulled them to the side, out of earshot from the other innocent Andaerians. "Something changed this morning. It's a long story, but I need you to sign up."

"You're going to have to do better than that," declared Erluc. His expression was one of disbelief. "We aren't in any hurry, so, *by all means*, explain."

Alisthír nodded. "Trust me, it's better this way."

The unease that Asten was reading from him wasn't at all like the old swordsman he'd met several days before. *What's so bad that it could rattle even this guy?*

"Is there some danger? Does this have to do with us being the Trinity?" asked Asten.

Alisthír scowled. "*Everything* has to do with you being the Trinity." He paused, regaining his composure instantly. "But you're correct: there is danger. It is your responsibility—

188 of The Promise of the Warrior

as the Trinity—to watch over the people of Eärnendor and protect them from potential danger."

Renidos frowned. "Hate to break it to you, but we already know that." He sat cross-legged on the lush grass. "But I was of the impression that saving people didn't involve electrocuting them"—Asten winced—"or impaling them. Mistakes don't hurt any less than the real thing."

The old warrior closed his eyes, exhaling deeply. "Ever heard of Uldarz?" he began. Erluc raised an eyebrow, and Alisthír continued. "The highlord of the dark elves and his son, Ulmûr, are going to be taking part in this tournament."

"Dark elves!" burst Erluc. "In Inthyl? What's Elandas thinking?" His hand had shot right to Telaris' hilt. Renidos shot him a warning look; the High King wasn't too far away.

"Quiet!" spat Alisthír. "Elandas doesn't know about them, and it's going to stay like that." Asten's lips parted as he was about to ask something, but Alisthír cut him off. "Because no king worth his crown would take us at our word, *obviously*."

"And why have they come here now?" questioned Erluc.

Alisthír looked at Erluc, his face carrying a grave expression. "I don't know. But it's not for a friendly discussion." Renidos rolled his eyes; the theatrics were starting to get out of hand. He continued, "I have... encountered the highlord on multiple occasions before, and it wouldn't be much of a stretch to say that we don't get along very well."

"What? Did you do something to offend him?" questioned Erluc, sighing in anticipation.

"That doesn't concern you," he snapped. "If the highlord attacks here, in Inthyl, there is nobody in the city who would be safe. If Elandas perishes, Aenor will be thrown into anarchy, and the ensuing struggle for power will give the dark elves the opportunity that they have been waiting for." He gritted his teeth.

Erluc furiously ran a hand through his hair. "So, what can *we* do about all this?"

Alisthír kicked a stone, sending it clattering onto the pavement. "You are Adúnareth's chosen. Your powers are our best chance at overcoming the dark elves."

Asten tapped a foot. "I suppose this is the part where you tell us why you can't do it?"

"I'll try, obviously," snapped Alisthír. "But Uldarz and his son—" He clamped his mouth shut, then started again. "The two of them together are too strong for me alone, now that the years have started to catch up with me."

"You wouldn't know it, watching us fight," muttered Renidos.

"Regardless, I believe the three of us should prove more than a match for them in a fair fight," Alisthír went on, "Which is why they won't give us that fight. If they find the opportunity, they will kill you and anyone else who stands in their way."

Erluc snorted in frustration as if he was getting tired of people threatening his life. "The Blade, he and every other dark elf alive." Erluc's eyes glinted, and Alisthír almost let slip a smile.

"Uldarz *is* the Blade of Atanûkhor," he revealed, and Asten nodded along, already having guessed as much.

The Trinity exchanged glances. Uldarz must have been one of the servants of Atanûkhor that Adúnareth had mentioned. "How do you even know that they're dark elves?" asked Renidos. "And how do we make sure that they don't kill us in battle?"

Alisthír held out a hand. "Did the Falcon tell you nothing after you received your gift?" The Trinity looked at each other, unsure of what advice Adúnareth had given to aid them.

"Yes. He had said to master our powers," recalled Asten. "But what's that got to do with anything? We've already done that!"

Alisthír snorted. "You think that *this* is the extent of your power? You are the chosen—your individual power will one day be great enough to face down entire armies."

Asten kicked a small pebble into the grass. *If only.*

"Really? Well, feel free to tell us when that day is," offered Renidos. "Meanwhile, what can *we* possibly do to fight off these monsters?"

Alisthír sighed. "Have you ever taken a life?" Renidos shook his head, but Erluc and Asten suddenly found the glittering stars extremely interesting.

Renidos' eyes widened. "You've killed people?"

"Not people. Dark elves. Undead skeletons." Asten shivered as Erluc said the words. The Vale of Shadows was one memory that he would love to forget. "It was for survival."

"Was it?" Renidos shook his head. "Dark elves are monsters, but you can't go around executing them no matter what."

Alisthír interrupted. "I'm not going to disagree with you, young Spectre. Just know that your friends aren't monsters. They've faced hardships that others would only face in their worst nightmares. It is probable that you will eventually find yourself in a situation where you must sacrifice your humanity to ensure the safety of the world. What will you do then?" Renidos said nothing, but Asten could see his fist clenched around a clump of grass, slowly tearing it out of the ground. The old combatant turned to the Warrior. "It's not right of me to ask this of you, but I must. For the sake of the people of Eärnendor, I implore you to honor your promise to the Falcon and help me rid the land of Uldarz for good."

Asten and Renidos stopped to look at their leader. Asten knew that Erluc had been thinking about this very decision since he had accepted the spirit of the Warrior. Heroes were only heroes if they could protect what they loved, and they both understood that. But protecting all of Eärnendor? Erluc was just sixteen—not even a man. How could he live with himself if he agreed to this?

Adúnareth's words echoed through Asten's mind. *Go forth, defend the Council and defeat the power of Atanûkhor here before he succeeds.* The Blade of Atanûkhor. *Your powers will be vital in your conquest against Atanûkhor's servants.* A sea of images flooded his mind while the Falcon's words resonated in his thoughts. He saw a large, helmeted creature brutally run an aging man through with a jagged, black sword, a massive horde of dark elves sweeping across the Manos, the villages of Lindrannon ablaze and wasted, and finally, Inthyl's grand temple reduced to ruins.

He opened his eyes, watching Erluc's troubled expression. "I'll do it," he said quietly, surprising even himself. Erluc turned to face him, wide-eyed, and Renidos looked like he had just been punched in the gut. "I'll enter the Trial and fight them." Asten paused, briefly deciding whether to continue. "I might not be a fighter, but I'm willing to face the risks." He locked eyes with Erluc, hoping he could read the rest of what he wanted to say from his face: I can't do this without you, but I will if I have to.

Erluc nodded once and looked back up at Alisthír. "I'm with Asten. I couldn't in good conscience let monsters like these roam free in the city. And if they bring the lives of innocents into harm's way.." He took a deep breath. "Then I'll do what I have to."

Asten and Alisthír grimaced, accepting his decision. Renidos looked at Erluc as if he had just agreed to kill Renidos himself. The younger boy stared blankly, his eyes filled with hurt and disbelief, and a moment later, he was no longer there. Asten sighed, Renidos was too young to understand. But if he were to be the force of change, the embodiment of darkness, he would have to come to terms with this decision on his own.

Erluc cleared his throat. "How do I fight them without revealing myself?"

Alisthír exhaled deeply and turned to Erluc. "Trust me. I shall teach you to control your powers, and this tournament is the best way to do that."

They held each other's gaze before Erluc slowly nodded. "Alright. You better know what you're talking about, because if you don't, you may have irreversibly scarred Renidos."

Alisthír shook his head. "The Spectre is much stronger than he lets on."

"I don't suppose you plan on telling us how we actually enter the Trial?" cut in Asten, a seemingly obvious question finally occurring to him. "Don't you have to be hand-picked by one of the provincial lords?"

"I know some people." Alisthír smiled.

Before Asten could question him further, the old swordsman continued. "Many of the champions in the Steel Trial follow a code of honor—at least, enough to spare the lives of boys. As long as you don't bleed out, you probably won't die." Asten mocked an expression of relief.

Erluc ran his hands through his hair. "Fine." He looked at Asten, then at Alisthír. "When is the Trial?"

"It's always held on the forty-seventh day of the second division, once every decade," Alisthír responded.

Erluc's brow furrowed. "There's half an hour left of today, and it's the thirty-ninth, which leaves us with… a week." Alisthír nodded gravely.

Asten raised a hand in mock courtesy, "Isn't it a bit late to sign up?"

"Yes." Alisthír shrugged. "But you can leave that to me." He led them around the majority of the crowd, to the far end of the Gardens, and into the interior of the compound. A troop of men was standing guard outside the main structure, but they said nothing when Alisthír led them onto the flat steps that extended into the palace.

Erluc shot Asten a quizzical look, and the older boy shrugged in reply. As long as they weren't doing anything dangerous or stupid, they should be safe from any sort of trouble. And while Alisthír had seemed relatively sensible to him at first, even Erluc looked like he was starting to have his doubts.

At the end of the corridor that they were passing through, two men sat on a bench, occupied in a hushed discussion. One of them rose immediately as they saw the old warrior, while the other took his time.

"Alisthír," acknowledged the latter, half-heartedly.

"Therglas," returned Alisthír. "Erluc, Asten, meet the General of the Twilight Legion—Therglas of House Illard." Asten's arms trembled as he shook hands with the man, who seemed slightly put off. Alisthír turned to the other man, who bowed in front of him. "And Euracis of House Solovar, the keeper of records for the Council of Nine." Erluc greeted the man, who nodded in acknowledgment.

"So," started Therglas. "It's been a while since I've seen you around the palace. To what do we owe the pleasure of this meeting?"

"Actually, I was wondering whether it would be possible to sign these boys up for the Steel Trial," Alisthír informed him.

The general turned to the other man, who seemed rather intimidated. "Well… registration has been closed for weeks, and we're in the final stages of preparation," supplied Euracis half-heartedly. Alisthír looked at the man once more before he nodded. "But I think we can make an exception in this case, sir."

He quickly scribbled their names and ages down on a scrap of parchment. Both Erluc and Asten were confused as to why the man had created openings for them, but the happenings of the past few hours had been so vexing that they didn't bother pursuing the reason. Given the circumstances, it was fortunate that things had worked out the way that they did.

Therglas looked Erluc over. "Well, I suppose I should wish you good luck. But it seems like you've had your share of luck already," he smiled at Alisthír, "with a Steel Champion watching over you."

"A champion?" Asten raised an eyebrow. "I thought *you* won the last tournament ten years ago."

Therglas nodded. "Aye, I did." He looked as if he was in pain. "I didn't, however, win the one before that."

Asten sighed. That explained why Alisthír was so respected at the arena and why the general seemed so intimidated by him. It would've been nice if the old warrior had thought to tell them about it before, but the man didn't seem to like discussing his past.

Just then, a loud trumpet blared into the air, and Erluc looked around, startled. Looking at Alisthír, he raised an eyebrow, to which the old combatant simply nodded. "Well, it was nice meeting you," dismissed Therglas immediately, patting Erluc on the shoulder. "Are you going to need an escort, or can you find your way back?"

"That's alright, sir, we know the way," assured Asten, anxious to leave a good impression. They left Alisthír with the men, making their way back to the inn.

"Did you know?" asked Asten.

"It's Alisthír. No one ever knows." Erluc shook his head. "So many secrets. I mean, I believe that he's a good person, but I don't think I can ever fully trust him."

"Are you sure this is the way?"

Asten nodded absently. "Just follow me." They walked past a row of houses, turning into the yard of a small villa. As they passed into the back garden, they caught sight of a familiar face.

"Finally. What were you boys up to this late?" asked Renidos' mother.

Asten smiled apologetically. "Sorry, Isabelle. Just got caught up at the inn," he lied. Erluc didn't understand what was going on, but he managed to return her smile.

"Renidos!" she called.

"I'll be right down, Ma!" came a voice. A second later, the younger boy burst out of the back exit. He jumped in surprise when he saw the rest of the Trinity.

"What are you doing here?" he asked. Isabelle poured them some cider, and Asten's gaze flitted between him and Erluc before he broke into a grin.

"I can't believe you *both* forgot," admitted Asten with a huge grin. "It's the fortieth. Happy birthday, guys."

Renidos raised an eyebrow. "When did you figure out that my birthday was on—"

"When I had this made." Isabelle produced a small locket necklace from her cloak. Renidos jogged into the lawn—at human pace, so his mother wouldn't suspect anything—and accepted the gift. On the end, a stone was carved with a rune he hadn't seen before: a circle with a curved four-point star inscribed in it.

"It's the Life rune. I thought it would fit you pretty well," added Asten. "I actually made it myself."

Renidos lifted it up to the sky. "I… can't believe it."

"Alright, I had *some* help from Lannet. I'm not that good yet, but I tried my best."

"Not that, you idiot." Renidos smiled. "Thank you. It's beautiful." He took a glass of cider from Isabelle, gulping down a lengthy sip. He turned to Erluc, "The fortieth?"

Erluc shrugged. "The fortieth. Who would've thought?" He shook his head, filling a glass with cider. "Happy birthday, then, I guess."

"You too," acknowledged Renidos, taking another sip. He hadn't fully recovered from their conversation at the Gardens, but he seemed to have decided to embrace the moment.

"I'm going to miss being the only man around here," joked Asten longingly.

Erluc opened his mouth to say something, but Renidos cut him off. "Let him have that one." Isabelle hugged Renidos, wishing him again. Both she and the Mage sang discordantly to the boys—Asten mumbled the words while Isabelle chanted loudly.

When they were done, he patted Erluc's back, whispering, "I got you the thing that you were asking for."

Erluc raised an eyebrow. "Really? Can I see it?" Asten grinned, and the Warrior waited in anticipation for him to reveal the gift. "I love it," he declared finally. "You know, I've always wanted an invisible present, but you just can't seem to find them anywhere."

Asten snorted. "It's back in the inn. But don't worry, she'll love it."

"She'd better," Erluc replied, stone-faced, before cracking a smile. "I'm just messing with you. Thanks, man."

"You're welcome," acknowledged Asten. "But when you dump her, I want it back." Erluc snorted, and both of them refilled their mugs with cider. "Oh, and there was another thing, for you."

Erluc raised an eyebrow in anticipation as Asten searched his pockets. Finally, he drew out a fine steel chain, just like the one he wore his red crystal on. "It's for—"

"My gemstone?" guessed Erluc, taking Asten by surprise.

Asten nodded, holding out his hand for the crystal. "I just thought you'd appreciate not having to carry it around in your pocket all the time." After tightening the clasp around the gem, he handed the chain back to Erluc.

After a little fiddling, Erluc was able to fasten the chain around his neck. "Thanks a lot, man."

"Don't mention it." Asten shrugged awkwardly, trying to pick out any sarcasm in his friend's voice. Unsure how to continue the conversation, he turned to his glass of cider and drained it, and Erluc seemed to get the message, instead heading over to talk to Renidos.

"How're you doing?" he asked. Asten set his glass down softly, turning to watch them. Isabelle had left the yard, probably to fetch something from indoors.

"Never better," answered Renidos softly, and he exhaled deeply. "I think I could've left things between us better, though."

"There isn't any shame in standing up for what you believe in." Erluc smiled, taking another sip of his cider. "Besides, I see where you're coming from."

Renidos nodded, slowly continuing. "So, you're not doing it?"

Erluc smiled. "I never said I would."

"But Alisthír—"

"Let Alisthír think whatever he wants," he interrupted. "I only said I would do what was necessary. If that involves doing something drastic, so be it."

"You really don't understand, do you?" Renidos rubbed his forehead with a finger. "I know we made a promise, and we should try our best to honor it, I do, but we can't kill people in the name of it. It's just an excuse, and I can't believe that we're the good guys if we have to kill people— any people."

Asten considered that, trying to organize his thoughts on the matter. He hated the fact that people had to die, and he had always considered it hypocritical to play a role in that death. But if he had to make a choice, would he be prepared to dirty his own hands to save innocent lives? Who chose who lived and died? Was that their decision to make?

There's always another way, his inner voice argued. That was what Renidos would have said, he was sure. But what if there wasn't? What if sacrificing a life that wasn't his to give the only way towards the good of the many? The question hurt his head to think about. For now, all he could do was trust in Adúnareth—at least until he could sort out his thoughts.

There was a silence, and Erluc took another sip. "So, I guess I won't see you at the tournament?"

Renidos shook his head. He looked to the door, where Isabelle was stepping back out into the yard. "If you change your mind about this, then come find me. I'll help you in whatever way I can."

Asten sighed, making his way over to the others. Maybe it was better that Renidos stayed out of this, at least until he understood what it really was that the Falcon was asking of him. *The force of change that emerges from the eclipse.* Asten had mulled over Adúnareth's words for days after their encounter at the Citadel, but only now was he really beginning to realize what they meant. Without darkness, there could be no evolution, because there would be no drive behind it. Renidos was like that; Adúnareth wanted him to be able to make the choices no one else could, in the name of the many. *You must master the call of the dark before it masters you.*

Erluc's voice jolted Asten out of his troubled reverie. "How about a toast?"

Isabelle topped up Asten's glass, and they raised them to meet the night sky. "To life," proposed Renidos, his fingers closing around his locket.

Erluc sighed before repeating the tribute, "To life."

They touched their glasses against each other's and drank till there was nothing left.

Chapter 12

One for Luck

Inthyl, Aenor

Erluc

"Again!" ordered Alisthír. Erluc and Asten threw their swords against each other, the impact sending sparks soaring into the air. Erluc ducked under the opposing blade, rising to full height behind the Mage. Telaris gleamed in the morning sun as Erluc brought it around to rap his opponent's greave before swiftly disarming him.

Asten swore for the thousandth time that day as his sword spun out of his hand, clattering to the ground. Both Erluc and Asten had received some swordsmanship training before—most youths in Sering had—but he was starting to get notably frustrated that his friend could render him defenseless with such ease. To be fair, Erluc had bested several full-grown men back home. If anything, he was glad that Alisthír had agreed to come to the courtyard so that nobody else could witness Asten getting humiliated.

Today was the last day before the Steel Trial, and even though his form had improved considerably, he didn't think that he had started to appreciate the feel of a sword in his hand.

"I think I'll take a little rest," Asten told Alisthír as he lazily walked to pick up the black-bladed weapon he'd found in the Vale. The worn-out hilt bled sweat into his palm. Erluc knew it sounded ridiculous, but compared to Telaris, Asten's sword was about as useful as a straw. And it didn't hurt that Telaris could bond with runestones, allowing Erluc to summon the elements.

Picking up his waterskin from where it sat, Asten collapsed on the grass next to Renidos. They had visited Renidos in the morning, and after half an hour of pleading, he finally agreed to aid their training.

Asten had even gotten excused from work—courtesy of Lyra—so his focus was primarily on the upcoming competition. Erluc always saw him in the courtyard, either fighting with the others or working on mastering the use of his ring. Even after barely a week, Erluc could see significant improvement. Now each blast taxed Asten only slightly, and he was constantly working on new and creative ways to use his lightning.

"Right." Erluc provokingly twirled Telaris in one hand, using the other to move the hair from his face. "Enough for one day, or do we still need practice?"

Alisthír pulled out a slim, curved longsword from a lavishly decorated silver sheath. "Ready yourself," he said, answering the question. He tossed his cloak to the side and extended his sword, eyes narrowed. Erluc crouched down to touch the ground before mirroring the old combatant's stance. They both charged simultaneously, Erluc leaping into the air, while Alisthír slid under his soaring feet.

They both speedily turned, and their swords clashed in front of their faces. Pushing hard against each other's blades, they found themselves in a deadlock before Alisthír kicked Erluc's knee back from underneath him. Reacting quickly,

Erluc shoved hard against Alisthír's sword, pushing himself away and unsteadily regaining his balance. He snarled, and the old swordsman's lip curved.

"The dark elves won't show you any mercy. The more realistic practice you get, the better it is for you," he declared. The man charged without warning, and Erluc had barely spun out of the way as the longsword passed a finger's breadth from his ear. He blocked a strike to the back of his head, rolling to put some distance between them.

Flipping his sword in his hands, he feinted at Alisthír's shoulder, but the old man saw through the bluff, immediately bringing his sword down to protect his legs. As their blades clashed again, Erluc twisted Telaris' hilt in his hand, shoving Alisthír's longsword out of the way before stabbing lightly at his bare shin. The man looked up at him in surprise as the cold metal traced the skin of his leg, before kicking Telaris back and drawing his sword across Erluc's stomach.

Erluc grimaced as he felt the sword pass through his chainmail and graze his skin. Alisthír had insisted that they practice with regular armor to make the duels as equally matched as possible. There was one problem with this idea—normal armor wasn't impregnable. Swinging Telaris around in a circle, Erluc leaped over Alisthír with inhuman strength and slashed downwards, but as the more experienced duelist had opted not to wear any sort of protection, he was easily able to twist out of the way.

The brawl continued until noon, both sides giving no quarter, before Erluc collapsed to the ground, exhausted. Alisthír's face was redder, and he grudgingly sat down with the support of a tree.

"Not bad. I've been practicing swordplay my entire life, and only a handful of people have the right to say that they've held their own against my blade." Alisthír sounded genuinely impressed. "If you continue to fight like this, then nobody—save Adúnareth himself—will be able to say the same about you."

Although both Asten and Renidos had both been fascinated by the bout for a while, they had lost interest far before it had ended, instead deciding to try a spar of their own. By the time Erluc and Alisthír had called a draw, both of them seemed to have independently decided to use their powers without telling the other in an attempt to bring the fight to a quick close. Renidos' speed made it almost impossible for Asten to see him, let alone manage to land a hit on him. The only thing keeping the Mage in the game was his superior experience and almost precognitive understanding of Renidos' fighting style.

After a few more minutes of this, though, it was clear to Erluc that Asten had had enough. In his left hand, a white ball of electricity appeared, and as he clenched his fist, a small shockwave exploded outwards, knocking Renidos off his feet and leaving him writhing in the dirt.

Erluc regarded his friend, impressed. "That's a new trick."

Asten raised his left hand, and his ring glinted in the sunlight. "I kind of like this one."

"It's okay," groaned Renidos. "I'm fine, thanks for asking."

By the time Asten got to him, Renidos was back on his feet, brushing the dust off of himself. He pushed the Mage back lightly before demanding, "Since when can you shoot lightning? I thought you didn't get any powers." His voice was more entertained than furious. Even Alisthír seemed intrigued by Asten's new ability.

"I just discovered this recently," he admitted. "I can bond runestones with the ring, and the rune determines the powers that I get." Renidos' eyes widened.

"How many do you have?"

"Just the one." Lightning sparked between Asten's fingers. "I tried the same thing with other runestones, but only this one did anything."

"I'd try the runes of Fire, Stone, and Ice if I were you," recommended Alisthír, surprising everyone present.

Asten narrowed his eyes. "Since when do you know how these things work?"

Alisthír didn't shed any light on the matter. "You seem to waste a lot of energy being surprised. From now on, just assume that I know what I'm talking about."

Clearly unable to argue with that logic, Asten turned to Erluc. "You don't happen to have those runestones on you right now, do you? I think I could master Stone by tomorrow if I practice enough."

"On the contrary, I think that you should spend more time *mastering* your sword," insisted Alisthír. He sheathed his sword. "A stunt like that, however spectacular, would get you immediately disqualified in the tournament and imprisoned as an alchemist."

Erluc rolled his eyes. *Whatever.*

Asten and Renidos stayed with Alisthír to continue their training, while Erluc was collectively forced to leave and get some rest. Shoving Telaris back into its sheath, he turned and jogged back into the inn. Following a brief bath, he changed into his clean tunic, wandering off toward the square.

There were posters advertising the Steel Trial all around the city, with accompanying slogans like, 'Try your luck against the strongest in Aenor!' As if that would be an encouragement.

But Erluc had a positive feeling about the competition. His training with Alisthír had visibly improved his skill. He remembered swinging his first sword nearly four years ago.

His father, Neran, was a hunter, so he insisted that both Erluc and Asten learn to defend themselves so they could eventually take up hunting as well. He was the only person in Sering that could consistently prevail over Erluc in their spars, but when his age caught up with him, Erluc no longer had sufficient competition. Trying his hand against the '*strongest in Aenor*' would be a refreshing challenge. Offhand, he wondered who the champions from his home of Lindrannon would be. Maybe I'll know one.

A woman in a long satin dress—an unnaturally wide hat covering her hair—complimented his coat as she walked past, and he nodded in acknowledgment. She must have been from the aristocratic district or a friend of the princess.

Eventually, Erluc found his way to the palace. The guards were strangely absent, prompting him to wonder where they might have gone. It was only about three, and the Gardens of Inthyl were completely deserted as well. He cast a look around, wondering if they were closed for some reason, but he shrugged to himself and pushed the gate open. Just as he stepped through, though, a hand on his shoulder caused him to flinch, whirling around with a hand on Telaris' pommel. Rose smiled as Erluc exhaled in relief. She was wearing Erluc's faded leather jacket over her long, dark leggings and had a scarf over her head to protect her from the harsh sunlight. "Trying to break in?" she teased. Smirking, Erluc led her away from the gate, and they walked back in the direction of the square.

"Scared me a bit back there," he admitted.

"Did I?" teased Rose. "Who'd you think I was?" Erluc shifted uncomfortably before dismissing the question. His reaction caught Rose's attention.

"Come on! Who?" she pressed, and Erluc shook his head.

"Uh, nobody," he quickly mumbled, immediately trying to divert her attention from the topic. "Haven't seen you in a while."

"I've got other friends too, you know," she offered. He lightly nudged her arm, a smile tugging at the edge of his mouth. "Father was pretty mad after the last time I spent the night out," she admitted. Erluc's face burned red, as did hers. They walked a few paces in silence before she changed the subject. "How about you? Busy practicing?"

Erluc raised an eyebrow. "How did you k—"

"Asten, of course." She exhaled. "He said you're representing Lord Karustor of Lindrannon in the Steel Trial."

"I didn't think you and he talked," noted Erluc.

"I was looking for you in the courtyard," Rose explained. "But it was just him and your other friend—"

"Renidos."

"—sparring in front of the tree." Her brow creased. "Is that why you came to Inthyl? To participate—"

"Are you kidding? I was actually this close to not participating." Erluc took her hand, trying to be as reassuring as possible.

Rose smiled faintly, letting her arm drop. "The Steel Trial, though? Isn't that a little out of the league of someone like you?"

"I'm a fair swordsman. Trust me," assured Erluc with an arrogant smirk. And he was—Alisthír's training had been instrumental in improving his fighting ability.

Not totally convinced, Rose met his gaze, her eyes betraying her concern. "Just... be extra careful." Her hand grazed his arm, and suddenly, his cheeks flushed.

"Don't worry. I've had lots of practice," he reassured.

Rose tilted her head, unconvinced. "Promise. If you're in any danger, you'll forfeit. I don't care if you lose." She spoke faster than usual, flustered. "These men aren't like the people who you practice with—if they get a chance to hurt you, they won't hesitate to take it. They only fight for money and glory."

They continued walking in silence as Erluc considered this. He wasn't overly afraid of most of his opponents, but a certain pair of dark elves could pose a considerable threat to his life. And he liked his life—living was so much more… *lively* than being dead.

Erluc ultimately settled on using his powers as a last resort, but he knew he wasn't going to forfeit. He opened his mouth to say something, but someone crashed into him before he could.

"Watch where you're going, cretin!" yelled a boy, turning around to face Erluc. He didn't retort, as it would start a fight for sure. He simply stared the other boy down. The boy stood an inch or two taller than Erluc but looked about the same age. A falchion hung from his belt.

Unable to hold Erluc's gaze any longer, he snickered and walked away, his friends shouting mocking comments behind Erluc as they passed. Rose gripped his arm with both hands as they continued walking. "Forget about it." Erluc nodded. He'd dealt with proud, holier-than-thou groups of kids back home. Funnily enough, they always managed to pick a fight with him in Sering too. He returned to Rose, tucking an amber lock of her hair behind her ear.

"Alright. I promise," he agreed, unable to find a way out of the conversation.

"Thank you." Rose smiled, and her dimples reappeared, etching a smile over Erluc's face. "Now that that's over with…" She ran to the back of a large tree, pulling him next to her. Her scarf fell down around her neck, revealing her auburn hair. Reaching into the pocket of the jacket, she produced a small device and handed it to him.

A watch. Its strap was brown leather, and it had a silver dial. Erluc smiled, although slightly confused. "And what's this for?"

"Happy late birthday." She kissed him on the cheek, and two seconds later, he smirked in realization. His friends must have told her about the party last week.

"Thanks," he replied. Looking the watch over, he said, "There's no way this could have come cheap."

"Hey, you deserve it," she said sincerely. "And anyway, my father traded an antique vase for this, so I didn't have to spend anything. It's the least I can do for missing your birthday." Her voice soured slightly.

"Well, in your defense, I didn't remember it myself," admitted Erluc. They both let out a laugh, and he put on the watch. "What do you think?" he asked, turning to face her.

She took a moment to look at him. "Not bad, leather suits you."

"That's not what you said when we first met," he pondered with a smirk.

Pulling his old jacket closer to her chest, she shook her head. "What can I say? It's grown on me."

Erluc sighed, a content grin on his face, and they stepped away from the shade of the tree. "It's going to be tough to outdo this present."

Rose's cheeks pinkened, and she smiled. "Oh, I'm counting on it."

"Just so that I'm not caught off guard," started Erluc, brushing a lock of hair from his face. "When's your birthday?"

"Third-twenty-seven," she said, meaning the twenty-seventh day of the third division before stopping immediately. "Rats, I'm supposed to send out the invitations this weekend."

Erluc raised an eyebrow. "It's nearly a division away."

She nodded. "It's my seventeenth, so I suppose Father is making quite the occasion of it. A formal declaration of my growth into womanhood, or something of the sort."

"So, when am I getting my invitation?" teased Erluc. "If you deliver it personally, I might even consider showing up."

Rose rolled her eyes, "You wish." Her eyes narrowed playfully before she allowed herself a grin. They continued wandering the city, quietly making fun of passersby until night fell. A few hours before twilight, she wished him luck for the Steel Trial and disappeared back the way they had come.

"See you at the tournament?" he called after her.

She turned and flashed a mischievous smile. "Maybe," she shouted back. "If you win." Erluc shook his head as he turned around and began to jog back to the inn. He walked into their apartment to find an exhausted Asten already crashed on the bed. He gladly followed suit; a satisfying nap was just what he needed before the competition.

Chapter 13

WHAT ARE RULES FOR, ANYWAY?

INTHYL, AENOR

Asten

Asten couldn't take it anymore.

He rolled off of his makeshift chair-bed, quietly pulling a long cloak over his tunic. The stress was just too overwhelming—it was driving him insane. Next to him, Erluc was sleeping soundly, unevenly sprawled across the bed.

Stepping around him, Asten carefully opened the door, tiptoeing through the small crack. His hair was a sorry sight, and he hadn't slept a wink that night. How could he? Tomorrow he was going to have to fight the strongest warriors across Aenor, and he didn't have the faintest idea of what he was going to do.

Asten stealthily flew down the creaky wooden steps of The Broken Fang's staircase and strolled out of the front door. Not a soul was out on that cloudy night, and even the moon had taken cover in the clouds. He casually wandered around Inthyl, drowning his anxiety in the serenity of the silent city.

After about an hour of loitering, he stopped in front of the great staircase of Heaven's Citadel. *Why not? If I'm going to drown my fears, it might as well be here.*

Racing up the stairs of the temple, he reached the same room where the Trinity had received their powers. The beauty of the main atrium was somewhat diminished in the sparse lighting, but Asten's enhanced eyesight made up for it.

He felt the pockets of his cloak, finding a pair of silver queltras on one side. Asten frowned; it must have been Erluc's cloak. Well, what he didn't know wouldn't hurt him.

Asten carefully placed both coins into the opening in the central altar. He waited for a second, half-expecting Adúnareth's voice to thunder through his mind, but the rational part of him knew that the Falcon had more pressing matters to attend to.

Instead, he walked around the hexagonal room, examining the engravings on the walls. The nearest carving depicted the Falcon, locked in combat with the Wolf, claw meeting talon in a scarily lifelike rendition of their battle.

In all honesty, the fact that a being as powerful and ruthless as Atanûkhor existed scared Asten to death and beyond. The legend of the Wolf was one he hadn't heard before coming to Inthyl, but apparently, it was well-known here: the youngest of the Immortals, who had betrayed his own kind and turned on them, slaying them one by one. Now only Adúnareth, the oldest and strongest Immortal, kept the Wolf's dark power at bay in an endless battle.

Both sides were equally matched and could never be defeated by each other. A terrible thought entered his mind. What if Atanûkhor had been influencing their choices? What if the Wolf was influencing him now? If Adúnareth could give the Trinity his power, then could Atanûkhor do the same thing to his own minions?

The questions just got worse as he passed on to the next few images. He saw all the people of the three Mortal

Realms—Eärnendor, the Sea, and the Far Lands—kneeling as the Falcon descended from the skies, and all the souls of the dead standing ready as the Wolf howled into the night. He blinked hard, hurriedly continuing onto the adjacent wall.

The final carving was the most disturbing of all: a man suspended in the air, the silhouette of a massive wolf appearing around his form, as an enormous serpent lay dead at his feet. This must have been the ascension of Atanûkhor—the day he had risen as an Immortal. Asten reached out, letting his fingers brush against the marble wall. For a shrine to the Falcon, these people sure took equal representation seriously. Even the universe itself respected the balance between the light and the darkness.

He spent the next few minutes lost in thought, pacing around the Citadel. Above him, one of the clouds drifted away, allowing a single ray of moonlight to penetrate the glass pinnacle and illuminate the altar with a soft glow. Asten sighed, turning back to the depiction of Adúnareth on the wall. "Look, I..." he began before trailing off. "I don't know if you're listening, but if you're listening, we could really use some good luck for tomorrow." He twisted the ring around his finger. "I know Erluc thinks he could probably take on the entire Twilight Legion himself, but the truth is that even with these new abilities, we still don't know what we're doing." The carved eyes of the Falcon gleamed coldly, and Asten sniffed. "Truth be told, I'm not even sure what we've received these powers for."

He extended a hand, the marble icy against his skin as he touched the relief. "Please, if there's any way to make this easier..." he started uncertainly, before closing his eyes and beginning again. "What I'm trying to say is, it would be great if both Erluc and I survived tomorrow."

Opening his eyes, he exhaled and turned to leave, but as his eyes crossed the altar, a glint of silver flashed in the moonlight. As he stepped closer, he saw the queltras he had offered resting next to the hole. He blinked, rubbing his eyes to clear them, but the coins remained on the altar. *What in the world?*

Approaching cautiously, he picked them up and hastily returned them to their former place in Erluc's cloak, before descending down the steps of the Citadel. The sun had just begun to rise, and Asten hurried back to The Broken Fang to get as much sleep as he could before the Trial began.

About five hours later, Erluc woke him. "What did you do to my cloak?"

His hair was wet, and he had draped a soaking towel over the window ledge. Outside, the sun had risen prominently, and Asten estimated that they had about an hour before they had to leave for the arena.

The Mage shrugged, recounting the incident that had occurred at the altar. Erluc frowned once he had finished and brought the pair of silver coins out from the cloak pocket. "You're sure that you dropped them in?"

Asten nodded.

"*Man,* that's weird. But who knows? Maybe it's a good sign—we can use the money, anyway." He meticulously inspected the coins before turning to his friend. "What were you doing in the Citadel, anyway?"

Asten quickly replied, "I just stopped by while doing some practice for the tournament today." He wasn't going to tell Erluc that he'd gone to pray for good luck; the Warrior would laugh at him.

Erluc raised an eyebrow, pulling the cloak over his shoulders, carefully placing a metal contraption in a drawer of the cupboard, next to Asten's unopened birthday present. "At three in the morning?"

Asten shrugged, jumping out of bed. He tossed the bag of armor that Alisthír had lent him onto the bed, next to Erluc. He hurriedly washed up, and they made their way down to the lounge. Erluc bought them a loaf of bread, along with two large tankards of some foamy beverage. "So, I heard the news," admitted Erluc, trying to be as nonchalant as possible. "I'm sorry, man."

Asten raised an eyebrow. "What news?"

"About Lyra?" tried Erluc, still trying not to state it explicitly. This time, it seemed to have worked, and Asten sighed.

"Oh… that," he acknowledged, burying his face in a chunk of bread. "Well, this sort of thing happens all the time, anyway. It's no big deal."

"Speaking of no big deal," sighed Asten, trying his best to change the topic of the conversation, "how's it going with Rose?" Asten had come to terms with her relationship with Erluc—if one could even call it that—and both he and Rose had agreed to be more hospitable to one another. To be completely honest, Asten was surprised that Erluc hadn't moved on yet. This had to be the longest he'd gone without getting bored of one girl.

Erluc frowned. "She said that she might come to the tournament, and I talked to her just two days ago." He shook his head. "But never mind that. I have exactly what you need to get over Lyra." He pushed one of the mugs, filled to the brim, towards Asten.

"Now? Before the tournament?" asked the older boy after glancing into the tumbler, grimacing. "Are you serious?"

"Why not? It's not like it's going to help *after*." Asten couldn't even count the number of reasons not to touch the foaming ale in front of him. "Besides, if we die painfully today," continued Erluc, "at least we won't feel too bad."

"So, if I drink this, will you stop talking?"

"Would that work?" Erluc shrugged. "To each his own, I guess."

Asten closed his eyes and took a sip. A cold, bitter snake slithered down his throat, and he made a gagging face, pushing the tankard away from himself. "Blech!"

Erluc took a sip as well, shivering as the strong liquid invigorated his body.

Asten furiously wiped the alcohol off his tongue with a cloth, while Erluc leaned back in his seat. "You happy now?" questioned Asten. "If I die today, it's your fault." He turned back to the tumbler. "And who even pays for that stuff?"

Erluc nodded in agreement. "Come on, let's get to the arena."

He called the barmaid over, reached into his cloak to pay for their breakfast, and he brought out the pair of silver coins. He put the two queltras on the table, half-expecting them to disappear.

As the barmaid reached the table, she picked up the coins and handed them back to Erluc. "You two don't have to pay today, my friends," she said with a toothy grin. "Just don't win—I've got big money riding on Therglas. And anyway, this gives you a little help with the rent you're due."

"Thanks a lot, Thea," remarked Erluc sarcastically, as they rose.

Once they had exited the inn, Erluc turned to his friend. "Maybe these coins are just lucky." With the bag slung over his shoulder, Asten led the way to the arena.

They shoved their way through the assembled throng and passed into the pavilion where the contestants were to gather. Dozens of other combatants had already gathered, with another one following them in. Two bearded men slipped past the gate, and a guard finally pulled it shut, locking it behind him.

"You ready for this, friend?" asked a bearded man. His northern accent was familiar, and Asten smiled in recognition. "I've come down here all the way from Geldran, just for this, and I'm going to win it all."

Erluc turned to Asten, before replying, "I'd wish you luck, but it seems like you don't need it." They promptly shifted to the other side of the tent.

Asten looked around, but there was no sign of the dark elves anywhere. If there were four contestants to a province, as he remembered, there must have been sixty-four people in total. A man in decorated robes jumped atop an overturned crate, a scroll in hand, and Asten recognized him as the man who had entered them into the Trial. The aged man called out names, marking them off if he received an affirmative answer. All contestants were accounted for, and he called for quiet when he was done.

"Welcome to the Steel Trial. My name is Euracis," he started. "I understand many of you have traveled a long way to be here"—the man from Geldran beamed and twirled his loopy mustache—"and we wish you the best of luck. Now…"

Euracis spent another five minutes explaining the rules of the Trial. "In the Steel Trial, all of you will be fighting one other simultaneously. The Trial will end when only one warrior is left standing. Contestants may be eliminated in one of two ways," he began. "Apart from being killed, any champion who exits the marked area will be eliminated. Additionally, you will also be disqualified if you lose your weapon inside the arena."

Seems simple enough. Just stay inside and hold on to your weapon.

"Attacking a surrendered warrior will not only disqualify you, but also land you in a different kind of trial with the Council of Nine." There was wry laughter around the room, but Euracis remained expressionless. "The Steel Trial will be the deadliest challenge many of the warriors present will face in their lifetime. Every champion in this room was chosen for a reason and is among the elite of the kingdom." His tone took on a grave air, and Asten shot Erluc a glance. "The Council has no desire for so many of Aenor's finest warriors to fall in the name of entertainment. Thus, if anyone of you wishes to forfeit his stake in the Trial, he may willingly do so by exiting the marked area or dropping his weapon," he continued slowly. Asten raised an eyebrow— the idea seemed a tad risky, not to mention impractical. "To win, one must remain in the circle, and not lose their weapon for the entire duration of the Trial." Once everyone had understood, Euracis gave them ten minutes to prepare, after which they had to proceed into the arena.

Asten saw Erluc slip behind a tree, reemerging in his dark armor. With a smirk, the Warrior clapped his friend on the shoulder. "We'll be fine. Half these people are probably delusional travelers hoping to get their hands on some trophy."

Looking up, Asten slipped his mail coat over his head. "Like us?"

Erluc had no answer to that. "Do you have a plan?"

"Defend against anyone who attacks us."

"Obviously."

"Have each other's backs."

"Of course."

"And stay defensive," added Asten pointedly.

"Ye…Wait, what?" inquired Erluc. "Where's the fun in that?"

Asten scowled. "We're here to defeat the elves, not fight sweaty thirty-year-olds. Focus!" he whispered harshly. "We find the elves and expose them before all of Inthyl. Deal?" Outside, Euracis had begun to announce the names of champions, and one by one, they were ushered out of the pavilion. Asten thought it best to press Erluc further on the point; there wasn't much time left. "And remember—we can't use our powers. Not at all, or we'll get singled out as alchemists or dark spirits or something."

Erluc scowled. "And I was looking forward to this? You're taking all the excitement out of this tournament for me."

Before Asten could snap back a retort, Euracis' voice called out, "And now we have the chosen of Lord Karustor, of Lindrannon!"

His heart leaped into his mouth. This was it. If he was going to run, it would have to be in the next fifteen seconds. "Jorlend, son of Avdar!"

Erluc squeezed his shoulder. "Don't worry. We'll be fine."

Asten took a deep breath, wanting more than anything to believe him. "Erluc, son of Neran!" echoed the voice of Euracis. Erluc locked eyes with Asten, nodding reassuringly, before letting his black helm materialize and striding out into the arena.

"Dalnor, son of Garranen!" Now it was just him, two guards, and the four champions from the province of Talanest left in the pavilion. As he waited for his own name to be called, a thought occurred to him: if they couldn't use their powers in the Trial, how were they any better than the other sixty-two warriors there?

"Asten, son of Neran!" Before he could give himself time to hesitate, Asten clenched his fist around the hilt of his sword and stepped out of the pavilion. His mail shirt was too large for him, and it jangled uncomfortably as he walked. He joined Erluc along with the other fighters just within a massive, marked, white circle of chalk. Some way inside, a red halo marked a much smaller boundary, forming a sort of strange annulus. Scanning the competition for Uldarz, Asten spotted swords, spears, hammers, axes, and even bows. This would be interesting.

"The combat zone," Euracis announced, "is demarcated by the white chalk, as you can see. However, when the fight narrows to the final sixteen, a gong will sound, and you will have fifteen seconds to reach the red circle before you are eliminated. After that, whenever a contestant is eliminated, a horn will blow. You have one minute before the Trial begins. Fight well, warriors!"

Once again, Asten looked around at the people he would be facing—he recognized the man from Geldran, the army general Therglas and an old, silvery-haired man wielding a slim, fearsome longsword.

Alisthír. He'd wondered where the old warrior would be, and now he had his answer.

A roar erupted from the crowd as the contestants entered the circle, drawing their weapons. Asten took a deep breath before pulling his own leaf-bladed sword out of the sheath, the dark blade seeming the leach the life out of the world around it. To his right, Erluc drew Telaris, eyes narrowed in determination.

The sound of the gong snapped Asten out of his daze, and moments later, he was sprinting forward with his bloodsteel sword aloft to engage the young boy directly to his left. Erluc charged up to his aid, quickly disarming the youth with a swift, fluid maneuver.

Asten wiped his brow. "One down…"

"Sixty-one to go," finished Erluc, twirling Telaris.

"Sixty," Asten corrected. He indicated Therglas, who had just knocked a soldier unconscious. "We'll need to move fast."

Most likely by some earlier pact, a group of about twelve men surrounded Alisthír, who raised his narrow longsword grimly. Erluc wasn't overly worried. If he'd had to bet on a victor, the old swordsman would probably have been his choice. Grinning, he stepped forward, before Asten held out his arm. "Are you serious? What happened to the plan? Stay away from the competition?"

Erluc shrugged. "Honestly, I didn't like the plan in the first place."

Their attention was diverted by a pair of patrolmen; apparently, they hadn't been the only people forming an alliance. Erluc prepared to intercept them, but before he could take more than a few steps, Asten flung his sword at his attackers. The black-bladed weapon spun past Erluc towards the man on the right, slashing him across the cheek. As the soldier caught the hilt in surprise, Erluc smiled, understanding.

"You should've just let it drop," he remarked. Then he punched the other man back, knocked the bloodsteel sword out of the first one's hand and caught it deftly. After disarming both guardsmen with his dual blades in seconds, he tossed Asten's sword back to him. "Don't try that again."

Asten shrugged, examining the blade. "It worked."

Another combatant charged at Erluc, who deftly ducked under the first swing of his sword and punched him in the chest. The man flew back from the force of the impact, skidding several yards before rolling to a stop just outside the circle. Wincing at Erluc's superhuman display of strength, Asten turned to berate him, but a heavily armored man charged in between them. Even as Erluc twisted to engage him, Asten found himself face-to-face with a teenager as tall as he was and considerably more muscular.

Blast it. He took a few steps back, hoping to put some distance between them, but his attacker closed the few feet in his way with a single bound, slashing at Asten's unarmored head. Asten scrambled back, the tip of the blade missing him by inches, and fought to regain his balance, heart pounding. *Attack first*, reprimanded Alisthír's voice in his mind. *Neglecting your offense makes you look weak.*

If he wanted to give his opponent pause, he would have to present himself as a threat. Yelling, Asten lunged for the youth's midsection, a blow that was easily parried before being countered with a downward swipe. He brought his own sword upward, blocking the incoming weapon, and as both he and his adversary shoved desperately at their locked blades, Asten was forced back, step by step.

Erluc, who had routed the large soldier separating them, saw Asten struggling and sprinted to his aid, but Asten knew that he had only moments before he would be forced outside the circle. He closed his eyes in concentration, and closing his fingers, he swung his left hand at his aggressor's stomach. As his fist moved, a rush of power surged through his arm, and the contact caused a small flash, leaving the larger fighter temporarily dazed. Without missing a beat, Asten drove his elbow into his opponent's back, sending him stumbling over the boundary.

Asten winced as Erluc seized his upper arm, a scowl on his face. "Are you insane?" he hissed. "You can't use your powers here."

Shaking his arm free, Asten grimaced. "Since when was superhuman strength not a power?"

"You know I can't control that. And pushing a guy around is a bit more subtle than cooking him with lightning." Erluc turned away, rapidly ducking under a wide blade, spinning around as he slashed at the bottom of his opponent's arm. Although the man's bronze gauntlet blocked most of the blow, he winced as Telaris made contact. Erluc aimed another strike, but this time Asten intervened.

Taking advantage of the man's incapacitation, he slashed at his shins, knocking him to the ground. The falchion slipped out of his grasp as he fell, dancing in the air before piercing the dirt. Erluc kicked the blade outside the circle, remarking, "You know, this is more fun than I thought it would be."

"Stay sharp," reprimanded Asten. "We're going to have to save our stamina if we want to outlast everyone else." Erluc snorted, turning to look around for any other opponents.

A little way away, they saw Alisthír, who was simply a blur on the battlefield. The old warrior had successfully disarmed nine of his twelve attackers, but the other three had him on the ground, hard-pressed to defend himself. Asten watched as Erluc charged into the fray, blocking a sword aimed at Alisthír's chest. The silvery-haired man kicked his aggressors' legs from underneath them, leaving them with their faces in the dust.

Within seconds, they were back on their feet, swords at the ready, and then they had split into individual duels, sparks flying as the blurred web of flying steel shifted and undulated with the blades striking one another every fraction of a second.

With a quick flourish, Alisthír twisted his opponent's sword out of his hand. Asten deflected one blow after another, trying to get a clear shot at his own adversary's guard, but the other contestant's relentless offense made it near impossible for him to get in so much as a light jab. Over to the side, Erluc slammed the third fighter's blade downwards with such force that it was ripped out of his hands. *He really isn't letting up with the magic powers, is he?*

Unfortunately, without any physical advantage to fall back on, Asten knew almost immediately that he was no match for his opponent. With each swing, the sword grew heavier in his hand, and it was all he could do just to keep from being decapitated. A drop of sweat rolled down into his right eye, forcing him to squint, and while he was clearly tiring, the other champion seemed as energetic as ever.

Just as Asten was on the verge of defeat, though, a gloved hand caught the wrist of the man forcing him back. Erluc squeezed sharply, shoving the man away at the sound of a *crack*. Within less than a second, Asten had seized his sword and flung it to the ground.

By the time they had both caught their breath, Alisthír had dashed away to take on Therglas, two scouts, a formidable close-range archer and another teenager. "Proud fool," muttered Asten. "We save his life, and he challenges half the competitors in one go?"

Erluc shook his head. "He could have handled those guys. I'll bet you anything that he's faced much worse than Elandas' soldiers."

Asten hid behind his sword, turning to look for any other incoming assailants. Most of the competitors were fighting each other for control of the center of the arena, more than half already eliminated from the competition. A man in silver armor was cutting through the defense of multiple contestants at once, the weapons of his adversaries lying around him like a protective barrier. *What in the world?*

"Erluc," he whispered. The Warrior turned to look at the sinister combatant and nodded. They could see the maniacal rage boiling through the man's bloodsteel helm. His forehead bore a silver three-pointed crown. "Which one?" Asten had still not resigned himself to the fact that dark elves had actually come to Inthyl, but the creature before him had confirmed his fears.

"He doesn't look much different from the ones I fought in the Vale of Shadows," judged Erluc. "That's probably Ulmûr."

The dark elf twirled his slim blade in his hand, knocking away a spear being jabbed at him, and drove it ruthlessly through the stomach of one of his challengers. Erluc winced, and Asten's entire body tensed up as Ulmûr yanked out his weapon to deflect another sword aimed at him. "I think I'm going to be sick," he muttered. Erluc didn't say anything, but he seemed similarly unsettled.

Parrying a stab, Ulmûr grabbed his attacker's blade with a gloved fist, preparing to slash the man across the face. His opponent cried out and released the hilt of his claymore, scrambling away from the prince. He had forfeited—better the competition than his life.

Ulmûr sneered, violently turning away from the fallen man. He swung his blade at his next victim, the carnage threatening never to stop.

"You boys lost?" interrupted a voice. In front of them was a tall, dusky, bald man. A long, double-edged sword with an emerald set into the pommel rested in his hand. "The spectators sit up there," he taunted, gesturing to the stands.

Erluc smiled provokingly, responding with, "Aren't you a little old for this?"

The man charged, Asten briskly stepping out of the way. Erluc swung his sword in front of his helm just in time to block another strike, before twisting the man's sword out of his grasp. The tall weapon fell to the ground with a satisfying thump. The dusky man looked shell-shocked, staring incredulously at Erluc as he retrieved his weapon and exited the circle.

Before they could catch their breath, though, Asten and Erluc were immediately forced to fend off the attacks of a group of about seven warriors who had decided that the boys were easy prey. Erluc leaped into the air, firmly planting the hilt of his sword into a man's helm, knocking him backwards. He raised Telaris just in time to block two swords aimed for his shoulder before Asten knocked the blades out from underneath. They made quick work of the rest of the warriors and sighed as the last man passed the white boundary.

Asten turned back to the center, where Ulmûr had considerably thinned the herd as well. If there had been about sixty warriors to begin with, he'd defeated at least twelve by himself.

Turning to the left, Asten froze, his eyes widened. "Great Falcon."

Across the arena, an unbelievably tall, sturdily built man in gray-black armor was keeping at least fifteen opponents at bay with a massive battleaxe. As far as Erluc knew, not even Alisthír could handle that many foes at once and be assured of victory.

Asten made a slight whimpering sound. "If that's not him, then I'm going to forfeit right now."

"No…" Erluc squeezed Telaris' hilt. "No, that's definitely him. We're both going to die."

The five-star crown on Uldarz's helm beamed into the light, as brilliant as it was ghastly. Asten bit his tongue, scanning the rest of the fighters nervously, anything to take his mind off of Uldarz's rampage. "How the *hell* are we going to fight those monsters without our powers?"

Erluc shrugged uncertainly. "If he's about to kill you…"

"Damn right! You can bet I'm going to fry his vile hide." Asten's voice was extra squeaky. He swung his sword at an incoming man, pushing him out of the marked circle. "But…" he started, incredibly conflicted, "with this few contestants, we'll be noticed." He challenged a duo of soldiers, Erluc joining him in a quick, fevered tag battle.

"Better noticed than dead." Scowling, Erluc tripped his opponent and shoved him out of the boundary. "We could team up with the others to take him down."

Alisthír was now dueling Therglas along with one of the patrolmen, while simultaneously deflecting arrows from the masked archer. Ulmûr—or at least who Asten assumed to be the dark-armored warrior who had diverted Therglas' attention and was now facing him—was fighting like a whirlwind, leaving the general hard-pressed to hold his own.

The gong sounded to mark the final sixteen contestants, and Asten leaped into the red ring immediately. Erluc followed him, circling around to assist Alisthír, and Asten charged into Therglas' fierce showdown with Ulmûr, locking blades with the dark elf and shoving him away and regrouping with Erluc. As the elf staggered back, he kicked Therglas in the chest, sending him stumbling out of the circle.

A horn blew as Therglas was eliminated, followed by two more blasts as Erluc and Alisthír dispatched their opponents.

"Hey, check it out." Asten felt Erluc tap his shoulder. The bearded man stood about fifteen yards away, thrusting at an opponent with a lance, its polished color the same jet black as Erluc's hair. "Do you want to or should I?"

Asten hesitated, before nodding. "I'll give it a try." He jogged up to the man, just as he'd eliminated his previous opponent.

The man seemed surprised to see him so late into the competition, but he smiled sheepishly, revealing a glaring hole in his crooked line of teeth. "Still alive?" He spun his lance in the air, the dark weapon surprisingly clean considering all the action it had seen. "Tell you what, I'll try going easy on you," he promised.

Asten pretended to be relieved. Charging, he slashed his leaf-bladed sword at the man's face. The bearded man ducked away from the blade, leveling his lance at Asten.

He stabbed ferociously, and Asten was only barely able to slip away sideways, losing his balance in the process. He rose from the dirt and stumbled away as the man charged at him.

He knew that he wouldn't be able to fend off someone this strong for long, and he immediately found himself wishing that he'd let Erluc do the fighting instead. Unable to properly parry the heavy lance, he instead found himself constantly jumping back, rapidly giving up ground as the two of them edged around the circle.

The next thrust of the lance was slow enough that Asten was easily able to step out of the way, and it was in that instant that he realized why he hadn't been skewered yet: lances were horseback weapons, too bulky to be used efficiently on foot. The sheer power of this man's attacks came at the cost of mobility. Asten scrambled away from another jab, and the bearded man advanced, grinning. "Sure you don't want to call it quits yet?"

"I'm really strongly considering it," muttered Asten to himself. If it weren't for Uldarz's stupid surprise visit, he would have been happy to throw in the towel right then and there. The man lunged with his lance, and Asten ducked under the weapon, stabbing at his hand. The razor-sharp blade just traced his wrist, slicing into his flesh, and the man howled in pain, reflexively releasing his weapon with his injured hand. Not wanting to miss his window of opportunity, Asten sprang up, bringing down his sword with all his strength onto the lance.

"Impossible!" The man's eyes widened in shock as his weapon tumbled to the ground.

Asten kicked it away, and Erluc stepped up to join him just as the horn blew.

"After everything I've been through, that word shouldn't exist," he said quietly, and Erluc let out a short laugh. As the man from Geldran stumbled out of the arena, clutching his wrist, Asten felt a little concerned. "I'm thinking maybe bringing a poisoned sword wasn't such a great long-term idea."

Erluc shrugged. "It's okay, that guy was kind of annoying anyway."

Asten flashed a guilty smile, and they both turned to Ulmûr, who had just forced another man to the ground, locked in a tense grapple.

The crowd cheered loudly as he spun backwards, denting the other man's chestplate.

Asten's eyes narrowed. *If these people could see behind that helm, you'd have the devil to pay.* The crowd watched with bated breath as his opponent brandished his hunting knife, striking at Ulmûr's waist.

Undaunted, the elven prince twisted away, allowing his armor to block the weapon, and stepped back in with a series of vicious attacks at the man's face. It was only moments before the man was forced to the edge of the red circle, desperate for any opportunity to strike back. Ulmûr snarled, and a mighty swing of his bloodsteel sword slammed the other blade out of his opponent's hands. As the sword landed in the dust, bent slightly by the blow, the man raised his hands before his face defensively. The prince's eyes gleamed behind his helm, and he snarled. Raising his jagged blade, he prepared to bring it down on the man. The bloodsteel whistled through the air, and Asten snapped his eyes shut, unable to witness the attack. He braced himself for the cries of pain, for the horror, but the moment never came. Instead, he heard a growl and the sound of swords colliding.

He opened his eyes to find Erluc standing on top of the disarmed man. Telaris had stopped the bloodsteel blade mere inches from the man's head, the swords locked in a stalemate. Ulmûr seemed shocked that his blow had been averted, but Erluc wasted no time at all in retaliating. Throwing his weight against the jagged blade, he kicked the dark elven prince's legs out from underneath him. "Go!" he shouted toward the other man, who hastily scrambled out of the circle.

Alisthír challenged Uldarz to single combat, and Asten watched as Erluc returned his attention to Ulmûr, swinging forward at the dark elf's shoulder. After his stroke was deflected, he stabbed at the dark elf's chest, his sword again stopped by the armored warrior. Suddenly, Ulmûr began to slash at Erluc with startling ferocity, forcing the Warrior to the edge of the combat zone.

Another long, deep, tone from the horn.

Erluc blocked a strike to the face, Telaris clashing with Ulmûr's dark blade before their eyes, blinding sparks springing out from the contact. The prince retreated before immediately striking again, sending Erluc sprawling to the ground. His helm tumbled off his shoulders, and he groaned.

Come on, Erluc. Asten dodged a strike from another adversary, shoving him out of the circle before turning back to Erluc's brawl. *You can beat this guy.*

Ducking under Ulmûr's next strike, Erluc pushed him towards the edge of the red circle. He followed with several consecutive attacks, forcing the dark elven prince to retreat. He feinted at Ulmûr's leg, slashing into the elf's shoulder.

Without allowing the dark elf to recover, he advanced diagonally, aiming a blow at the chink between the elf's chestplate and helm. Had it landed, the wound would have almost inevitably killed Ulmûr. Instead, he ducked under Telaris, aiming a strike to Erluc's back. The bloodsteel glanced off the divine armor without leaving so much as a scratch. Erluc turned, flipping Telaris in the air, and catching it with his other hand.

Asten grimaced. Erluc wasn't going to defeat this opponent easily, and he was going to have to try another approach. Slicing at Ulmûr's shins, Erluc threw a punch at the dark elven prince's helm. But in doing so, Asten realized with mounting horror, he had left himself wide open for an attack. Midway through, he seemed to realize his mistake, but by then, it was too late. Just as his gauntlet crushed his enemy's helm, the dark elf lunged forward towards Erluc, the edge of his blade just tracing the side of his neck. As the bloodsteel bit into his skin, blood began to spill from the cut, and Ulmûr was knocked to the ground, groaning.

Staggering back, Erluc cried out in pain, clutching his neck as he slowly fell to his knees. *Erluc!* He rushed forward to help, but two combatants stepped in between them, pushing him back. *Don't give up.* He held his sword at the ready, planning to take them on one at a time. The sooner he could get to his friend, the better their chances of winning would be.

Grunting from the effort, Erluc pushed himself up to his feet, even as Ulmûr rose alongside him. The elven prince seemed heavily winded by the strike, and that was the advantage Erluc needed. Ulmûr snarled, charging towards him, sword outstretched in front of him. He brought the sword down at Erluc's neck once more, springing in the air. With a spontaneous burst of strength, Erluc shoved Ulmûr's chest and grabbed his sword arm, flinging Telaris higher into the air than was possible for any normal human.

Drawing upon his strength, Erluc swung a fist at Ulmûr's head, twisting his sword arm slowly to the right. In response, the elf caught his punch and retaliated with one of his own. They grappled for a moment until Erluc finally managed to force Ulmûr to drop the sword, reaching up and catching Telaris even as Ulmûr tried to knock his arm away. The elf dove for his bloodsteel sword at the last second, but he missed it by a hair even as the horn blew again.

In the next moment, realization dawned upon Asten. Ulmûr was there, vulnerable, weaponless. All Erluc had to do was summon a single shard of frost, and just like that, the son of Uldarz would be beyond help. No one would know until it was too late. Placing one hand lightly on his own wounded neck, the Warrior seemed mere inches from calling on the power of Telaris in a move he could never take back. Even though he knew it was wrong, a part of Asten egged Erluc on as well, urging him to rid the world of the highlord's heir.

But Asten knew he wasn't a killer. Stepping back, Erluc turned to Asten, who was being forced back by another man, grimacing in pain and effort as they exchanged blows. As Erluc moved to help, though, Asten spun his sword and slashed the man's wrist, causing him to drop his weapon, howling in pain. The horn blew once more.

As the pair of them engaged another warrior, Erluc called, "Take it easy—bloodsteel."

He grimaced. "Bloodsteel hurts more than you can imagine."

"There are cures," assured Asten. "There would have to be, given the number of dark elven raids."

"There had better be." Erluc indicated his neck, where a dark gash breathed into the air. "And I'm going to need some of… whatever I need."

Asten grimaced at the sight, shaking his head. "That's going to leave a mark." Erluc glared at him, and Asten smiled apologetically. "You don't seem like you're going to pass out, at least for the time being, but make sure you don't exert yourself too much."

Erluc snorted and tackled an incoming man. Asten mimicked him, and the two of them shoved their opponents across the boundary before they'd even had time to react. Three more blasts of the horn left them with only five other competitors: Uldarz, Alisthír, a tall, swift, agile teenager who had dodged every blow, never returning with one of his own and a pair of archers.

"We'll need everyone on our side to take down Uldarz," urged Asten. "You reason with them while I hold him off."

"You can barely fight," pointed out Erluc.

"True, but I'm not exactly charismatic, either." He dodged another strike. "And you need to save your energy."

Erluc hesitated, then nodded briskly, clapping Asten on the shoulder with one hand. "Be careful and stay alive."

"One tries." Then he was gone, joining Alisthír against Uldarz, slashing, rolling, and stabbing in a desperate fervor. Turning, Erluc ran to the archers, who were firing on the teenager.

Alisthír seemed to be doing remarkably well by himself, neither him nor Uldarz giving an inch to the other. Even the spectators were enjoying the exchange between them.

Asten turned back, and Erluc was still trying to reason with the others.

I have to do something. Shaking his head, he charged into the battle, aiming a strike at Uldarz's arm. The highlord seemed to be caught off guard, but the shaft of his battleaxe blocked the blow, and the force of the impact sent Asten to his knees.

Just then, the horn blast out three times in quick succession, and Asten knew that Erluc had eliminated all the other contestants. *It wasn't as if they were going to be much help, anyway.* That left just Asten, Erluc, Alisthír and Uldarz.

Asten felt his gemstone pulse under his mail, and Uldarz turned to face him after pushing Alisthír back. The highlord bent down, grabbing Asten's neck, his fingers slowly tightening around it. "This one," he growled, his voice powerful, yet discordant. "Weak."

Erluc, who had been sprinting to their aid, stopped in his tracks at the sight of his closest friend an inch from death. "You can't kill him here," he challenged. "Not before everyone."

"You doubt me?" With his free hand, Uldarz ripped off his helm, revealing a slim, handsome face with eyes so dark brown that one could barely notice that they were solid; they had no pupils. "I call upon Atanûkhor, the true master of the Five Realms, Emperor of the Night, to make his might my own."

Instantly, his irises darkened, along with the whites, until his eyes were nothing but endless, soulless voids, dark, empty pits of eternal damnation. When he spoke, his voice was mingled with another, once filled with fury and hatred and an insatiable hunger for the whole of the Mortal Realms.

Asten's eyes widened, but the iron grasp around his throat rendered his struggles useless. He already knew what was coming. And if he was right, not even Adúnareth could save them.

Chapter 14

The Downside to Being Alive

Inthyl, Aenor

Erluc

Uldarz raised his axe high above his head, and after a brief pause, he slammed the butt of his axe haft into the ground, and a sphere of darkness expanded from the point of contact, consuming them, the arena, the horizon. In place of the daylight from moments before, the sky was the color of ebony, with an aurora of violet spreading as far as Erluc could see. In the stands, the spectators seemed frozen in their seats, unable to move.

"No…" Alisthír stepped back in horror.

What the hell? Erluc's eyes widened, and for the first time, he truly realized who it was standing before them. As the highlord spoke, he instantly recognized the Falcon's overlying tone, but with a merciless, cold edge. Uldarz wasn't just called 'the Blade of Atanûkhor' for lack of a better name.

"*Is this better?*" demanded the creature, in that same raspy, terrifying voice. "*Adúnareth's chosen, I had expected so much more! And you, Exile. I have sought you ever since you fled from me, so long ago—*"

Before the elf could continue, Alisthír took a runestone out of his tunic and cast it to the ground, crying, "Ryzae!"

A jagged streak of lightning split the air, drowning out Uldarz's next words. "You will not tell them what you have found, Wolf," warned Alisthír. "That stays between us."

Erluc couldn't understand what was happening in the least. "What is this place?" he questioned, his voice awfully labored. "What happened to everyone?" He remembered the day in the Citadel when Natalie had been frozen just like these spectators. Uldarz must have cast the same spell that Adúnareth had.

"*Yet the cursed meet the destined at Twilight's frontier,*" whispered Alisthír, and Uldarz nodded slowly. Asten's crystal shone brightly around his neck, and Erluc felt his own gemstone pulsing at his chest.

"*Mortals. They do not understand their gift.*" The contempt and malice in the voice of the Immortal took Erluc aback. "*But they cannot withstand the energy within the Twilight Realm—while you and I, we creatures of the Void, we have the strength to do so.*"

Erluc held his sword at the ready, wary of a sudden attack. "Twilight Realm?"

"A shadow of the Void, cast over our world." Alisthír's face was tinted a ghostly purple by the lights in the sky.

Behind the massive battleaxe, Asten's eyes traveled to Alisthír. Understanding immediately, Erluc pointed at the old swordsman and pressed, "And him? How is he still able to move?"

"*So, you haven't told them?*" Alisthír's jaw clenched, and the highlord laughed in Atanûkhor's voice. "*I have already told Uldarz,*" he jeered, as though Uldarz were another person and not the dark elf threatening them himself. "*That is why he came to Inthyl, you understand—to find and kill you.*" He sneered. "*And them... I was furious when Uldarz allowed them to escape the Vale of Shadows. But I never expected* you *to lead me to the very people that I want to kill the most. I should have known Adúnareth had you watch over them.*"

Erluc gritted his teeth, looking to Asten, who was still dazed. *This is going to end well.*

"Let him try," retorted Alisthír. "If you know who I am, you know what I am capable of."

"*Yes, but do you understand who I am and what I am capable of?*" Uldarz stepped forward, locking eyes with the swordsman. "*Surrender or you will bear witness to the true power of the Emperor of the Night.*"

Sensing his opportunity, Erluc leveled Telaris at him, charging forward. He swung the sword at Uldarz's neck, but the dark elf waved his hand, and he was launched back, barely inside the circle.

"*Are you really so eager to die?*" threatened Uldarz. His fist clenched, the color beginning to return to his eyes, and all around them, the eerie light faded slightly.

Alisthír scowled. "This practice is unimaginable heresy, Highlord. Even among your kind."

"Not for the Blade of Atanûkhor," countered Uldarz, his voice now a mixture between his own, and that of the Wolf. "You know little of my people. And who are you to speak of heresy?"

"Quiet," ordered Alisthír. "You will say no more."

Uldarz ignored him. "You are a traitor, Exile. How could you have dared to wet your lips with the water of the—"

"Silence!" roared Alisthír, drowning out the words of the dark elf.

"We tarry for far too long." Uldarz readjusted his axe against Asten's neck. "Your precious prophecy fails today. If you insist on fighting me yourself, you too shall be slain."

Alisthír's eyes narrowed. "You know who I am, Highlord. Your power cannot match even the smallest part of mine."

"Yet even you cannot stand against the Emperor of the Night," Uldarz declared, his hollow eyes boring into Alisthír's. "Surrender to the Twilight, Exile. You need not die today."

If there had been any doubt in Erluc's mind as to the power inhabiting Uldarz's body, there was no trace of it left. Much as he hated to agree with his enemies, he was forced to admit that no matter how much strength Alisthír was keeping hidden, it could not triumph over that of Atanûkhor himself.

The old warrior locked eyes with the dark elf, and Erluc watched apprehensively as a silent battle of wills took place between them.

Finally, Alisthír dropped his longsword in disgust and kicked it away from him. "You can't win. The prophecy will be complete." He turned to Erluc, their fierce gazes meeting for a moment. "You can do this—the Trinity are more powerful in the Twilight. But remember, channel your feelings—don't let them control you." Erluc nodded hastily, and Alisthír exhaled, stepping out of the circle.

With a contemptuous shove, Uldarz sent Asten to the ground, still clutching his sword. Alisthír closed his eyes, and the air around him rippled before leaving him frozen in place like the spectators.

"*A shame*," remarked Uldarz. He waved his battleaxe at Alisthír, but the blade just passed through him as though he were not there. His eyes darkened once more, and whatever had remained of his own voice was replaced with that of the Wolf. "*I had hoped that the old man would remain defiant; I could have killed him, too.*"

"Yeah, real pity," agreed Erluc mockingly.

Asten scrambled to his feet, raising his sword. "You can't affect the rest of the world from within the Twilight Realm," he guessed.

"*True enough, boy,*" Uldarz's mouth twisted into an ugly smile. "*But that also means that you two are alone here. With the Exile gone, how can you hope to survive?*"

Erluc looked to his friend, who was just as exhausted as he was. There was no way that they could defeat Atanûkhor, not when they were so close to collapsing.

He had to buy them some time.

"That… is an interesting question," admitted Erluc, and Uldarz's smug expression melted away, replaced with momentary confusion. "But you're in for a surprise if you think that we're just going to fall on our swords." And then, the thing that Erluc least expected to happen came to pass—Uldarz broke into a laugh.

Not a genuine, amicable laugh, but an ugly, mocking sneer. "*Of all the mortals in Eärnendor and the Far Lands, Adúnareth chose the one that could talk down to an Immortal.*" He shook his head. "*However ill-advised, I can't say I don't admire your courage, boy. I was once very much like you.*"

"I'm flattered," Erluc whispered to himself, just so Asten could hear. His fingers tightened around Telaris, and he took a step forward.

Just then, two things happened simultaneously. A spark exploded in Erluc's neck, sending him down to the ground, just as Uldarz charged towards them. Slowly raising the battleaxe, he took a mighty heave at the Mage.

Ducking under the blow, Asten slashed at the elf's plated gut, leaving a long, pale scratch along the folded bloodsteel armor. He emerged from the other side, crouched in a defensive position.

Erluc's entire body tensed as he fought the mounting agony—he had to get up. There was no way that Asten could hold his own against Uldarz, and he wasn't going to let his friend die. Not like this. Mustering his remaining strength, he pushed his shaking arms against the ground, slowly rising to one knee. An ocean of sweat had formed inside his armor over the course of the Trial, and Erluc blinked hard to stop a few salty drops from blinding him.

The voids that were Uldarz's eyes burned with malice, and Erluc only saw his muscles tense for a moment before he lunged at Asten, his axe cleaving downwards. Before the blade could touch him, though, he yelled, and a shockwave of energy blasted Uldarz several feet back. Asten sidestepped another swing of the mighty battleaxe, slashing hard at Uldarz's waist. The dark elf growled in pain, and he stumbled backwards. For a brief moment, it looked like Asten would be able to hold his own. Their gazes met, and Erluc stumbled, falling back down to his knees. Suddenly, Uldarz barked out, and the blade of his axe passed a hair's breadth from the top of Asten's head. The edge just barely caught against the mail of his gauntlet, tearing it off of his hand. Reflexively, Asten clenched his fist as his ring glowed eerily in the purple light, exposed to the world.

Taking another step toward Asten, Uldarz raised his axe, his hollow, lifeless eyes as intimidating as ever. Asten swung his leaf-bladed sword, but it was easily knocked aside by a twitch of the powerful axe. The elf lashed out once more, and Asten was forced back yet again.

Three more swings of the battleaxe found Asten on his back, his sword held protectively before his face in a gesture he had to know would be futile. Uldarz raised his axe, preparing to bring it down one last time. "*Weak, both of you*," taunted the voice of Atanûkhor. "*It used to be an honor, reserved for only the most extraordinary mortals, to wield the power of the Void. Now it is squandered on the likes of children.*"

The ring! Erluc wanted to yell out. *Use the ring!* But as he opened his mouth, only incoherent groans escaped his mouth in place of words. The pain had finally reached a climax, a point after which it could become no more unbearable, and only his sheer exhaustion was able to keep him from screaming.

Even as the axe descended, Asten threw up the hand with his ring, shouting, and a bolt of lightning so powerful it illuminated the whole arena split the air and struck Uldarz. The dark elf yelled in pain, staggering backwards, and Asten took the opportunity to struggle to his feet and hastily back away. Erluc groaned, shaking unsteadily as he pushed himself to full height. *Hold on.* Exhaling deeply, he willed his helmet to form over his head and stumbled to Asten's aid. As Uldarz slashed at him, he deflected the blade with Telaris and punched the dark elf in the chest. To his surprise, the force of the blow sent the elf flying, crashing into the ground ten yards away. Maybe the old warrior had been right after all.

Uldarz stood once more, axe at the ready. "You are stronger than I gave you credit for, Warrior."

"It's the Twilight Realm," Asten realized. "Our strength comes from the Void, and you just brought it closer to us." His ring sparked, and lightning began to course up and down the length of the sword, before he aimed it at Uldarz, firing a deadly bolt at his chest.

Quick as an arrow, Uldarz blocked the energy with the flat of his axe, grimacing as it dissipated into the ground. While he was distracted, Erluc leaped forward to engage him with a downward strike, which he countered with a quick swipe before slashing at Asten once more.

Bracing himself for the shock that was sure to come, Erluc stepped forward and punched the axe out of the way. Still, though, nothing could have prepared him for the jarring force where his fist slammed into the bloodsteel, surging up his arm like a tidal wave. Without wasting a moment, Asten stepped in close and went for Uldarz's head. Though the dark elf twisted aside just in time, the blade just barely traced his cheek.

When Uldarz turned to face them again, the purple light highlighted the thin cut which was starting to seep blood.

"What's the matter?" posed Erluc, a wry smirk on his face. "You don't look so good."

Uldarz grimaced. "Choose your words wisely, Warrior, for you never know which may be your last." His bearing remained as confident as before, but he did seem rather on edge.

"Is that right?" asked Erluc. "Well, I have some advice for you too—take that wonderful axe of yours and stick it through your neck. It would certainly save me some trouble."

"*You dare!*" roared the voice of the Immortal once more. "*I am not to be meddled with, human. I will destroy every last thing that you love until there is nothing left for you in this world.*" He held out his axe, and the shadows all around seemed to bend and warp into a sphere of darkness the size of Erluc's head, just above the point. In response, Asten summoned a white ball of energy between his palms, and the pure power in the air caused the hairs on the back of Erluc's neck to stand on end.

Then in an instant, both orbs exploded into shockwaves of energy, light and dark, and Erluc was forced to summon his full body armor to avoid being disintegrated. The sheer power of the two waves in tandem threw Asten back like a rag doll and knocked Uldarz off of his feet. Asten's sword shattered in his hand, forcing Erluc to spin his sword to knock aside a shard flying at his face.

The dark elf stood, breathing heavily, and Erluc could see the whites of his eyes returning, no longer the soulless voids they had been moments before. The combination of the light and dark energies must have banished Atanûkhor from his body. But without the Wolf's power holding it in place, the Twilight Realm was beginning to collapse. All around them, the purple sky shimmered, threatening to trap them in darkness forever. Even as he watched, Alisthír's frozen form began to dissolve, his very flesh vanishing completely from sight.

As Uldarz raised his battleaxe and stepped towards Asten's listless body, Erluc charged, his heart pumping, fire coursing through his veins, his entire body pure lightning. Raising Telaris, he dropped and rolled past the elf highlord, slashing as he passed. A roar of pain told him he had succeeded.

He sprang up, only just in time to deflect the battleaxe spinning towards his eyes. Though the blade just missed his face, the impact jarred his shoulders and caused him to stagger back in pain. Ducking under the next sweep of the axe, he shouted and swung his sword overhead. Though Uldarz blocked the blade easily, Erluc disengaged just as rapidly and willed his armor away for mobility. He struck again and again, knowing fully well that the dark elf's heavy battleaxe didn't have the speed to counter every attack and still maintain an offensive.

There's no way I'm getting close enough to land a direct hit with that monster weapon in the way. He feinted and lunged with Telaris, intending to sever the shaft, but his aim was just a hair too high. His sword clanged off of the axe blade, leaving him unsteady.

Roaring triumphantly, Uldarz smashed his axe flat into Erluc's chest, sending him flying across the arena and wrenching his sword out of his hand. He crashed into the dirt, each tiny pebble scoring across his back and tearing his tunic. As he struggled to stand, each breath like a stab in the chest, he glimpsed Telaris lying just a few feet in front of the dark elf.

He scrambled to his feet and dashed up to Uldarz's left, but as he reached for his sword, he was forced to roll away to avoid being decapitated. Yet, while Erluc's strength was fading, Uldarz seemed virtually unscathed save for the scratch on his cheek and a light hip wound. He barely made it to his feet once more in time to dart past the whirling battleaxe and snatch up the shield of a fallen combatant. As he lifted the heavy steel plate, its owner dissolved into the air, along with the other defeated warriors.

Blast! Erluc didn't know what would happen if everyone frozen within the Twilight disappeared, but he didn't think it was anything to hope for. *We have to get out of here.*

Uldarz, meanwhile, had retrieved Erluc's sword and was holding it in his left hand, though it looked like a knife compared to his immense form. Erluc charged once more, but at the last second, he hurled the shield at Uldarz's legs and kicked him in the chest. The combined force of both attacks caused the dark elf to stagger back, while Erluc used the impact to lean forward and leap up. As he began to drop, Uldarz swinging his axe upwards in hopes of cleaving him in two, he summoned his gauntlets and drove both elbows into his adversary's skull.

"Agh!" Stunned, Uldarz took a few more steps away, Telaris slipping from his fingers, before shaking his head and raising his axe. Erluc allowed himself a smile—maybe this dark elf wasn't invincible, after all.

Erluc hefted the shield, trying to decide whether it could withstand a blow from Uldarz's battleaxe. Above him, the violet streaks of light began to intensify, their color shifting to blue and green and back again. The cut in his neck had stabilized, but he still felt a monochrome throb of pain. Either that or the heat of battle had allowed him to ignore the pain.

He gritted his teeth, and he could feel his hand tighten around Telaris' hilt. "Last chance—surrender or else." He felt his gemstone grow hotter against his skin, and his vision tinted blue for a second before fading back to normal. It didn't seem like much had changed, but the effects of the cut in his neck seemed to have been almost completely neutralized for the time being.

A diagonal swipe at his head forced Erluc to drop into a crouch, but reacting quickly, he sprang forward, grabbing Telaris as he rolled past. A flash of red at the corner of his eye caught his attention—Asten's crystal was shining through his tunic. Almost at the same moment, he felt a burning sensation against his skin just to the right of his heart. Wincing in discomfort, he stood again, resisting the urge to look down at his chest.

He stepped in to engage Uldarz once more but was driven back by two wide slashes. *For heaven's sake!* How was he supposed to do this? Thanks to his superhuman strength, he was able to match the elf almost blow for blow without either of his arms breaking, but fighting him to a standstill would be of little use if he couldn't find a way to escape the Twilight Realm. And to make matters worse, Uldarz's attacks were relentless enough that every time Erluc tried to summon fire with Telaris, he was distracted by a deadly swipe of the battleaxe before the air around him so much as warmed up.

No, magic couldn't help him here.

Uldarz's battleaxe swept over his head as he dropped into a crouch and slashed at the exposed haft, but Telaris barely dented the iron plating. Even as he stood, Uldarz thrust out his axe, barely missing Erluc's neck. Moments later, though, his breath was violently cut off, an agonizing pressure chafing against his throat.

It's the necklace, he realized. The battleaxe had caught against the back of the silver chain, and now, as he scrabbled at his neck, trying to free himself, Uldarz raised the weapon, nearly lifting Erluc off of his feet. He looked up, the dark elf's pupilless eyes boring into his, and even as he rotated Telaris in his hand, he returned Uldarz's piercing glare and spat in his face.

Wiping himself off with his free hand, Uldarz lifted Erluc even higher, so that the tips of his toes barely brushed the ground. "You can ignore dignity in life, and it will ignore you in death."

"Dignity?" Erluc choked, forcing his lips into a smile, "Okay. I'll give you one more chance to give up." Behind his back, he continued to shift Telaris' hilt in his hand, aiming the tip upwards. All he had to do was keep Uldarz fixated on him. The edges of his vision began to fade to black, and the world began to blur and flicker.

"Unfortunately for you, boy," snarled Uldarz, raising the axe another few inches. "I wouldn't presume to show you the same mercy."

Erluc didn't reply. Instead, he focused every last scrap of energy he had on keeping Telaris steady, directed straight at the chain drawn taut behind him by Uldarz's battleaxe. *Perfect.* Even as Uldarz opened his mouth to speak again, Erluc clenched the fist of his free hand, and Telaris' point shot a focused beam of white-hot flames at the chain.

When the necklace snapped, several things happened at once. Uldarz stumbled back as his axe came free, Erluc dropped to his knees, gasping for air, and his crystal flew off its chain, landing with a clatter several yards away. He stood, his black armor forming like liquid around his body, and lifted his sword once again. "That's better," he remarked. "Does it feel like that when Atanûkhor holds your leash too, or do you actually enjoy it?"

Uldarz's eyes narrowed. "No more leashes, Warrior. Nothing to protect you. Rest assured—*this* I will enjoy." Almost faster than even Erluc's enhanced vision could follow, he dropped into a crouch and swung at his shins. Even as Erluc prepared to jump over the axe, though, the cut in his neck throbbed painfully and his vision blurred, his knees buckling. Unable to quite clear the axe, his left foot caught against the blade, and while his enchanted armor protected him, he fell flat on his face, rolling onto his back.

Before Erluc could bring up Telaris to defend himself, though, Uldarz brought his axe dangerously close to his head. "Tell me." He shook his head. "Which words can save you now?" As he raised the weapon, twisting it so that the flat was facing Erluc, the air around Telaris' blade began to shimmer.

The axe descended, and with all of his strength, Erluc stabbed straight through the flat with the superheated blade, yanking it out of Uldarz's grip and scrambling to his feet. As the weapon clattered to the ground behind him, he called on Telaris' power to summon a spike of ice the length of his arm and launch it at Uldarz. The highlord easily caught it with his left hand, though, and as he hurled it back, Erluc was only just able to throw up a gloved hand to protect his face before it shattered against his armor. The force of the impact threw him back, and he skidded several feet in the dirt before coming to a halt.

Unable to breathe, he watched blood rush out of his arm, leaving it completely listless. Uldarz turned to face him, breathing heavily. Erluc struggled to crawl away from the dark elf, crying out every time he moved his left arm before he reached a fallen patrolman just before he too vanished from sight. Reaching for the man's sword, he forced himself to his feet. He cried out, his listless arm grazing his side and flaring up with pain. The ground was changing too, the fine sand of the arena slowly fading to a cold, dark material.

Grudgingly, he brought his good arm back, preparing to hurl the blade at Uldarz. "Please don't miss," he prayed silently. Just as he was about to release the weapon, a blinding pain shot up in his neck, and he immediately collapsed to the ground.

Uldarz hobbled closer to him, while Erluc writhed in pain, paralyzed. He saw the shadow of the dark elf cover his own, and the sound of the battleaxe being lifted against the air. He clenched his hand around Telaris, but an inch from the ground.

Suddenly, his vision tinted blue, and the entire world started shaking, Uldarz falling down to his knees. The dark elf cried out, looking up to the sky. Erluc saw that the elf was shaking, lines of steam escaping his skin. A strange mist began to rise from the ground, and as the last of the spectators turned to dust, the only people left in the world were him, Uldarz, and Asten.

Erluc didn't waste a moment, his body charged with newfound energy. Ultramarine wisps surrounded his body, and he hobbled towards where Asten was lying, clutching his injured arm all the while. The red gemstone on the Mage's chest was also glowing brightly, pulsing even more violently as he got closer. "Asten," called Erluc weakly, brushing his friend's arm. He pulled the stone closer to him, hoping for something, anything to get them out of this place. "Come on," he urged uncertainly. The air grew colder all around them, and Erluc's eyes widened. *What the hell?*

To his great surprise, his palm started heating up, and he felt Asten's red gemstone glow brighter than ever before, a rune shining out in clear, white light. In front of his eyes, Asten's unconscious form started to fade away into nothing. They were alone.

You don't have much time. The voice in his head didn't seem completely his own, but it still rang true with every bone in his body. Before long, the Twilight Realm would simply cease to be… along with anyone inside it.

Some distance away, his discarded crystal began to blaze even brighter.

As Uldarz continued to advance, now disarmed, Erluc struggled to his feet and sprinted at him with Telaris. The poisoned cut in his neck burned, his entire torso stung from having scraped against the ground, his vision was starting to blur, and perhaps worst of all, his armor was starting to melt away as though he no longer had the strength to maintain it. The highlord smiled cruelly, almost inviting Erluc to charge to his death.

A wave of exhaustion washed over him, and even as he swung his sword overhead, Uldarz was already moving to swat it away like a twig with his gauntlet. Telaris was knocked aside easily, and without so much as a pause, Uldarz grabbed Erluc's face with his free hand and slammed his head into the ground. A pain like a stab shot through his skull, causing him to scream into the dark elf's bloodsteel glove.

Uldarz lifted Erluc's head roughly, smashing it once more into the dirt. Erluc tasted blood in his mouth, and the force of the impact had come close to knocking him out. He grasped uselessly at the highlord's wrist, but what remained of his strength was rapidly fading. Unfazed, Uldarz dragged him off the ground, gripping him by the throat, and punched him viciously in the face. His vision was rapidly fading, and he could just barely sense a trickle of mixed blood and spit trailing from the corner of his mouth.

Erluc. There was that voice again. He blinked, trying to focus, and Uldarz punched him again, this time in the stomach. *Take it.* The more he thought about it, the more certain he became that he recognized it from somewhere.

"Is that really the best you can do?" he mumbled, forcing his eyes open and trying to manage a smile. Uldarz laughed shortly, unaffected by the taunt, before seizing Erluc's shoulders and flinging him brutally several yards away. Even the pain was leaving him now, replaced with an overwhelming urge to give in to his exhaustion.

He groaned, rolling over onto his back, even as Uldarz strode purposefully toward him. The dark elf knelt to pick up his discarded axe, and Erluc braced an elbow against the ground, struggling to sit up. *Not like this.* He coughed, spitting onto the dirt and staining it dark red. Clenching his fists, he threw a punch at Uldarz's head, but the highlord caught his wrist effortlessly, swinging him overhead and slamming him once more into the ground. His ears rung, and he could barely move. Despite his best efforts, his eyes fluttered shut.

"You're resilient if nothing else." Uldarz chuckled to himself. "I'll give you that." On the left of the blackness that was all he saw: a faint red glow was beginning to materialize. He rolled over onto his side, commanding his eyes to open, and immediately a blue light like a beacon blinded him. In that instant, everything fell into place. Asten, the crystal, the voice of who could have been none other than Adúnareth—finally, there was hope. His right hand brushed against the hilt of Telaris just next to him, and as he gripped it, a surge of newfound energy coursed through his limbs. His pain and fatigue forgotten, he forced himself to stand once more, facing Uldarz defiantly.

The dark elf's eyes widened in surprise, and he rushed at Erluc once more, slashing downwards with his axe, but Erluc dodged to the side and drove an elbow into the highlord's face. At the cry of pain, he ducked under the weapon and sprinted for his jewel. If there was any salvation left to him, it was there.

Then without warning, Uldarz's axe blade smashed into his back, throwing him onto his face and winding him. Although what remained of his armor prevented him from being cut clean in half, he was almost certain that the force of the impact would leave a nasty bruise. It was a wonder his spine hadn't been broken, he thought as he crashed into the dirt, tumbling head-over-heels before coming to rest on his back.

Even as he sat up groggily, Uldarz was there, weapon poised to deliver a killing blow. "A pity," he declared, aiming the axe at Erluc's neck. "If only the Emperor had chosen you to serve him—you would have made a formidable ally."

The axe descended, and Erluc rolled aside, scrambling to his feet in a desperate attempt to put some distance between them. Uldarz was faster, though. As he stepped forward, his arm shot out, grabbing Erluc's shoulder and pulling him into a painful headlock.

Erluc didn't think. Instead, he turned Telaris in his hand, wincing, and drove it forward with all of his strength. Whether by the will of Adúnareth or through sheer luck, the blade found a gap in Uldarz's armor, meeting little resistance as it pierced the dark elf's gut. Uldarz shouted in pain, releasing Erluc and seizing Telaris' crossguard, shoving it away from him to keep the sword from stabbing straight through him. His axe dropped, clattering to the ground, and all around them, the stands faded into dust, and the ground cracked, falling away into nothingness. All that was left of the Twilight Realm was the two of them, their weapons, and the rapidly vanishing earth on which they were standing.

Both he and Uldarz dropped to their knees, and next to him, the gemstone blazed brightly enough to bathe the highlord's face in its clear, blue light. With his left hand, Erluc let go of Telaris, reaching down and grasping the ultramarine gem. The moment his fingertips made contact, everything seemed to slow down. A rush of energy surged up his arm, and the sky warped and shifted before returning to its natural red-tinged blue as the sun neared the horizon. The vanished warriors and spectators returned, and in an instant, time returned to normal, Uldarz yanking Telaris out of his body and shoving Erluc away.

His vision darkened as he stumbled and fell onto his back, and all the strength flooded out of his body, but he felt the coarse grains of sand rub against his fingers again. There was a steady pulse of pain from the cut in his neck, and he heard a faint echo somewhere to the side. Erluc tried to get up, but another figure gently nudged him down and shouted something vague to someone on the side.

Putting a palm on Erluc's shoulder, the figure whispered, "No, that's enough. Rest knowing that you have fulfilled your promise." Erluc's muscles tensed, and he tried his best to sit up, but all the energy in his veins had dissipated. His vision blurred, lined with a black haze. A battle cry pierced the air, and the darkness expanded, engulfing his entire field of sight.

Chapter 15

You Win Some, You Lose Some

Inthyl, Aenor
Erluc

O uch. When Erluc opened his eyes five minutes later, he thought he was flying.

Was he?

Not really. Two medics were carrying him away from the arena, and they patiently advised him to stay still once they noticed he had regained consciousness. His armor had faded, and his arm was suspended in a makeshift brace. He groaned as they promptly set him down on the ground.

Suddenly Renidos ran up to him and helped him to his feet. "Take it easy."

Erluc raised an eyebrow. "Wh… what are you doing here? What happened? Where's Uldarz?"

Renidos handed him Telaris and put one of Erluc's arms around his own shoulder. "Those are three completely different questions. There's only so much I can do at once." He grinned, and Erluc leered at him. "Fine. One at a time. You don't need to worry about Uldarz—he's being hauled away to Inthyl's dungeons. In chains."

Erluc's brow creased. "What happened to him?"

"Where are all these questions coming from?"

"Renidos, I swear I'll—"

"Ease up, I'm only pulling your leg," admitted Renidos. "But I was hoping you could tell me the answer to that. I only got here after you passed out."

"How did you know to come here?"

"I saw the spell that Uldarz cast. It had spread all around the city, and the entire sky had these weird lights. My gemstone was glowing like crazy, and everyone around was frozen in place," he explained. "It took me forever to make sure my mother was okay, and after that, I ran here as fast as I could, but it was already over." Renidos grimaced. "Uldarz was everything but dead, his skin all burned and steaming. Alisthír and the others saw to it that he was taken care of."

Erluc nodded. "It was probably an after-effect of hosting Atanûkhor for so long. His body must not have been able to handle the presence of something that powerful, especially when the Twilight Realm started falling apart."

"*What?*" Renidos' eyes widened. "Did you just say Atanûkhor?"

"Don't worry. I'll make sure to tell you everything later." Erluc shook his head, slightly amused. "What about Ulmûr?"

Renidos' brow creased, but he answered the question. "No sign of him," Erluc cursed under his breath. He would've liked to eliminate the threat of the dark elves completely, and the prince was definitely a loose end.

"Anyway, I wanted to say thank you," resumed Renidos.

He raised an eyebrow, wiping the dirt from his face. "For what? I didn't do anything."

"Oh, I know that," admitted Renidos, a sly smirk on his face. "But you didn't kill him, did you? Even after what you promised Alisthír. And for that, thank you."

As if I had a chance. Erluc steadied himself as he took his arm off Renidos' shoulder, and they stopped in front of the last of the Trinity. Asten was in conversation with Euracis, who quickly ran off into the stands when they approached.

"You alright?" asked Erluc.

"Not good, but not terrible. Uldarz has quite the death grip," replied Asten. "What about you?"

"I'll live. Probably." Erluc adjusted his arm brace once more, carefully scanning the arena. Mention of Alisthír hadn't gone unnoticed, but despite his best efforts, Erluc couldn't spot the old warrior anywhere.

"Good." He nodded. "Are you ready?"

"For what?"

Asten turned to Renidos, who smiled sheepishly. "You didn't tell him?"

"Tell me what?" questioned Erluc, flustered about being kept in the dark.

"Well… you won," he disclosed. "You passed the Steel Trial. They're going to crown you champion."

"What?" demanded Erluc. He looked to Renidos, then back to Asten. "If you're joking—"

"I wish," admitted Renidos. "But even Uldarz was taken away. You and Alisthír were the last two contestants, and he said that you disarmed him. So yes, you won."

What? There was no way that Alisthír would do something like that.

Asten shook his head. "You want proof? There." He gestured behind them at the party that was approaching from the stands. "Look sharp, my friend. Or at least try your best." Erluc snorted, turning back as the contingent reached them.

Erluc frowned. "I could've sworn Elandas was here."

"He left a long time ago on account of some conflict in the city. Duty doesn't stop for teenagers and elves hacking each other to pieces," explained Asten. "But the Council and the princess are still here, so you're not completely off the hook."

Making a face, Erluc turned to the approaching group. Before them, a young woman, hardly more than a girl, around the age of sixteen, maybe seventeen, gracefully made her way to the center of the arena, where the Trinity stood, flanked by half-a-dozen patrolmen. She had an aura of serenity, and Erluc couldn't help but notice the way her straight hair, complemented brilliantly by a silver circlet, curled before it ended just below her shoulders. She definitely looked like a princess.

Another member of the contingent approached them, and Erluc recognized Euracis. "Congratulations, Erluc," wished the man. "Now I know you must be exhausted, but you're going to have to bear with us for a while. You'll be alright, won't you?"

"I-I guess." Erluc shrugged, unsure of what to say.

He nodded, turning to the crowd—most of them had calmed down by now—and called for silence. Immediately, the crowd lost their jubilance and sat soundlessly, tense with anticipation.

A bead of sweat ran down into the corner of his mouth, and Erluc muttered a curse as he spat it out. *Never a towel when you need one.* Obviously, there was nothing useful in sight, so he settled for wiping his sweat on his dirty tunic. *This is going to be embarrassing.* His confidence hadn't completely abandoned him just yet, but somehow he found it hard to meet the maiden's deep, piercing, brown eyes.

"People of Inthyl, the Steel Trial has ended," announced Euracis. "Erluc, son of Neran, has emerged as the Steel Champion." The crowd thundered around the arena, and he called for silence once more.

Once the roar calmed, Euracis turned to Erluc and continued, "By revealing the murderous Uldarz, who came to Inthyl in his fair guise as a man to slaughter our people, he has defended the people of Inthyl from a terrible menace."

If you say so. Erluc wasn't one to reject praise, but this ceremony was getting a tad too grandiose for his liking.

Another councilman, whom Erluc couldn't recognize, called for quiet. "Erluc, son of Neran. Your actions on this day have earned you a title: Lord Heroblade. Hail, citizens of Inthyl, Lord Erluc Heroblade, bane of dark elves, defender of Inthyl!" He announced the last few words such that it could be heard throughout the arena.

Heroblade? Erluc shook his head. *No. Absolutely not. If you're going to knight me, you might as well have come up with a good name.* To the left, he could see Princess Roxanna suppressing a smile as well.

The crowd rose as one, standing in anticipation, leaving Erluc all the more confused. Then the princess raised one hand, and beside him, both Asten and Renidos knelt, Euracis after them. Then the soldiers dropped to their knees, and all around, up in the stands, Erluc could see people kneeling… before him? Even Council members were down on their knees.

No, it probably was the princess. It had to be the princess.

That must have been it, because she was the only one still standing in the end. Erluc began to fall to one knee, but Roxanna spoke for the first time, clearly, but softly. "Rise, Lord Heroblade. These people kneel before you."

Erluc frowned, certain he'd heard that voice before. But no, that couldn't be right. He would definitely remember meeting a princess. It took him a moment to regain his composure, but once he managed that, he stood self-consciously. He settled for unsheathing Telaris and holding it up, which seemed to have a good effect. It was better than nothing in his opinion. A cheer started in the crowd, as everyone stood up once more, and all around him were faces full of admiration.

Wow. For a moment, Erluc found it hard to think. Then he allowed himself a small grin. Roxanna blushed slightly, round dimples appearing on her cheeks. Erluc's heart stopped for a moment, and a single bead of sweat trickled down the back of his neck. *Rose.* His smile faded.

Princess Roxanna… How could I have been so stupid?

Erluc just stood rooted to the spot, shell-shocked. It all made sense now. Everything. Now that he was looking more closely, he could recognize Rose's hair neatly brushed instead of its usual mess that he was used to seeing. Her simple tunic and leggings were replaced by an elaborate, aqua dress, which brought out the green flecks in her hazel eyes.

He almost swore aloud, but he caught himself in time. The whole city was watching. He chanced a glimpse to his friends, and Asten seemed to have reached the same conclusion that he had. It took all his willpower to keep from going red. Roxanna—*Rose*, whatever it was—sensed his discomfort and whispered discreetly to Euracis, who once again announced, "The Steel Trial is over!"

The crowd went wild again, and the gate lifted once more. Erluc turned to leave the way he had entered, through the competitors' pavilion, but Roxanna's familiar light-brown eyes indicated him to follow as she led the procession out of the arena by the main gate.

Erluc did so, and once they were well out of the arena and he could hear the gate being closed behind them. With an air of command, Roxanna gestured towards the soldiers and the herald. "Leave us."

The man didn't look happy about it, but he barked a command to the troop, who marched with him toward the barracks. Once they were out of earshot, the princess seemed to relax and began to look more like Erluc was used to. There was a short silence before Rose finally spoke. "Aren't you going to say anything?"

He shook his head, unable to form a sentence. It was probably better that he couldn't; it probably would have been something unbelievably unintelligible. Luckily for him, a councilman caught up with them.

"Princess Roxanna," he acknowledged, bowing quickly. "Lord Heroblade." Erluc nodded awkwardly, and the man turned back to Rose. "The High King had requested that I escort you back to the palace before sundown, your highness."

"In a moment." Roxanna turned back to Erluc and continued in a hushed tone. "If you'll still talk to me, then meet me in the courtyard in half an hour."

He nodded absently, and without another word, she followed the councilman back into town. Avoiding all crowded streets, Erluc traveled through postern alleys in an attempt to evade any other people. Before long, he entered The Broken Fang, moving swiftly through the building, hood cast over his face to avoid being recognized. Once he made it out the back, he checked to make sure no one was watching, and as always, no one ever was.

The courtyard's beauty was undiminished, but Erluc found it harder to appreciate the lush grass and the familiar trees, as though they had soured somehow.

What is wrong with me? It wasn't like him to get so worked up about a girl. And it wasn't as if this was the worst he'd ever been through. Just hours ago, he'd been fighting for his life against Uldarz. *All she did was protect her identity—the exact same thing you've been doing.* He shook his head. *And now I'm talking to myself. Great.* For some reason, this was bothering him to the point of… madness.

To make matters worse, the cut in his neck flared up once more, and the overwhelming pain tinted his vision red for a moment. He growled in frustration, but he felt more like yelling. Instead, he raised his sword and began slashing and whirling furiously to blow off steam. Occasionally, Telaris' adamantine edge would slice a gash in the stone walls, but he really couldn't have cared less. He set the blade alight, gazing into the flames as they swirled up and down the length of the sword.

When the hidden door swung open again, Erluc stiffened, surprised that Rose should appear so early, but he sighed when he heard that the soft voice that he heard belonged to Asten instead.

"Well, I certainly didn't see this coming," commented Asten.

Erluc willed Telaris' flames to die out, and when they did, he slowly sheathed the sword. "Save it," he ordered. "I'm in no mood to argue with you right now."

Nodding hesitantly, Asten tentatively continued. "You know what you're going to do?" he asked.

Ignoring the question entirely, Erluc walked over to the edge of the courtyard, watching as the sun finally dipped under the horizon. *I will kill everyone you love until there is nothing left for you in this world.* Atanûkhor's words echoed in his mind, now more real than ever.

Unsatisfied, Asten made another attempt to get through to his friend. "I-I know you don't want to hear this, but I guessed this about a week ago. The way she talked, her bearing—it gave her away."

Erluc didn't take his eyes away from the distance. Without turning around, he asked, "Is that right?"

He could almost sense Asten's shrug. "It was a wild guess." The Warrior gritted his teeth, refusing an answer. "Come on, Erluc, talk to me," pleaded Asten.

"You're right. I don't need to hear this right now," he agreed. "This doesn't concern you."

Erluc thought he heard the Mage's golden ring crackling and sputtering with electricity. "If I want to stay and talk to you, I will," proclaimed Asten. Erluc's hand rested on Telaris' hilt, his fingers tensed in anticipation. Asten's gaze flickered to the sword, his eyes flashing in defiance. "I'm only trying to help."

"I don't need your help!" growled Erluc, turning away from him. "I don't want your help. Just leave." He drew Telaris, the blade glistening despite the sparse lighting in the courtyard.

Asten's eyes flashed angrily, and his fist clenched, his ring releasing a burst of light that made Erluc's vision blur and his hands thrum violently before hurling him backwards into the ground. Telaris clattered to the ground. Erluc's eyes glazed over with the crimson mist of battle rage, and in one smooth motion, he yanked Telaris out of the dirt, whirled around, and extended its point to Asten's collarbone. "Go," he hissed quietly, "I don't want to do this, but don't test me."

Stepping away from the Warrior, Asten shook his head. "Congratulations, Erluc," he whispered, his voice shrouded in pain. "You won." He didn't look back as he exited the courtyard, closing the gate behind him, leaving Erluc alone once more.

Breathing hard, Erluc fell to his knees, staring at the flowing patterns on Telaris' blade and willing the haze of fury to calm, before hurling the blade at the grass in disgust. A single tear fell from the corner of his eye, tracing his cheek until he finally wiped it with his sleeve. Crying out softly, he collapsed to the ground with the support of the great tree, and he held his head in his arms as he waited for the seconds to pass into minutes.

When he finally heard the wall crack open, the sun had completely set, and there was darkness all around. The tension permeated the atmosphere, and it reflected on his face, which wore a steely expression. It showed on hers too but in the form of regret.

He didn't even trust himself to speak. And from her silence, neither did she. She tentatively approached, sitting against the tree beside him. "I'm sorry," she confessed at last.

The pause that followed was even heavier than the last, the very lack of words weighing down the entire courtyard. Eventually, Erluc looked up, staring blankly at nothing in particular. "I told you that I knew what it was like to keep a secret." Rose frowned, uncertain about what he was getting at. "I know what it means, what it does to you."

"What do you mean?" She didn't seem any more relieved, but he continued, his gaze lost in the distance.

"I made a big mistake, Rose," he started. "And now I'm going to make it right." Erluc nodded, finally turning to meet her confused brown eyes. "But before I do, I want you to have this." He loosened his thin belt and removed the small box of brown wood that he'd received from Asten for his birthday. He handed her the box, which she tentatively accepted.

Slowly opening the wooden seal, she revealed a silver chain and pendant, a rose engraved into the circular stone. "Oh, it's beautiful." Her expression turned from surprise to happiness to somewhere in between. "You shouldn't have."

"I did promise, didn't I?" he reminded her. "With your permission?"

She made a half-smile, turning around so that her back faced him. He brought his hands around her, slowly clipping the ends of the chain behind her neck and pulling the stone up to her chest. He lifted her hair and flinched as his hand made contact with her warm skin. Rose gasped, and Erluc fought a smile. Her hair was more made-up than he was used to seeing, but its natural brown glaze was not lost. He let her locks fall, and she turned around to face him.

Suddenly, Erluc stopped, and she raised an eyebrow. "What's wrong?"

He shook his head. "Nothing," he lied. What he didn't say was that he was actually trying to preserve this picture in his mind. Taking a deep breath, he continued. "Were you *ever* going to tell me?"

Her face fell slightly, but she seemed ready to answer the question. "Of course, I was," she spoke softly. "I was just afraid if I told you too soon, you'd react... you'd freak out." She paused, the leaves rustling in the trees behind them. "I'm sorry for what I've done, but you knew me as the person that I am. A few clothes and a title don't change what's underneath."

Erluc's face fell, and he couldn't bring himself to meet her eyes. "I wish that were true." He shook his head. "But... this does. This changes everything, Rose. Some secrets are just meant to be kept."

When she replied, her voice was shaking but measured. "But now you know mine, don't you?"

I wasn't talking about your secret. He bit his tongue, trying his best to stay composed. "It isn't as simple as that."

"Then make it simple!" she cried. "Please, tell me what the problem is, and we can fix it together!" Erluc's heart ached as she said the words, and a part of him wanted to just fall into her arms. He gritted his teeth, cursing Adúnareth with every word he knew. He wasn't even sure who or what he was angry at anymore: her, Ulmûr, Asten, Uldarz, himself. But all he knew was that this unforgiving, forbidden world that he'd been thrust into would inevitably tear them apart.

"I-I can't," he finally spoke. "I never meant for things to be like this," he whispered. "But we… we can't do this anymore." The wind whistled above them, but instead of passing over the hidden courtyard, as it always did, it reached down, caressed their cheeks, and caused the leaves of the tree above them to sway and whisper insistently.

Her eyes glistening with tears, she shook her head. "You can lie to me, but at least don't lie to yourself." Erluc looked up, his brow furrowed. "This isn't… this *can't* be because of a secret. No, you've got some other reason for this—something you're not telling me."

Her words affected him more than he thought they would. "You didn't really expect this to work, did you?" challenged Erluc suddenly, standing up. "How could it ever? You're a princess, and I'm just… just a regular guy. This could never have lasted, and you would have seen that eventually."

"Then how come you're the one pushing me away?" she demanded, rising as well. Erluc's vision blurred around the edges, the colors of the night flowing into one another, their borders undefined.

He took one of her hands, holding it tightly in his own. "You deserve better than this, Rose." Erluc gritted his teeth.

She pushed him backwards, and he stepped away, evidently not expecting the reaction. "That's my decision to make, not yours," she decided, her voice shaking hesitantly.

Shaking his head, Erluc stepped away from her. "Actually, it is." He turned around, unable to meet her eyes, surrounded by nothing but silence.

"Why didn't you just do this from the start?" she whispered back, her voice painfully soft. "Why did you wait until today?"

"What is that supposed to mean?" questioned Erluc. "I wanted to give us a chance."

"No, you didn't!" she cried. "Forget about us—you didn't even give *yourself* a chance. This is all a game for you. And now that you're starting to realize that it's real, you'll find any excuse to quit." She shook her head. "Well, I'm sorry, Erluc. I'm sorry for *actually* caring, and I'm sorry that you think you're doing the right thing."

He waited for her to leave, but instead, he felt her small, warm hands cover his. And a moment later, he felt the soft pressure of her lips on his. Startled at first, he regained his balance and drew her in again, kissing her with even more passion, losing himself in the minty taste of her lips, a stirring rising deep in his chest. He released her hands and brought his around to her back, pulling her closer. A small sigh escaped her lips.

The wind seemed to stop, and the entire Earth stood still for a moment. Everything except her. Erluc leaned in once more, and they lost themselves in each other, running their hands through each other's hair, savoring the moment. When they couldn't hold their breath any longer, they broke apart, and Erluc finally opened his eyes.

"Erluc—"

"Take care of yourself," he whispered. "Please." Their gazes met long enough for him to see the hurt poisoning her brimming brown eyes. Not trusting himself to say anything else, he simply watched her walk out, hearing the door close lightly after she'd left.

Erluc closed his eyes, painfully letting his head rest on the trunk of the tree behind him. His vision flashed red, and the wind echoed throughout his mind. He didn't want this to be the end. In fact, he didn't want there to be an end at all. But she was the princess of Aenor, and Erluc would never be willing to place her in any danger. And if that meant that they couldn't be together… it was a sacrifice he was willing to make.

The stars twinkled brightly, not a cloud in the sky, but Erluc buried his head in his arms once more, embracing the darkness before he finally slipped into poisonous slumber.

Chapter 16

THE MURDERER'S GAMBIT

INTHYL, AENOR

Asten

Asten's eyes snapped open. In a flash, the previous day's events came rushing back to him. The Trial, Roxanna, the fight… *Erluc*.

He twisted to face the bed but found it perfectly made, just as he'd left it the night before. His brow creased in concern, and he rolled off the pair of stools he had been sleeping on. Before anything, he would need to find Erluc—if nothing else, to reconcile with him. He struggled to his feet, fumbling around for his key, and burst through the door once he had located it.

It wasn't unheard of for Erluc to spend the night in the courtyard, especially when he was talking to Rose, and Asten was certain that they had met at some point after he'd left. With luck, they'd manage to work out whatever issues they had. Making sure no one was watching, he pushed his way into the courtyard, only to see that Erluc had fallen out of the hammock, clutching his throat with both hands.

"Erluc!" He sprinted to his friend, who was twitching uncontrollably, and managed to gently roll him onto his back in the soft grass. Though his eyes were open, they were glassy, unfocused, and he seemed to be unable to hear anything Asten was saying.

"Erluc," he urged again, and finally, his friend's eyes seemed to focus.

His spasming gradually stopped, and he whispered back, "That did not feel good."

"What happened?" asked Asten urgently, kneeling down beside his friend.

Erluc coughed violently, lowering his arms, and Asten grimaced. Most of the veins on his neck had turned purple, a small gash at the epicenter of the contamination. "Poison," Erluc managed. "Ulmûr's blade cut me in the neck, and I think… poison."

Of course. He'd been stupid to forget about Erluc's injury. Though his seeming resistance to pain had kept him from feeling the full effects of the venom since the Steel Trial, the poisoned bloodsteel sword had been working away at his system. The cut itself had clotted, but the skin around it was tinged an ugly shade of purple.

Asten nodded frantically. "Does it go all the way?" he asked. Erluc threw off his tunic, and even he couldn't keep looking down. The purple lines traced down till his shoulder, but they hadn't reached his chest yet. "Okay. Okay, stay here. I… I think there's a runestone for healing." Asten didn't know the cure for bloodsteel poisoning, but he had to start somewhere.

Erluc nodded vaguely, gritting his teeth as the Mage ran out of the courtyard.

Asten flew up the stairs, throwing open the door to their room. In the corner, Erluc's pack rested against the wall. Grabbing it, he rummaged through until he finally found the pouch which contained the runestones. Emptying it on a table, the pieces clattering all over, he flipped over as many as he could, desperate for anything that could help. "Sight, Bind... damn," he muttered to himself, slamming his fist into the wood.

What am I going to do? If there wasn't a runestone to cure him, how was Erluc going to recover? He dashed down to the courtyard, racking his brain for anything that might present a solution. As he saw Erluc's suffering once more, he looked up helplessly, his fists curling. "We'll get you to a healer. Maybe they might know something."

"Let's hope," managed Erluc. He held out a hand, and Asten gripped it, helping him to his feet. Together, they managed to drape Erluc's arm around Asten's shoulder and stumbled out of the inn. As they made their way along the streets, Erluc pulled his hood low over his face—now was far from a good time to be recognized as the newest Steel Champion.

By the time they reached an infirmary on the far side of the city, Erluc was barely conscious, and Asten was forced to practically drag him the last few steps. As they burst in, Erluc collapsed on a cot, and Asten called for a healer. A young woman clad entirely in light brown hurried to their side. "What's wrong with him?" she asked urgently.

"Bloodsteel," Asten explained, pointing at the cut. "Almost a day ago."

The healer's brow furrowed. "Bloodsteel?" A tense moment passed as she seemed to put the pieces together. "You don't mean this is—"

"Who he is or isn't is none of your concern," cut in Asten sharply. "And you'll say nothing of this to *anyone*. Your job is to keep him alive. Understood?"

The nurse hesitated, then nodded assent. "I'll do as you ask, but I should warn you that bloodsteel poisoning usually kills in hours, if not minutes, depending on the severity of the wound. He's lucky to be breathing this long after being cut."

"All I need is for you to keep him that way." Asten's expression steeled. "Can you do it?"

"I'm not sure," admitted the healer. "I've never dealt with a cut this severe, nor this late. It's likely he won't make it." She met Asten's gaze.

The news came as a shock to Asten. There it was—his last hope, vanished into thin air. If there wasn't a runestone for healing, and even an experienced nurse knew no cure, then he had no options left.

Except, he realized, he knew someone who could help on both counts.

He turned back to the healer. "How long does he have?"

"Till sundown, maybe longer." The young woman shrugged. "Maybe a few hours less. I'm sorry, but I can't be sure."

Sundown. That wasn't unreasonable. Fishing around inside his cloak, he located his pouch and counted out seven queltras. "I'll be back at dusk, at the latest." He handed her the coins. "If he's still alive by then, I'll take him from here." The nurse nodded again, and Asten spun on his heel and took off running, out the door and into the streets of Inthyl.

Hang on, Erluc.

He slipped and weaved between the droves of passersby, sprinting for all he was worth towards the colossal arena on the outskirts of the city. Of all the people in Aenor to ask for help, the one he was seeking out was near the very bottom of the list—but it wasn't as though he had a choice. If there was anyone who knew of the cure, it would be Alisthír.

Asten didn't trust many people. He trusted Erluc with most things—though he might push his boundaries at times, he usually knew when to toe the line and take a situation seriously. He trusted Neran, the man who had given him everything from life itself to a friend close enough to be a brother. He *had* trusted Lyra, at least up until it had turned out that she'd been using him simply to make her previous boyfriend jealous. Renidos? Sure, to an extent, he supposed, but somehow he found it hard to be open with the younger boy. But did he trust Alisthír? Hells, no.

In Asten's opinion, a man who kept so much to himself wasn't worthy of the faith of others. Trust went both ways—if Alisthír wanted to be privy to everything the Trinity did, it wasn't unreasonable to expect him to share something of who he was or how he knew who *they* were or why he even cared.

The main gate was open once again and the devastation of the previous day forgotten. Asten could easily spot the man at the far side of the arena, and he quickly ran towards him. He recognized Renidos as well, who was sparring with the old combatant. They both stopped once they saw him, lowering their weapons.

"What's wrong?" asked Renidos. Judging by Asten's face, it was a fair assumption.

The older boy swiftly pulled both of them to the side, filling them in on the events of the morning. As quickly as he could, Asten gave them the rundown of the situation. "And I couldn't think of anyone else who might know," he finished. "You knew about the prophecy, our powers, and where we came from. You must know the antidote."

"I do have some experience in this area," responded the man. "Normally, bloodsteel to the neck leads to instantaneous death or permanent unconsciousness, depending on the variety of the poison. However, my assumption is that your blessing has somehow enhanced your healing capabilities, and his body is resisting."

"So, how do we save him?"

Alisthír grimaced. "There are two natural cures for bloodsteel poisoning, but unfortunately, neither of them will be accessible to us before the Warrior meets his fate." Asten was about to open his mouth in protest, but Alisthír wasn't finished. "The only other way to heal Erluc's wound… well, let's just say that the people of Aenor are wary of its use."

Unconsciously, Asten twisted his ring around his finger. "Magic," supplied Renidos.

Alisthír nodded. "Now, I know that as of right now, you only command the power of lightning… I suppose it's time to remedy that." Asten opened his mouth, but the old swordsman had already turned away, Renidos tailing him closely. "Follow me."

Keeping up a brisk pace in order to avoid being left behind, Asten let his left hand drift to the handle of his dagger. If it turned out anything was amiss, he needed to be able to defend himself—at least long enough to get to safety.

Without looking back, Alisthír said, "You won't need your weapon."

Unsettled, Asten released the handle, quickly catching up to Alisthír. "Aren't you going to at least tell us where it is we're going?"

Alisthír raised an eyebrow, his eyes fixed on the horizon. "You'll see for yourself when we arrive." The sun was nearing its zenith, its soft spring rays warming the back of Asten's neck. Only a few more hours until… no. He couldn't hope to save Erluc if he was already planning for failure.

They left the grand marble colossus that was the arena, passing the mud and shale shanties of the city outskirts and finally reached the small forest that served as Inthyl's main source of lumber. Without a second thought, Alisthír disappeared beyond the treeline, Renidos easily keeping up and not even looking back to see if Asten was following. Cursing, Asten picked up his pace and slipped into the trees.

Catching up to Alisthír a second time, Asten pressed, "Okay, we're out of earshot. So now, if you'd like to tell me where we're going, I'd be much obliged."

The old warrior barely glanced over at him. He ducked under a branch, and Asten followed him into a wide clearing, where they finally stopped. Asten seemed to be the only one that felt any sort of fatigue by the time they had arrived, sighing in relief, while Renidos simply started to regard the clearing, his eyebrows raised.

"We walked all the way here for this?" asked the Spectre, evidently not impressed. The entire site was made up of several pieces of time-worn, jet-black stone scattered around a clearing. Perhaps something of importance had once stood here, but it had been decades since it had been destroyed, thick layers of dust covering the stone. "What is this place?"

Stepping lightly into the middle of the circle, Alisthír brushed away a layer of dust that had built up on one of the rocks. What must have been millennia of isolation had left its sure mark on the ruin. "It might be easier to say what it *was*," he sighed. "Thousands of years ago, before Eltar's first landing, this site was a temple to Adúnareth—much like the one that now stands in Inthyl."

"Heaven's Citadel?" offered Asten, only slightly recovered.

Nodding, the old warrior continued. "In the war against the clans, Elthormen's army looted and pillaged this temple, burning it to the ground. The barren relic before you is all that remains."

Asten nodded; he'd heard stories of Elthormen, son of Eltar. He was the first High King to also serve as General of the Twilight Legion, but he was more famous for driving the clans out of South Aenor.

"History remembered this event as the Minithoan War, but it was more accurately a six-year massacre." Alisthír's eyes glinted. "The clans rallied behind Inro Ryloch, the largest of the clans, and after years of fighting, were driven into the North. When the dust cleared—"

"Inro Ryloch had been completely exterminated," finished Renidos. At Asten's expression, he added, "What? I studied history, you know."

Alisthír nodded in approval, while Asten simply glanced around the site. "He destroyed their most sacred site," guessed Asten. "He wanted to make an example of them."

"And it worked," agreed Alisthír. "The war ended soon after, and peace was declared."

Renidos grimaced. "If there's nothing left, what are we doing here?"

"Some things can't be stolen or destroyed." Alisthír knelt down on the ground, reaching into his coat and producing a small, red chalk. "This site still has a strong connection to the Void, and that means lingering magical potential." He started tracing a large circle with his chalk and inscribing a triangle within it, as the two of them looked on in intrigue.

Asten nodded, beginning to understand. "That explains why the blessing took place at Heaven's Citadel." Transfixed, he lightly placed his left hand on one of the stones. It might've been his imagination, but he could almost feel a thrum of power, running like a current beneath his fingers.

Alisthír inscribed a second circle into the triangle and began to draw a three-armed spiral from its center. Just as he finished drawing three lines connecting the triangle's points to the inner circle, he stopped, the chalk almost completely diminished in his hand. "Brace yourself."

"For wha—"

Alisthír placed his palm into the symbol, and the red chalk started to glow. For a moment, everything was still, and Asten could hear the sound of the noonday breeze.

His next words were lost as the symbol on the ground erupted into light, and the world around him *bent,* twisting and folding in on him. And then he simply… wasn't.

"You can get up now," he heard a voice. Asten opened his eyes, a dim, orange glow creeping into view. He was on his knees, cold, dark stone against his skin, in a chamber. *What in the world?* Shakily, he stood, and his surroundings came into focus. He was in a large cavern, walled by the same black stone as the ruins of the temple. All around, old wooden shelves lined the walls, and the center of the room was taken up by a large, hexagonal altar. In the back of the room, a roughly carved stone table was covered almost completely by scraps of parchment.

Immediately, his thoughts turned back to Alisthír, and he whirled around to find the old swordsman sitting hunched against a step, exhausted. "Welcome," he managed. Although the man didn't seem hurt, his face had sunken, and he was breathing heavily.

Renidos rubbed the back of his head, slowly rising to his feet. "What the hell is wrong with you?" He stretched his back, picking up his spear from the ground.

"What just happened?" demanded Asten. "Where are we? How did you…unless…" He trailed off, realizing that he had answered his own question.

Like a river filling a pond, everything fell into place. How else could Alisthír be so familiar with magic, except as one who wielded it himself? And this, Asten realized, was why he could speak Telmírin and why he had concealed his true name. It even explained the moniker he'd chosen—the Exile—and most of all, how he'd been able to summon lightning against Uldarz.

Renidos raised an eyebrow. "Unless what?"

"You are, aren't you?" demanded Asten, speaking directly to Alisthír now. The older warrior sighed, holding his gaze. "Blast! It was right in front of us the whole time, and I never once thought of it."

Alisthír seemed a little on edge as if he recognized that Asten might have been onto something. "Is that right?"

Scowling, Renidos pulled Asten's tunic. "What are you talking about?"

There was a tense moment of anticipation before the answer was spoken. "He's an alchemist," revealed Asten, and Alisthír flinched.

Renidos coughed. "Excuse me, a *what* now?"

"An alchemist," informed Asten. "Someone who artificially manipulates arcane energy in place of—"

"I *know* what an alchemist is, Asten!" snapped Renidos. Though he'd done an admirable job of masking his tension up until now, he seemed to have finally reached his breaking point with this revelation.

Alisthír snapped his fingers, and torches along the walls of the chamber burst to life. "For your information, alchemists served in the Golden Armada up until the rule of Eldorien, son of Eldrath," said Alisthír. "One monarch started getting cold feet about magic, proclaiming that its power was too great for mere mortals to wield, and all alchemists were immediately treated as outlaws, hanged on sight."

Asten knew what the old warrior was talking about. Eldorien had also disbanded the Golden Armada after defeating the dark elves, forming the Twilight Council between men, elves, and dwarves. It wasn't until Elandas decided to rebuild the army as the Twilight Legion that Aenor would once more have a single protective force.

"Laws are laws, but as long as nobody knows what we're doing, I don't see why we should have a problem." He turned back to them. "And nobody's going to find out, are they?"

Asten gritted his teeth. He had no love for alchemists, and he wasn't overly fond of Alisthír, but the old warrior was the only chance that they had to cure Erluc. "No," he decided grudgingly.

Renidos nodded hesitantly, approaching a wide, oaken table behind them. He was obviously not satisfied with how the situation had gone down. And how could he? Alchemists were berated the most in Inthyl of all places; he'd grown up hearing tales of their atrocities. Still, he didn't say a word, probably realizing the same thing that Asten had—they needed Alisthír's help, and until Erluc was safe, they had to stay focused.

"Now, what you're looking for is inside that cabinet," continued Alisthír indicating the very back of the room. "Second shelf from the top."

Walking over to the cabinet, Asten pulled on the handle. "It's locked."

With a scoff, Alisthír closed his eyes, muttering a short incantation, and Asten felt the air next to the cabinet shimmer. A moment later, the alchemist opened his eyes. "Try again."

This time, he'd barely touched the handle when the door opened swiftly. Looking back at Alisthír, Asten shook his head incredulously. He didn't want to like the alchemist, but even he had to admit that this magic was impressive.

He grabbed a long box from the second drawer, setting it down next to Alisthír. The man blew at it, and unsettled dust polluting the air. Taking a deep breath, his eyes closed, the alchemist began mumbling quietly, and Asten watched intently as the lid of the box started to light up, bright red characters periodically illuminating as he chanted. Finally, Alisthír paused, opening his eyes.

"What was that?" questioned Asten.

Alisthír sighed. "That," he began, "was a rune seal. An almost impregnable magical barrier summoned by magicians to protect what are often their most valuable possessions." He wiped a bead of sweat from his brow. "They're quite possibly the most complex spells in existence."

"So, what are *you* protecting?" demanded Renidos. In answer to the question, Alisthír slowly slid the lid off, revealing three small, engraved slate stones.

"Runestones," breathed Asten.

Alisthír nodded. "The most precious runestones in my collection. Vistre, Moren, and Dimahr."

Renidos raised an eyebrow, indifferent, but Asten's eyes gleamed. "And that means?" questioned the younger boy.

"Life, Death, and Thought," Alisthír explained. "There is much I'll have to get you up to speed on if you're to truly master your power." He turned over the runestone in his hand, revealing an engraving of a four-pointed star inscribed within a circle. "Here," Alisthír handed him one of them. "Try not to drop that." He closed the box once more, setting it to the ground.

Asten instantly recognized it the rune of Life. *This is going to work.* He closed his eyes, cautiously touching his ring to the stone.

Sometimes Asten felt like there was someone in control of them, and that this person occasionally orchestrated particular moments so that Asten would look incredibly stupid. This was one of those moments.

The stone touched the cold metal and absolutely nothing happened. "What? Why didn't it work?" he asked.

"Because bonding runes to objects isn't as simple as that," responded Alisthír accordingly, taking a deep breath. "Only the most basic elemental runes bond through mere direct contact with an object. Several runes—the more powerful ones—can only be bonded to objects after you discern the true essence of the rune. In essence, the more complex the rune, the more difficult it is to bond it to an instrument. Similarly, some of the more powerful runes exact a heavier toll on the caster."

"Like the one you used to get here?" guessed Asten.

"Xanthon," confirmed Alisthír. "Yes, that one especially so. But rather, I was referring to these stones in particular. Some runes are particularly draining for the user—like Wind, for example. And some, like these three, simply *cannot* be bonded to physical objects without the use of alchemy."

"But can't we just cast the runestone?" pointed out Renidos, raising a hand slightly. "That sounds faster than messing around with alchemy."

Alisthír sighed, breathing deeply. He hadn't regained his energy from the previous spell yet, but the man was determined. "Runestones are *made* through alchemy, Renidos. Give that here." Asten passed him the runestone and the ring, and he placed them both on the altar. Steadily rising to his feet, he approached the altar at the side of the room, upon which Asten placed both his own ring and the runestone. Retreating to the table, Alisthír selected a bottle half-filled with dark-blue powder, and another, larger one that seemed to be completely filled by metal—quicksilver.

For the first time since the blessing, Asten found himself without his magical ornament, and it left him feeling helpless and vulnerable, just as if he was the same person that had left Sering so long ago. His cheeks heating up, he took a few steps back, watching as the old alchemist poured the silvery, metallic liquid into the depressed circle in the center of the altar. Gradually, it began to spread through the grooves in the table, and when all of the channels had been filled, the bottle was almost empty.

"What's that for?" blurted out Asten, before he could stop himself.

Alisthír didn't respond—instead, he pulled out the stopper from the second bottle and tapped it lightly, spilling out a thin circle of blue dust around the runestone, and another around Asten's ring. With another line of dust, he connected the two circles and replaced the bottle on the shelf. He produced some more chalk from his cloak, and Renidos put out a hand, restraining him.

"Please tell me you're not going to use that spell again," insisted Renidos. Alisthír shrugged the hand off, shaking his head. He drew a rune on the line of dust connecting the two objects, the red and blue together, granting more color to the room than anything else in sight.

"Maleryar," barked Alisthír quietly, hovering his hand on the rune.

Asten frowned at him. "Excuse me?"

"I don't think he was talking to you, genius," whispered Renidos sharply from behind him. The younger boy had made sure not to distract the alchemist, his eyes wide open to make sure that nothing was going wrong.

On the altar, the circles of dust began to glow, and a strange, violet mist rose from the quicksilver-filled channels across its stone surface. Slowly, the vapor gathered around the runestone and began to swirl around it insistently. With each moment, the round stone was further obscured by the mist, and suddenly, the line of dark-blue dust connecting the rings lit up.

Then the mist dissipated, and the runestone was gone. The quicksilver filling the altar's grooves had vanished as well, and the circles of dust had lost their vibrance, now a weak grayish-blue rather than the rich indigo from earlier. The air around the ring itself was shimmering as it would above a bonfire.

"So that was it?" Renidos stepped up to the table. "Did it work?"

In response, Alisthír snatched up a pair of tongs hanging against the wall and gingerly lifted the ring off the table. "See for yourself." Gently, he turned the tongs so that the side of the ring with the lightning rune was clearly visible. Next to the symbol he already knew so well, though, Asten could see another sign: a curved four-point star inscribed inside a circle, delicately engraved into the gold.

The Mage grasped the ring, quickly returning it to his finger. Though the surface was by no means burning, the metal was noticeably warm. He spun it around, and his eyes glinted. Besides Ryzae, the power of the rune Vistre had been fused to the ring, and finally, he would be able to bring Erluc a faint sliver of hope. "Let's go," he said with finality.

"In a minute," mumbled Alisthír. The effort seemed to have tired him even more, and he was on the verge of collapsing. He pointed at the box beside him. "Put this back in the cabinet, would you?"

Renidos nodded, walking over. He picked up the box of runestones from the ground and placed it back in the cabinet where they'd found it earlier.

Placing a hand on the table behind him, Alisthír slowly got to his feet. Several beakers were racked up, bits of parchment and ancient scriptures sprawled all over the desk. Pressing his palm against the wall, he inhaled deeply, and Asten could see the vigor flowing back into his face, his limbs. When he turned back to Asten, any trace of his fatigue had been utterly eliminated.

"What was *that*?" asked Renidos, his resolve slipping for a moment.

"An etherinite shard embedded in the cavern wall," explained Alisthír. "It's a rare crystal that stores energy, which makes it immensely useful when it comes to magic." He wasn't lying—the lines on his face had vanished, and he looked completely re-energized. "That's why it's used in the creation of runestones." He raised his red chalk. "It's primarily what this is made from." Asten nodded; it made sense that the chalk was made of some magical substance. "Casting rarer runestones is a waste, and I usually like to avoid it unless absolutely necessary. The etherinite provides an efficient alternative."

"Must be pretty hard to get a hold of, though," guessed Renidos, taking a look around.

"Indeed," confirmed Alisthír. "It took me countless years to get what little I have, and it is harder still to get more now." Taking a moment, he shrugged. "That said, this laboratory probably has the highest concentration of etherinite that you will come across. Its crystals power all my spells and enchantments, as well as control the entrance. If anyone else were to find out about this place, they certainly wouldn't be telling anyone about it." Asten grimaced, and the alchemist shrugged. "Better to be safe than sorry."

Asten shook his head. "But wait—this still doesn't explain how you were able to survive in the Twilight Realm.

284 • The Promise of the Warrior

The way I understand it, you need to have a connection to the Void in order to exist there, right?" He shook his head incredulously. "How come you didn't freeze like everyone else?"

"There are many things that you still do not understand about the Void," was all Alisthír would say. "But I will tell you this—the less connected you are to it, the more likely you are to stay alive." With a wave of his hand, he extinguished the torches burning throughout the laboratory, and kneeling, he began to draw the same sign that had brought them to the cavern. *Xanthon*, Asten remembered. "Brace yourself," warned the alchemist. Asten closed his eyes, and Renidos gripped his spear tightly, holding on for dear life.

The man covered the rune with his hand, and gravity turned off. For a moment, the three of them hovered in the air, marveling in tranquility and wonder. When he opened his eyes, he was crouching on the ground, not a scratch on him.

He smiled, still in awe of the wondrous magic. *One day… one day I'll learn to cast a spell like that.*

"Get off your tail, we've got a Warrior to save," urged Renidos, pulling Asten up off the ground and checking his watch. "Half-past three," he reported, looking up. "Wait, what? We were gone for almost *four hours?*"

"Well, you do know what they say about time when you're having fun," said Alisthír, his tone dripping sarcasm. He pocketed his etherinite chalk, turning on his heel.

Renidos' brow furrowed in confusion. "Care to explain, alchemist? Or are you just going to leave us in the dark about this too?"

Alisthír's expression didn't betray a hint of an answer. "When you find out, I hope you'll understand why I didn't tell you." They walked for a few more minutes in uneasy silence, the direness of the situation on all of their minds, but none of them were willing to put it into words. Even Alisthír, the ever composed, was clearly struggling to hide his fear. Whatever the old man's ultimate plan was, Erluc's condition had almost certainly put it in jeopardy. All of them had too much at stake to fail now.

When they reached the outskirts of the city, the sky was totally overcast, rendering Renidos' watch useless. By the swiftly fading light, though, Asten guessed that the time was just after five. They kept moving, their pace becoming ever brisker, and within the half-hour, the infirmary was in sight. Taking a deep breath and twisting the ring around his finger, Asten stepped over the threshold into the structure.

Several corpses were desecrated on the floor, less blood inside than out. The white tiles were now smeared with red, and Asten flinched. Behind him, Renidos and Alisthír hurried inside, gasping at the sight of the bodies.

Then, a terrible thought entered Asten's mind. *If the medics are dead, who's keeping Erluc alive?* He knew it was selfish, and he should've been thinking about the slaughtered men and women, but the worry tugging at him was too strong to think of anything else.

"Who… who killed them?" whispered Renidos from behind.

Asten shivered. He unsheathed his dagger, pointing his ring out in front of him. *If I'm not wrong, we're about to find out.* They cautiously stepped around the cadavers on the ground, making their way to where Erluc was being treated. Asten pushed the door open, and he gasped.

No. Not you. It can't be you.

There he was. With a blade rested on Erluc's chin, the dark elven prince sat on the bunk, snarling at them. "Move a muscle, and he gets it through the neck."

Ulmûr was wearing a hood to avoid being recognized, but he'd forsaken it completely when they had entered. The elf looked strikingly similar to his father, the same chiseled jaw and pupilless eyes.

Asten grit his teeth. *Stay calm.* He turned back to face Renidos, and the younger boy nodded. Slowly, they both lowered their weapons. About a million questions were swimming around in Asten's head, but he settled for asking, "What do you want?" Alisthír's hand tightened around his sword, ready to pounce.

"No chivalry among warriors, I see," mocked the elf. "It's nice that all three of you blessed fools are here together." He relaxed his hand, laying the flat of his blade on Erluc's face. "And you brought me the Exile, too, how nice."

Alisthír glared, "Leave. You know you are no match for me."

"No." Ulmûr shrugged. "But I won't be fighting you. They will."

"You want us to fight each other?" Renidos echoed sardonically. He had sensed an opportunity. "What if we refuse? You'll kill us?"

Ulmûr snarled, gesturing at Erluc. "I'll kill him as well as everyone else in the city. Without your protection, Inthyl will fall." He twisted the sword in his hand, and the edge of the blade scraped Erluc's skin.

"Wait!" cried Renidos. Their main goal right now was to heal Erluc, and they had to do it before sundown. "What about your father? If we set Uldarz free, will you let Erluc go?"

"An admirable attempt, but with him out of the way, I will become the leader of my own tribe and crush all those who dare oppose me among the *Irmaera*." Ulmûr smiled perversely, and Asten had never seen a more hideous sight.

"And honestly, the pleasures of being king far outweigh my sentiment for my father."

Asten was repulsed. *What a monster.*

Suddenly, a nurse rushed into the room from behind them. Laying eyes on the prince, she became paralyzed instantly, rooted to a spot. She opened her mouth, but no sound came out. A second later, the hilt of a knife was protruding from her heart, and her lifeless body fell to the ground. Ulmûr didn't even flinch.

Both Asten and Renidos were shocked. He really was a monster.

But by virtue of the woman's entrance, Alisthír had found the opening that he had been patiently waiting for. He ripped his sword out of his sheath, and both Asten and Renidos crouched to the ground as the man jumped at the dark elf.

The assault worked.

The prince brought his sword up to defend against the blow, exposing Erluc. Alisthír kicked Ulmûr away, and the elf fell backwards, knocking over several flasks as he flipped over a table.

Asten turned to Renidos. "Go! I'll get Erluc!"

Renidos nodded, jumping to his feet and running off towards the other two. Asten scrambled to the cot, where Erluc had been resting. He'd lost consciousness. *Please don't be dead.* Asten tucked two fingers behind Erluc's ear, and the weak but persistent beat of his friend's pulse throbbed against his skin.

He sighed in relief. Asten looked at the battle raging mere feet away from him, his comrades pushing the dark elf back. Ulmûr dodged Alisthír's strike, rolling away from Renidos' spear. He lashed out, knocking both of them backwards, charging after them.

Normally, Alisthír alone could've easily bested the elf, but for all the spells he had cast, the old combatant was far below pristine condition.

Asten turned the ring on his finger. *Now or never.* He placed a palm on Erluc's neck, where Ulmûr's jagged blade had incised his skin. He had no idea how this procedure would work, or even how to start, but he had to try something. Right now, there was only one person who could defeat Ulmûr, and they needed him back.

He concentrated, pushing down on the wound, and waited for the spell to take place. Ten seconds passed, then a minute, and Erluc hadn't even shifted. *Damn!* Suddenly, Erluc's shoulders flickered to life, and his mouth contorted into a grimace. The muscles in his good arm tightened and loosened at their own will, and he struggled in place, tossing back and forth on the cot. *What's happening?*

It looked like their time had run out. Erluc was dying. Asten frantically covered the wound again, channeling the power of the ring, snapping his eyes shut. He breathed heavily, putting all of his will into it, but his friend's expression didn't relax for even a second. *Come on!*

He opened his eyes, and nothing had changed. *Blast!*

Placing his hand on Erluc's chest, he pressed the ring against his friend's cold tunic. "Vistre," he whispered lightly as if he were begging his friend to live. His fingers tingled, and he felt an ocean of power flow through his veins. His palm started to heat up, and slowly, the warmth began seeping out, down into Erluc's body.

The Warrior's eyelids fluttered, and his fitful limbs slowly relaxed. Asten let out a smile of relief. He pressed down further, and color returned to Erluc's ashen face. Slowly, a small groan escaped Erluc's mouth, and he shook his head, sitting up on the bed. "Ouch," he grumbled, looking around. "Where am I? What happened?"

"The bloodsteel poison in your wound started taking effect," explained Asten. "I only just managed to bring you back." He sighed, taking deep breaths. The spell had certainly taken its toll on him, but at least it was worth it.

Eyebrows furrowed in discomfort, Erluc nodded. "Thanks," he muttered. "Maybe I *did* need your help."

"You don't say," replied Asten. He gestured to the far side of the hall, where Renidos and Alisthír were being pushed back against the wall. "Now, you should probably rest. They should be able to take care of him." He wasn't confident at all, but he didn't want Erluc doing anything stupid. Of course, it wasn't as if it mattered.

Erluc gritted his teeth, his eyes glinting at the sight of Ulmûr. He rose to his feet and unsheathed Telaris. In one swing, he cut his cast open, freeing his left hand.

"What are you doing?" questioned Asten immediately, taken off guard.

"I don't know what you did to me, but I think you healed my arm too," he explained. He'd really wanted to use his powers against Ulmûr in the tournament, but the rules had forbidden him to do so. Now, he had the opportunity he had longed for.

Stretching his shoulders outwards, he turned back. "You coming?"

Asten nodded, turning the ring on his finger. "This ought to be interesting," he muttered.

Admittedly, four against one wasn't the most balanced contest, but up till that point, Ulmûr had had the upper hand. Alisthír was leaning against a wall, panting, while Renidos tried his best to hold the dark elf off alone.

His enhanced speed was keeping him a step ahead, but Ulmûr's superior swordsmanship and raw power were wearing him down. Up until that point, he had dodged most of the dark elf's attacks, but he couldn't keep it up forever. As he ducked under the bloodsteel sword, a knee to his hip brought him to the ground. He had managed to avoid being cut by the blade but had suffered several bruises whenever the prince of the dark elves had managed to land a physical blow.

He swung his spear upwards, but Ulmûr blocked it with his sword and twisted it out of his hands. He brought the bloodsteel sword an inch from Renidos' eye but hesitated. "You." He shook his head, and his gray teeth popped outwards as he snickered. "I recognize you. You were the boy who helped capture my father." He nodded, agreeing with himself. "Yes…"

Renidos grimaced. Now was not a great time to irritate the elf, and his spear was too far to reach before Ulmûr would notice his movement and impale him through the eye. Even with his speed, it wasn't a chance he was willing to take.

"Well, I suppose I should thank you," decided Ulmûr. "You saved me the trouble of killing that vile miscreant myself." Suddenly, a bright ray blasted him in the chest and sent him sprawling backwards.

"You know what they say—like father like son," completed Erluc, running up next to his fallen friend. Renidos almost jumped in joy—he was alive! And his timing was impeccable as ever. Erluc bent down, helping the Spectre to his feet. "You okay?"

"I'm fine," he nodded. "I guess we've all saved each other now." Erluc shook his head, a wry smile on his face, just as Asten ran up from behind them. "Looks like the spell worked," remarked Renidos, turning to Asten, who nodded his confirmation. He jerked his chin up, beckoning towards where the dark elf had risen to his feet.

"Actually, I changed my mind," declared Erluc, turning back to the others. "Would you mind standing down?"

Asten shrugged. *Just escaped potential death, still cocky as ever.* He decided that he would stay alert, just in case Erluc's confidence was misconstrued.

Ulmûr spat, and a dark, viscous liquid contaminated the floor. "Well, well. It looks like you were holding back during our first encounter."

Erluc grinned. "And here I was, worrying that you'd forgotten me."

"I don't care about who you are," barked the elf. "And I don't care about the Immortals that watch over you. But I know I'll take special pleasure in killing you." He glowered confidently. "You know why?"

"No," conceded Erluc. "But I bet you're going to tell me."

Ulmûr snarled, advancing towards the Warrior. "The most satisfying victories are those won when you can see the light leave your foe's eyes, knowing that they could've done nothing to stop you."

"You're psychotic," muttered Erluc, shaking his head in disgust.

The dark elf leaped at him, enraged, Telaris and the bloodsteel blade clashed once more. Erluc's eyes glinted— this was going to be so much more fun than last time.

He pushed Ulmûr backwards, lighting Telaris up in flames. The elf's eyes burned, and he charged, swinging his own sword at the light. Erluc shifted Telaris in the air, slicing through Ulmûr's wrist. The bloodsteel sword fell to the ground, and the elf howled, pulling his arm close to his chest. There wasn't even any blood—the smoldering blade of Telaris immediately cauterized any cuts it made.

Erluc frosted Telaris over, quickly cooling the blade and placed the tip on Ulmûr's chin. "You were saying?" he asked, breathing heavily. He pointed the blade down, stopping just in front of the dark elf's abdomen, and kicked the prince's bloodsteel sword away. Cautiously, Asten knelt down, picking it up and holding it at the ready.

"You don't have it in you," goaded the prince of the dark elves. "You're weak, spineless, just like every other man."

Erluc gritted his teeth, obviously jarred. "You'd be surprised."

"Those are the words of a coward," spat Ulmûr. "A frightened boy who is afraid to embrace the truth of the world. True strength is written in destiny, and yours is cursed to live in the shadow of those who have the courage to do what's necessary."

Erluc steamed, and in that moment, he extended Telaris further, stabbing the elf through the stomach. Ulmûr caught his breath, inhaling deeply as the steel blade passed out of his back.

He scoffed at Erluc, his voice painfully stinted. "Are... are you really so naive? You allow even your enemies to tell you what to do?"

Erluc narrowed his eyes. "What enemies?" he whispered to the dark elf. "Your father is padlocked in the dungeons, and you're not exactly in fine condition." He looked pointedly at Telaris. "You've lost. It's over."

"It hasn't even begun," retorted Ulmûr, a smirk creeping onto his grotesque face. "Word of my father's defeat would have reached her by now," he proclaimed, the terrible smile on his face threatening to enlarge. "She..." He shook his head and broke out in a fit of maniacal laughter.

Erluc grit his teeth, gripping the dark elf's neck with his free hand. "Who is she?" he demanded.

Ulmûr snickered once more, and Erluc tightened his fingers around the elf's neck. The laughter stopped, and the Warrior finally released the pressure. The prince sighed, taking in a deep breath. "*Ere the traitors unleash the true power of fear*," he finally proclaimed, and Alisthír flinched. Asten felt his gemstone start to pulse and glow at his chest, Erluc's and Renidos' following suit as well, before slowly fading once more. "The Traitor… she will come for you. All of you."

The Traitor? Asten's mind went directly to the words of Invardui, back before they'd even arrived at Inthyl. He'd said that the Traitor had taken control of Inro Forthel, almost seven years in the past.

They all simply stood there, unsure of what to say back. Even with a sword through his abdomen, Ulmûr was gloating as if it was them who had just been stabbed. "And when she does…" He stopped, his eyes smoldering as they met Erluc's. "You will all burn."

Erluc tensed, ripping Telaris out of the elf's stomach. A dark, viscous fluid leaked from the fatal wound, and Ulmûr sneered once more, his eyes rolling back into his head. "I'll take my chances," cursed Erluc, slowly sheathing the blade. He turned around, and Renidos had an uncomfortable expression on his face. "Listen, I didn—"

"No, it's fine. This one time, I think you did the right thing. A beast who would readily slaughter scores of innocent people… he was never really alive in the first place." His face remained sour, but Erluc knew better than to press the subject.

Asten sheathed Ulmûr's sword, strapping it to his belt. Though he was reluctant to wield a weapon that had done so much evil, the sword had felt perfectly balanced in his hand—and anyway, he needed a replacement for the blade Uldarz had destroyed. He supported Alisthír's arms, and with his help, the man slowly made it up to his feet. "You all did well today," he acknowledged. "But I'm afraid that this is not the end."

Erluc turned to Alisthír. "How do you mean?"

"The prophecy is not yet over," explained Alisthír. "You must continue to protect Eärnendor as emissaries of the Falcon. I don't know of the woman that Ulmûr spoke of, but be on your guard, for it may be anyone—" He turned to Erluc. "Anyone at all. And you must be prepared for what lies ahead of you."

Asten nodded. After the day he'd had, how could he not be alert?

"Now I must take my leave," continued Alisthír. "I am certain you will all grow into great heroes, and I wish you all the best in your conquests."

"Wait, you're leaving?" asked Asten. "As in leaving Inthyl?"

"Think of it as… a retreat. Going underground." Erluc raised an eyebrow, but Renidos nodded in recognition. "I promise you we will meet again." Alisthír raised his hand to his head, then up to the sky in a salute of farewell. "Vor té dryln."

"Vor té carast," Erluc called after him. And just like that, he was gone.

Asten shook his head. "We can never catch a break, can we? This Traitor—whoever she is—sounds like she's stronger than both Uldarz and Ulmûr."

"I'm counting on it," Erluc assured him. Asten snorted, and Renidos smiled in awe of the Warrior's confidence. He turned around, facing the rest of the Trinity. "Now come on, we have to clean this place up." Looking around, the infirmary was littered with bodies, the walls dented, ruined furniture and equipment shattered against them.

Asten groaned. "This is going to take a while."

Renidos raised an eyebrow. "You two have any money on you?" Erluc found a half-dozen queltras in his pockets, as well as the two queltras that were still in his cloak. Asten found a daeral, probably a part of Erluc's prize money that had been delivered the same morning. They collected the money, holding it out.

"How much do you want?"

Renidos started slowly counting. One, two, and then he grabbed all of them. "That should be enough."

"Oh, thanks." Erluc snorted, his palm empty. "Aren't you going to tell us why we were just robbed?"

He slipped the coins into his cummerbund, handing Asten the spear. "Don't drop that." His form flickered, and he returned to his place, grabbing the spear back. "Alright, the building's clear. No one inside."

"Of course not, it's past sundown," reminded Asten. "Only the Royal Infirmary stays open through the night."

Renidos looked to Erluc, and a silent conversation passed between them. Then, Erluc closed his eyes, turning away. Normally he could stare down a lion, but truth be told, the same thought had been running through his mind. "Fine, let's go."

"What?" asked Asten. "We can't leave this place like this."

"We're not." Both he and Renidos walked out, and Asten sprinted after them. They passed around to the back, and after making sure that nobody could see him, Erluc lit Telaris.

"What the hell are you doing?" burst Asten. Erluc ignored him, and Renidos pulled him aside, just as Erluc set the building alight. They backed away, watching from afar just to make sure that no one had been roasted alive.

"How were you planning to explain the dozens of bodies on the floor? The shattered equipment? And the corpse of the prince of the dark elves?" asked Renidos.

Asten grit his teeth. "Ulmûr—"

"Ulmûr's dead!" Erluc interrupted. "And he deserved it. But sometimes, not everyone needs to know everything. Having the public believe that the infirmary burned down will conjure up less panic than telling them about this." He cooled Telaris, returning it to its sheath. "After the Trial, after Uldarz, people are scared. The Twilight Legion is off fighting alongside the dwarves, and… we're not ready for a war."

Frowning, Asten turned to watch the fire slowly engulfing the infirmary.

"The best thing for us is to train, hone our powers until we're sure that we can hold our own against the Traitor, whoever she is," he paused. "We had Alisthír this time, and we were lucky. But we can't keep relying on others to save us."

Asten scowled. "The Traitor," he spat. "It's just one challenge after another with us, isn't it?"

Renidos raised an eyebrow. "What do you mean?"

"Ever since we left Sering." Asten picked up a pebble and flung it into the burning building. "I get captured, and assuming I survive that, then what? We'd come to Inthyl and live our lives. But no—now there's a prophecy, and we have to get to the Citadel in a month. And after that?"

Erluc placed a hand on his shoulder, but Asten brushed it off. "When does our fight end, Erluc? We didn't sign up for this."

"Didn't we?" Erluc looked down. "We made a promise, all of us. We swore to protect the innocent, the defenseless. Right now, this is where that promise takes us."

"So, we're trapped?" Asten laughed mirthlessly. "Are we stuck *protecting the innocent* until we die? Charging into danger every time someone's in trouble, never knowing if any fight will be our last?"

There was a sullen silence, and they looked to the building. The wooden structure had crumbled, the roof caving in on itself without the support of the walls. The timber had ignited, and their great bonfire burned throughout the night until a group of neighbors hosed it down. The bodies were indistinguishable, and the dark elf's murderous rampage was just one more secret that the Trinity had to keep locked away in their hearts.

After a few minutes, Renidos turned to Asten again. "What you said about us not knowing if we would survive? What about the prophecy?"

"*The Trinity shall rise to the Council's defense?* I thought about that too," admitted Asten.

"So then?" Renidos shrugged. "We know we're going to save the Council, right? Isn't that confirmation enough to you?"

Asten shook his head, and his eyes burned—whether from the smoke or from the first hints of tears, he couldn't have said. The past two days had been extremely clamorous for the three of them, and Asten felt a little guilty, but the fire seemed to help restore his concentration a little. The flames rose up into the sky, and he lost himself in the dark cinnamon inferno as his thoughts ran wild in his mind.

Asten noticed that both Erluc and Renidos had remained silent as well, probably consumed in their own feelings.

He didn't know how long it had been when Erluc finally spoke. "Nothing's confirmed, not really," he remarked. "And I couldn't care less about the prophecy. But I know one thing—if there's something that we can do with our powers to help save someone, then we don't have a choice. If that means we're in danger, so be it, but I'll be damned if we don't try."

Chapter 17

LIES OF OMISSION

INTHYL, AENOR
Renidos

Asten spun his sword, desperately trying to fend off the lightning attacks of the spear being thrust at his throat, his chest, even his eye. Of course, Renidos wasn't trying anything too serious, only to keep the older boy on his toes.

The ebony-hued blade of Ulmûr was a blur, slashing left and right, twisting, and spinning, but the Spectre was *inhumanly* fast. And after a series of particularly vicious blows and a feint, his spear was at Asten's throat, forcing himself to leap back to avoid being skewered through the neck. He crashed into the ground, scraping his back on a crooked fallen branch, which snapped loudly.

Erluc, who was asleep lying against the ancient oak, woke with a start. He immediately moved to draw Telaris and stand simultaneously, but the blade was stuck in the sheath, and he lost balance, tumbling onto his back. Asten rolled to the side and stood, snorting with laughter. Erluc rose to his knees, grinning apologetically, and Renidos stepped back and lowered his spear enough to relax and start laughing as well.

Asten seized on the moment and lashed out at Renidos' leg, but the Spectre's reflexes were too quick, and he leaped over the blade and put his weight on his spear shaft, pressing the flat into the earth. Feigning panic, Asten wrenched his sword out of the soil, stepping backwards towards the tree as he deflected the spear again and again. His basic tactics were starting to bore Renidos, who had deliberately started to fight slower so that he wouldn't hurt his friend.

"This is disappointing," Erluc snorted, shaking his head.

Asten's voice was strained from the exertion. "I told him I wouldn't use magic. Forgot about his superspeed for a moment." He was too busy to look, but Renidos could clearly picture Erluc's face of exasperation as he inched backwards so his shoulders almost scraped the bark of the oak.

Asten feinted at Renidos' gut, then planted his foot against the tree trunk and sprang forward, slashing. And as a startled Renidos stumbled back, trying to avoid the blade, Asten curved his sword around the right and neatly tripped him with the flat, causing him to topple backwards and crash onto Erluc, who was too surprised to move out of the way.

He stood, dusting off his tunic. Erluc groaned and shoved Renidos off of him. "Brilliant footwork, Ren." His expression was one of frustration as he clambered to his feet.

"Not a compliment," cut in Asten, grinning. He passed Renidos his spear with one foot.

Renidos glared and got up, picking up the weapon. "Cheat."

Asten shrugged. "To be fair, no one actually called off the fight."

"Who cares? That doesn't justify losing to Asten," dismissed Erluc, running one hand through his hair, which was horribly spiked from his nap. Renidos snorted, a grin spreading across his face, while it was Asten's turn to glare.

Ordinarily, they would've had some kind of exchange, and Asten would've inevitably lost the fight that would have followed. But on that particular day, Renidos noticed that Erluc didn't seem like his customary, provoking self. "You okay?" asked Asten, also picking up that something was wrong.

"What?" Erluc seemed slightly distracted. "Y-Yeah, of course, I'm okay," said Erluc, adjusting his scabbard on his belt. "Probably still recovering from the whole bloodsteel poisoning coma." Asten nodded, even if he wasn't fully convinced. Something definitely seemed off about Erluc, but they'd find out what it was soon enough. "Anyway," transitioned Erluc, "I think I'll go get some breakfast."

"You sure you don't want to spar a bit?" offered Renidos.

Erluc considered this, but he spotted the strings lying in the corner of the courtyard and shook his head. "I think I'll just rest today," he decided. "But I'll see you guys for lunch." With that, he disappeared into the inn to get dressed.

Renidos seemed as perplexed as Asten was. "I really don't think he's okay," he remarked. "You think this is because of yesterday?"

"Could be," agreed Asten. After all, fighting Ulmûr had certainly taken a toll on all three of them, but since it was Erluc that killed him, it could explain why he was acting so strangely. "He'll come around."

Nodding, Renidos twirled his spear around his torso. "Ready?"

"Bring it," replied Asten, initiating the brawl. Instead, he dropped into a slight crouch and began circling him, scouting for flaws in his opponent's stance. "With powers?"

"Why not?" decided Renidos with a smirk. "Two queltras say that I win."

Asten snorted. "You're on." Renidos made the first move, shifting to a one-handed grip and leaning to put more reach and power into his arcing strike to the side. Asten was hard-pressed to deflect the blow, and the impact almost forced him to drop his weapon.

Shaking off the pain, he drew back his sword and began a series of quick attacks towards Renidos' left shoulder, but the Spectre effortlessly blocked the strikes. Not wasting a moment, he lunged and struck Asten's sword just above the crossguard.

Reacting quickly, Asten fired a blast of lightning at Renidos' face. As he stumbled back, he dropped, rolled, scooped up his sword, and came up on one knee.

Renidos, having only been temporarily stunned by the lightning, feinted towards Asten's right leg, then shifted his weight and lunged for his opposite side. Without hesitation, Asten sidestepped and spun his sword, and a thin line of crimson appeared on Renidos' thigh.

"Someone's getting slow," he teased. Renidos turned to face Asten, a grim smile on his face. *Alright, if that's how you want to play.* He suddenly pounced, aiming for Asten's unprotected forearm. In panic, Asten flailed, trying to dodge the assault, and in turn leaving his defenses wide open.

With a quick rap on the flat of Asten's blade, Renidos extended his spear, so the point lightly rested on Asten's collarbone. "You were saying?" taunted the younger boy, brightening up.

Asten scowled. "You were holding back?"

"Well, not a *lot*," admitted Renidos. "But I tried to keep it as fair as possible. You did pretty well, considering you lost your old sword."

Rolling his eyes, Asten placed his palm over Renidos' wound, whispering lightly in Telmírin. When he took his hand away, the blood had faded away, and the cut of the bloodsteel seemed to have left no trace.

"Wow, you've gotten good at that," acknowledged Renidos. And it was true; Asten had practiced his spell for the better part of the previous night. Unfortunately, he still had a series of unhealed bruises along his calves from failed attempts. "Now, come on, you owe me two queltras worth of krill."

After a quick bite, Renidos spent some time at home, and Asten said he'd return to work at Galimin's smithy. Of course, he didn't really need to continue working—the prize money from the Trial was enough to live on for more than a year. But Asten knew that he needed to do *something* with his time, even if it was painstakingly awkward to be around Lyra. Besides, with the king's order finally completed, work was a lot more relaxed than it had been earlier.

Renidos had even suggested for them to move into a fancier place, or purchase their own house, but the Fang had started to become their home. And after everything that had happened, he could understand that it was nice to have something constant and normal in their lives.

A few hours later, the Trinity met at the courtyard behind The Broken Fang, Erluc leisurely swinging around in his hammock while Renidos and Asten were sprawled out on the grass.

"So, guess what happened at the forge today?" started Asten. Renidos shrugged, and Erluc didn't even acknowledge the question. "Lannet introduced me to this girl."

Renidos raised an eyebrow. "I thought he didn't like you."

"Well, he doesn't hate me," countered Asten.

Erluc snorted, rolling over his hammock. "How fast did you get rejected?"

Asten's eyes narrowed. "I have a date in three hours," he taunted. "You tell me."

"Lucky you," commented Erluc. "Get me something to eat on the way back."

"We can go in and eat if you want," offered Asten. "But you haven't done anything the whole day, so I don't know what you're complaining about."

Rolling his eyes, Erluc sat up. "I was at the arena for a couple of hours," he conveyed with a shrug. "Not that I had much practice. I was mostly just shaking hands with all kinds of people that wanted to meet *Lord Heroblade*." He enunciated his new title as sarcastically as possible.

"Really?" remarked Renidos, with a sarcastic expression. "That's unexpected, seeing as you've passed the Steel Trial and are arguably the best swordsman in all of Aenor."

Asten didn't seem to be in a mood to flatter. "What were you doing at the arena? I thought that you would have wanted to stay as far as you could be from fighting after yesterday. That's why you were so lost this morning, right?"

Erluc tilted his head. "What are you talking about?" he questioned. "Ulmûr deserved what he got, and I don't regret that I killed him." He turned to Renidos and then back to Asten. "And you guys don't have to worry about me, I'm fine."

Renidos rolled his eyes. "If you don't believe us, you should go talk to Rose. At least you'll listen to what she says." Erluc didn't look up, but Renidos saw his jaw tighten.

"He's right, of course, *Lord Turcaelion*," mocked Asten, emphasizing each syllable for maximum effect.

Raising an eyebrow, Renidos looked to Erluc, who hadn't even seemed to notice the Mage's adaptation of his title. "What in the world does that mean?" he demanded.

"Turcaelion?" he confirmed. "It's Telmírin for Heroblade. And it sounds a hell of a lot better, too." Asten had spent a lot of time studying Telmírin—something he'd never shut up about—and he'd made remarkable progress.

"Whatever." Erluc looked away in disgust and twirled in his hammock. A weak fire burned half-a-dozen yards away from the hammock, while the strong breeze made Asten's hair ruffle like leaves in the wind.

Renidos shook his head. "And how is it that you get to be a lord, again?"

"Why do you think?" questioned Erluc nonchalantly, eliciting snickers from both Asten and Renidos.

"Let's see, I seem to recall you inches from death before the Twilight Realm collapsed," inserted Renidos. It wasn't so often that one had the opportunity to tease Erluc.

Asten nodded, a growing grin etched on his face. "He's right," he agreed. "If it weren't for sheer luck, you probably would've lost."

"Oh yeah?" retorted Erluc. "Well, you were lots of help, weren't you? You really saved the day when you passed out."

"Atanûkhor fired a shockwave at me!"

Erluc shook his head. "That sounds like a pretty sorry excuse to me."

"You mean like having your enemy defeat themselves?" interjected Renidos, and Erluc narrowed his eyes playfully.

"Well, at least I didn't lose to Asten," decided Erluc at last, and Renidos broke into a laugh, shaking his head.

"He got lucky. But since *his lordship* is so confident in his abilities, why don't we have a little spar?" he jested. He sprung up from the smooth stump he was sitting on and picked up his spear.

It took him a second to make up his mind, but Erluc finally got up. "Fine, I won't reject a chance to practice. And look on the bright side; if you win, you get to say that you defeated—" started Erluc smugly before he was interrupted by an assault from Renidos' spearpoint. Anyone else would have lost a finger, but Erluc had the reflexes of the Warrior. He jumped back, rather inelegantly, and fell on his back.

"Oh, I'm sorry. You were saying?" was the snide remark he heard as he landed with a soft thump. Salvaging the rest of his pride, he rose and charged toward Renidos. Asten, who was leaning on the edge of a tree, was on the verge of bursting into laughter.

Renidos didn't know this at the time, but he'd come to learn to never fight an irritated Erluc. With a flick of his wrist, a bend of his knee, and an exhaled breath, Erluc was kneeling with his sword behind him, while Renidos had fallen backward into the grass, rubbing his head.

"Erluc!" shouted Asten irritably as he rushed to check the severity of Renidos' injuries. By the time he reached him, Renidos was already on his feet, a provoking smile on his face.

"I'm not losing in just one stroke, *Lord Turcaelion*," declared Renidos, now determined to stay on his feet. The wide gash near his stomach stung a bit, the fire offering him some strength as the wind died down. Asten stepped away from them and returned to his previous spot, a concerned look on his face.

Erluc rose, now calmer, and smiled, "Of course not. What fun would that be?" He walked back and picked up his blade. They advanced, and the battle commenced once more, neither giving any quarter to the other. Not even his speed was enough to keep Erluc at bay, which made the older boy's skill that much more impressive.

Finally, they both retired in exhaustion, panting, and out of breath. After healing their wounds, Asten dragged them to the room and filled the bucket with icy water, insisting that they smelled worse than Skyblaze's droppings.

After they'd washed up, they returned downstairs for a late lunch. All three of them had smartened up in new tunics and trousers, courtesy of the prize money. Renidos noticed that Erluc even had a watch, which brought a smile to his face. They sat near the door, filling Erluc in about the happenings of the time he was incapacitated.

"What's a rune seal?" he questioned, with just barely enough curiosity to keep the conversation going. Renidos understood his boredom; after two days of constant danger and fighting for their lives, today seemed starkly calm.

"It's actually really interesting," provided Asten, and Renidos caught Erluc's attention, shaking his head.

The corner of Erluc's mouth curled up, and he sighed back into his chair. "Go ahead," he prompted reluctantly.

"They're basically locks—except they can only be formed and unlocked by magic. That alone makes them much more secure than regular modes of security, but they also are some of the most complex spells ever created. Alisthír has one in his laboratory to protect some runes. I'm not sure, but I have an idea to potentially break one of them." He paused, unable to hold back a smile. "I can explain it out if you want."

Erluc and Renidos looked at each other, and the older boy shrugged. "Not like we've got anything better to do."

They had only just gotten up when a pair of guards marched into the inn, bowing before Erluc. "Lord Erluc Heroblade, son of Neran. By charge of the High King, we are here to escort you to the royal palace, where the Council awaits your presence."

The Trinity looked at each other in surprise, and Asten was the first to ask, "Is there a problem?"

The guard who had spoken earlier simply shrugged his shoulders, and Renidos sighed. He probably didn't even know what they were being called for. "I'm sure it's just to talk," provided the younger boy, tentatively standing up. "After all, it's not like we did anything wrong."

That wasn't entirely true, especially considering that they'd burned an entire infirmary to the ground just the day before. Perhaps someone had recognized Erluc and reported it to the king.

"Alright," agreed Erluc finally. "Of course, we'll honor his majesty's call." He made sure that his sword was strapped to his belt before hastily following the guards out of The Broken Fang. Either way, it would have been a bad idea to refuse the king's summon to the palace. At the very least, now people would think twice before accusing them of anything.

They walked briskly through the primary gate of the palace, attracting the watchful stares of all passersby. Several of them cheered for Erluc, who nodded in acknowledgment, sending them into a bigger frenzy.

Near the main building, Renidos saw a maiden, completely covered in clothes and a headscarf, talking to someone who looked like one of Rose's handmaidens. Once her conversation with the handmaiden ended, the woman looked up and saw the three of them. He noticed her eyes narrowing as her gaze fell on him. Her ice-blue eyes. They were the only visible part of the maiden's face. Renidos estimated that she was in her early twenties, but she was practically invisible, and he could've been seriously mistaken. He blinked, and suddenly she had disappeared, leaving no trace of her existence.

"Did you guys see that?" questioned Renidos, obviously wondering what he had just seen. Ignoring him, Erluc shook his head, taking a deep breath before continuing to follow the guards. Asten, now recovered, grabbed Renidos and ran behind as well. The guards led them through the center corridor and to a grand set of double doors.

Renidos sighed, straightening his tunic, and his watch seemed to catch Asten's eye. "By the way, I'm meeting Myrena later, and I'd really appreciate not missing that date," he proclaimed firmly. Renidos nodded his head in mock obedience, while Erluc snorted. Ever since they had arrived in Inthyl, Asten had been extremely reclusive. Aside from Renidos and Erluc, he knew practically nobody in the entire city. He spent all of his leisure time in the library or exploring the city.

Renidos had grown up in the city and was familiar with the boys his age around the city, and even Erluc wouldn't hesitate to strike up a conversation with anyone he met. This was good progress for Asten.

"They are ready for you," informed a guard from behind them, and Erluc nodded, pushing his hair out of his face. He pushed the doors open and advanced down the crimson-lined carpet in the center of the chamber, followed by a confused Asten and a nervous Renidos. As soon as he entered the room, a cool drift hit him and all signs of perspiration disappeared from his face. He let go of his cloak, the hood relaxing behind his neck.

As he continued walking, Asten's eyes widened in recognition, but he quickly returned to assume his usual guarded expression, much to Renidos' amusement. High King Elandas sat upon the throne of Inthyl, a calm smile resting on his regal face. This wasn't the first time Renidos had seen the king, but it had been close to a year since he'd had the opportunity. He had to say that the king looked as royal as ever. As the Trinity reached the throne, they each bowed and fell to one knee. Asten and Renidos made sure to stand behind Erluc to attract as little attention as possible.

"Rise. You need not kneel to me, my children," directed Elandas, his magnificent voice echoing off the walls of the chamber. As they rose, all with honored expressions painted on their faces, Elandas allowed himself a small smile. "At ease."

The Trinity relaxed slightly, but Renidos could see that the king's confident bearing made Asten a tad nervous. Erluc, on the other hand, was radiating a similar aura to Elandas.

"Lord Heroblade," began Elandas. "I express my congratulations on your victory. Your performance at the Steel Trial is worthy of more praise than I can bestow. Not only did you best two previous champions—including a member of the Council of Nine—but you were also the youngest contestant to ever succeed in the esteemed battle of blades." Looking around, Renidos could see only eight members of the Council—Therglas was probably leading the Twilight Legion against the moon elves in the west.

Erluc nodded sincerely. "Thank you, your majesty." Renidos recognized that Erluc would not have been used to addressing others with respect, but he seemed to have pulled it off. At least they'd been summoned for congratulations rather than retribution.

"However," The High King's face steeled, "this tournament was not the same as the others held over the years. It seems our patrolmen have been ineffective—so much so, that even the highlord of the dark elves was able to march into Inthyl without our knowledge."

Asten swallowed, trying his best to not speak out of turn, and Renidos nodded. The fact that Inthyl was so horrified by Uldarz's presence justified Erluc's decision to keep Ulmûr's rampage a secret.

"Nevertheless, your heroic actions helped save Inthyl from a terrible fate, and we all owe you our gratitude." Erluc allowed himself a smile, but he otherwise remained as impassive as possible. "Tomorrow, there will be a banquet in commemoration of your victory and the capture of Uldarz, here in Inthyl's palace."

Immediately, Renidos' eyes widened. *A royal banquet?* That was definitely not what they had thought they had been summoned for.

"All of the Council—save for the general, who is en route to the Kre'nagan—will be in attendance, as well as my daughter and a few other dignitaries."

Erluc's expression flickered at the mention of Roxanna, but he managed to regain his composure before the High King could notice. Renidos had heard meeting with the parents of a girl was often overwhelming, but he was sure that nobody would have had to go through what Erluc was at that moment.

"And I'd like you to be present as well," continued Elandas. "Of course, you can bring whomever you wish."

Erluc hesitated for a moment, but Asten didn't falter and answered in his stead. "Thank you, your majesty." Erluc glared back at Asten, but the older boy simply gritted his teeth and continued. "We would be honored to attend, and that you would think to invite us in person."

"Very good," Elandas nodded, "Shall I send a troop to escort you back to your residence?"

Renidos shook his head. "That will not be necessary, your majesty. Thank you." The Trinity bowed, quickly making their way out of the court.

As the doors closed behind them, Erluc shoved Asten backwards. "What do you think you're doing?"

Asten was about to push back, but Renidos stopped them. "I didn't do anything," insisted the Mage.

Erluc shook his head irritably. "We can't go to this thing."

Renidos grimaced. "Elandas invited you *in person*—I don't think you had a choice."

Straightening his collar, Asten continued. "Besides, I thought you'd want a chance to meet Rose without having to hide in the courtyard."

"No, you *parrots*," spat Erluc. "She's the reason why I can't go."

"What do you mean?" Shrugging, Renidos patted his shoulder. "Surely it can't be *that* bad."

Erluc covered his face with both hands, evidently trying his best not to punch them. "We broke up," he finally explained.

Renidos grimaced, trying his best not to meet Erluc's gaze. "Okay, that's pretty bad," he muttered to himself.

"Only you," remarked Asten, pushing Erluc softly. "Only you would be stupid enough to break up with the princess of Aenor." Turning to Renidos, he whispered. "I totally called it, for the record," Erluc growled back, walking faster.

Catching up to him in seconds, Renidos tried again. "Wait, is this why you're acting so weird?"

Erluc scowled in annoyance. "I told you that I'm fine."

"There's no way!" exclaimed Asten, immediately alert. "Please don't tell me that you're depressed because of a girl."

"Are you ignoring everything that I'm saying?" questioned Erluc, thoroughly aggravated. "I'm not depressed."

Asten shook his head, turning to Renidos. "I'd usually stay, but I'm running late. Try your best to make him see reason. If it still doesn't work, I'll see you in a bit." He dashed away to the inn, leaving Renidos with Erluc.

"So how—"

"Can we talk about something else?" interrupted Erluc.

Renidos nodded. "Sure." He tried thinking of something else to talk about while they walked, and about a minute passed in absolute silence. "Alright, I have one last question." Sighing, Erluc nodded for him to continue. "Why did you guys break up?"

"Renidos—"

"I'm just asking!" justified the younger boy. "Did she cheat on you or—"

Erluc's eyes widened. "Veras-tí!" he exclaimed, and Renidos raised an eyebrow at his sudden adoption of Telmírin. "Of course not! It wasn't even her fault."

Renidos considered this. "You didn't cheat on her, did you?"

"I broke up with her because she's the princess of Aenor, and I'm the Warrior, and she'd always be in danger if people found out we were together," explained Erluc in a hushed tone. "Nobody cheated on *anyone*."

"Oh," was all Renidos could say. "I guess that makes more sense." There was a lasting silence as they walked for the next few minutes. "But wait—"

"No more questions," overruled Erluc. "Ever."

When they returned to the inn nearly half an hour later, a flustered Erluc went directly to the bar. He ordered himself a drink, and Renidos spotted Asten sitting at a corner table with a girl who was probably Myrena. He nudged Erluc, who sneered.

Suddenly, the girl stood up, said something softly into Asten's ear. She then turned and exited the inn, a cheerful expression on her curved face. Standing up, Asten slowly approached the bar. "So, you look like you're having fun," remarked Renidos with a grin.

Asten nodded, a genuine smile on his face. "We were talking about dwarven history. Apparently, we have a lot in common. She moved to Inthyl with her family recently as well."

"Sounds great." Erluc nodded, only vaguely paying attention, and turned to the barmaid. "I'll have a beer," he called. "Pint size." Renidos grinned to himself—at least it would keep Erluc's mind away from everything.

As Thea prepared the drink, Renidos turned away from the bar, his back resting on its edge. He had so many questions, and he didn't know where to start. "So, you dumped her, just like that?" he decided to ask. Out of the corner of his eye, he could see Thea look up, and he decided it would probably be better to say as little as possible until they were in the courtyard.

Erluc scowled, taking a gulp from his foaming tankard. "We are *not* talking about this." Once he'd downed another couple of tankards, they returned to the courtyard. It had gotten quite late, and although they'd started to make a habit of late nights, Renidos was really starting to get heavy-eyed.

"Well, I hate to interrupt this joyous night, but some of us," he pointed at himself, "are due for a nap."

Erluc nodded, looking around the courtyard. "We really should leave some blankets down here," he said, unsheathing Telaris slowly. "But, I think a fire would do fine for now."

"Wait," Asten held out a hand. "I'll do it. I could use the practice, anyway." They all knew that Telaris could easily light up and create a big enough fire for them, but that took all the fun out of the situation. Asten turned his ring around, aiming it at a bundle of broken branches. But before he could move, Renidos dissolved into a blur, and a shower of sparks fell into the bundle of sticks. Materializing next to a small bonfire, he tossed two rocks to the side and stepped back. Asten gaped at him, amazed, while Erluc just shook his head and smiled.

"You're welcome," declared Renidos, yawning as he climbed into his hammock.

"Show-off," muttered Asten, as he turned around, shifting his weight to balance the tarp. The three quietly drifted into a listless slumber, with only the rustling of the leaves to lullaby them.

Chapter 18

Food for Thought

Inthyl, Aenor

Erluc

The brightest ray of sunshine that fell down from the heavens that day landed directly on Asten's face. Just his luck. He scowled and tried to shift his position, rolling around in his hammock. But, as usual, the loosely woven cloth flipped over and dumped him into the damp soil.

"Bloody thing," he muttered, climbing to his feet.

Disturbed by Asten's complaining, Renidos yawned, blinking his eyes open grudgingly. He was now scratching his head, a bemused expression on his face. "What was that about?" he asked. Then he looked into the sky, realization flooding into his face. "I should probably go home and get dressed for the feast." His expression soured. "I don't know what I'm going to tell Mother."

Asten snorted. "Good luck with that." Renidos leered at him, and Asten raised his hands in surrender.

Renidos snorted. He stretched his arms, flipping forward once in the air to stretch. "I'll meet you guys back here in a couple of hours," he muttered. He dashed back home, and Asten took one look at Erluc—still persistently asleep—before going up to their room.

Within an hour, Erluc was awake. According to his watch, it was nearly eleven-thirty already. *Fabulous.* He quickly sprinted up to the room, and once Asten had bathed, he followed suit.

A few hours after noon, the Trinity was all clean, fed, and suited up. Erluc and Asten had spent some of their prize money from the Steel Trial to buy dress robes from the town center, and Renidos had devoted almost a full hour to teaching them how to put those on, Erluc grumbling all the while.

When they finally started making their way to the palace, most of the crowd appeared to be going to the same destination, and the streets were jam-packed as people pushed and shoved their way towards the palace. "I swear, if these people don't stop, I'm going to kill somebody," muttered Erluc quietly, so just Asten and Renidos could hear him. Luckily for the public, Renidos navigated the Trinity through a series of alleys, completely avoiding the chaotic traffic. Suffice to say, Erluc's temper ceased dramatically.

Within five minutes, the palace was in plain sight. According to Renidos' watch, they had made it with a quarter-hour to spare. Just as they were about to enter the grounds, a scream pierced the sky. Immediately, all of them spun around, alert for any possible danger.

"There!"

In response to Renidos' call, Erluc's vision focused on a dark-robed figure fleeing into a side alley. Before he knew it, they were all in hot pursuit, his suit drifting upward with every stride. His clothes had reduced his speed, but even then, he flew past the gathered crowd.

Renidos rightly didn't slow himself, and with each stride, he gained on the assailant until he could finally lay a hand on him. But as soon as his fingers touched the man's skin,

Erluc saw him sent flying, his back impacting hard against a stone wall. Renidos rushed off with renewed strength, adrenaline pumping through his veins. Suddenly, the man turned a sharp corner and exited their field of vision. *Damn!* Renidos' shoes screeched as he abruptly came to a stop, which came as a surprise to not only Erluc but Asten, too. Alas, as he turned the corner, he saw only one thing, and it wasn't the man.

By the time Asten and Erluc had finally arrived, panting, Renidos was already kneeling down, his brow furrowed in disgust and grief.

"What happened?" asked Erluc. Renidos said nothing. In front of him was the withered corpse of a young girl.

Anger flashed in Erluc's eyes. Who would dare do such a thing! What coward would take the life of a girl, a child, no less! Renidos was shaking his head in disbelief. They spent a minute in complete silence, mourning for the young girl.

Finally, Asten looked down at her body, and he caught his breath. "Guys," he began. "Guys, look at her face."

In more confusion now, Renidos lifted the girl's chin, so that they could get a better look at her. Her skin was ice cold, eliminating any slivers of hope that they had left. Asten was correct. As the light shone on that unfortunate girl's face, Erluc immediately recognized her. He recalled the handmaiden talking to the robed stranger in the palace two days prior. The stranger with the azure eyes.

Erluc glanced at his watch; there were five minutes till the feast started. He bit his lip. With all of his focus, he jumped up on top of two large trash containers. His watchful eyes scanned the area between his friends and the palace, looking for the garbed man. If the man had existed, he left no trace of it.

Renidos checked his watch as well, "I hate to say this, but we have to go."

Erluc turned to him, furious. "We can't let whoever did this just get away!" Asten put a hand on his shoulder, and Renidos nodded.

"Of course not," he agreed. "I'll inform a patrolman about this, and as soon as the banquet ends, we can come back here. But right now, you have to clear your mind—you have enough to worry about today."

Still frowning, Erluc slowly nodded, and the three of them ran back into the palace grounds. The guard on duty had barely given his salute, when they raced past him, leaving behind just a battered trail of dirt on the pavement.

"Where do you think it is?" asked Erluc.

Asten sighed. "In the banquet hall, where else?"

They rushed into the corridor, Renidos catching up to them halfway. As they entered the hall, they were greeted by several dignitaries, all of whom congratulated Erluc on his victory. He noticed the guards, solemnly standing under the chandeliers, probably armed to the teeth. As Asten and Renidos greeted the High King, Erluc looked around until he finally spotted Roxanna.

She was standing behind Elandas in a green, sleeveless gown, her hair flowing down below her shoulders. Suffice to say, she wasn't too hard to spot. When she saw him, her expression hardened, and she immediately turned away, talking to some minister or the other.

Just then, a hand clapped around Erluc's shoulder, and as he turned to see who it was, his heart jerked violently.

Oh, no.

"Ah, Lord Heroblade," welcomed the High King. "I'm glad to see you here." He turned, gesturing to Rose. "Have you met my daughter, Roxanna?"

Erluc felt a line of sweat forming on his brow. "Um—"

"We met a few days ago, on the day of the Steel Trial," offered Rose, and Erluc quickly nodded.

"Yes, that's right. I'm quite sorry that I didn't get to see the end," continued Elandas. "And our meeting yesterday was quite formal, I'm afraid. Before all this starts," he gestured at their surroundings, "I want to personally say thank you. You saved a lot of innocent lives that day, and you should know that Inthyl is in your debt."

"Thank you, your majesty," was all Erluc could fathom. Elandas nodded, and the three boys made their way past the entrance, towards the banquet table. As they took their seats, a handmaiden offered them water, which Erluc gratefully accepted.

They sat at the grand maplewood table, Elandas at the head, flanked by Roxanna and Verdanis, the royal advisor. Totally, about thirty faces were present around the table.

"Welcome," pronounced Elandas. "I understand that many of you are tired and hungry, so please take your seats." There was a large commotion in the hall before everyone finally settled. "For generations, the boundaries of the kingdom of Aenor have been regularly infringed, our peaceful towns looted and massacred."

Erluc grimaced. *Not the best way to start a feast.*

"The single cause of these atrocities is a heinous race of miscreants: the dark elves. For fear of starting a war akin to that of our ally, the dwarves, and the elves of the Archanios, we have hesitated to retaliate in kind and allowed such atrocities to continue." He rose. "But no longer."

Erluc didn't know if the room had gotten warmer, but he'd certainly felt it. A few eyes flickered in his direction, but he managed to keep his calm.

"Two days ago, the highlord of the dark elves, Uldarz, planned another daring attack—but this time, he struck directly at our heart. At Inthyl. He attempted to sabotage the prestigious Steel Trial, and in turn, tarnish the auspicious tournament." He paused, turning to where the Trinity was seated. "And he would've been successful, if not for a young warrior. Inthyl will forever be in your debt, Erluc Heroblade."

There was a round of applause from around the table— louder in some places than others—and Erluc nodded respectfully in acceptance. Roxanna's eyes met his for a moment, and he did his best to stay composed.

Once the applause had receded, Elandas continued. "Thanks to his heroic efforts, Uldarz—the greatest threat to the kingdom of Aenor—is now being held captive in our dungeons." He smiled. "Friends, this is a cause for celebration." He raised his goblet to the sky, and all around the table, people rose to their feet and mirrored the High King. "To a new age, an era of peace throughout our kingdom."

"To peace," everyone echoed around the table.

Renidos took a deep sip from his cider, and he leaned to Erluc's shoulder. "See? Nothing to worry about." Erluc nodded tentatively, taking a sip from his own goblet.

"Without further ado," boomed Elandas, "let the feast begin!"

As Erluc took his seat once more, a flicker appeared in the corner of his eye. His head whipped around instinctively, looking for its cause, without avail. Looking around, he saw everyone digging in, enjoying the feast. Asten looked up slightly, raising an eyebrow, and across the table, Erluc just shook his head and settled back in his seat.

Suddenly, a sharp cry escaped from the side of the table, and Renidos was instantly on his feet. Elandas had slumped back into his grand chair, his eyes closed. Asten seemed to have frozen in panic, but Erluc reacted quickly, leaping to the man's side and immediately checking for a pulse.

As he pressed his fingers to Elandas' neck, hunting desperately for the steady beat of life, his thumb brushed a piece of cold metal.

"Over here!" he called to Asten. "Now!" Asten seemed to snap out of his stupor and sprinted to him. Carefully extracting the shard of metal, he identified a black steel dart with jagged, offset flights.

Bloodsteel.

Looking up, he vaguely saw Renidos sprinting to the other end of the hall, and within seconds, Asten ran to join him. He got a glimpse of the hooded figure that they had pursued and clenched his fist. *Go! Catch that bastard.*

Erluc slammed a fist against the table in frustration and propped Elandas up, frantically checking the barely bleeding wound for shards of the poison metal, but thankfully finding none. However, the old king's pale, bloodless complexion was now tinted with a sickly-looking lavender hue.

Erluc snatched the tablecloth, creating much noise and causing many of the untouched delicacies to tumble to the ground. Swiftly, he tied it around the width of the old king's chest.

This should help keep pressure on the wound. He called for a handmaiden and had her summon a medic, a sliver of hope still alive in his heart, however futile. Erluc could hear Roxanna's sobs, as the councilmen restrained her from gazing upon her father's tarnished state. A figure appeared beside Erluc, causing him to jerk backward in surprise. The medic had arrived.

Better late than never.

She gestured at the cloth, and Erluc nodded. Its silky, white texture had faded to a fatal crimson. As Erluc untied the cloth, she analyzed the wound. The bleeding had stopped, to Erluc's great relief.

The medic, however, seemed to be rather fazed by the situation. After she'd performed many complicated procedures, Erluc finally caught a glimpse of the wound. The entire side of Elandas' sternum had become streaked with violet and his mouth was foaming.

Erluc grimaced and felt the wound, but as soon as he made contact, he pulled away, as if he had touched a smoldering iron. Roxanna had fought free of the Council members trying to restrain her and squatted alongside Erluc next to the medic, helpless. Erluc restricted the urge to look at her, trying his best to improve the situation.

His eyes burned as Asten stumbled into the hall, gasping and shaking his head. Erluc spat an oath and watched his friend race to Elandas' side. Though Asten was obviously drained and suffering from a painful stitch, Erluc couldn't stop himself from whispering sharply, "Heal him! Heal him now!"

Asten nodded quickly, his ring glowing, and he placed his hand flat against Elandas' burning forehead. But he had only just spoken the incantation when the glow of the ring faded away, and the Mage collapsed from exhaustion. And barely moments later, the healer let out a sharp cry, Roxanna rushed to her father's side, and Erluc's heart clenched with dread.

There he was, and there he stayed, lying at the king's feet, completely helpless to save him. And in that final moment, he let his silent tears fall. Ulmûr's last words roared through his mind. *And when she does… you will all burn.* The Traitor. She'd come for them.

Chapter 19

ONE LAST NIGHT

INTHYL, AENOR

Renidos

Though he'd been well and truly roused by the bloody rooster, Renidos was still reluctant to open his eyes. He blindly fumbled to his side in a futile attempt to reach his spear. Though his fingertips barely brushed the shaft, he couldn't get a grip.

What the hell is that thing even doing here?

With a groan, he rolled over, promptly falling out of the bed with a *thump*. Grumpily, he stood and snatched up the weapon, then headed over to get dressed. Slipping on a fresh tunic, he strolled out of the room. His mother was nowhere to be seen, so Renidos assumed that she was out on an errand run.

The moment he was out of the house, he hurled the javelin at the infernal chicken, skewering it through the neck and exacting his revenge. After retrieving it, he stepped into the streets, admiring the beauty of Inthyl. Though he had lived here his whole life, the dazzling city never ceased to amaze him.

On the day of the feast, three fortnights ago, all kinds of hell had broken out across Inthyl once they'd found out about Elandas' death. The Council of Nine—now Eight—had held an emergency meeting that very night, and it was decided that as the late High King's heir apparent, Princess Roxanna Laethon would ascend to the throne.

However, fifty days had remained until Rose turned seventeen—until she became eligible to be crowned Queen. And when she did, she would become the ninth Council member.

Now, only eight days remained.

Nearly the whole city—not to mention dozens of additional grief-stricken Andaerians—had attended Elandas' funeral the day after the feast. The late king, as was the tradition, had been cremated on an island in Comet Lake. The custom dictated that his pyre was to be lit by a flaming arrow fired with a sacred longbow by the king's heir from Heaven's Citadel, but as Roxanna had little to no skill with the bow, they had allowed another archer to shoot.

As a gesture of respect, the princess had had her father's long, keen-edged sword set into the marble behind his throne to honor his memory. Since the capture of Uldarz, though, there hadn't been any dark elf raids—at least until now. That was one less thing to worry about.

Passing through the marketplace, Renidos found his way to the butcher's shop to sell his rooster. He pocketed the four queltras from the transaction and headed for the courtyard, twirling his spear in his hand. Sure enough, both Erluc and Asten were asleep, Erluc in the hammock and Asten on the grass beside it. Their weapons were propped against the tree.

He shook his head and slipped the spear through the leather loop on the back of his tunic. Snatching Asten's waterskin from the ground, he emptied it over their faces.

Asten jumped up immediately, alert and ready, but Erluc groaned and twisted around in his hammock. "Not today, Ren. Please… just for today, let me sleep."

Renidos sighed and slashed at the hammock's cables, causing Erluc to fall to the ground. "I did. It's almost noon," Erluc stretched lazily, "and we're supposed to go meet Rose."

Erluc stared up into the sky for a while, as if he hadn't heard Renidos, but he eventually got to his feet. The princess of Aenor had been kept under twenty-four-hour guard by a troop of patrolmen for weeks on end, never allowed to leave the palace grounds. After what had happened with Elandas, the Council decided that they wouldn't be taking any chances with the princess. That is, until the perpetrator had been captured and brought to justice.

Erluc had tried to visit Rose and pay his condolences the day after the feast, but he'd been refused admittance into the royal chambers. So naturally, they were all surprised when a patrolman informed them that they were invited to the palace after today's court session.

"Here." Asten tossed Telaris to Erluc, and the Warrior caught the blade, sheathing it on his belt.

Renidos held up the four queltras he'd just made. "I got lunch today." They quickly dressed up, stopping for some food at the Fang, and made their way to the palace.

They traveled mostly in silence, before Renidos asked, "So, you know what you're going to say to her yet?"

Erluc shook his head. "Haven't the faintest."

They crossed into the palace grounds at around three-thirty and greeted a guard, who grunted back at them. Renidos sighed. After Elandas' passing, the Gardens of Inthyl had been closed off, and there were to be no unauthorized visitors—without exception. Renidos didn't know for how long it would remain that way, but he presumed that the situation wouldn't change until Rose's coronation.

He'd grown up coming here with his mother, playing with the other kids in Inthyl. It would be a terrible shame if kids today would never know what it was like. They crossed the main corridor, stopping in front of the set of double doors. They could faintly hear the court session in progress, so they decided to wait outside until it concluded.

Retreating to the Gardens, both Renidos and Asten relaxed on a bench. Erluc stretched out on the grass; the calm, natural vibe soothed his mind, cooling the blazing furnace within. Bored, Renidos raised his spear and swiftly planted it into the ground. Erluc sat up, perplexed.

Renidos sighed, "Give me a second."

He jogged about a dozen steps back, picking up several small rocks. Eyes widening, Asten raised his hands in surrender, a shocked look painted on his face. Renidos just raised an eyebrow, signaling him to get out of the way.

Selecting four of the stones, he hurled them one by one at the weapon. The first collided with a vase, shattering the delicate designs. Two glanced against the side of a tree, while the last met its mark, bouncing off of the north pole of the shaft, landing on a shard of the vase as it hit the ground. He pumped his fists in jubilance, shot down by a venomous glare from Erluc.

"My bad," he added, looking away, embarrassed.

"Next time, maybe don't use your weapon as target practice. Adúnareth help you if you cut the thing in half." Asten obviously wasn't amused either. His frown melted, and he added, "Nice throw, though."

Cracking up, the three of them took turns flinging the rocks at a thick oak tree, the projectiles flying around wildly, hitting everything else in sight.

Renidos' every throw landed right on target, while Asten's horribly inaccurate shots refused to travel anywhere near the thick bark. Erluc himself usually missed two times out of three, though one particularly sharp stone flew so deep into the tree that not even he was able to yank it out again.

Erluc absently looked towards the horizon. The orange of the afternoon sun reflected off of his dark hair, tinting it a milky brown. For the first time since the feast—besides his best efforts to hide it—sadness became abundant in his eyes. He bit the side of his bottom lip, diverting his attention, as well as the pain.

Suddenly, the doors flew open and several ministers, representatives, and the members of the Council of Nine exited the Royal Hall. The last to exit were Rose and Verdanis. Erluc let out a long breath as he saw her, and Renidos sighed. The princess turned and nodded once she saw them. She quickly bid Verdanis farewell and approached them.

She frowned once she saw the damage they had done, but she said nothing of it. "I apologize for keeping you waiting, Lord Turcaelion." Renidos only just managed to hold back a laugh. It'd been long since Erluc had decided that the Telmírin translation of his title would become official, but Renidos could never manage to keep a straight face when he heard it. The thought that one of Asten's jokes would actually make it so far was unbelievable.

Erluc raised an eyebrow, confused, before he realized that they couldn't talk freely in her palace. "Of course not, your highness. I had wanted to extend my deepest condolences to you upon the High King's passing." She nodded, her jaw clenched. Her carefree, independent attitude was completely washed away, revealing a distant, broken shell. "How come you asked to meet us?" asked Erluc.

"I was informed that you had visited the palace," she explained. "I wasn't taking visitors at that time, but I can meet with you now if you still want."

Nodding, Erluc tried continuing. "I'd prefer if we went somewhere more private, your highness."

Roxanna considered this. "Wait here," she directed. Disappearing into the palace halls, she returned in old clothes, the ones she wore when she was just *Rose*, carrying a few dust-brown cloaks over her shoulder. She tossed him the cloaks and led the way, pulling a hood over her own head. Erluc took a cloak and quickly fastened it, tucking it near his hip to conceal Telaris. He passed one to Asten, who struggled for quite some time until Renidos was forced to come to his aid.

As she approached the gate, a guard approached her. "Your highness, shall I summon a troop to accompany you into the city?"

"That won't be necessary, Jon," ensured the princess with a tone of authority. "I'm just stepping outside to get a little air. Besides, I have the Steel Champion to protect me in case anything goes wrong." The guard glanced towards Erluc, before nodding and stepping back.

They quickly exited the palace, skirting around the edges of the city to make their way back to the Fang. "How're you holding up?" asked Erluc softly. Both Asten and Renidos walked behind them, but they were close enough to hear the conversation.

"How do you think?" Rose tried her best to keep a straight face.

Erluc shook his head. "Look, I'm here for you. We—"

"If that's all you came to say, then you might as well go back," she cut him off again. "You want to help me?" she questioned, and he nodded without another thought. "Then help me understand. Give me a reason."

Erluc's face immediately fell, and he could feel her gaze on him. "You know I—"

"Have a secret," she finished. "And for some reason, this secret means that you can't be with me." She tucked a lock of hair behind her ear. "And I thought that I could accept that awful excuse, but apparently I can't." He met her determined gaze, unsure if he should speak. "With everything that's happened, I have no one left." She paused, shaking her head. "If I'm losing you too, don't you think I deserve to know why?"

Biting his tongue was all Erluc could do to prevent himself from revealing his secret. He hated that he was putting her through all of this, and she definitely deserved a real answer. But he knew that telling her like this wasn't the right thing to do. From behind them, Renidos and Asten were whispering among each other, wondering whether or not Erluc would. "You deserve to not have to deal with it," he told her.

Rose glanced back at them, and they both immediately turned away, pretending to not have been listening. "Do they know?" she asked suddenly, turning back to Erluc.

He tried his best not to look directly into her eyes, which gave her the confirmation she didn't want. "Rose, I swear it's not like that."

She clutched his arm, and he turned to meet her large hazel eyes. "I trust you," she confided. "Do you trust me?"

"Of course," he replied immediately.

"Then tell me."

Erluc's jaw tightened, and he placed a hand atop hers. "I can't," he whispered back. "I just can't. I'm sorry."

Her expression melted away, and she slowly let go of his arm. "Can't," she echoed softly, almost to herself. She broke away from his gaze, quickly wiping a tear with her cloak.

"What happened to us?" she asked, but Erluc didn't think that it was for him to answer. "I used to think that this was it—that this was what I wanted. And now... it can't be." She shook her head.

Erluc didn't trust himself to say anything, but he couldn't just watch her suffer alone. "If you ever need anything, I'm here for you. I always will be." Reaching forward, he wiped a tear from her face, her dimples reappearing for the smallest of moments.

"Hmm." She nodded absently. "Could you do something for me?"

"Anything."

"Pretend," was all she said. "Just for today, let's pretend that nothing happened." She met his gaze again with her strong, brown eyes. "Forget all of this, just for a few hours. And after tonight, we never have to see each other again."

He wasn't expecting that. "Never?"

"Never," she confirmed.

Erluc considered it for a moment, but deep down, he knew that he could never reject something like that. "Okay, I think I can do that. One last night."

"Alright," she said with a sense of finality. "We don't have much time, so let's get on with this." They entered the Fang, sitting together in a booth near the wall. Erluc ordered a whiskey, while Asten filled a mug with wine. Rose ordered a gallon of ale as well, to Erluc's great surprise. She'd never drunk a glass in her life without someone watching over her, and there was no way that Elandas would have approved of it. She drank nearly as ferociously as Erluc, draining two large tankards before the others cut her off. Renidos, however, still underage, settled down with a flagon of foaming coffee. Technically, Rose was underage as well, but she definitely didn't look like it. Thea had nothing to suspect.

They drank and drank, not noticing the lights in the corners of their eyes getting fuzzier. Erluc turned to the others in the middle of his second whiskey. "You sure you don't want to try some of this stuff?"

The boys declined, and Asten raised an eyebrow. "You ever had that before?"

"Not nearly as often as I would've wanted to."

Rose peered over, "It can't be that good." She took a long sip from Erluc's tankard, before grimacing and pushing it away, amid an uncomfortable laugh.

They'd lost all sobriety.

Asten smirked. "Rose," he began. "Did Erluc ever tell you about the 'Night of the Four Tumblers'?"

The princess raised an eyebrow, taking another sip from her glass. "Four tumblers? Pray, do tell."

"Do *not* tell." Erluc asserted, which Asten promptly and completely ignored.

"I think it was the seventy-first day of the last division, just before my sixteenth birthday. The neighbors had thrown a little party, and all of the youths in town went down to the River of Fire around midnight, where a boy named Arthur had set up a separate affair." He snorted. "Erluc and I went with two of our friends, Hayden and Celia."

Renidos let loose a small laugh. He remembered the last time Asten had recited this story, on the night of his and Erluc's birthday. It was certainly worth hearing again.

"And Erluc—being Erluc—picked a fight with a drunken Arthur the second we got there. Both of them ended up in the river, soaking wet." He smirked as he said the words, and Erluc winced as he drained the last of his whiskey. "Anyway, Celia, too, had gotten drunk that night and was making eyes at… guess who?"

"You?" tried Rose before her composure broke and she let slip a laugh.

Asten grimaced, shaking his head. "Haha," he mimicked sardonically. "It was Arthur. And Erluc did *not* appreciate it when he started making out with Celia."

"You more than me." Erluc snorted, turning to Rose. "Asten fancied her," he explained quickly, provoking a sharp kick from his friend. Then again, if Erluc were sober, he probably wouldn't have allowed this story to be told to Rose of all people.

"This again?" questioned Asten. "It was a long time ago. Leave me alone."

Rose rolled her eyes, pushing her glass forward for another refill. "Not that I'm not entertained, but what's so special about this story, anyway?"

"Give me a minute." Asten nodded. "So, then Juliana— Arthur's sister—arrived at the party." He turned to Erluc, who was trying his best to mask his smile.

Rose's expression flitted from embarrassment to envy and then to surprise. "Really? You don't strike me as that type of person," she remarked, eliciting howls from both Renidos and Asten.

Erluc started another glass, shivering as the cold liquid slithered down his throat. It was their last night together, so there was no point in hiding this. "That's why it works."

Shrugging, Rose took another sip. "Well, what did you tell her?"

Asten broke into another laugh, and Erluc cleared his throat. "I bet her that I could drink four tumblers of gin before she could and that I'd do whatever she wanted for the rest of the party if she won."

Rose shook her head, letting out a soft laugh. "And then what?"

"I lost—on purpose, of course," he continued. "But she was wasted by then, and we ended up kissing for a *long* time."

Renidos rolled his eyes. "I still think that there's no way that worked."

"I don't know what to tell you." Erluc shrugged, but his face betrayed a kind of subtle happiness. "Dated her for a while, maybe a fortnight, before Arthur came by and apologized to me."

Rose raised an eyebrow. "He asked you to dump his sister?"

"More like begged me not to."

Renidos snorted, shaking his head. *You're going to regret this tomorrow.* Calling for a refill on everyone's glasses, Erluc set one in front of each person. "What are you doing?" questioned Renidos.

"Just a game that we used to play back in Sering," he explained, and Asten suddenly broke into a grin before nodding.

"I guess I can start," he decided. "I have never… been questioned by patrolmen."

Rose and Renidos looked at one another, perplexed, before Erluc took one sip from his glass. "Oh," he realized, noticing their confusion, "If you *have* done what he said, then you take a sip. The first one to finish their glass wins."

"When did you get questioned by patrolmen?" questioned Renidos, mildly surprised. But then, it *was* Erluc—he had probably done something incredibly stupid.

"That's a story for another time." Shaking his head, Erluc turned to Rose. "Now, it's your turn."

"In that case," Rose nodded, taking a moment to think. "I have never cheated."

Raising an eyebrow, Asten extended his hand in protest. "That's a bit too vague. *Cheated* can mean a lot of things."

Rose flashed a sly grin. "Either way, your answer should stay the same. Unless, of course, there's something we should know…" Collectively, everyone turned to look at Erluc, who sighed in exasperation.

"Come on, guys, you know I don't cheat," he appealed. "You don't trust me?"

"No," started Rose. "We just—"

"Shut up and drink up," called Asten. His confidence had certainly been boosted by his drink, but Renidos was surprised, nonetheless. Erluc snorted, taking another sip from his glass. He turned back to Asten, who grudgingly took a sip from his glass as well.

"Really?" asked Renidos. "How did that happen?"

Asten groaned. "Believe me, it's not what you think," he assured them. "It was at a fair in Sering, and Erluc made me sneak behind the stage to sabotage an act. I only agreed to do it because I hated that guy too."

"It was hilarious, but still technically cheating." Erluc grinned. "Right, I'm next. I've never gone out with someone that wasn't extremely attractive."

Rose broke into a grin. "I'm flattered." She took a long sip from her glass, as did both Renidos and Asten. "Last year, I had to go to lunch with the son of the Duke of Fyrne," she explained. "The worst experience of my life."

"I hate pretty much everyone I've dated," Asten clarified, turning to Renidos. "All one of them." He grimaced, taking a big sip as well. His relationship with Lyra hadn't exactly ended on the best terms, but Renidos didn't know that Asten was still hung up on it.

"I wouldn't say *extremely* attractive, but I did go out this one girl back before I met you guys." The younger boy shrugged. "So, for my turn… I've never been in love with anyone before."

As he said the words, he could feel the entire room grow warmer. He saw Erluc's jaw clench, and Rose blushing crimson behind him. Asten closed his eyes, pushing his glass away before covering his face with both hands. "So *that* game's over," he mumbled through his fingers so that just Renidos could hear.

What? Renidos was slightly confused. *Was it something I said?*

Erluc's knuckles whitened almost imperceptibly. "I'm going to get some air," he muttered. He grabbed his glass, draining all the rest in a single shot, and placing it up-turned on the table as he made his way to the door. Rose took a small sip from her own glass before pushing it away from herself.

"Rose," Asten started. "He didn't mean it like that. He's just always been… sensitive about the subject."

She tried her best to not reply and turned to Thea, who fortunately didn't recognize her as the princess. "How much?"

"A daeral and… eight queltras," she calculated. "You lot almost emptied my stock."

Asten grinned, almost too happily. "Well, yeah, it's extra hard to get drunk with the blessing." Renidos' eyes widened, and he stomped down on Asten's foot, eliciting a sharp cry from the Mage.

"Blessing?" asked Rose.

"Oh, it's nothing really," Renidos spoke quickly, trying to be as convincing as he could. "That's just what Asten calls the wine that he drinks." It wasn't his best work, but it wasn't as if she'd remember anything that had happened tonight.

She shrugged, placing two daerals next to the glasses, turning to the other boys. "Come on." Renidos sighed in relief. That was close. Once Asten sobered up, he'd be sure to conk him on the head with his spear. They all hobbled outside, the twilight beams of the moon soothing their throbbing heads. A light drizzle clouded the night, and the friendly droplets hugged Renidos' skin as they impacted.

They caught up to Erluc, who was wiping a strand of wet hair out of his face in front of the inn. "Well… that night was certainly memorable," mumbled Roxanna, a cheerful but distant grin on her face.

Erluc nodded. "I almost forgot how much I enjoyed this," he agreed. He seemed to have recovered from the previous incident, and both Asten and Renidos looked at each other in agreement.

"I don't think you'll remember how much you enjoyed *this* either," returned Asten. Everyone cracked up at that, except for Renidos, who looked on smugly, tapping his foot.

I think I like drunk Asten more than regular Asten.

As they hobbled up a narrow street, leaning on each other for support, their minds were carefree, released from the bondage that life had enforced upon them. For the first time in a while, they were truly happy. It wasn't even the liquor talking; fate had wound them up to a twisted road, where they had definitely lost themselves.

The silence of the night hadn't been broken, but a shadow stealthily broke into the tranquil scene, unnoticed by the weary wanderers. High upon a rooftop, the shadow's intense, icy gaze tunneled through the air to behold the princess and her companions. The shadow leaped onto the next rooftop, now almost directly overhead them. It landed soundlessly, its cloak flowing freely with the gentle breeze of the night, rising to full height with cat-like grace. Looking up to the cloudy moon, the shadow closed its eyes, round sapphires, and kissed a soul goodbye.

One Last Night • **339**

Alert as he was, Renidos knew instinctively that something was wrong. A small *swit* in his left ear freed him from his confusion, a sense of urgency and defensiveness entering his walk. Suddenly, he turned around, his anticipation proven true. In the corner of his eye, a sharp projectile screamed down towards them, poisoning the air around it.

He swiftly kicked Asten to the ground with his right leg, who groaned as he rolled out of harm's way. Yet in a split second, he registered that the piece of death was aimed at Erluc and that there wasn't time to yell, no time to knock it out of the air.

In an instant, he charged at the Warrior, the shard slowing down as it neared his throat, Asten's recovery looking as though he were trying to get up through honey. The dimly lit street bent and warped around him as it always did, and they collided in an instant, time returning to normal, leaving both of them groaning in the dust. The force of the impact caused Erluc to slide a few feet, leaving friction scars on his arms and hip.

Just then, a subtle moan escaped from behind them. Upon the rooftop, the shadow grimaced, melting into the darkness. With his lightning reflexes, Renidos leaped to his feet and whirled around to see Rose collapse. Moments later, Erluc stood and sprinted to their side, while Asten regained his balance and dashed over as Renidos identified the black dart, akin to the one that had claimed Elandas' life, lodged in her shoulder.

Erluc opened his mouth, presumably to yell at Renidos, but he was cut off by Roxanna trying to speak.

"E… Erluc," she whispered, her entire body shaking. Erluc dropped on his knees, anger, regret, and great worry burning in his eyes. He took her frail form into his hands, carefully extracting the projectile. His hands met the wound, veins of crimson streaking her once-fair skin.

"Rose... Rose, you're okay. You're okay," he pleaded helplessly. "Stay with me. You're okay." A torrent of tears flowed down his cheeks, each one stinging as it reached his bloody hands. But that didn't matter. "Hey, just stay with me... stay..."

The heavens cried, and the drizzle escalated into a cascade of blue, thundering down all around them.

"Not again... please," he begged. "Not...No..." Erluc rested his head upon her chest, hiding his face from the rest of the cruel world, sorrow ushering him towards the precipice that marked the boundary of sanity. The twilight rays grayed in grief as the last of House Laethon's eyes finally closed.

And all became still.

Chapter 20

GUILTY OF POWER

INTHYL, AENOR

Erluc

"She's alive."

Erluc glanced at Asten, who stood wiping the mud off of his soaking leggings. He felt as though he could hug him right now, but he suppressed the urge. The worry squeezing his chest temporarily subsided.

"How can you be sure?"

"Her neck. There's a pulse, but it's painfully slow. Almost as though she were in a deep sleep." Asten stepped back, perplexed. "I don't know for sure. You should wait for the healers."

"Renidos should be back soon." Erluc was too distracted, too distressed to yell at Asten or make a sarcastic remark. "How long will she be like this?"

"I'm sorry. I've got no idea." Asten's eyes scrambled to abandon the gaze he was holding, looking anywhere but at his friend.

Erluc studied Rose's face, which had become deathly pale even compared to Asten's. Her breathing was shallow, yet she seemed to inhale no faster than he. His blood boiled in his veins. "First Elandas and now Rose? If I ever find the person doing this, I swear I'll rip their throat out with my bare hands," he spat forcefully.

Not only that, but if Roxanna died, then the line of Eltar would have finally failed. Erluc knew as well as anyone that it was said that the fate of the Andaerians was bound to the bloodline of their kings—if Eltar's last descendant fell, so would Aenor. Asten, he was sure, didn't believe a word of it, and neither did he, but even so, the thought left him feeling even darker than before.

A young woman in a creamy skirt approached the alley, tailed by Renidos. With a respectful curtsy to Erluc and the words, "Lord Turcaelion," she swiftly made her way to the princess and examined her gently. With one look at the wound, she crushed several herbs into a poultice and bandaged the cut.

Looking up, she asked them, "Is it infected?"

Erluc had no idea, but Asten responded, "I don't think so. But we have the poison to worry about as well. Though the dart was tipped with bloodsteel, it was clearly crafted differently, probably a custom-make." All the time in the library and the forge had eventually paid off, after all.

The healer nodded. "If it were bloodsteel in the usual sense, the princess would be dead by now. Thank the Falcon that it is not so."

If only that had been the case—Asten could have healed her in seconds.

Reaching into a pocket of his tunic, Erluc produced the dart and turned to Asten. "Take this to the weaponmaster and see what he can make of it."

"I could show it to Galimin as well tomorrow," Asten offered. "He should have something to say about it."

Erluc considered this for a moment and nodded. "Do as you will, but *do not* lose it." His statement ended with an edge of poison and ferocity enough to derail the sternest of men. With sound assurance, Asten sprinted away in search of the weaponmaster.

Two more healers arrived shortly, just as the one attending Roxanna grimaced faintly. "Lord Turcaelion, the good news is that whatever poison was in her blood dissolved some time ago. Unfortunately, it may have affected her brain."

Her brain? Erluc almost fainted in shock. "What…" he began uncertainly.

The healer quickly directed her companions to fetch several things. "It means that she is alive, but only just. From what I could tell by examining the blood left on the dart, the venom slows down her body processes to a bare minimum. This means that she could live virtually indefinitely in this state, as long as no disease takes her. We will see to that."

Erluc grimaced. *You'd better.*

A second healer turned to him with a gentle smile. "At least for tonight, we should take the princess to the Royal Infirmary. We shall inform you of any progress in her highness' condition by morning."

Although the last thing he wanted to do was to leave Rose's side, he nodded, soaking, exhausted, and grudgingly returned to the Fang. The bed seemed strangely cold, unwelcoming as ever. Erluc fought tears as his head hit the pillow. He didn't even bother changing clothes. And though he had been thoroughly completely drained by the events of the day, he couldn't sleep till well after midnight.

Even his dreams were fitful and troubling. He was in the courtyard with Rose, long before the events of the Steel Trial. The moonlight had been a clear white that night, and he distinctly remembered a soft breeze blowing through his hair. But everything else was a blur, and he'd completely lost himself in her deep, brown eyes. As usual, her lips tasted like mint, and he sighed contentedly as he sat up against the trunk of the thick tree, her hand clasped in his.

Suddenly the moonlight became obscured by thick clouds, and his vision turned completely black. He felt the warmth from his hand fade away as she was forced from his grasp. "*You do not deserve her love,*" growled a deep, powerful voice, which he immediately recognized as Atanûkhor. "*You failed her.*" Just then, Erluc managed to rouse himself with a supreme effort, heavily breathing as he rested up against the headboard.

I'm sorry, Rose. I'm so sorry. He silently swore to himself, *You... you'll be okay.*

"I promise," he swore, this time aloud. "Even if I have to kill Atanûkhor himself to do it, I will find a cure." His eyes glinted. "And I won't ever fail you again."

Slowly lifting himself out of bed, he changed into a fresh set of clothes. Elandas' killer and Rose's attacker, whoever she was, had to be dealt with. And he would do it himself. He didn't care who it was—anyone who dared to commit such heinous acts didn't deserve to live.

So, he decided he was going after the attacker. Today. No matter what.

Just as he was about to leave, he glanced at the desk beside the bed. Asten had been back here, and he'd left a piece of folded parchment. Erluc carefully unfurled the message, squinting as he read through it.

"*Didn't want to wake you. Summoned to the palace by the Council. They didn't tell me why, maybe something to do with Rose. Should be back before lunch. Please don't do anything rash until then.*"

Erluc raised an eyebrow. What would the Council want to talk to Asten about? Either way, he was not being left out of this. Tucking Telaris into his belt, he dashed to the town center and knocked on the door of the fourth house in the second avenue.

"Yes?" came a voice, and a woman opened the door. "Oh, good morning, Erluc. Haven't seen you in a while."

Erluc nodded. "It's nice to see you, Isabelle. Is Renidos home?" Five minutes later, Renidos was striding with purpose beside the Warrior, and they passed through the gates of the palace.

"Where can I find the Council?" Erluc asked urgently as a handmaiden passed them.

"The Council of Nine are in the Royal Hall, Lord Heroblade," she replied. They thanked her, making their way to the grand set of double doors yet again. A pair of guards stood ready, blocking their way.

"Let us through," demanded Erluc. "I'll only ask once."

The guard didn't move. "Nobody is allowed inside while the meeting is in session." Erluc growled, ripping Telaris out of his sheath, quickly disarming the guard and jabbing at his temple with the butt of the blade. As the other guard jumped up to block his way, Renidos kicked him in the chest, sending him flying against a wall. After hitting the concrete with a *crunch*, the unsuspecting man dropped to the ground, unconscious.

Erluc pushed the doors open, keeping Telaris handy. If things went rough, he might still need it.

"But we don't have the authority to m—" Verdanis was in the middle of a sentence when they burst into the hall. The eight councilmen were sitting around a wooden table at the side of the court, deep in conversation. Asten stood a few feet away, hands folded behind his back.

Therglas immediately stood, "You! What is the meaning of this?"

346 • The Promise of the Warrior

Erluc gritted his teeth. "Councilmen." He bowed stiffly, trying to keep the scowl off of his face. "It seems that none of you thought to invite me to this meeting. And why would you? It's not as if I was present *during the attack*."

The general leered at him. "Guards!" he called. There was an awkward silence before Erluc answered.

"As I was saying," he continued, indicating for the general to sit.

Therglas glared at him, and all the councilmen around him looked at Erluc, stunned. The general snarled, and Erluc tightened his grip around Telaris, spinning it around in his hand.

"Wait!" Asten interrupted. Everyone turned to look at him, and he continued. "Both of them were present as well, weren't they? Don't you think they should be allowed to give their own version of events?"

The general shook his head. "A schoolboy and a Steel Champion? We can't convict either of them without starting a rebellion!"

"Convict?" asked Renidos, turning to Asten. "Is this a hearing?"

"This is a meeting," cut in Cephine, another Council member. "At the end of which we will identify the culprit and give him the due punishment."

"What?" challenged Erluc incredulously.

"Oh, look around you, boy," snapped Therglas, exasperated. "If you truly were a witness, then you saw what happened to the princess. Yes, she's still alive, but the last descendant of Eltar is *gone*. Comatose."

Erluc's grip around Telaris tightened so much so that his knuckles whitened.

"And any assault on the family of Eltar is an assault on all of Aenor, all men," finished Cephine. "We must find the perpetrator and put him to justice." Her tone steeled as she ended.

"So, unless you have something new to say, I suggest you leave before I throw you in a cell." Therglas showed no sign of calming.

Renidos scowled. "Then maybe you ought to let us speak."

"Therglas," the voice of Tarsidan, the loremaster, rang out through the hall. "They were both witnesses at the scene of the attack, and it would be wise to hear what they have to say." Murmurs of agreement escaped around the gathering, and Therglas finally gave up, sitting back down. It seemed that he was slightly more put off by his loss at the Steel Trial than he let on.

"Very well," conceded the general. "You can start by telling us why the princess was outside the palace grounds without her guards, and what you were doing with her."

Erluc grimaced. "We've been friends for a while, and I had wanted to convey my condolences upon the passing of Elandas. As you know, she'd been confined to the palace until recently, and I only receieved an invitation to visit her two days ago. I didn't think she'd be in danger while she was with us, and we weren't expecting to stay out so late."

"What about the attacker?" Therglas nodded. "You're saying it's just a coincidence that you were also present when Elandas was attacked with a bloodsteel dart?"

A spark ignited in Erluc's eyes. "What are you trying to say?"

"Now, Lord Heroblade," continued Tarsidan, "Nobody is making any accusations just yet. But unless you have any information that can help this investigation, it would be best for you to leave."

Erluc's jaw tightened. He didn't have anything else to say, but he couldn't bring himself to concede and simply walk away. He had to do something.

Luckily for him, Asten seemed to have noticed his hesitation. "Speaking of the dart," he began, gesturing toward the flechette that lay on the grand oak table in front of him, "after consulting with the weaponsmaster and a blacksmith, we have traced this to a remote mountain in the Grônalz range, far to the north, the very edge of charted Eärnendor." Several murmurs appeared throughout the room. "The Vale of Shadows," continued Asten, "was never the home of the dark elves—it was simply a forward outpost, for reasons unknown to us. They have always been settled in the Grônalz Mountains for the whole of recorded history—thousands of years before Eltar ever set sail from Andaerion."

Therglas put up a hand. "I'm sorry, this is all very helpful, but if the intruders do not intend to contribute, perhaps we should consider closing the doors to this conference once more?"

Erluc gritted his teeth, but he knew that Therglas was right. He'd charged in here without even the seeds of a plan, and now he'd be humiliated in front of the Council. He could feel an urge to back away from the table, to run away, but he found the strength to stand still. "On the contrary, councilman," responded Asten. "Erluc has devoted every moment of his time since Roxanna's incident to finding her attacker. In fact, he was the one that retrieved a map to the mountain." He turned to Erluc. "You brought the map, didn't you?"

Erluc was lost. "What?" he muttered.

"The map," enunciated Asten pointedly, flicking his eyes towards Erluc's pack. Quickly understanding, Erluc rummaged through his bag until he found the map that he had gotten from the Ancient. He whispered the name of the mountain range, and an image formed, revealing the mysterious sierra. A peak at the southernmost tip of the range—'Bone Mountain' it was called—was depicted alongside a small skull. Surprised, Erluc took this as insurance, laying the map flat onto the table. *That must be where the assailant was based.*

It seemed that they had piqued the interest of the Council, and even Therglas looked impressed with their foresight. Stealing a glance at Asten, their eyes met for a moment, and Erluc could tell that his gratitude had been conveyed.

"It seems you have the floor," conceded Therglas.

Taking a deep breath, Erluc announced, "We have to go there and bring this perpetrator back," he paused, and then softly added, "dead or alive. I can lead the expedition."

Therglas seemed to regain his composure and stood, fixing Erluc with a stern look. "You will lead an expedition?" He wasn't having it. "You have proven yourself a decent fighter, but you have no experience as a leader and wouldn't last a second in the real world." He turned around, looking at his fellow councilmen. "Assuming your information is even correct, a mission as important as this should be trusted to someone who could actually do justice to the princess."

"Someone like you?" spoke out Asten, rising as well.

"Why not?" challenged Therglas. "As General of the Twilight Legion, I am the most respected warrior in Aenor. It is under *my* leadership that the Legion drove the cowering elves out of the Kre'nagan and southern plains, back into their forest. I could storm that mountain, *effortlessly*, and bring back the fiend in less than a week."

"And leave Aenor undefended?" Erluc interrupted. "You would send your army to fight a needless, avoidable war and sentence hundreds of honest troops to death, when I am offering do the same task myself?"

"You w—"

Erluc didn't let him intrude. "And for what? Just so you can prove to me here that you have more power than I do?" He looked around the circle, and the councilmen shied away from his gaze.

Tarsidan stood, gesturing to the map. "I do not know how many of you know of this place, but Bone Mountain is no mere hill. It is home to the fortress of Ghâzash-Byrrn, which was the main staging point for the attacks of Ulraz, the first Blade of Atanûkhor." The rest of the Council rolled their eyes; it seemed that they didn't believe in what the loremaster was conveying. "Now is not the time for your tales of the supernatural, Tarsidan," remarked Therglas, and it was obvious that many others agreed.

"Supernatural?" questioned Asten, glancing at Erluc exasperatedly. "I'm afraid you're mistaken, Councilman. Ulraz was, and more importantly, Uldarz is, the Blade of Atanûkhor—he almost killed Erluc and me during the Steel Trial." It was obvious that Asten was trying to reveal as little about the blessing as he could, but they were venturing into dangerous territory.

Therglas rolled his eyes. "I suppose we should take your word for it?"

Asten raised an eyebrow in defiance. "If you don't believe us, you can go ask Uldarz himself. I'm sure he'd be delighted to have a visitor after all this time in the dungeons. Maybe he'd even give you a demonstration of his power."

"That is a discussion for another time." Tarsidan put up his hand. "Regardless, the fortress is sure to be heavily guarded. We can also take this to mean that whoever is responsible for this has the support of the dark elves."

"We knew that when we saw that the dart was of bloodsteel," pointed out Asten. "The secrets of its forging are not bandied about to all.""It is a confirmation," retorted Tarsidan, looking mildly offended. "My point is that no one should go alone to this place. It is a deathtrap, especially for one man.""I would never allow another to ride alongside me if it meant he was riding to his death," retaliated Erluc. "Few are experienced enough for an expedition so arduous, and fewer possess the expertise required to survive."

"Neither do you," pointed out Verdanis, "Though you are a masterful swordsman, there are many here with far more experience than you."

True, but I'm the Warrior. "Yet no one in the city defeated Uldarz," he shot back instead, nettled. "Where was their experience then?" Therglas glowered at him but remained silent.

"Most of the soldiers in the Legion have been training their whole lives. Do you truly think that you can face up to that with your limited experience?"

Erluc didn't reply. Instead, Asten took over. "So, you would send the Legion instead? A force strong enough to defend Aenor for centuries, against any kind of attack—you would endanger that to capture one man?"

Woman. But Erluc wasn't about to interrupt him. There was a silence around the room, and no one knew how to respond. Asten was right.

Asten shifted in his seat as though to rise before being signaled otherwise by a sharp glance from Erluc. None of the Council seemed to have noticed. Arryth, the treasurer and a man of few words, bowed his head. "Who is in agreement?"

Nobody moved, before Tarsidan tentatively raised his hand, followed by Verdanis. Arryth didn't look overjoyed about the plan either, but the fact that he was putting up his hand indicated his approval, however faint. One other Council member seemed to be in agreement, and Erluc recognized him as the weaponsmaster.

Therglas seemed firmly set in his decision, as did Cephine and another member. Euracis, the record-keeper, looked like he wanted to raise his hand, but he was not going to go against Therglas.

Four against four.

Just then, the doors opened once more, and another figure entered the Royal Hall. Erluc turned around, and he gasped.

The figure approached the table, and not a soul protested. "The boy is right," announced the man. "To make up for his lack of experience, I offer my own, and I propose to accompany Lord Heroblade. Together," he stopped to nod at Erluc, "we are more than capable of completing this quest. And on the off chance that we fail, you can do as you will."

"Alisthír," hissed Therglas. "I suppose that anyone can just stroll into the Royal Hall now."

If there was anyone whom the general despised more than Erluc, it was the alchemist. But on the other hand, if there was anyone whom Euracis admired more than Therglas, it was Alisthír. Actually, everyone else in the room seemed awed by his presence.

"Sir—" began Euracis.

"I know all about the situation," affirmed Alisthír. "Now you need to consider a solution."

"We have," Therglas started.

"Have you?" asked Alisthír. "You think it's wise to send the Twilight Legion—the army that Elandas had subdued for a score of years—to attack the Ghâzash-Byrrn? You of all people should know how long the High King had been trying to put off a war with the dark elves, and instead of honoring his memory, you would throw away his efforts?" He stopped, looking straight at the general. "Perhaps you'll reconsider your solution." Stressing each word, he looked around the circle. "Everyone in agreement?"

This time, seven hands flew up into the air, leaving Therglas staring at Alisthír in disgust. The alchemist nodded, and he clasped Erluc's shoulder.

"Very well." Tarsidan announced, "You shall accompany Lord Heroblade. Together, you shall embark on an expedition tomorrow, to capture Princess Roxanna's attacker and bring him to justice. May your success restore the honor of House Laethon and Aenor."

With that, the Council dispersed, everyone in a hurry to broadcast the news, while the Trinity took Alisthír back to the courtyard.

"What happened?" he asked, turning to Alisthír. "How come you're back?"

The alchemist shrugged. "When I heard that Elandas had been killed, I had to talk to you. Now that Roxanna, too, is incapacitated, the situation has become worse than I ever could have imagined." He turned to Erluc. "With you gone, Inthyl's going to need me more than ever."

Renidos raised an eyebrow. "What do you mean?" He paused. "Aren't you going with him?"

Alisthír shook his head. "I'm afraid not—those were simply empty words to steer those fools towards making a decision." He shook his head. "This is undoubtedly the work of the Traitor—the one that Ulmûr spoke of. Under no circumstances can we allow Inthyl to fall to her. In the event of an attack, you two will need all the help you can get."

"You're right." Erluc nodded, allowing himself a wry smile. "Thank you... for coming back." Alisthír grimly nodded, but Renidos wasn't done.

"Do you even have a plan yet?" he asked.

Erluc grimaced. "I know I'm leaving tomorrow, and I have Skyblaze," he started. "I'll fly through the Manos—it's the fastest route—and then I'll search all of Ghâzash-Byrrn for the Traitor, starting with Bone Mountain."

Asten raised an eyebrow. "That's it?"

"Pretty solid, huh?"

Renidos sighed. "Are you sure you want to go alone?" he asked again. "If you get into any trouble, we won't be around to save you," he reminded.

"Yes, I'm sure," confirmed Erluc. "And stop worrying about me. I need you two to be alert. If there is *any* sign of the Traitor—"

"We know," affirmed Asten. "We'll take care of it." Erluc nodded before taking his leave. He went up to the inn, starting to gather his provisions.

It was evident that Roxanna's incapacitation had taken a visible toll on all of Inthyl, most of all, Erluc. There was a settled sadness in his eyes that radiated a gripping sense of permanence. He looked worn, almost as if he had already passed his prime at seventeen, with an unspoken ruthlessness in his demeanor that was destined to remain there forever. Of course, Renidos didn't want that for his friend, but he didn't know what he could do to help.

In hope for the princess' recovery, the entire city had left flowers at Heaven's Citadel, a silent prayer for Adúnareth's aid.

The remaining three of them dined together, before Alisthír took his leave as well, promising that he would stay in the city. Around four, Asten left to help Erluc, and

Renidos went home to train. The sun was already asleep
when Renidos had finished. Looking around the room, there
wasn't a single artifact that didn't have a hole ripped into
it. Target practice was always exhausting, not to mention
extremely destructive. Drowning his sweat-soaked face into
a barrage of soft towels, he sighed in relaxation.

He hurled his spear at the wall, dust rising as it sank a
foot into the concrete. When he yanked it out, cracks spread
from the hole where it had entered. Collapsing into his cot,
he pulled the blanket over him. His mother was going to
have his head. With a satisfied grin, he slowly dozed off.

Suddenly, he was surrounded by a vast expanse of water.
Clawing his way up, he felt himself depart the particles
of frosty liquid, dragged by invisible strings. His feet now
rested upon the surface of the pool, his body hovering over
it. Around him, not a soul was present, not a tree in sight,
not a ripple in the water. The constellation of the Swan
looked down accusingly at him from above, the moon's
glare beating down against the water.

Comet Lake. He knew the site instantly.

He frowned. What could he be doing here? He hadn't
visited Comet Lake for years, definitely not since he'd
received his powers. An immense wave crashed into him,
pushing him backwards, but leaving him surprisingly dry.
In its wake, a deep hollow drilled into the lake, not a drop
rushing to fill the gap. Renidos tried to get closer to see
what was happening, but his feet just wouldn't move. It was
as if iron ropes were bound around his calves, constricting
all movement. No amount of struggle would set him free.

A large figure abruptly emerged from the basin, and
Renidos' heart stopped abruptly. The figure was shrouded
in darkness, its features completely unidentifiable. Renidos
watched as the man-thing looked around the lake as if it was

expecting a visitor. He called out, trying to get its attention, but no sound escaped his mouth. He waved his arms around, but it was as if he was invisible to the creature. Its gaze passed his own, and it froze. It turned to look directly into Renidos' eyes, and a single word reverberated through his mind.

Come.

A piece of the wall broke off and fell on his nose, causing him to cough violently, releasing him from his slumber. He sat up, breathing heavily. *It was only a dream. The creature and the lake.* He drew the curtains of his room and sighed. It was still night.

Suddenly, he faintly heard a knock on his front door. Raising an eyebrow, he frowned. Who could possibly be visiting so late? *If this is Erluc or Asten, I swear I'll tie them to trees.* Throwing on a fresh cloak, he went downstairs to investigate. He pulled the door open, and the last thing he felt that night was the cold apathy of steel against his skin.

Chapter 21

The Two Traitors

Inthyl, Aenor

Erluc

Erluc's cloak flapped wildly as he sprinted to the royal stables, ducking behind pillar after pillar to avoid the guards. No one save the Council, Alisthír, and the Trinity knew that he would be leaving.

He had left by the back of the palace, passing the servants' quarters, exiting straight into the building with the small skylight where the royal horses were kept. Glancing at the scroll that he had taken from the Ancient's pack so many divisions ago, he noted that the journey would almost be a straight flight due north. He quickly made his way to Skyblaze and untied the looping knot holding him to the fence. In an instant, he was on the pegasus' back and flying out of the structure.

Thankfully, the clouds were low and covering the moon, so Erluc was able to conceal himself without too much difficulty. Now that he was away from the blazing lamps of the city, he could see the stars in all their glory. He knew only a few constellations—the Falcon, the Swan, the Pegasus— and spent roughly half an hour trying to identify them. Maybe he had some sort of aptitude for creatures of the sky.

The moon was already on its voyage downward when the lush vegetation of the Aenor Peninsula began to fade to a dusty wasteland. He knew this terrain well, though he was far from his original home in Sering. He shivered, wrapping his cloak tighter around himself, and leaned down to tighten the leg straps. Eight hundred feet in the air, he knew it would be less than fortunate if he slipped.

By the time the sun came up, Skyblaze had landed in an oasis in the Manos Desert, and Erluc was setting up camp under a flowing date tree. Just that previous night, both he and Asten had snuck down to the stables and smuggled supplies into the pegasus' saddlebags. Now it came in handy as Erluc bit into an apple, letting the cool juice flood his mouth, at odds with the glaring sun.

Renidos had seemed incredibly distracted before Erluc had left, but he was probably just worried about Rose like the rest of them. Still, it was strangely uncharacteristic of Renidos to be so downbeat. What was worse was that he had refused to talk about it and denied anything different about his behavior. Asten, on the other hand, was openly averse to the idea of Erluc traveling to Bone Mountain alone, but nobody gave him much attention—he worried far more than was good for him. The truth was that Erluc didn't know if this lead had any substance to it, but he couldn't ignore a chance to avenge Rose.

Once Erluc was finished, he had Skyblaze lower him near to the palm until he reached the graceful leaves and large branches. With a hand on the trunk for support, he drew Telaris and slashed down a cluster of dates. They landed on the sandy ground next to his pack, but Erluc didn't think that the runestones would mind the disturbance. When he got down, Skyblaze drifted off to a weary slumber, and Erluc enjoyed the dried fruit. Taking a hint from the pegasus, he eventually dozed off, propped against the large tree.

For the next two days, he was out of commission while the sun shone, but when it went down, it wasn't long before the silhouette of a great winged horse could be seen against the moon. Finally, as well as he could make out with his enhanced vision, the fine sand gradually began to give way to rough, gray-black gravel. The clear sky thickened to a dark fog, obscuring the barely visible crags in the distance. Rowan trees became steadily more frequent on the progressively hillier terrain.

Though the sun hadn't yet come up, the sky was brightening, and Erluc assumed that day would break in half an hour at the most. The trees had already begun to vanish from the tops of the hills, but no stone or snow was visible except for the towering summit he was approaching. He checked his map again to confirm. There it was—the southernmost peak of the Grônalz—Bone Mountain. Now that he was closer, Erluc could see the fortress built into the side of the mountain out of the same strange, black stone as the rest of the range.

The person who had killed Elandas, injured Rose, and mutilated that young handmaiden—he would find that monster here. Finally, he'd get justice. Blood rushed to his muscles, tensed for a fight.

Diving into the cover of the shadows, he touched Skyblaze down underneath a small overhang below the fortress. A cave yawned out of the mountain, and Erluc dismounted, tethered his pegasus behind some rocks, then lit a torch and stepped into the cavern. Pushing the sleeves of the cloak back to his elbows, he unsheathed Telaris with his free hand.

It was his first time inside a cave, which would have been scary enough, not counting the fact that the stone was as black as night. Erluc wasn't exactly thrilled about the darkness, either. He walked slowly, constantly expecting to be ambushed, hoping that this tunnel opened out into a system that might lead up to the fortress—Ghâzash-Byrrn.

He pulled out his map and opened it with his free hand, desperately thinking, *Ghâzash-Byrrn, show me the way to Ghâzash-Byrrn.* He examined it by the torchlight, but apparently, the map's magic didn't extend to underground caverns.

Frustrated, Erluc rolled up the scroll and continued, his left hand gripping the torch, his right tensed on the hilt of Telaris. In the guttering flame, the shadows of the rocks appeared to be dancing, making it seem as though there was someone there.

Suddenly, Erluc whirled around, summoning a dark gauntlet as a spear whizzed past him. Extending Telaris, he released a column of fire, illuminating his attacker. The fiend tried to dodge the flames, rolling off to the side of the cavern before Erluc sent a shard of ice through his stomach.

Breathing heavily, he approached his foe. The man was clad in dark clothing, and his lifeless eyes were a solid fuchsia. *Dark elf.* At least this meant he was going the right direction. Erluc advanced with caution, allowing his gauntlet to dissolve. If there were more elves, he'd need to be as agile as possible.

The faint sound of weeping interrupted his thoughts. He strained his ears, trying to listen more intently—yes, there was the sound of a young girl crying. He gritted his teeth, turning the corner more quickly, to find a maiden of about twelve chained to the ground. Behind her, there was a staircase shrouded in darkness, leading upwards—probably into the fortress. *Has she been taken prisoner? Is she being held for ransom?*

The young girl was sniffling into her tattered, blue dress, but when she saw Erluc, sword drawn, her eyes widened in fear. Before she could cry out, he hastily put a finger to his lips and whispered, "Hey, hey, it's okay," he comforted her. "My name's Erluc. I'm going to help you get out of here."

He quickly stepped up to the girl and swung his sword at the fetters.

CLANG.

So much for the element of surprise.

He helped the maiden adjust the cuffs so that they touched the sleeves of her dress instead of her skin, then asked tentatively, "Okay, now could you do something for me?" She looked slightly shaken but nodded. "Just close your eyes," he told her.

The girl squeezed her eyes shut, all too gladly, and Erluc exhaled deeply. He set down his torch, ignited Telaris, and held the blade to the chain where it met the metal loop in the wall. He focused, willing the sword to heat up even more, and the dark steel chain began to glow red hot, snapping almost immediately. He quickly cooled the chain using water from his waterskin before it could touch the girl and helped her stand.

"I would free your hands too, but the fire might burn you. We'll have to get you out of here before we do anything. I know an oasis in the Manos Desert where we can rest for a bit. Understand?" The maiden nodded fearfully. Erluc knew that he was wasting time, but he couldn't play with the life of this girl. Maybe he could leave her in the care of the Guardians until he was finished here and then take her back to her family.

He stepped away from the wall, but the girl didn't move. Instead, she curled her hands around her knees, shaking her head in fear.

Sheathing Telaris, he bent down so that he could talk to her. "Hey, it's going to be okay," he assured. "I promise." Just as he said the words, he bit his tongue.

Still, his words seemed to have some effect on the girl, who would now at least look up to face him. "You promise?"

Exhaling deeply, he gave her a slight nod of assurance. "What's your name?"

The girl sniffled, pulling her hair from her face. "Brooke," she whispered weakly.

Nodding, Erluc helped her to her feet. "Don't worry, Brooke. You're going to make it out of here safe and sound."

Leading the way, he guided the girl through to the entrance of the cave, careful to avoid the corpse of his previous attacker. But as they passed that same area, he noticed that the corpse had vanished. As far as Erluc could tell, dead people didn't just get up and walk away. *There's someone else here.*

Just then, there was a flicker in the corner of his eye, and Brooke collapsed to the floor. Instinctively, he drew Telaris, crouching down protectively next to her. His fingers came in contact with her cold skin, and he flinched in defeat. A small dart was barely visible, protruding from the side of her neck.

"I wouldn't bother if I were you," came a voice.

Looking up, Erluc was face-to-face with a young woman, clearly in her early twenties, with pale skin that resembled Asten's and piercing ice-blue eyes. He froze. He'd seen those eyes before. His thought went back to the maiden he'd noticed with his friends that day so long ago… the day Elandas was murdered.

The woman sighed exasperatedly. "There's no reason to be so dejected. That poor thing would have suffered a far worse death in here." She pointed behind her. "Or even out there."

"Who are you?" he demanded.

The young woman smiled slightly. "Really? Don't recognize me?" The accent was definitely Andaeric, but one that didn't speak the language frequently enough to call it their own.

Was he supposed to? Erluc said nothing.

"Ah, well. No one would have mentioned me, I don't think. Especially not those—what do you call them? Guardians? They even refuse to say my name, believe it or not. Being banished does tarnish one's reputation, does it not?"

"You," Erluc's voice rang with accusation. "The Traitor, who took Inro Forthel?"

"Traitor?" The maiden's expression flickered angrily for a moment. "There's no one alive left for me to betray." She stole a glance at the fallen girl, and Erluc gritted his teeth.

"Ulmûr warned us about you."

The woman's smug facade broke for a second, and he could see the annoyance on her face. "He talked, did he?" she questioned. "I should have killed that despicable weasel when I had the chance."

Erluc grimaced. "He's dead."

It took her a moment to understand what had happened, before the corners of her lips curved upwards into a chilling smile. "Not bad at all," she commended him. "The hero has a spine. Maybe I should've given you a slightly larger welcoming party."

Erluc shook his head, still in shock. His hand rested on Telaris' hilt, ever-ready to spring into action. "How did you know I was coming?"

The corners of her mouth curved upwards deviously. "That's a good question." She waved her hand, and thirty or so dark-haired, olive-skinned men emerged from the shadows, wielding bloodsteel scimitars. "I know all there is to know about you, Erluc *Heroblade*." Erluc held his sword ready, but he couldn't fight this many. Not alone. He summoned his armor, which glowed molten in the firelight, and thrust the torch out from his body as though to ward them off.

"An impressive trick, the enchanted armor," mused the maiden. She looked at his sword, smiling grimly. "And quite the blade too—fire and ice, was it?"

His jaw tightened. "How do you know all this?"

"Let's just say that we have a… mutual friend." Her voice reverberated in his head, even as it was spoken so softly.

"Friend?" His eyes widened in incredulity. Erluc immediately thought of Asten, but there was no way the Mage would betray him, and there was nobody that she could threaten for him to cooperate. Slowly, realization dawned upon him, and the maiden knew it. "I don't believe you. He wouldn't."

But even as he said the words, his resolve slowly wore away. His friend's absence of mind finally made sense; he was thinking about this witch the whole time!

Her eyes radiated a certain crude empathy as if she had been betrayed once as well. Turning to the men, she hissed something in an alien tongue, and three of them broke off, charging out of the cave.

"Trust never is absolute, is it? Everyone has a weakness, something that makes them helpless to do anything. It wasn't too hard to find his." Her voice had an edge of supremacy as if she had already won, and this was all just entertainment.

"After all, how else could I know?" The remaining men stepped closer, swords extended.

He felt a sudden spark of anger towards Renidos, betraying him to this treacherous, sadistic gorgon. *How could he? So much for the honor of the Trinity.* Fresh hate gripped Erluc, and his eyes glazed over with red. "Who are you?" he roared again. He would have killed her right then if he hadn't been surrounded. A flash of blue seemed to wink into existence for a split second around his hand, but it vanished just as quickly as it had appeared. He settled for hurling his torch at her, which she sidestepped easily. The shadows seemed to shrink away from the brand as it vaulted through the cavern.

"If I told you that, I'd have to kill you." The young woman merely returned his fury with another smile. "But my friends—and enemies, for that matter—call me Vyrnaur."

"Fire serpent," Erluc translated. *So, she speaks Telmírin too?*

She nodded, a faint smirk of amusement playing across her lips. "Deadly creatures, fire serpents." She abruptly looked away, as if someone was approaching. "I think that's enough chatter for today. If you'll excuse me, there's someone I need to kill." Vyrnaur's keen eyes narrowed, and she stepped forward, tapping Erluc's shoulder. Frost spread from the point where her pale finger made contact with his chestplate, covering his body with a thin glaze.

Erluc reacted quickly, setting his sword alight and pulling it back to melt the ice creeping up his neck, but even his enhanced reflexes were too slow. In an instant, Vyrnaur drew two long hunting knives and struck, twisting Telaris' blade so it flew out of his hand. The flames were extinguished the moment the weapon reached the cave floor. One of the men picked it up and stepped back, even as the last tendrils of frost captured Erluc's look of rage in a pristine sculpture.

Chapter 22

Renidos Takes a Dive

Inthyl, Aenor
Renidos

"Go!" shrieked Renidos as he slammed a gray-cloaked man in the forehead with his spear. He pushed his mother through the doorway, only to be cornered by two other infiltrators.

"She promised!" he cried. "She promised to leave us alone!"

They simply ignored his appeals, beginning to advance in unison. He kept them at bay with his spear, while his mother escaped into another room from behind him. Two men abruptly charged at him, and he quickly ran them both through before they could react. They crumpled, but Renidos couldn't kill them. He wasn't ready for that.

Yet, despite this victory, he was losing. In his concentration, he had forgotten about the last assassin, who had taken advantage of this opportunity to follow his mother.

No!

He utilized his heightened speed to pursue the last man, both of them reaching his mother in the same instant. The mercenary had just drawn his sword along her arm, leaving a long, deep cut, when Renidos drove his spear through his hip, its dark head emerging from the other side. His lifeless carcass fell to the ground as Renidos rushed to his mother's aid.

Her wound was bleeding heavily, and Renidos removed his tunic and tore a piece off. He thoroughly wrapped the cloth around the wound, slowing the crimson flow.

"Renidos…" was the weak cry from his mother.

"Don't worry, Mother. It's going to be alright," he whispered back solemnly.

Next to him, the man's dark-bladed sword caught his eye. *Bloodsteel.* Almost immediately, the thought occurred to him to find Asten, but he knew that even he wasn't fast enough to scour an entire city before his mother bled out or the poison took her. And more importantly, he wasn't about to leave her side.

"Renidos…" she tried again, with a frail, waning voice. "Listen to me." He nodded, a single tear starting to escape his eyes before being followed by a cascade more. "You have to be strong," she breathed. "I won't be there for you anymore, so you need to look out for yourself."

He shook his head adamantly. "I won't let you go."

"I… I am proud of you." Her hand caressed his face. "Your father would have been as well." He flinched, and another stream of tears flowed down his face. "You're so much like him." She looked into his eyes, but it seemed like she was farther than ever. "You're strong, Renidos. You'll find him. I know you will," she revealed softly.

"What?" Renidos' eyes widened. "Mother, what are you saying?"

"Promise me—" she winced. "You'll find him." Her hand brushed his chin weakly.

"No, Mother, it'll be alright. Hold on, just…" He couldn't complete the sentence; he didn't know what he could do to save her.

"Be strong, Renidos." She mustered the strength to put a finger on his cheek. "Promise…"

Renidos' eyes steeled as his mother's hands cooled to marble. The hand fell from his face, and he fell to the ground. Kneeling, Renidos turned back to the broken body on the floor, not even bothering to fight the impending tears.

He sat there crying until time became irrelevant, at the end of which he carried her outside, where he cremated her himself. He clutched the locket that hung from his neck, studying the star-shaped rune of Life, before ripping the thread that held it around his neck and throwing the stone into the fire. He had lost faith in life, and it could burn away with everything else.

After the fire had burned out, he returned home to dispose of the infiltrators. He took the three of them and threw their lifeless corpses into an alley. The savages had murdered his mother; the dogs could have them.

He couldn't go back home after that. No, he would stay in the courtyard. Asten would definitely be working late that evening, and Renidos prayed that the Mage didn't intrude. He couldn't face him—not after all that had happened. Luckily for him, Asten never showed, and he spent the night on the lush grass by the fire.

That night, he received another vision: the same shadowy figure summoning him to Comet Lake. However, this time, it was followed by a vision of an unconscious Erluc in a dark cell, frost covering his skin. She was there, Vyrnaur, whispering outside of his cell, and Renidos suddenly felt like he was falling.

He sat up, shaken. The sun had just risen, and he scowled. *Dawn. The start to the day that could end your life.* He hated dawn. But he rose, locking the courtyard behind him, and ran.

Something. I have to do something. Anything. If he continued to sit there, wallowing in guilt and grief, he would never leave. He ran, and he kept running towards the very edge of Inthyl. Keeping up a sprint with the spear was a challenge, but he was much better off with it than without.

Gently gliding through the town, Renidos finally saw Comet Lake at the horizon of his vision. The sun's rays beat down upon the water, producing a blinding reflection: a warning to discourage visitors. He doubled his pace, dust soaring through the air. As it always did, the world seemed to bend and tilt around him as he ran, time slowing down, until it finally reformed into the banks of the lake.

Just like in his dream, nothing disturbed the tranquil environment. Unfortunately, the shadowy creature didn't appear either.

In the center of the water, Renidos could see a small island—the Pyre. He closed his eyes, a silent tribute to all the past High Kings of Aenor and one for his mother. Without stopping, Renidos used his huge momentum to dive into the crystal-clear water. The morning water was cool and cleansing, and his sorrows washed away within its countless ripples. His spear didn't help the experience, but he wasn't taking any chances.

The last time he'd been here, his mother had brought him for a swim. Not much had changed—after all, it was a lake.

As he re-emerged, he met the warm rays again, and he pushed his hair out of his face. Renidos dove into the water once more, testing how long he could stay under. His eyes stung as he looked around, the cold water obstructing most of his view. A minute later, he rose to the surface, unable to hold his breath any longer, and all was engulfed in darkness.

I couldn't have been down there for that *long.*

To his great terror, Renidos noticed that only the water surrounding him was flowing with incredible speed. Just as he was about to take a breath, he was met with an immense barrage of water. As he wiped the droplets from his face, he felt the water underneath his legs, pulling him downward to his watery grave.

The struggle barely lasted a second.

Renidos might have held his own, but the attack was unexpected, and his powers couldn't help him. He struggled helplessly as a huge splash of water covered his head, dragging him underneath the steady surface. Once the last bubbles reached the surface, his eyes beheld only darkness.

It was official. Water was definitely Renidos' least favorite element. As he came to, he immediately felt himself suffocating, swallowing a mouthful of water, coughing into whatever came out of his mouth. Not a bubble of welcoming air greeted him as he struggled violently.

Suddenly, he felt a pull at the back of his soaked tunic and watched helplessly as he was hurled to a wet, solid surface. The coarse terrain scarred his palms as he pushed himself up, and he found his legs decorated with cuts. He could breathe, but there was still water everywhere. His amethyst was glowing a bright violet, tinting his entire field of vision.

What the heck is happening!?

As the strength of the Spectre returned to him, he slowly rose to his feet, and his heart stopped. In front of him balanced the shadowy creature he had seen in his premonition—a merman. He could only now make out the creature's man-like head and serpentine tail. *So not a merman. A snake-man.*

A pang of dread vibrated through his heart, and he frantically retreated from the beast. Although the enclosure was dark, the scaly skin of the creature radiated sufficient light for Renidos to make out that it was holding a thin javelin with a polished platinum point.

Where's my spear?

Drifting into a defensive stance, he croaked, "Why did you bring me here?" Ordinarily, it wouldn't have made sense to speak underwater. But after… whatever it was they'd done to him, it sounded like he was talking on land.

The creature grunted loudly and began to slither towards Renidos. Terrified, Renidos backed further away from the leviathan, feeling cool water shift against his head once again. Swiftly turning around, he noticed that he was at the edge of the surface.

After the stone platform, Renidos saw… Comet Lake. He was inside Comet Lake! In his defense, it's quite difficult to notice *anything* while being stared down by a scaly monster twice your size.

Once the creature finally reached Renidos, it simply gestured for him to follow it, and slithered onto a line of connected platforms. As it turned around, Renidos regained his confidence.

"Where are my weapons?" he called after it. The creature simply ignored him, as if nothing had happened. With a deep breath, he muttered to himself, "What a sock." And he dashed after the creature. He crossed the arch, passing onto another platform. He had just noticed, if not for the luminescent white light emitting from the platforms, the city would be awfully dark. He looked around, and there were several odd-looking structures across all platforms, and several other snake-people were slithering about.

After several minutes of chasing his 'guide' around several hovering platforms, they finally came to a stop in front of a spotless, white wall.

"Well, reptilian nightmare, where to now?" asked Renidos incredulously.

Suddenly, the platform underneath his feet started to descend rapidly. Sensing the change, Renidos leaped upwards and kicked against the wall, launching himself extremely high from the surface. While he was still airborne, the platform finally came to a stop on a lower level, next to another floor. Deflecting off of the white wall, Renidos spun in the air, landing on the platform adjacent to the humanoid. His feet landed with perfect balance; perks of being the Spectre. Just then, a voice escaped from behind him.

"Renidos. Welcome." The voice was level, perfectly moderated.

Sharply turning around, Renidos saw about a dozen serpent-men. On a sparkling coral throne, the king of serpent-men sat—or balanced—surrounded by a dozen of his kind, all armed to the teeth with lethal javelins.

"I'm sorry. Where are my manners?" The king raised a scaly finger, and his guards eased. From behind Renidos, the last serpentine warrior joined the guards.

"You speak Andaeric?" started Renidos, shaking his head in confusion. "Who are you?"

The king laughed royally, a genuine smile etched across his pale-white lips. "I am known by many names, young hero, but you may call me Oztarr." While he spoke, his tone was soft, yet demanded full attention. "As for your first question, we istroce are fluent in all the languages that are spoken across Eärnendor and the Far Lands."

Istroce? Oh, you mean serpent-men.

"Alright, Oztarr. What am I doing here?" As he blurted the words, he suffered the piercing gaze of the istroc guards. "Your majesty," he added hastily.

Oztarr's smile melted, and he rose from his white throne. His serpent tail was a glittering white, and his scales a radiant silver. A tall staff materialized soundlessly in his open hand. "Come, we have much to discuss."

The battalion of soldiers led Oztarr and Renidos through another set of twisted platforms, to what seemed to be the royal chambers. As the guards left them, Oztarr gestured for a curious Renidos to sit.

"You have extremely tangled streets here."

Oztarr half-smiled. "Indeed. Many istroce spend the greater part of their lives roaming the streets of Lutens Braka, learning all of the paths."

"Do the istroce have any other cities, besides Lutens Braka?"

Oztarr's expression closed faster than Renidos' superspeed. "You ask many questions," was the short reply.

Renidos simply shrugged. *An underwater city! Who wouldn't be curious?*

Yet, from the king's tone, it sounded like something Oztarr didn't want to talk about. Instead, he tried, "What about the platforms? That glow isn't natural—do you use some kind of magic?"

"You're a perceptive one," admitted Oztarr. He gestured at his staff, "It is an ancient magic, drawn from this staff, passed down to me from the previous leader of our people. The entire Lutens Braka—the prosperity of our kind—is drawn from the Vulyra. Yes, it illuminates our passages, serves as nutrition for our crops and herbs, and has powers which even *I* don't understand completely."

Renidos whistled. "Pretty important then." The king nodded, his face not betraying his emotions in the slightest. "And, not that I have a problem with this or anything, but how come I can breathe?"

"There are several herbs in Lutens Braka which produce natural juices that affect the drinkers' bodies." He started, "The herb we administered to you goes by the name of Jygras Brilexa. It allows your body to adapt to any outside conditions. Its impact will eventually wear off, but for now, you can breathe, talk, and move around here."

Renidos nodded. "And wh—"

"I think that's enough questions for now," commanded Oztarr. "The reason that I summoned you here is that I need your help. And you, the one with the power of the Falcon, are oath-bound to aid those who are in need."

"How exactly do you know so much about me?" Oztarr's expression remained entirely neutral as if he wasn't even going to consider giving him an answer. Rolling his eyes, Renidos decided to ignore the king. "Fine, what do you need my help with?"

"Vyrnaur," explained the king. "In the language of the elves, the name means—"

"Fire serpent," breathed Renidos through sealed lips. The corners of his vision flickered black as poisonous grief crept back at him. Closing his eyes, he could feel his heart pounding and his skin heating up against the cool water all around him. Thinking about what he would do to Vyrnaur when he saw her was all he could do to keep himself from exploding.

"Yes, and a fitting description it is," confirmed the king, looking at Renidos in surprise. "How do you know of h-?"

"Never mind that," interrupted Renidos. "What do you want with her?"

Oztarr's gaze met Renidos', and he could see the pain in the istroc's eyes. "Well, young hero, that is why I have called you here. The serpent kidnapped my daughter."

Renidos' temper flared monumentally. *That witch!* She was already going to pay for hurting his own family and Rose's. He would die before he would allow her to destroy another. The fire in his eyes was matched only by the rage in Oztarr's.

"Your Majesty, I will help you in any way I can."

The old monarch coiled his tail up, taking a seat on top of the makeshift throne. "This is why I asked for your help over the other two. Your resolve is unwavering, and there is something of steel about you." His heart pained as the istroc spoke the words. He'd betrayed his friend. How could he possibly be trusted for such a task? "And I believe… we have a common enemy." Renidos' eyes narrowed slightly. He couldn't possibly know about that. "The thing is, Vyrnaur is keeping my daughter hostage. And before you ask, I know not why."

Renidos shook his hair through with both hands. *At least she's alive.* "Do you know where?"

"That is no secret. Vyrnaur has a fortress, Ghâzash-Byrrn, that resides on the southernmost peak of the Grônalz—you Andaerians call it Bone Mountain." Renidos' eyes widened. That was where Erluc had headed as well. "I would go myself, but the route to the Grônalz is too lengthy and treacherous for me to travel along. Vyrnaur is no doubt attempting to lure me out to the surface, to expose and eradicate the istroce once and for all." Oztarr seemed to be conflicted inside. "Besides, I must remain in Lutens Braka. I cannot and will not allow anarchy to engulf my people."

Well, aren't you the best father ever? Except what right did Renidos have to judge anyone else? What did Renidos know about being a leader? Or a friend? Or even a good person? All he'd done was throw Eärnendor's fate into turmoil with both hands.

He shoved the thought out of his mind—he was going to find Vyrnaur. That was why the istroc had appeared in his dreams. He would love to thwart whatever moonstruck scheme that she was planning, and saving a princess didn't seem too bad to him. After all, his other friends wouldn't be too glad once they found out about his betrayal—some redemption was probably in order.

"So, I'm to go to Bone Mountain. I don't suppose you're going to give me a ride?" He looked up hopefully. To this, Oztarr brightened up.

"As a matter of fact…" he began, rising from his tail-throne, he slithered into a secluded chamber. Unsure of what to do, Renidos began to follow, when Oztarr re-emerged, tailed by a large, pale, silver wolf. Its eyes were storm gray, and it had wings akin to a bat's.

Renidos found himself slip into a stance as it approached, its intimidating glare instantly brightening the room.

"This is a grmmn. One of my informants found it near the edge of the Kre'nag mountains, alone. We raised it here in Lutens Braka. It is fully trained. As I have nothing else to offer you, I would propose that it accompanies you on your quest."

Renidos wasn't having it. A vicious animal following him around—he was more than a little wary of the idea. He was in enough danger as it was. But refusing the istroc king's gift wouldn't be the smartest move, either. "I appreciate it, your majesty. Thank you."

He knelt down and extended his arm towards the grmmn's snowy fur. As soon as he made contact with the first strand of hair, he swiftly pulled his hand back, gasping in pain. The color from two of his fingers had drained away, and they were tinted icy pale.

"Hey!" cried Renidos. The grmmn lightly growled back in return.

"Don't worry, that isn't uncommon. Grmmna have extremely low body temperatures due to their mountainous heritage. You will grow accustomed to it in time."

I'd better. Renidos wasn't going to have much luck riding a wolf that could freeze him into an ice sculpture. The thought reminded him of Erluc, and he forcefully shoved it out of his mind.

"What do I call him?" he asked instead. Oztarr shrugged.

"The istroce that raised him never spoke to him, so I suppose you may name him as you see fit."

After some silent thought, Renidos announced, "Frostbite." He held a triumphant look on his face, but it seemed like he had forgotten how to smile. "It's perfect."

Oztarr smiled in approval despite himself. The king then called for an istroc guard, who returned all of Renidos' weapons to him as well. His eyes gleamed as his spear returned to its place in his palm. Renidos took Frostbite with him back to the edge of Lutens Braka. Looking upward, he asked, "How have you managed to remain hidden for so long? Why?"

"We prefer to stay away from the conflict on the surface. Do not misunderstand me; we istroce are accomplished warriors, but why fight without significant reason?" Renidos was impressed. "Eventually, our time to ascend to the conflict will arrive, but until then, we are content merely observing and learning from all of you on the surface."

"Speaking of the surface," continued Renidos, glad that the conversation had progressed in the way that it had, "how am I supposed to get back?"

"Your grmmn," Oztarr explained. "Frostbite can swim you up. Although, I would advise that you take care to hold on tightly."

Renidos snorted, looking up at the never-ending expanse of water that obstructed his passage to the surface. "All right," he sighed. "So, I go to this *Bone Mountain*, and I look for your daughter—that part seems pretty straightforward. Once I find her, I'm to bring her back here?" Oztarr nodded slowly, alien to the incredulity in Renidos' voice. The boy threw his arms up in frustration, unsure of what to do. "This is probably the most guarded prisoner of the most dangerous individual in all of Eärnendor. Not only am I to free her, but also escape this mountain fortress and return with her on the back of a living block of ice. I have no reinforcements, and this is my first time outside of Inthyl!" he exploded.

"I believe I can help you with that," replied Oztarr thoughtfully. He raised his staff, and a smaller, silver scepter crowned with a pearl appeared in his empty hand. He offered it to Renidos, who accepted it gratefully.

Renidos spun the rod in his hands. "How can I use it?"

"You cannot. Only an istroc may wield it." The corner of Oztarr's mouth twitched. "As it happens, none of my subjects are worthy to bear a royal scepter either. But if you can find my daughter, give this to her. She will know what to do with it."

Suppressing a groan, Renidos continued, "Can any of your warriors accompany me? After all, if I were to be captured, Vyrnaur," Oztarr's features tensed, "would know exactly where to find you, your numbers and how you are armed, as well as have possession of your daughter's scepter."

Oztarr grimaced, and the staff in his hand flashed once, its light escaping back into the city. "Very well. You may take seven of my most elite istroce. They will meet you on the surface immediately." He placed a scale-lined hand on Renidos' shoulder. "Kera means everything to me, and I can't lose her. My complete faith is in you."

Kera? Well, it's better than Oztarr.

Renidos remembered something that he wanted to say to the istroc king. "Just for future reference, your majesty, there are fewer *crude* methods of invitation." He was obviously referring to the istroc that had forcefully pulled him under Comet Lake's surface. "I wouldn't be averse to a simple sign that says *dive here.*"

The old king guffawed and patted Renidos' shoulder. "As it is, we mustn't tarry any longer," the king finished, and Renidos agreed whole-heartedly. He'd had enough istroc exposure for the next fortnight, and traveling with the istroc warriors was likely going to be a disaster. He carefully mounted Frostbite, to the grmmn's obvious discomfort, and turned to Oztarr again.

"Are you *sure* that this is safe?"

Oztarr smiled. "Don't worry. It should be fine."

Oh, it should *be. No worries then.*

"And one last thing," added the king, and Renidos turned to him in anticipation. "Never forget—death is not the end," were the words that escaped Oztarr's bronze tongue. Raising an eyebrow in surprise, Renidos nodded hesitantly. After all, Oztarr wasn't the most straightforward person he'd met. It'd probably be better to ignore him and focus on getting back to the surface.

He grabbed Frostbite's flank and barked, "Now!"

The grmmn silently narrowed his eyes. With one flap of his wings, Frostbite was off the ground. Instantly understanding, the grmmn launched upwards, and his Spectre reflexes alone were keeping Renidos steady. The icy droplets ripped across his face as Frostbite ascended. He was forced to close his eyes, the darkness outside wasn't going to be much help anyway.

He felt his grasp start to give away, and he tightened his other hand, fingers tensing around his spear. His ears exploded, and just as he felt the last bubble abscond his lips, sweet air burst back into his lungs and he broke the surface.

Renidos felt the loving touch of dirt and pebbles against his back as he rolled onto the ground. Gasping, he didn't even notice Frostbite hovering above the calm surface of Comet Lake.

"Well, that was fun," he groaned. As he stood, he brushed off the mud from his soaking clothes. Suddenly, Renidos fell to the ground once more, a stone impacting his shin during the descent.

What in Atanûkhor's name? His grasp over his body started slipping away. He couldn't feel his toes. The rest of his legs quickly followed suit while Renidos lay helplessly on the soil. A blinding pain erupted in his shoulders and quickly spread all around his body. A second later, Renidos hazily glimpsed a band of warriors standing above him. One of them bent down and pushed a leafy supplement through his numb lips, and Renidos couldn't have resisted if he wanted to.

Fortunately, the greens were some kind of medicine. Renidos' nerves burned as the blood flowed back through, reinstating his control over his limbs. He groaned as he sat up, rubbing the dirt out of his hair. The man who had helped him looked relieved and offered a hand.

Renidos grabbed on and hesitated as he rose to full height. Something in the man's palm cut into Renidos', but he didn't feel it—the herbs had seemed to have had a lasting effect.

"Thank you," he groaned. Wiping his bloody palm on his tunic, he looked around. There was nothing in the man's hand, which surprised him. Taking a moment to think, he looked the men up and down, before he realized what had happened. The elite istroce that Oztarr had sent—they had somehow been altered to look like humans.

Six men were present, armed to the teeth with spears, scales, and shining daggers. He swiftly met their hands, careful to avoid overt squeezing for fear of more scars on his hard-worn palms. They quickly receded back into their formation, with the exception of the one istroc that had healed Renidos.

"Not at all, sir. Captain Rawek had advised us to bring along the Prima Brilexa, just in case. After all, you were the first alien to be invited into Lutens Braka." The istroc had an accent similar to Oztarr's. His brilliant purple eyes burst with electricity.

Renidos raised an eyebrow. *Interesting.* He had always wanted to be the first person to explore a place, even if he was being called an alien. But he knew that his achievement was not as pionerring as it was made out to be—after all, Vyrnaur had not only managed to find and enter Lutens Braka uninvited, but also kidnap their princess and escape without the help of any magic herb. "It is an honor. I look forward to meeting Captain Rawek," he replied instead. "And you are?"

"Kroyo, sir."

Nodding, Renidos turned to the istroc, who was waiting respectfully. "Please stop calling me sir. It's Renidos, or

Ren—if you will." He paused. "And King Oztarr told me about these herbs—he'd said that one of them had helped me to breathe in Lutens Braka."

Kroyo nodded. "Jygras Brilexa, I believe it was. We use it to breathe on land." He smiled. "But Prima Brilexa acts differently on one's body. Instead of adapting to its surroundings, the body returns to its regular, healthy self. Both are extremely pivotal in maintaining the health of our citizens in Lutens Braka."

I could definitely use some of that. He turned back to the istroc, "What does 'Brilexa' mean?"

"In Kyesti—our chosen language—it means 'flower'." Looking up at Frostbite, Kroyo smiled. "I was the one who brought him back from the Kre'nagan. I'm glad that he has found a worthy master." Renidos nodded, slightly embarrassed.

"Frostbite!" he called, and the grmmn grunted in recognition. Spreading its wings, it swooped down in a spiral of concentric circles, eventually landing by his side. As it neared them, the air around the beast seemed to dampen, and both of them could feel the frigidity it radiated.

Kroyo let loose a laugh. "Frostbite, indeed!" he agreed.

A low grumble escaped the rest of the istroce as they stood at attention. Another istroc walked toward them, carrying an ornate axe. His eyes were a dark pewter, absorbing the dusk light.

Captain Rawek's raspy voice barked a command, and the entire group were immediately at ease. To Renidos, he questioned, "Everything okay, Spectre?"

"Yes. Thank you, Captain."

He swiftly turned to Kroyo, as if Renidos had ceased to exist. "How far?" His voice was violently severe in comparison to the other istroce, including Oztarr. Renidos didn't think that istroce were this aggressive, and Rawek seemed to be the only exception.

"Three dozen leagues—give or take a few, Captain." Rawek grimaced. He barked a command, and the band started to rapidly dash away. Renidos looked at Kroyo, who was to be his voyage partner, in astonishment. The speed at which the istroce were traveling was incredible, even if the grmmn could probably better them, and even Renidos didn't know if he could consistently run at such a fast pace.

"The Captain may seem to be slightly extreme at times, but that's just determination. Princess Kera and he—well… they were close friends."

Renidos' eyes narrowed, but he didn't care enough to ask. "Right. Well, don't worry. She'll be fine. We'll get her back in no time." But to be fully honest, Renidos didn't know whether he was reassuring himself or his new friend. "I just hope you have more of that… flower herb."

"Prima Brilexa."

Renidos nodded. "We could really use some of that."

Kroyo had a cryptic expression on his face as he tried to nod and shake his head simultaneously. The istroc settled for remarking, "The Prima Brilexa is irreplaceably helpful in a fight, true. Unfortunately, that means that we're only given so much at a time." Renidos sighed. Without the reinforcement from the rest of the Trinity, at least a miracle herb would have been nice. It seemed like Adúnareth was testing him somehow—only a celestial, metaphysical force could hinder him with such bad luck. Unless it was Atanûkhor making his life more miserable than it already was on purpose.

Either way, the cause of his suffering was definitely an Immortal.

The Spectre suddenly wondered whether the herb could awaken Roxanna from her coma, but his wishful thinking halted abruptly at the thought of her waking up just to find that Erluc had been murdered by the same person who had assassinated her father.

And that it was all Renidos' fault.

Shoving the thought out of his mind, he leaped onto Frostbite, who growled at contact, and with Kroyo energetically slithering at their side, they sprinted forward with abnormal speed under the crimson shade of a dusk sunset.

Chapter 23

THE SPECTRE STRIKES BACK

NORTHERN MANOS DESERT, AENOR
Renidos

"Sir? Renidos?" a voice called. A sudden stop threw Renidos' into Frostbite's snowy fur. Launching himself off, Renidos brandished his spear, crouching down on one knee. Only then did he realize that he was in the middle of nowhere, surrounded by a handful of surprised istroc warriors. Kroyo mockingly raised both his hands in surrender, breaking into a grin.

"We've reached the Grônalz, Spectre," declared the gruff voice of Captain Rawek. Renidos rose to full height, tucking the spear back under the rope on his waist. *Well, that's not embarrassing.* He gave an affirmative nod and scanned the surroundings. The istroce were making the final preparations for the assault, with Rawek and another senior istroc bent over a map in intense discussion.

Sighing, Renidos looked out into the distance. The sun had just dipped under the horizon in the west, and darkness was descending over their camp.

The last two days had been a haze. Frostbite and the istroce had raced across the Manos, only stopping for food during the day and sleep in the night. Renidos practiced sparring with an exhausted Kroyo each night before dinner, and the istroc was on par with the Spectre. Other warriors often joined in, lengthening the brawl, but Renidos always came out on top. After all, Erluc was a much more formidable opponent, and sometimes Renidos surprised even him. Either that or the istroce were going easy on him.

During the day, Renidos usually passed out on Frostbite or practiced flying the grmmn. And slowly, they advanced through the desert. Crossing the Diamond River had proven to be a slight problem, but the istroce ultimately managed to traverse the powerful current.

Renidos silently prayed that Vyrnaur had left Erluc alive, just so he could apologize to him. He pushed the thought out of his mind. Erluc was the Warrior. For all he knew, Vyrnaur had caught the bad end of Telaris and was gathering moss in the ground somewhere.

Looking out one last time, he guessed that they were probably less than half a day's journey away. Kroyo approached, offering his waterskin. Renidos gladly drained half of it before returning it to its owner. "Kroyo, I have a question, if you feel like answering."

The istroc was slightly confused, but he nodded. "Certainly, master Renid—" He paused at a sharp look from the Spectre. "Ren."

"Thank you," acknowledged Renidos. "Now, King Oztarr said something to me, and I haven't been able to make any sense of it. Something about… death and how it isn't the end."

Hastily nodding, Kroyo adjusted his wavy, blond hair. "It's an ancient saying among our people, dating back to our ancestors of the Golden Bay. It concerns the afterlife, but between you and me, the phrase has become a mere expression of condolence in recent years."

Condolence? Then what reason did Oztarr have to ask him to remember the phrase? Sighing, Renidos nodded. "So, what's the plan?" he asked his istroc friend.

"I believe that we are to infiltrate the Ghâzash-Byrrn. Without alerting any guards, we are to free Princess Kera and escape without the dark elves even knowing we were ever there." Renidos snorted.

"Precisely. In and out without any disturbances," interrupted a voice. Captain Rawek had concluded his discussion and slung a bag over his gray shoulders. He let loose a guttural growl and bolted towards Bone Mountain, flanked by the istroce, a ravenous expression on his face.

Renidos flinched as he ate their dust, covering his eyes his both arms. Kroyo laughed, and Renidos would have—only his heart was still not ready for any kind of amusement. He mounted Frostbite, and they blasted off behind the group.

An hour before midnight, they arrived at the foot of the first mountain in the Grônalz. Renidos whistled—the sheer size of these mountains gave him goosebumps. Even Adúnareth, in all his glory, might be in trouble if one of these came crashing down upon him.

"This is it," announced Captain Rawek. Renidos raised an eyebrow. *If you're going to have a fortress in a mountain range, why choose the most accessible mountain?* But he simply told the istroce that he would circle the hill, looking for a vantage point.

Frostbite glided around the mountain, and nearly opposite to where Rawek had set up camp, Renidos discovered the entrance to a cave. Jumping off of Frostbite, he examined the ingress. There were lines of footprints in the moist loam, rows of blades of grass trampled. Spear out, Renidos was beginning to enter the enclosure, when a low moan escaped from behind him. He turned to see Frostbite clawing at a large figure.

In a second, he materialized beside his grmmn but stopped in his tracks.

"Frostbite, stop!"

Renidos quickly untied the grand pegasus from the tree, all the while stroking its white snout. This pegasus was going to survive, and he was going to ensure it. His master must have tied him to the tree before entering the cave.

"It's alright, Skyblaze. I'm here now."

Erluc had once introduced them. He had even tried riding him before. But now, thanks to Renidos, Skyblaze's master was likely dead.

"Find anything, Renidos?" interrupted a voice. Renidos froze, believing that Skyblaze had just spoken to him. To his great relief, Kroyo had walked up from behind him, followed by the rest of the istroce.

"This pegasus belonged to a good friend of mine," began Renidos softly. "This may be too much to ask, but could you—"

"Could I get someone to take him back to Inthyl?" inserted Kroyo with a smile. "Definitely. In fact… I'll see to it myself." He produced an apple, which the pegasus gladly bit into.

Renidos eased into a grateful expression, and he patted Kroyo's shoulders, careful not to bruise his hands. "I am in your debt." After all, if Erluc had indeed died inside the fortress, at least now Skyblaze would have a home to return to.

Rawek grunted. "One less warrior won't hurt our chances. Go forth, Kroyo." The istroc bowed to his captain and then to Renidos.

He handed the Spectre his satchel, "This has the last of our Jygras Brilexa, and it should be more than enough for you to re-descend to Lutens Braka." Renidos nodded, gratefully accepting the pack, throwing it over his shoulder.

Several minutes later, Skyblaze was soaring above the Manos, Kroyo fiercely charging through the sand below him.

It took them some time, but the istroce and Renidos finally made it to what looked like the entrance to Ghâzash-Byrrn. A rather surprised battalion of dark elves was quickly obliterated as the group made their approach. The sole survivor was pinned to the ground, while Rawek barked harsh commands in a rough, guttural speech. The elf seemed fazed by Rawek's knowledge of his language, but he weakly returned a phrase.

In one fluid motion, Rawek jumped into the air, and the illusion shimmered, his scaly tail whipping the dark elf in the face, winding him. He landed upright and looked at Renidos.

"There's an abandoned entrance to the fortress there," the istroc pointed at an enormous boulder several dozen yards to their left. "We can find the dungeons once we make it inside. That's where the princess will be."

They dashed to the boulder, but even the combined strength of the istroce wasn't enough to displace it. Renidos jammed his spear under the boulder's side and pushed upwards, but it still refused to budge. He considered the scepter in his opposite hand, though abandoning the notion after consideration.

Grimacing, Rawek put one hand on the boulder, closing his eyes. Renidos felt the ground under his feet give away for a moment, and suddenly the boulder crumbled down to fine grains of sand. The istroce seemed more entertained than surprised, but Renidos just mumbled, "How?" Shaking his head, he tried to stay as focused as possible. They were here to find the princess. Spear in hand, he dashed into the cave.

Rawek was right, the entrance had been abandoned long ago, but at least it still led them into the fortress. Charging through the dusty corridor, he followed a row of torches that led down deeper into the mountain, before he finally reached the dungeons.

The first face that greeted him was not pretty.

Another party of three dark elves stood guarding a corridor filled with containment cells. The one directly in front of him barely had enough time to scowl before being impaled by the shining tip of Renidos' spear.

The other two weren't as idle. They charged in parallel while Renidos wiped the grime off his spear. Lifting himself off of the ground, he kicked the wall of the cave and brought the weapon down on the assailants.

A moment later, the istroce entered to find Renidos standing amid three dark elven carcasses. Swarming inside, they all split up to find Princess Kera. As his burst of power slowly diminished, Renidos managed to search three cells, all without any success. With a sigh, he turned around, and his eyes widened. This wasn't what he was looking for—he didn't dare to dream to find this here, but his eyes couldn't possibly have been deceiving him. The Warrior lay unconscious in the center of a cell, completely unaware of the occurrings around him. *Please be alive.* Renidos tried breaking the latch of the door with his spear, but the bloodsteel proved too sturdy. Not even picking the lock with the head did any good. An istroc called out from behind him, a familiar sword in hand.

Telaris.

He dashed to retrieve the weapon. Apparently, the sword had been left with Erluc's pack in a crate near the end of the corridor. The istroc seemed slightly uncomfortable around the weapon and was overjoyed when Renidos snatched it from his hand. But while sprinting back, the Spectre was confronted by Captain Rawek.

"Who is this?" he indicated towards Erluc. "We are only supposed to free the princess," his firm voice commanded.

"A friend. Trust me, Eärnendor will be much worse off if I don't save him. And I owe it to him," returned Renidos. Rawek remained unconvinced. Frustrated, Renidos snapped, "You can't stop me. Go find the princess."

Rawek scowled. Clearly, he was a stranger to taking orders. An intense battle of wills raged between their blazing expressions before the istroc Captain walked off to find the princess, a defeated glower on his face.

Renidos quickly slashed at the lock, and Telaris cut it into two with ease. Erluc, who had suddenly begun to stir, leaped to his feet and kicked the door across the hallway, slamming the Spectre against the opposite wall. As he crumpled, Erluc grabbed his sword back and had it at Renidos' throat in seconds.

"You!" Erluc's temper didn't abate when he saw his old friend. "Why? You have five seconds. Explain yourself!" he snarled. Behind him, the band of istroce leveled their javelins at his back, Rawek at their head. He turned back and laughed harshly. "And who the hell are they supposed to be?"

Rawek looked like he wanted to say something, but Erluc's glare was smoldering with enough rage to make the entire Twilight Legion flee from the field of battle in panic. The istroc simply grunted.

"You're working with Vyrnaur now, is that it?" Erluc's expression was now a chaotic blend of fury and disappointment.

"No!" Renidos threw up his hands. "She threatened my mother!"

For the first time, Erluc lowered his sword. "What?" His heavy breathing was the only sound in the cavern for that moment.

"Vyrnaur. She threatened to kill my mother if I didn't play informant," spat Renidos back, pushing Erluc away from him. "The day before you left Inthyl, she showed up at my house and threatened me. I tried to resist, but she... I couldn't defeat her. So, I told her—I told her about the dart and that you were coming *here*." The istroce slightly relaxed, but they kept their javelins at the ready. Renidos' strained eyes were brimming. "And after she had taken you, she went after my mother anyway, and I wasn't able to protect her." His voice broke, but he dragged himself forward. "I'm sorry about this, Erluc, but I had no choice." There was an uncomfortable silence, and Erluc sheathed Telaris, an apologetic expression on his face. Although he had not known Renidos' mother for a long time, he remembered her as a kind lady, and Renidos had spent his whole life with her as his only family.

"But why would she attack instead of keeping the leverage against you?"

Renidos dropped his gaze. "She told me to convince Asten to go with you, and I thought if I could at least keep him safe, I would be able to figure something out before you reached the mountains. I'm sorry." He collapsed into Erluc's arms, and the friends found comfort in each other's grasp. Erluc lightly consoled him, whispering soothing words, patting his back.

The Warrior's eyes gleamed. "It's no wonder you look so tortured." He gritted his teeth. "Vyrnaur will answer for this. For all of this."

Renidos' face darkened. "She will." Erluc sighed.

"Remember: we're a team. I have your back… no matter what," added Erluc with a smile. Renidos actually wanted to smile back, but only the sides of his mouth curved up as if his body was rejecting the momentary happiness.

Injuring their moment of camaraderie, Rawek howled a sharp command, and the rest of the istroce scattered, searching the cells. He tried holding Erluc' gaze unsuccessfully and proceeded to continue searching the cells.

"I know," replied a recovered Renidos. "The istroce can be a slightly… acquired taste." He quickly summarized his entire journey from Comet Lake to Lutens Braka, across the Manos, and the climb up Bone Mountain.

Erluc whistled. "You deserve more credit than you get. The journey sounds like it was perilous." Renidos nodded, but he didn't know what to do with that. "Now, about this princess," continued Erluc. "I didn't see any other prisoners. How do w—"

Suddenly, a loud noise reverberated in from the entrance. A massive battalion of dark elves had swarmed at the opening to the tunnel, blocking their exit. They both crouched down into battle formation, but Captain Rawek cried, "No! There's too many! Back, Spectre!"

Both Renidos and Erluc hated fleeing from the battle, but they heeded the advice of the istroc Captain and retreated further into the cavern. They rallied with the istroc warriors and formed a defensive formation at Rawek's command. As the fighting began, the illusion around the istroce flickered back and forth, before fading completely, exposing their true forms to the world.

Taken by surprise, Erluc backed into the corner of the corridor, tripping backward on a mossy rock. His back collided with the wall farthest from the entrance, and he felt it give way slightly. Regaining his balance, he pushed it with all his force, and the wall wasn't a wall anymore.

"Erluc!" called Renidos, after rapping a dark elf in the head with the shaft of his spear. "A little help would be appreciated!" Erluc grabbed his friend from behind, passing through to the next passage.

"Erl…Where are we?" he looked towards Erluc, who simply pointed to the false wall that they had crossed over from. Renidos went back across and saw that the istroce were about to be overwhelmed by the storm of dark elves.

"Go, Spectre! Find the princess! We'll hold them off!" shouted Captain Rawek over the noise of the brawl.

Erluc grabbed Renidos back, whispering, "You've got to see this."

On the other end of the wall, a long spiral staircase winded upwards, probably up to the rest of the Ghâzash-Byrrn fortress. But behind the staircase, a single cell stood alone. Renidos rushed to the cell door, only to be denied by a grilled gate.

"Stand back," said Erluc as he raised Telaris, and a rune lit up at the base of his sword. He then pointed the sword at the gate, frost creeping around the metal, instantaneously freezing the whole net. A single swing of his sword and the gate was a mound of scattered fragments on the cold dungeon floor.

They quickly passed on towards the cell, which had heavier fortifications than all the others. A single elf burst through the false door, and Renidos turned just in time to drive his spear through its sternum. Just then, the rotating door burst into splinters, as the entire army of dark elves burst through. Captain Rawek was in the middle of seven enemies, his axe decorated with the blood of hordes of dark elves. A few elves were sinking into the stone floor, still struggling to escape just as Rawek dispatched them.

How is he doing that? No other istroce could be seen anywhere.

"Ren! Try to get the cell open. I'll go help out," decided Erluc. Telaris flared up, the second rune shining brightly. Flames came to life, spontaneously dancing along the length of the blade. Erluc let loose a blast of inferno, engulfing the approaching wave of dark elves. Between Erluc and Rawek, they rapidly thinned the ranks of the attackers, but the hordes kept replenishing from what seemed like an endless supply.

As Renidos approached the cell, he finally saw the princess. She had flowing, unnaturally straight, dark-brown hair. Her scales were a rich, iridescent green, and she had a clear, white tiara in one hand. Unfortunately, she was unconscious—without the Jygras Brilexa available to her, she probably couldn't breathe on land for so long.

He focused on the lock, which was held in place by five bars. Raising his spear, he daggered the bars as fast as he could. Erluc whirled Telaris in a figure-eight, slashing two approaching dark elves across the chest. Out of the corner of his eye, he saw the istroc Captain fall to his knees, backed against the wall of a closed cell. Erluc ran Telaris through another elf, finally summoning the black armor of the Warrior. Every dark piece surrounded his limbs, except for the helm—it would only get in the way while fighting these soldiers.

The first bar was finally broken.

He bulldozed through the dark elves towards Rawek, but not before three assailants had surrounded the Captain. Blasting another column of flame, Erluc engulfed two of elves just as the third pierced Rawek's neck with a poison-barbed arrow. He cut the creature down, but it was too late—the istroc had breathed his last.

He was Renidos' terminal line of defense. They were alone.

Clang. The second bar gave way. Three to go. A dark elf charged at Renidos, who dashed behind it with inhuman speed, slashing it across the back. Erluc had been pushed back a few feet closer to Kera's cell.

Renidos ran to his friend's side, brandishing his spear with both hands. "I'll hold them off. Just break the rest of the bars!" he proclaimed. With a last blast of frost, Erluc ran off to break the princess out. Telaris glowed red as he approached the cell, and in one stroke, the third bar melted away.

The Spectre kicked two dark elves through the door of a cell, decapitating another. Now faced with five dark elves at the same time, the Spectre swiped under the legs of the two on the right, swiftly circling around the other three. He skewered two on his spear, while the third scratched his shoulder before being thrown back into a wall. About fifty more dark elves had burst into the cavern now, and Renidos was forced back to the cell. From his other hand, he clobbered an elf with the butt of the scepter, knocking it out cold.

The fourth bar snapped, and Erluc swung his sword one last time, breaking the last bar into fragments. The lock flew open, and just as the dark elves had surrounded them, Renidos dashed into the cell.

Please work. He carefully placed the scepter in the hands of the princess, and in a sudden, blinding flash of light, everyone was instantly thrown back. Her scales flashed white, and all the elves hovered upwards and were thrown sideways into the cells. Whether they crashed into the cell doors or the inside of the cells, everyone either passed out or were killed by the impact. The green returned to her scales, and Erluc pulled open the cell door. Renidos wiped the grime off of his face onto his tunic.

The princess took a long, labored breath before turning to the others. "What took you so long?" she chided. Her voice was impatient but friendly at the same time.

"You knew we were coming?" asked a perplexed Renidos.

Kera sighed. "It's a long story," she tried. "When she first brought me here, I dreamed of a stranger arriving at Lutens Braka—I take it this was you."

"Lutens what?" asked Erluc.

Renidos shook his head. "I'll explain later."

"Yes," she agreed, tugging on Erluc's sleeve. "We have to get out of here before that harpy finds out that you've broken in," offered Kera.

She had only stepped out of her cell, before a voice whispered, "Come now, I thought we were having fun." They all froze as a steady rhythm clattered down the steel steps, finally dying out with a soft landing on the sandy tunnel floor. "I'd hate for you to leave so soon." The young woman spat the words out, taunting them.

Erluc and Renidos scowled in unison, which just widened the expression of hubris on her face. Kera aborted her formalities; she wasn't taking a chance with Vyrnaur. She raised her scepter, but her scales seemed to refuse to metamorphose—the green remained.

"You seem to have exhausted yourself, Princess. Pity! I would have liked to witness your little trick." She looked down at the fallen dark elves. "And I can't tell you how refreshing it is to see you walking free again, *Lord Turcaelion*." She turned to Renidos, who shot her his most loathsome stare possible. "If it isn't the Spectre to the rescue. I'm rather surprised that you survived," she admitted. "But I suppose it is better this way. I truly enjoyed our last encounter." She flashed a sadistic grin. "I hope the family is doing well."

"Don't you dare!" Renidos shot back with a scowl. "We had a deal!"

"And you didn't keep your end of it," pointed out Vyrnaur. "I'm sure I told you to bring the Mage, too, didn't I?" Renidos' eyes flashed a dangerous red, and his muscles quivered, but he didn't move. The woman seemed to relish his rage. "Where is he? Cowering back in Inthyl?" She looked directly at Erluc. The natural blue in her eyes had faded since the first time they'd met, so that white was more prominent. "It's amusing, this… *Trinity*. You think that you're heroes just because of a *poem*." Kera seemed intrigued at this point, but she dared not interrupt. "Do you ever stop to question it? Who you're fighting," she challenged. "Who the real villains are…"

Renidos couldn't help but consider what she was saying, and it definitely threw him off a little. Beside him, Erluc gritted his teeth, probably going through something similar.

"As it is, I loved that one line of the prophecy. Didn't you?" Renidos flinched, and she smirked, her gaze boring into his eyes. "*Ere the traitors unleash the true power of fear.*" Renidos' gemstone began pulsing at his chest, and he saw Erluc's familiar blue glow at his side as well, illuminated for the briefest of moments before fading away.

Erluc's eyes burned with rage, and Renidos' hands tightened around his spear. Ulmûr had recited the same line before dying. Renidos certainly hadn't expected it to be from the prophecy.

"The Immortals know what's going to happen. They always do. The only difference between the two of them is whether they have the fortitude to intervene." She flashed an unnerving smile, revealing perfect, white teeth. "The Falcon didn't stop me from killing Elandas. He didn't protect the young Spectre's innocent mother." Renidos's knuckles whitened around the shaft of his spear. "He didn't help the princess when she needed it, and now she's almost dead." Erluc's skin seemed to radiate cold fury, and his sword began to glow white-hot, the air shimmering around it. "Of course, *my* master wasn't happy about that. When I'm done with you, I'll have to pay her another visit."

A terrible scream of rage tore through the dismal passageway, and the light from Telaris grew blinding, releasing a rippling wave of blue fire toward Vyrnaur, who was only just in time to react with an icy jet of light. The bolts met in a beautiful explosion, the force of which blasted all three of them backwards.

Renidos spun and landed lightly on his feet while Vyrnaur put down a hand and skidded back. When the smoke cleared, Erluc was still standing, Telaris casting a blue glow over his face. And when he looked up, Renidos gasped aloud.

His eyes were blazing a brilliant ultramarine.

"*When you're done with me?*" Erluc's voice was strange, alien, and somehow yet still his own. "*Don't make me laugh.*" As Renidos watched, the blue light first spread across Erluc's face, then began to cover his body, giving his black armor an eerie sheen. The corridor was tinted blue by the force of the aura surrounding him.

"What…" Renidos breathed. Vyrnaur seemed equally shocked, but she recovered quickly, leaping forward with her knives outstretched. Erluc stepped up to meet her, swinging Telaris down to contact the blades, pinning them to the floor. His eyes flared, Telaris' glow becoming unbearable, and Vyrnaur was barely able to wrench out one of the daggers before the other one melted into the air.

She leaped back against the wall, pushing off and stabbing down at Erluc's head, but the Warrior parried the blow and responded with a thrust of his own, which Vyrnaur was only just able to dodge. Even so, Telaris' white-hot blade sliced open her cheek, causing her to stagger back in agony.

Renidos lunged forward to help, but Kera called him back, and he hesitantly retreated to the other end of the hall.

Erluc seemed to be wreathed in flames as he attacked again and again, forcing Vyrnaur to the defensive. He turned, and Renidos could see the fury of Adúnareth mirrored in his every action; this was the Warrior, leader of the Trinity, and it seemed his powers had escalated to even higher bounds.

He deflected a strike, then seized Vyrnaur by the neck and slammed her against the wall, his body blazing with a final surge of power. In response, Renidos dashed toward them, leaving Kera behind alone. While one hand held his spear at the ready, the other shielded his eyes from the terrible heat.

Renidos lifted his spear, preparing to charge to his friend's aid, but Kera called out to him just in time. "Stop! You'll be incinerated if you get anywhere near him!" The Spectre gritted his teeth but lowered his arms. Instead, Erluc darted forward, twisting behind her, Telaris ripping through the thin fabric on her back with blinding speed.

Vyrnaur flinched as her blood met the air, and the energy in her palms dissolved. She screeched as she unleashed her hunting knives—one slash, and Renidos fell backwards in retreat. The distraction was enough for Erluc to regain his breath. His eyes blazing cobalt, Erluc stepped forward with a thrust of Telaris, and though Vyrnaur's lightning reflexes were enough for her to twist in time to avoid being impaled, the blade grazed her side. She dropped to the ground, crying out in pain, and Renidos didn't wonder—the sword looked like it could cause them all to erupt in flames.

Erluc's armor burned black, and he fired a bolt of white, electric fire, storming through the air. Vyrnaur's eyes widened as she caught its impact, barely able to retort with an icy blast of her own. The collision of their two beams blasted her five feet back, her back slamming against a cell door. Before she could recover, Erluc leaped into the air, bringing Telaris' razor edge screaming down towards her, but Vyrnaur's reflexes were too quick. She turned immediately, dodging the blow, her hand summoning a clear, cold energy. The temperature in the room dropped a few degrees. Erluc feinted towards Vyrnaur's waist, before slashing her right shoulder. Her skin burned open as the blade cut across it.

Crying out, she furiously lunged towards Erluc's arm, surrounding Telaris with her long knife, gripping his neck fiercely with her hand. Where her pale skin made contact with his glowing flesh, steam issued, as though she had tried to freeze him, but his aura had been too powerful. Taken aback, Erluc staggered—just long enough for Vyrnaur to slash at him once more. Though the dagger glowed in the heat, it held together long enough to trace a long cut on Erluc's upper arm, even as he punched her back with a gloved fist. The dagger burned through his gauntlet and pierced his skin.

The effect was instantaneous.

Even though the wound was not deep, Erluc's aura began to fade away, his armor melting into his tunic. His eyes returned to their normal, human brown, and he fell to one knee, breathing hard. Renidos ran to his side protectively, and this time Kera did not interfere. Meanwhile, Vyrnaur had finally regained her footing and was studying Erluc carefully, though it was evident that she had received a crippling injury.

"The power of an Immortal." Slowly, she rose to her feet, gripping her long, curved dagger. "It's no wonder the Emperor wants you dead." Vyrnaur's face, though contorted with pain, betrayed signs of amusement. She wiped the single bead of sweat from her brow. She violently sheathed her knife before tossing her hair back, revealing her pale, strikingly beautiful face. She flashed an unsettling look at Renidos, before returning her attention to Erluc. Kera hissed, and Vyrnaur smiled coldly. "Oh, I haven't forgotten about you, Princess. In fact, you've served your purpose quite well. Tell everyone back home to expect a visit soon."

Renidos grimaced, opening his mouth to say something, before Vyrnaur interrupted him.

"I look forward to working with you again in the future," she taunted. "And for what it's worth, you've given me all that I want." His expression contorted, unsure of how to take the comment. "Until next time, Adúnareth's chosen," she stepped back. Twisting her cloak, she spun in a sphere of darkness. A blink later, she was gone.

Erluc clutched Renidos' shoulder. "Don't—" he gasped, "don't let her get away!"

Swearing, Renidos dashed the way she had come, but his way was soon blocked by four gray-cloaked men—in the same attire of those that had destroyed his mother's home.

Without wasting a moment, he darted at the first man's legs, knocking him over, and caught him on his spear, flinging him at his neighbor. Dodging a sword strike, he charged in and impaled the offender, then kicked out at another man, whirling around and spearing him through the chest.

A whistle behind him—Renidos rolled, narrowly avoiding the sword aimed at his neck, then slammed the blade aside with such force that it was wrenched out of its owner's hand. The man scowled and swung a fist at his head, but Renidos reached up and caught it with his left hand.

The man's eyes widened. "How did you—"

"Magic." Renidos grinned savagely, wiggling his spear, then drove it into the man's stomach. He turned, and with another whistle, came another battalion of assailants. Grimacing, he called out to Erluc, who was leaning on Kera for support. "We have to leave—she's called reinforcements."

"We have her on the run," croaked Erluc, taking deep breaths between each word. "We can still defeat her!"

Renidos slashed at an incoming warrior. "If we don't leave now, we won't make it out!"

Footsteps sounded from either side of the corridor. Raising her scepter, Kera shouted out a command word, and two barriers of energy flared into existence, shielding them from both sides. She was making a valiant attempt, but Renidos knew she couldn't hold out for long after all the energy she had expended earlier.

"We can't hold them off forever," he whispered urgently, "You have to cut us out of here with Telaris." Erluc hesitated for a moment, then stabbed downward, burying his sword to the hilt in stone. Yanking it out, he peered into the gash.

"We're just above the caverns," he confirmed. Gray-cloaked men swarmed into the passageway from both sides, pausing at the glowing walls. One of them touched the barrier, then jumped back, crying out in pain.

Without wasting a moment, Erluc slashed at the floor, carving out a rough square. "Hurry!" urged Renidos.

One of the men cautiously fired an arrow at them. Though the barrier vaporized the projectile, both walls flickered, and Kera gasped. Erluc tried to stomp on the square until it fell loose but to no avail. Roaring in frustration, he summoned his obsidian gauntlet and smashed his fist into the stone. Dust rose from the floor, and fissures appeared in the stone.

Two more men shot arrows, and the barriers vanished entirely, Kera dropping in exhaustion. Erluc slammed his fist into the ground once more, and the stone fell through the floor, landing with a crash in the cavern below.

The men charged, raising their swords, and Renidos leaped lightly into the hole. With the last of her strength, Kera lowered herself through with magic, while Erluc dropped down and froze over the gap with Telaris as soon as he'd landed in the cavern below.

They stumbled through the cave, reaching the entrance within minutes. "Skyblaze," choked Erluc.

"He's fine," assured Renidos. "Now, come on!" He loosed a piercing whistle, and Kera winced, just as a hulking Frostbite swooped down towards them.

Chapter 24

Tides of the Heart

Lutens Braka, Comet Lake, Aenor
Renidos

"Okay, I can't hold it off anymore," blurted Renidos. "How did you do that back there?"

Erluc raised an eyebrow, settling on top of a relatively soft piece of leather. "Do what?"

"The blue shine thing?" clarified Renidos. "When you suddenly became insanely powerful and lost all control?"

"Warrior powers, probably," replied Erluc softly. He shook his head, too worn out to think about it further. "Thanks for the assist, by the way. You really saved me back there."

Renidos grinned apologetically. "I honestly would have helped, but I couldn't get close with all the fire everywhere," he justified with a shrug. "The princess didn't think much of my spear-throwing idea, either. It seems like you did alright without my help as it is."

Erluc snorted. "Remember the Steel Trial?" he began, between deep breaths. He still hadn't recovered completely from his episode, but at least he could breathe. "And how Uldarz finally lost all his power before he defeated Asten?" Kera seemed quite lost, but Renidos nodded grimly. "When he summoned Atanûkhor, he became unimaginably powerful, but only for a short time. Do you think that I could have—"

"You could have summoned Adúnareth when you were fighting?" questioned Renidos. "I'd say there's a fair chance. Does that make you 'The Blade of Adúnareth'?"

"If that catches on, I'll kill you." Erluc glared at him. "Besides, I don't think this was a part of my specific ability. After all, glowing isn't really a quality one looks for in warriors." Kera smiled, her grin fading when she looked at the others. "No, I think that this is something different," continued Erluc.

"And there's another thing," remembered Renidos. "*Ere the traitors unleash the true power of fear.*" Both their gemstones glowed brightly, and Erluc's eyes widened.

"Did you know that would happen?"

Renidos shrugged. "Not really," he admitted. "But every time someone says those words, my gemstone starts glowing. It's got to be related somehow."

Considering this, Erluc took a moment to think, before his brow furrowed. "During the Trial, Uldarz—or Atanûkhor—summoned the Twilight Realm, and Alisthír said something that did the same thing." He closed his eyes, trying to recall the words. "*Yet the cursed meet the destined at Twilight's frontier.*"

Sure enough, their gemstones were illuminated once more, and Renidos' eyes widened. "Well, *that* can't be a coincidence."

Kera waved her hand in front of them, and Erluc turned to face her. Truthfully, he'd forgotten that the istroc princess had been listening. "I don't know if this helps, but those two lines rhyme," she offered, and Erluc realized she was right.

"She's right," agreed Renidos. "Wait, you don't think—"

"Yeah." Erluc nodded. "The prophecy." Shaking his head incredulously, Renidos took a moment to consider, reciting all four lines together.

> *"In the Temple of Inthyl, one thousand years hence.*
> *The Trinity shall rise to the Council's defense.*
> *Yet the cursed meet the destined at Twilight's frontier.*
> *Ere the traitors unleash the true power of fear."*

Erluc felt his gemstone grow hotter at his chest, the blue light emitted from its glow visible even through his tunic. Renidos had to remove his purple gemstone from his neck, growing uncomfortable from the blinding light.

"I guess that's it," concluded Kera uncertainly. "What does it mean?"

Erluc looked to Renidos, who seemed as confused as he was. "Absolutely no idea."

The younger boy scratched the back of his own head, pushing his hair down. "There could be more lines," he offered. "I guess we could ask Alisthír, but I don't think we can do much else about it." All three of them seemed rather surprised by the sudden discovery, but they agreed to let the matter sleep until they had more time to think about it.

As night fell over their desert camp, Renidos and Kera took turns describing to Erluc the wonders of Lutens Braka. She explained how her father's scepter had been passed down for generations, and that its elemental magic was the salvation of the istroce.

Both Renidos and Erluc were surprised to learn that istroce—despite their chosen environment—did not need to drink water, while Kera was amazed that humans did. However, istroce always needed Jygras Brilexa to breathe on land, unless they were of royal blood. The magic of the royal scepters allowed any royal istroc to adapt to whatever conditions they found themselves in. That was why she had been able to breathe after she was in contact with her scepter.

"Watch this," she presented. Taking Erluc's empty waterskin from him, she covered the opening with her scaled palm. When she lifted her hand, clear water was brimming to the top. Both Renidos and Erluc were momentarily stunned, before Kera offered an explanation.

"Each generation, a few istroce are born with power over an element. I was born with power over Rain, my father has full control over Sight, while a friend of mine—who eventually became Captain of our land forces—had power over Stone."

Erluc and Renidos looked at each other, ultimately deciding not to tell her about Rawek. At the very least, now Renidos knew how the istroce he had fought alongside had been cloaked. Then again, the sheer range of the enchantment must have meant that Oztarr was an incredibly powerful spellcaster.

After several assurances from the istroc princess, Erluc took a sip from his waterskin. "I can only summon water when there is considerable moisture in the air, but I can transport and manipulate it with much greater finesse." To prove herself, she levitated the remaining water out of Erluc's waterskin and doused Renidos with the entire fluid. It took Erluc several minutes to get back onto his stump; he was captured in such a great fit of laughter.

"Finesse," repeated Renidos as he wiped the water away with a spare shirt. "Sure."

"So, Kera," started Erluc, now slightly more open regarding the princess. "How old are you?" The istroc princess thought for a moment, before finally answering. "By the standards of human maturity, I'm about eighteen."

Erluc nodded, but Renidos was not satisfied. "How old are you really?"

Kera blushed, slightly embarrassed. "Nine," she whispered. They all broke into light-hearted laughter.

Finally, Erluc—at Kera's persistent request—painfully recounted the story of how the Trinity had received their powers, with frequent interruptions from Renidos.

"You knew the princess?" inquired Kera as Erluc skipped past the Steel Trial.

He didn't trust himself to say anything about Rose, so Renidos took it upon himself to softly explain how Vyrnaur had shot her with the poison dart, and the significance of the watch. Erluc was nearly in tears by the time Renidos had completed that part of the story. Renidos continued to add his quest to Ghâzash-Byrrn, explaining how Vyrnaur had blackmailed him into her service in Inthyl, and how he had failed to protect his mother. His face steeled when he spoke of her, but he didn't stop talking.

Erluc only impeded him once, to tell Kera about Rawek's death. He felt that it was his responsibility, as he was the one who had seen it, even if he didn't approve of the istroc Captain. Kera paused, taking a moment of silence to mourn for her fallen comrade, before whispering something in Kyesti which sounded so foul that Renidos could only assume was a curse.

"Death is not the end," he told her softly, and she raised an eyebrow in surprise. He explained how Oztarr had mentioned the old saying.

She raised an eyebrow. "That sounds like my father," she admitted, trying to explain when Renidos asked why. "I already told you that my father had the power of Sight. He probably searched your mind and found that you were mourning someone." Shrugging, she turned away. "Either that or he saw something regarding you."

"Like what?" asked Renidos, slightly panicked. "Something good?"

"I'm joking," she assured with a small laugh. "It's probably best not to pay it too much attention. Between you and me, my father isn't the most straightforward person in the world."

That I can believe. Renidos grudgingly let it go, and they continued with the story.

When they were finally done talking, it was nearly morning, and they all set off once again. Renidos once again offered Kera to ride on Frostbite with them, but both of them knew that not all three of them could ride the beast together. Besides, as Renidos had learned while traveling with Kroyo, the istroce were incredibly fast travelers over land. Even if Kera couldn't consistently keep up with Frostbite, they only had to stop a couple of times for her to rest.

As the sun banked at an angle, Renidos leveled his watch, to notice the nine o'clock shadow. Frostbite skidded as Erluc directed it to a halt, while Kera slithered up from behind.

There's a sight for sore eyes.

Since he'd been constantly occupied, Renidos hadn't noticed that he was homesick. However, as Inthyl's Citadel towered above the city in the distance, he felt a bit warmer.

That said, it was already the third division, and winter wasn't far. The nights were going to start to get colder from now on, even this far down south.

He flicked his jaw in irritation as he realized that he couldn't go back home just yet. A few hundred yards ahead lay the waters of Comet Lake, and Lutens Braka was anxiously lying in wait for its princess. They all stopped at the banks of the lake, and Kera had a hesitant expression on her face. Erluc simply looked into the water in anticipation, but nothing happened.

"Last time, I just jumped in to take a dip in the lake, and an istroc pulled me down." Renidos hadn't cherished the memory. "We definitely can't swim down, that's for certain." Erluc shrugged, turning to Kera.

"Well, I can," the istroc princess was stumped. "But there's no way that you're getting out of going down there with me," she quickly slipped in before the thought could enter Erluc's mind. Their voyage through the desert had sown the seeds of a friendship, and Kera knew it.

"Wait!" Renidos burst out. "Oh, I'm such an idiot." He grabbed Kroyo's pack, producing the flask of Jygras Brilexa.

Erluc grimaced at the sight of it. "What in the world is *that*?"

"Just drink it," ordered the Spectre. Erluc didn't have nearly enough energy to argue back, so he did. Both of them winced as the cold, bitter liquid passed down their throats. *Blech!*

Erluc punched him lightly in the shoulder, spitting out on the ground. "I am never, ever drinking that again." He agreed, mouth contorted in disgust. "So, now what? I don't feel any different," proclaimed Erluc. "And I don't know about you, but I can't swim."

Kera groaned. "For the saviors of Eärnendor, you are surprisingly incompetent."

Both Renidos and Erluc turned to glare at the princess, who held their exhausted gazes. *Don't forget that we ended up saving you, too.*

Suddenly, Kera's eyes widened, and a radical idea started to form in her head. She explained her plan to the boys, who first reacted with shock, and then with angst. Following excessive assurances and reassurances, they tentatively agreed to the arrangement.

The istroc cracked her scaled knuckles and backpedaled a few yards, before closing her eyes. She stretched her arms forward, almost hugging the air. Both Erluc and Renidos crouched ready at the bank of the lake.

Comet Lake was relatively still, a light flow the only disruption to perfect stillness. An unnatural ripple started to form, and the tranquility of nature was suddenly infringed. A single point in the lake, near where Erluc and Renidos were placed, served as an epicenter from where all water was repelled away from. Kera slowly started moving her outstretched arms away from each other, and the ripple started to burgeon violently, forming an area of water that was shallower than the rest.

A steady trickle of sweat ran down from Kera's brow, and her eyes clenched even tighter than before. The trough was now unnaturally deep, and Erluc had to crane his neck to see the bottom.

Kera exclaimed as she exerted more force, and the depth of the narrow passageway was now immeasurable. "That should be enough! Do it!"

Renidos and Erluc gave each other a hesitant look before diving headfirst into the deep, shadowy space, possibly to a very wet coffin. Their streamlined forms screamed through the air, before impacting into the dark water. Renidos held in a shriek as the cold droplets pushed him upwards, and he lingered in the water, between two worlds. *I'm going to die here.* He felt the pressure on the inside of his throat push upwards, almost unbearable, threatening to release his breath with each passing moment, before he finally felt himself fall headfirst towards the marble platforms of Lutens Braka.

He gasped, air flooding back into his lungs, and he tried blinking his eyes open as he fell towards the surface below. Renidos managed to right himself just as he regained his sight, and just as he was about to hit the ground, he bent his knees. The impact from the hard stone was insulated by his landing, his shins and forearms taking most of the blow. He rolled forward twice before coming to a stop.

Ouch.

Erluc was luckier. He flailed around in the water, and when he could see the faint lighting of Lutens Braka's platforms below, he landed on his feet, before falling to his knees in pain, gasping for air. They both furiously blinked their eyes open, glad they'd finally reached Lutens Braka.

A large whoosh emitted from behind them, and Kera gracefully slithered up, helping them to their feet. "I told you it would work, didn't I?" She was honestly enthusiastic.

Her jet-black hair vaguely resembled Erluc's, but the water lithely drained out of hers, while his looked like he had just jumped thirty yards downwards into a lake.

"Never again," reminded Renidos.

Kera rolled her eyes. To Erluc, she cheerfully declared, "Welcome to Lutens Braka."

"And welcome back, Princess Kera. I'm sure that everyone will be comforted that your rescue was completed without any hitches," intruded an istroc with a purple hue. Renidos grinned widely as he ran to his friend, and they performed an obscure embrace.

Kera was as surprised as Erluc to discover that they knew each other, but nobody provided an explanation. Renidos grimaced at his scratch-bejeweled hand by the time it ended.

Never going to get used to that.

"Kroyo!" recognized Kera. "Weren't you a part of the land forces?"

"He offered to take Erluc's pegasus back to Inthyl," explained Renidos.

"Who—you'll be glad to hear—is safe and sound in the stables of Inthyl, Master Renidos." Kroyo declared with a smile. They had grown close over their voyage across the Manos, as Erluc and Renidos had with Kera on the way back.

Renidos shook his head solemnly as the istroc asked where the rest of his force were. Kroyo's grin seemed to fade slightly, but he quickly recovered and introduced himself to Erluc, who thanked him for escorting Skyblaze safely.

"Not at all, sir," he replied. "Your steed is great company, in fact. We had some very interesting conversations over our voyage. He speaks very highly of you and was more than willing to wait in the stables."

Tilting his head in disbelief, Erluc obviously thought that he'd heard him wrong. "You can talk to Skyblaze?"

Kroyo smiled affirmatively. "Are you another chosen one of the Trinity?"

Erluc looked at Renidos, who shrugged in confession, before replying, "We don't exactly like to advertise ourselves, but yes, I am the Warrior." Renidos smirked. Erluc never could resist an opportunity to show off.

They were all escorted through a twisting set of passageways which Renidos recognized, before finally stopping before the clear, white wall. As the platform descended, Renidos perfectly mimicked his maneuver from his previous visit, using the wall to curve through the water above, before landing on the adjacent platform. Erluc's hand went straight to Telaris' hilt as the platform moved, but he eased after Kera assured him that it was safe.

They were rejoined by Renidos, who had turned around after his stunt, and they finally beheld the sight of the istroc king.

"Welcome home, Kera." He smiled warmly as she ran to give him a small hug. "It's great to have you back." He turned to Renidos, who bowed slowly. Kroyo whispered something into Oztarr's ear before the old king sighed. "That's terribly calamitous."

Oztarr turned back to Renidos, who bowed again. "Captain Rawek and his team fought bravely, and they gave their lives so that we could be successful."

"They will be remembered as heroes," the istroc king declared. All of his guards banged the bottoms of their javelins to the ground together.

"Nevertheless, our land forces must continue to function," he turned to Kroyo. "Congratulations, Captain." Kroyo bowed and nodded gratefully to Oztarr. Renidos winked a 'congratulations' to his friend, who smiled out of the side of his mouth.

Erluc clapped along with everyone else, and the istroc king finally turned to him. "I have heard great tales of your triumphs, Warrior. The Vale of Shadows, Uldarz, and now Vyrnaur. It is fortuitous that we finally meet." Erluc nodded in acknowledgment. "Welcome to Lutens Braka."

"Thank you, your majesty," was Erluc's stock reply.

"No, thank you. Without your aid, the quest might have led to an even greater loss than before. Besting Vyrnaur is nothing to be scoffed at." Erluc replied with the same answer as last time.

Oztarr rose from his throne and placed a sparkling-white hand on Renidos' shoulder. "I am forever in your debt, young Spectre. If you ever are in need of anything, I promise that it will be granted." He looked like he wanted to hug him too. Kera smiled fondly.

"Not at all, your majesty," replied Renidos, Kroyo suppressing a laugh as he used his traditional response.

"I made a promise to serve, and I don't intend to break it." Renidos had worked out that answer for instances like this.

Oztarr chuckled, before offering, "At least accept this." He raised his grand scepter, and a moment later, a long, beautiful, purple spear appeared in his opposite hand. Both ends of the shaft had silver spear points, and the shaft itself was flexible but sturdy.

"This is Zythir," proclaimed Oztarr, as Renidos took the spear into his own hands. "It is enchanted to never break, and its points consist of a rare metal from the Far Lands. It's one of the most valuable items in Lutens Braka and has rested here for generations." He smiled. "It is yours."

Renidos had stopped listening as soon as the spear landed in his palm. It fit perfectly, and he felt that this spear was meant for him. The conciliatory part of him thought of refusing the gift, but the rest of him won out. "Thank you so much," he managed. Kroyo, Kera, and Erluc all looked at him with pride—he deserved it.

Erluc yawned behind him, and Renidos understood it as a signal to leave. Just as he was about to bid the king farewell, a thought popped into his mind. "Before we go, could I borrow some Prima Brilexa, your majesty?" Oztarr was slightly confused but called for some of the miracle herb to be brought in. One of his istroc guards scurried in and handed Renidos a small pouch.

Erluc seemed to be the only one that didn't know what was going on, but he didn't want to interrupt whatever Renidos was doing, so he resisted the urge to ask a question.

"Out of curiosity, what do you intend to use it for?" questioned Oztarr. The istroc king wasn't about to go back on his recent promise, but his interest was piqued. Renidos tucked the pouch into his bag.

"The princess," Kera looked up at him, and he shook his head before continuing. "The princess in *Inthyl* has been in a comatose state for more than a fortnight now. The herbs helped me atop Comet Lake, so maybe they can help her recover as well."

Erluc's face flushed red, and he was taken aback by Renidos' consideration. If there were any chance that Roxanna could be recuperated, he would dive at it with both hands. Unfortunately, his moment of celebration was immediately cut short by Oztarr.

"The Prima Brilexa is a powerful herb—there's no doubt about it—but unfortunately, even its herbs won't be able to free your princess from her coma," the king seemed truly apologetic about crushing their endeavor. "In all my years, I have only heard whispers of a single item that can return an individual from the brink of demise—and even that would be impossible to get."

Erluc was insatiably intrigued. "What is it? Where can I find it?" His voice came out slightly harsher than he meant, but he didn't care.

Oztarr raised an eyebrow from his throne. "It fascinates me that you're so determined to heal this princess." His voice was speculatory, and Erluc gnashed his teeth against each other.

"My reasons are my own," spat Erluc. "But if there is any cure for her, I will find it—with your help, or without. It's your choice, take your time."

Several guards around the throne growled but were silenced by a raised finger from their king. Before her father could further agitate Erluc, Kera quickly whispered in Oztarr's ear. Though the words were clearly not meant for him, Renidos could easily hear them with his enhanced senses. "Father, they were friends. He was present when she was attacked."

Oztarr clenched his jaw, gesturing for all of his subjects to leave, except for Kera. Kroyo waved goodbye to Renidos, who quickly waved back as the istroc wandered behind a doorway. With a sigh, Renidos tucked his new spear into his belt.

When they were the last four in the room, Oztarr continued. "It has only ever been heard of in legend, and I know miserly little about it." Erluc impatiently gestured for him to continue. "The legend says that the elves of the Archanios are in possession of an ancient crystal. History is littered with subtle references to its existence, but I have heard no word or whisper of it since the dawn of the Tiren Calmar. The powers of this crystal are unknown, and its potential undiscovered, but there is a chance that you could make use of it to save your princess. Your Mage will be able to help you out there."

"Very well. What's this crystal called?" tried Erluc, his temper subsided by now.

Oztarr paused. "The Heart of the Moon."

Erluc nodded slowly, grasping the information. Renidos, on the other hand, was excited. *The elves!* Roxanna had always been kind to him, and he knew if there was a cure, Erluc wouldn't stop until he'd found it. Renidos would surely accompany him. And if it meant that he had the chance to travel to the land of the elves, then there was no way that he was missing out.

Erluc was about to turn, when Oztarr put a hand on his shoulder. "I apologize for before. I didn't mean to bring back unpleasant memories." On the side, Kera and Renidos were frantically whispering about whatever rumors they had heard about the Archanios.

"I understand, your majesty. I apologize for the way I reacted as well," replied Erluc. It was obvious that the istroc king had the right intentions, but if Erluc hadn't said what he had said, then they probably wouldn't have heard of this crystal. Kera and Renidos had also finished their conversation, and Erluc bid Oztarr farewell. He had already turned around, when a voice echoed through the chamber.

"Wait!" Kera had slithered up behind them. "Father, I have something to ask of you." Oztarr nodded in anticipation. "I would request that… you allow me to leave with them." She hurriedly continued before the istroc king could intrude. "They have already agreed to it, and I wish to go to Inthyl with them."

Renidos stealthily turned so that his back was towards Oztarr, facing Erluc. "We have?" he whispered out of the side of his mouth.

"Apparently," whispered Erluc back.

The princess took her father's hand. "I was already kidnapped once, and if not Vyrnaur, someone else could be the aggressor next time," she argued. "As things remain, I cannot be a princess forever. I want to make a life for myself, just like they did." She gestured towards Erluc, who made sure not to meet Oztarr's gaze.

Kera continued, "I would be as safe as possible and traveling with the Trinity. The three of them together could protect me with ease." Oztarr flicked a tooth with his narrow tongue.

"The istroce have remained a secret for generations: Am I to reveal our entire race based on a mere whim of my daughter?" he challenged. "I would even alter your appearance, but I am not familiar with human females."

Erluc coughed. "Your majesty, if I may interrupt. My friend Asten—the Mage—has the power to conceal appearances. With his help, Kera would look like a regular human girl." Renidos raised an eyebrow but didn't interrupt. "I promise, the istroce will remain hidden." They had grown to appreciate Kera's company, and Renidos could understand her not wanting to live below Comet Lake for another fifty years or so.

Oztarr considered this. He had power over Sight and could probably understand what Erluc was proposing. "I will hold you to your word." He looked around at the three of them. "All of you."

Kera smiled in delight before kissing her father's cheek. "Don't worry, I'll visit soon." The istroc king managed a wry smile, and his face steeled as he dismissed them.

Renidos nodded respectfully, and together, they walked back to the edge of Lutens Braka. "Umm… Kera?" he began. "Not that I don't love the idea of you coming with us, but next time maybe try, I don't know… *asking* first." The istroc princess smiled and lightly caressed his face with the tip of her tail as she passed him. Renidos seemed to stop breathing for a second, blood rushing to his face, before he casually continued walking. "Never mind."

When they reached the last platform, they were faced with the dilemma of their passage to the surface. Since they had left Frostbite on the surface, Kera offered another plan. Without the availability of a substitute option, they agreed to her plan for the second time in the same day.

They stood at the very edge of Lutens Braka, the tips of their brogans peeking off of the stone platform. Renidos gulped, and they jumped off the structure, down into the depths of Comet Lake. The second their feet left the ground, Kera willed the water to slowly raise them upwards to the surface.

As they broke the surface, they found themselves gasping for air. As Renidos swam to shore, he waited for sickness to drown over him, but nothing ever happened. He had probably been rising through the water too quickly last time. Climbing onto the bank, Renidos noticed that a large portion of dirt near the lake was damp—possibly from the water that Kera had spread out when they had jumped in earlier. He grimaced, shaking his hands in the air to clean off the mud. *I really need a bath.* Kera broke the surface, nimbly swimming to the bank of the lake, her hands whirling through the water.

"Alright. That wasn't so bad," admitted Renidos. "Let's get back home as fast as possible: I want to sleep on a real bed tonight." He jumped on Frostbite, who had been taking a well-deserved nap near where they had emerged from.

"Not so fast," warned Erluc. "We have a massive problem." Kera looked at him in anticipation. Erluc sighed before explaining, "We still have to figure out how you're going to enter the city unnoticed."

Kera hesitated, before trying, "I thought your Mage friend can make me look human." Erluc smashed his fist to his forehead.

"About that," he started. "I might just have lied a *tiny bit.*"

"Exactly how much is a tiny bit?" she asked, unsure if she wanted to know the answer. Erluc made an uncertain face, and Kera groaned, looking up to the murky sky. This was not going to end well.

Luckily, Renidos came to the rescue. "Wait. Do you have a runestone that could conceal her appearance?" he asked Erluc.

Erluc shrugged, and Renidos realized that it would have been a miracle for him to remember the runestones at all—he hadn't been exactly jobless in the past couple of weeks. There was probably some kind of reference to the runes in Inthyl's library, but that had always been Asten's area of expertise. They ultimately came to the conclusion that once they reached the city, Renidos would run into town and get Asten, along with the runestones. They continued their journey, and a few hours later, they stopped near Inthyl's main gate.

Taking shelter behind a few tall trees and some shrubbery, they dismounted from their beasts. Renidos sprinted into the city, leaving behind Kera and Erluc. Taking a seat on an uneven stump, he uncomfortably swept a hand through his hair. "Thank you for lying," she confessed, breaking into a nervous chuckle.

Kera's attempt to make conversation really surprised Erluc, but he just nodded. "I knew what you were saying, that's all," he said flatly, not trusting himself to say more.

"All the same, you helped me." His tone had probably indicated his feelings on the conversation, and she gracefully decided it was better to let him be.

Erluc felt a small sadness inside of him. The truth was that Kera reminded him of Rose. Apart from her serpent tail and green scales, they were indeed quite similar. What was worse was that he couldn't help but form the opinion that Rose's condition was his fault. And Kera was a constant reminder that everyone around him—however innocent— would be in danger. If Erluc could help Kera in any way, maybe that meant that he could help Rose too.

"I'm sorry about what happened to her," Kera told him.

Erluc frowned. "How did y—"

"There's no other reason that explains why you would look so terrible," she disclosed.

"Thanks, I feel loads better," remarked Erluc.

Kera sighed. "You know what I mean." She paused. "But yeah, that probably sounded bad."

Erluc smirked, shaking his head. "No, it's alright," he conceded. "But this is one wound that I can't have left open. You saw what Vyrnaur did—she manipulated me, and I just…"

Kera grimaced. "I saw." She touched his arm, and he flinched, breaking the contact. "And I can't even imagine what you're going through, so I'm not the right person to help you. But your friends—they respect you, trust you, and I'm sure they'll help you get through this."

A light rhythm of thumps sounded as Renidos ran back, trailed by a panting Asten. In his right hand was the pouch, while his left, as always, held the Mage's ring. When he finally stopped to gasp for air, he looked up and nearly fell on his face.

"Calm down, you big baby. She's a friend," chided Renidos. "This is Kera, the princess of the istroce. She's going to be a part of our team." Asten stopped to stare blankly at Renidos, who was tired of people asking him the same question. "I'll tell you the whole story when we get back," he spoke sharply. "Right now, we need you to work your magic." He sketched quotation marks with his fingers in the air.

Snatching the pouch of runestones from Asten, he emptied them out on his lap.

"Nice spear," was his sole comment, not at all surprised that he had been left behind while they had received new weapons. He was used to it by that point.

Renidos wasn't listening, and Erluc bent down to look at the stones. Asten turned to the istroc, managing, "Well, nice to meet you, Princess Kera."

"Nice to meet you too, Asten," she wished back, and Asten smiled. For a princess, she certainly was very down to earth. They would probably get along well. "What are your powers then, as a member of the Trinity?"

"Well, I can—"

"He turns into a dragon," tried Erluc, laughing as Asten pushed him back. He turned to Renidos, who only had three stones left to check. "No, he has a magic ring."

The Spectre finally raised the stone he was looking at, "I think this is Sight. It should work fine." The stone's rune vaguely represented an almond, and he tossed it to Asten.

"You're right, it is," he confirmed. "What do you want with this?"

"Not me, you blockhead. We need you to use the rune on Kera." *This could take a while.*

"Hold on." Asten pressed a hand to his forehead. "First of all, I have no idea what you're trying to accomplish here, and even if I did, I wouldn't help you unless I knew what was going on." He scowled. "You can start with why you left the city without telling me." Erluc and Renidos looked at each other, before Erluc shook his head, and Renidos agreed.

"Later." Renidos would have had to admit that his best qualities weren't represented in that particular story.

Asten crossed his arms, slightly suspicious. "What even happened on that blasted mountain?"

"Well," offered Erluc. "It was a spine-chilling experience."

Renidos shook his head, grimacing. "A real backbreaker."

Kera shrugged. "Make no bones about it."

"How humerus," Asten mocked. Everyone paused, turning to look at him in confusion. "What?" he asked obliviously. "The humerus is a bone in th—"

"Well, way to kill that," muttered Renidos. "Now, I would really appreciate sleeping on a regular bed today, so if you're done…" He pointed at the runestone in his hand.

The Mage was unmoved, stubborn as ever.

Renidos took a deep breath, before explaining, "The istroce—Kera's race—have been hiding from the rest of Eärnendor for generations. We promised her father that we would ensure that this remained as it was."

"And?"

"If you cast the Sight rune, then maybe you can make everyone think she looks like a human," he concluded irritably.

Asten sighed. "Who knows what that rune can do, Ren? You do understand that it could blind her or sprout an extra pair of eyes somewhere on her body." Kera finally intervened, slightly frightened by his statement.

"If the spellcaster isn't sure about the result, then the outcome itself will almost certainly be something other than what he is trying to do. We're not going to do this if you're not up to the task." She had some experience with spells, and she clearly wasn't keen on placing her life in the hands of an amateur.

Asten wiped his brow. This princess made a convincing argument. If he didn't do it, then he would be admitting that he was incompetent. However, if he agreed, then he would be endangering a princess' life.

"Don't worry, I'll be fine as long as you concentrate on your goal," reminded Kera. Asten sighed in resignation. He shut his eyes as he reluctantly slammed the runestone into the ring, and once again, it melted out of existence. His sight wavered for a second, but he opened his eyes with spots dancing in them.

He turned the ring around, and there it was, next to the others—the rune for sight. He smiled, still in disbelief of how miraculous the whole process was. Renidos and Erluc both patted his shoulder in encouragement.

"Right. Now the hard part," warned Kera. "Try not to kill me."

Asten gave her a sarcastic, "Thanks for the vote of confidence," before closing his eyes. Erluc and Renidos turned around, unable to watch. The Mage focused on his breathing and pictured the Sight rune in his mind. He visualized Kera and blurred her istroc features in his mind. He pictured her without the spotted emerald scales, but instead with human skin.

His ring grew unusually hot in his hand, and he yelped as he opened his eyes in pain. Luckily, his finger was fine. He turned to Kera, about to apologize for the delay, before he froze. The istroc princess looked… she looked great. If they had met her at the Fang, he would have gone up and talked to her.

Kera looked down, and she saw the same thing that she always did. But when Asten looked at her, he saw someone else. Her green scales had faded to smooth, white skin, her tail replaced by a long, woven skirt that rounded around her brand-new ankles. She looked like a girl.

"Guys, I don't think it worked," she informed wistfully with a tilted head. Both Erluc and Renidos slowly turned around to see what Asten had wrought.

Renidos gasped and let out an impressed gust of air. "You have no idea," he returned.

"Great job, man." Erluc congratulated Asten.

Kera was still slightly awkward about it. "I don't feel any different."

Asten tried his best to explain what his spell had done. "If you did, then I probably would've been on the hit list of an entire species right now. No, my spell just masks you with the image that I imagined. I think the spell should last as long as I will it to, but you shouldn't wander too far away from the ring, just to make sure."

Renidos coughed in surprise. "Seems like your powers aren't useless after all, Asten." He scampered away before the older boy could retaliate, leading the istroc princess into Inthyl.

Erluc consoled his friend, throwing an arm around his shoulder. "You won't believe what happened while we were gone."

Chapter 25

Nature's Missed Call

Asten

They spent another hour catching Asten up on why they had left so abruptly and without notice. Everyone present collectively leered at Renidos when he spoke of his betrayal, but they all seemed to understand his intention when he spoke of his mother. He finished the story, adding how Erluc had defeated the Traitor with his cerulean glowing fit—which they had dubbed 'the Awakened form'—and their journey to Lutens Braka.

"Do you remember what triggered it?" asked Asten. "Seems like it would be extremely useful in a fight."

Erluc's face darkened, and he told them about what Vyrnaur had said. Renidos grimaced as he heard the words again, but the Warrior kept a straight face.

"So, an emotion?" brainstormed Asten.

"I…" Erluc paused, and he made sure that he averted his gaze from everyone else's. "I need a little more time to figure that out." Asten raised an eyebrow but didn't push it further. "Until then, we'll need to come up with something else."

Asten spun Zythir around in his hands, knocking a vase off of a pillar. Renidos dove down to the ground, catching it a second before it impacted the dirt. He laid it down onto the grass and snatched the mystical spear back from the Mage. "You better hope that nobody heard that."

They had met outside the royal stables, where they could keep an eye on Frostbite. All of them could agree that Renidos' beasts needed to be someplace isolated, and they couldn't waste any time looking for a place to hide them right now. And even though the palace was officially off-limits, nobody was going to ask *Lord Heroblade* to leave. Besides, they'd made sure to stay far enough away from the main palace to make sure not to attract any unwanted attention.

Asten sighed in exasperation, "Aren't we going to discuss this?" They were all burned out, having spent the last couple hours explaining how the situation had changed while they had been away. He had particularly liked Kera's scepter but found it hard to shake off how Renidos had betrayed Erluc. Asten faced an unwelcome development in the form of Zythir, too. Now the other two had both received sacred weapons, and yet again, he was left with nothing. He wasn't sure if Kera was now officially a part of their group, but even she had her own mystical weapon.

Erluc snorted. "There's nothing to discuss—I'm going."

Kera sat up onto the bench—at least that's what it had looked like to everyone. The sight spell hadn't worn off yet, luckily for all of them. Her silver scepter was tied across her back, and her hair glowed gold in the artificial light.

In their absence, it had been decided that the Council of Nine—or rather, Eight—would be in charge of Aenor, at least until Roxanna recovered. In the time since news had spread of her condition, Asten had noticed there had been lots of discontent with the arrangement—citizens wanted someone with the blood of Eltar running through their veins to occupy the throne. But without a High King or a successor, the Council had the highest authority, and there was little that anyone else could do to stop them from seizing power.

"I *know* I'm not sitting this one out," declared Asten.

Renidos and Kera nodded in agreement. "So, when do we leave?" asked the istroc princess, while Erluc put on a new tunic.

"As soon as possible," he replied with a muffled voice.

"But before that, I need a favor," proposed Renidos. Erluc re-emerged and tucked Telaris into a new belt. "Mhmm?"

"My house. Someone needs to make sure it stays standing while we're gone." His voice wavered, but he managed to continue. "It's been in my mother's family forever, and I can't be the reason that it falls to ruin."

Erluc nodded, and he patted the younger boy on the back in reassurance. "I'll ask Verdanis to do what he can."

Asten didn't know how that would work; it wasn't as if they were on great terms at the moment. In fact, Verdanis would not have been too glad that Erluc had returned without Roxanna's would-be murderer.

Either way, Asten's mind seemed to be triggered by his response. "That reminds me, the Council has been meeting frequently while you've been gone."

"You have any idea what they were discussing?"

The older boy grimaced, which didn't help the mood of the room. "Short of storming into the hall like you two did, I had no way of finding out myself," he admitted. "But there's been a lot of talk around the city, and it's not exactly encouraging." Erluc raised an eyebrow, indicating for him to continue. "In some of the larger cities across Aenor, the general discontent at the Council's rule has erupted into violence. The people in Fyrne, Lendrach, and Raelon have tried storming the homes of the nobility, hoping to seize control, and in the case of Tarrach in the north, the local duke threatened to secede from the kingdom." Renidos' eyes widened, and Erluc didn't seem too pleased either. "Unless we can save Rose soon, Aenor might collapse into a civil war."

Erluc scowled, taking a moment to digest the information. "Are the Council stepping down?" he inquired finally.

"Not even close. Instead, they're preparing for—" he began before being interrupted. A handmaiden rushed outside, hastily scampering past them.

"Wait!" called Erluc. The lady stopped, taking a moment to recognize him, and then tensely bowing. "Is something wrong?"

"Oh, thank goodness you're back, Lord Turcaelion. Something's happening, and we don't know what to do."

Her tone was urgent, and Erluc raised an eyebrow. "What is it? The Council? Are we being attacked?"

"No, sire." She paused as if she was about to deliver a death sentence. "It's the princess."

They all dashed behind the maid, Renidos pacing himself for the sake of appearances. She led them to a staircase at the far edge of the palace grounds.

"I thought she was behind treated at the Royal Infirmary so that the healers could work uninterrupted," clarified Erluc, clearly not impressed. He didn't like to be kept in the dark. The maid leveled her gaze at his feet, replying, "Councilman Therglas ordered us to move the princess here not a fortnight ago."

He turned to Asten, who shook his head. "Don't look at me. This was *his* decision. I didn't even know about it."

Erluc steamed, and Asten put a hand on his shoulder. "I'll deal with him later." He turned to the handmaiden, "What was the problem?"

"I'm sorry, sire, but I don't know." She faced him, but her answer was vague. "The medic that was watching over her tonight called for me to bring anyone in the Council, and that it was urgent." Looking towards the palace, she continued. "Should I still inform the councilmen?"

"No, it's alright," assured Erluc. "We'll handle this. No need to spread more panic than there already is. However, you can convey my personal request to Councilman Verdanis to maintain Wayron Manor for two fortnights. Tell him that I'd be in his debt and that my mission is close to completion." He nodded, dismissing her. "And wait… tell him tomorrow morning."

She curtsied, scurrying away. They dashed down the stone steps, confronted by half-a-dozen physicians crowded around a table, shouting over each other. They all seemed to lose their voices as Erluc entered the room. Bowing, they retreated away from the table so that the princess was in sight. Erluc flinched as he saw Roxanna's listless form.

One of the healers—Erluc recognized her as the one who was present when Elandas passed away—explained the situation. "Lord Heroblade," she greeted urgently, "Something—something is happening to the princess."

As if on cue, Rose jerked upwards and fell back onto the table like she was being restrained. Her eyes were closed, but her body was moving autonomously. Erluc rushed to her side, standing helplessly while she writhed in pain. When she finally stopped struggling, he felt himself letting out a breath.

"Why is this happening now? What did the dart do?" he demanded, turning to the healer.

"I-it must be the poison," she tried. "The toxin must be affecting her brain."

"And her body's fighting it," completed the Mage. He nodded, immediately starting to think up possible solutions.

Erluc turned to the healers, "I'm sorry, but I'm going to need you all to give us the room."

"But, sir, we've been given orders from the Council to never leave her highness alone," informed one of the physicians.

"It's okay," assured Erluc. "I have brought a specialist, and she might be able to help." He indicated Kera, who took a moment to understand what was happening, before she nodded.

"I prefer working without people watching," she concurred. "But don't worry, if all goes well, I shouldn't be too long."

The physicians looked at each other, finally conceding and tromping out of the room. Erluc waited until they were out of earshot and then turned to Asten. "Do it. Use the spell that you used to heal me."

"Oh, no," protested Asten immediately. "Not on her. You almost died the first time—"

"But I didn't, right? So, it doesn't matter." Erluc cut him off. "Do it."

Asten stopped and looked at him. He was definitely stressed and starting an argument with him right now would probably end up worse rather than better. But this was the life of Inthyl's princess, the last living descendant of Eltar. He couldn't make this decision.

"If not for anything else, do it for me," tried Erluc. He paused, adding, "You know I'd do the same."

Asten sighed and then turned towards Rose's lethargic body. He turned his ring so that the life rune faced forward.

The Mage closed his eyes and prepared to use the spell. "Vistre," he whispered.

He felt his senses heighten, unimaginable power coursing through his veins. Raising his hand above her body, he imagined her as he had known her before. Inthyl's princess, the girl who would gladly slap him across the face. He felt a small strain, and he opened his eyes. The tension had lifted from her face, and he was relieved when he felt her slow but steady pulse on his fingertips.

Renidos tilted his head. "Well?"

Asten suddenly collapsed, and the Spectre barely managed to catch him before he fell to the ground. He sighed, "I've prevented it for now, but I don't think I can remove the toxin fully without causing more permanent—" he turned to Erluc, "and *lethal* damage to her brain. I'm sorry, but that's all I can do."

Erluc ran his hands through his hair, a few dark strands breaking free as he brought them down. "What—" he shook his head. "How long does she have?"

"I don't know." Asten's bitter scowl seemed to heighten the tension in the entire room. "But if she's gotten this much worse in just a fortnight, I have a feeling that she won't remain stable much longer."

Erluc found himself biting his nails—something which he had never done before. "We need to get that crystal as soon as possible."

"Well, it's not like the elves are going to just *give* it to us," complained Renidos. "Do we even know who the leader of the elves is? Or where in the Archanios to look for this crystal, for that matter?"

"No and no," growled Erluc. "We haven't even had any contact with the elves for the last blasted century!" He slammed the heel of his palm into the wall, causing the wood to splinter in a foot-wide circle around his hand. "But it doesn't matter—I'll steal it from them if I have to." He opened and closed his fist, finally noticing the pain. Panting, he shoved both shoulders against the shut door, sliding to the ground in despair.

"We're with you," came a steady voice from beside him. Kera walked up, placing a hand on his shoulder. "We'll save her, don't worry." She helped him to his feet, and he smiled at her.

He turned to his friends. "Come on," Erluc called the physicians back in, who were relieved at the fact that the princess was not only still breathing, but more stable. He changed their arrangement so that at least two people must stay with the princess at all times of the day and requested that they should alert the Council or Alisthír immediately if she had another seizure.

Renidos ran to fetch the alchemist from the arena to let him know about what had transpired in his absence, but the old warrior was nowhere to be found. Erluc led them back to the stables, avoiding any and all patrolmen that he could see. Drawing Telaris, Erluc set the blade ablaze, illuminating their surroundings.

Renidos dashed to the corner where Frostbite was lazily licking his paws. The grmmn seemed to brighten when it saw him, standing up on all fours. A white stallion was asleep a few yards away but awoke at the noise of the group entering the stables. It neighed at Asten, who promptly decided to use Erluc as a shield. Leering at the Mage, who slowly took his hand off of his shoulder, Erluc knelt beside the stallion and stroked the hair on its neck.

The serenity of the scene was abruptly shattered when Frostbite growled ferociously at Erluc, almost causing him to fumble at Telaris.

"The fire! I don't think that grmmna do well in the heat," conveyed Renidos urgently.

Erluc grimaced, conflicted. "It's going to be terribly hard to see, not to mention freezing, if I put it out."

"Give me a second," informed Asten, stealthily dashing to where they'd left Skyblaze, leaving the others alone in the stables.

Bending down to pet Frostbite, Kera cried out when she touched his icy fur. Erluc looked up, "You okay?"

"I'm fine, just a bit shocked is all," she assured. "Forgot that grmmna do that." She turned to the Spectre, who shrugged. "Apparently, you get used to it."

Erluc chuckled, and Asten scampered back towards them with the pouch of runestones. He set them out on the floor, and Erluc crouched down next to him, as did Kera. "This is your great idea?" he asked.

Asten shrugged. "The two of you are already pretty strong, and I don't want to be a liability. The only way that I can be more of an asset is if my powers become stronger." He pointed at the stones. "Or if I get new powers."

Renidos nodded, spinning Zythir in his hands. "For the record, I've been saying this from the very beginning." He turned a stone around, examining it. "Which one is this?"

Squinting, Asten nodded. "I think that's Moren. Death."

Immediately dropping the piece, Renidos pushed it away from him. "Okay, let's leave that one alone, shall we?"

"Why?" asked Asten, picking the stone back up. "It's one of the most powerful runes, and it would probably help us a lot."

Erluc grimaced. "I don't know, man. It sounds pretty dangerous."

"Exactly," countered Asten. "And that means it'd be even more useful in battle. But you're the leader, you decide."

Erluc sighed in contemplation. "We can't afford to make this trip without everyone at full strength, and it's possible we'll lose more than we'll gain if we try using this." He paused, turning to Asten. "But, if we encounter Vyrnaur—or someone as strong as her—we don't stand a chance without me summoning my Awakened form, which I have no idea how to do yet." He shrugged at the Mage. "It's your risk, it's your call."

Asten turned to look around at everyone. They all had the same expression on their face: anticipation. He had waited forever to be trusted enough to make a decision, and now—when he was finally given the opportunity—he was terrified of it. What would happen to the people looking to him for an answer if he made the wrong choice?

A newfound respect for Erluc bloomed in Asten's mind. The Warrior had always been able to make the right judgment when the time came; that was why he was the chosen leader of the Trinity. Asten needed to start taking control of his own fate, influencing his future. He closed his eyes and exhaled deeply. "I'm going to do it."

He turned the stone over in his fingers, then tapped it against the ring. He frowned at Erluc, who shrugged and indicated Kera. The princess just sighed. "Moren is a powerful rune. I don't think that you possess the strength to join it to your ring yet."

Asten wiped his brow, turning to her. "Could you do it then?"

"I don't think that's how this works." Kera shook her head. "Some runes are so powerful that you need to use alchemy to bind them to objects."

"We know an alchemist," pointed out Asten.

Renidos grimaced. "I couldn't find him anywhere. There *has* to be another way."

Kera cleared her throat and indicated the stone in Asten's hand. "You can cast the runestone itself, too, if it comes to it."

Asten blinked. He'd forgotten that that was a possibility. "Is there a downside to that?"

"A runestone is destroyed when cast independently." Kera waved a hand as Asten opened his mouth to question her further. Nodding quickly, Asten snatched a stone out of Renidos' hand.

"What are you doing?" demanded the younger boy, clearly dumbfounded.

"Maleryar," explained Asten, and Kera's eyes glinted in recognition. "This is the Bind rune—the same rune that Alisthír drew with etherinite chalk to bond Vistre to my ring."

"And you're going to cast Maleryar to bond Moren to your ring?" clarified Kera, prompting a scowl from Erluc. He'd almost given up on the conversation entirely, but it looked like they'd found some kind of solution.

Asten nodded quickly. "Exactly," he confirmed. Placing the Death rune beside his ring on the ground, he knelt with the Bind rune in his hand. Everyone else fortified themselves behind him. Even the beasts seemed apprehensive, unsure of what was happening.

"Uh, Asten?" checked Renidos. "You don't know what you're doing, do you?"

The Mage slowly took a deep breath. "Not really," he admitted. "It's not like there are *instructions*."

"Just do the same thing that you do with the other runes," offered Renidos.

"No," disagreed Kera, "This does not work the same way as runes cast from your ring. First of all, you need to throw the stone. Second, you have to say its name.

And most importantly, it's completely meaningless if you don't know exactly what you're doing. You have to believe *without reservation* that it's going to work, or it won't. There is no room for doubt when casting runestones."

Asten gulped, closing his eyes. *I can do this. This is going to work. I'm going to make this work.* He raised the stone once more, clearly picturing the Death rune in his mind, etched into the gold of his ring.

The familiar tingle that he felt before using the power of lightning filled him, and he directed it into the stone. The runestone *would* work. A sudden surge of energy swept through his body, and he raised his head, his eyes snapping open. He flung the stone at the ground where his ring lay, chanting, "Maleryar!"

A shockwave shot out from the stone, throwing them all backwards. Frostbite growled, standing in front of Renidos, who was the closest to the collision. The runestone burst into a swirling orb of orange flame, surrounding the beast, who seemed to be more shocked than in pain.

A huge flash detonated in the room, and he raised his hands to shield his eyes. The Mage shook his head violently, fighting to regain his sight. His ears rang endlessly, and he dropped to his hands and knees. *What's happening?!* Just when he thought that he couldn't survive any more torture, the pain subsided.

The Death stone dissolved into a shower of golden light, which lanced toward the grmmn and entered its chest. The wolf's eyes narrowed, its teeth elongating into curved, razor-sharp fangs. Its body became longer and sleeker, the wings taking on an elegant delta shape. It tensed, its powerful muscles rippling, and howled, fearlessly announcing its presence to the entire world. It had silver fur surrounding its body, the bat-like wings of the grmmn protruding out of its sides. The curved fangs of the beast gleamed in Telaris' flames, like miniature swords. Frostbite's storm-gray eyes had given way to an unforgiving black.

Erluc twirled his sword in the air, causing Kera to jump backwards to avoid the searing heat. He helped Asten to his feet, who was completely shocked. "What the hell?" breathed the Mage. Nobody moved as the hulking beast turned to face them.

"Frostbite?" whispered Renidos. He tentatively extended an arm, inching towards the beast.

Unfortunately, before anyone could rejoice, the grmmn charged for the exit of the stables. Erluc pulled Kera out of the way just in time as the beast barreled past them. It pounced into the air, razor claws ripping through the wood as though it were cheese. It kicked the wall apart, debris clattering loudly across the paved palace grounds.

The Warrior acted swiftly, crystallizing his blade in ice and firing a non-lethal bolt at the beast. Frostbite growled as the icy blast contacted his fur, fighting to be free of the ice, but the glaze had frozen his leg to the wall, obstructing all movement.

Just then, a glass-shattering screech echoed throughout Inthyl. A handmaiden had come to check on the noise, and finding herself face-to-face with a seven-foot-tall beast, she threw her hands into the air, scampering away for her life. Renidos raced outside in time to see her run into the palace, yelling for help.

"Oh, boy." He turned to everyone. "I think it may be time to leave. We're not going to want to explain this to the Council." They hurriedly stumbled out, bounding out of the stables and to the edge of the palace grounds.

Renidos struggled to drag Frostbite out of the stables, breaking the ice with one of Zythir's tips. This time, the creature didn't flee but growled faintly. Renidos hesitantly touched its rough fur. The beast flinched at contact but slowly crouched down, as if it was inviting Renidos to mount.

"Asten, the ring!" called Erluc, and the Mage swore, scooping up the ring from the ground as he sprinted after the Warrior.

Renidos advanced tentatively. "Frostbite?" The beast growled softly, acknowledging the call. He leaped onto the beast's back, grabbing onto a spike between its wings for balance. Kera followed him up, her arms fastening around Renidos for support. "Erluc!" called the Spectre.

The Warrior turned as he followed Asten further into the stables. "Go! We'll meet you at the Pyre!" he yelled back. Renidos nodded as he heard a flurry of worried voices behind him.

"You're not afraid of heights, are you?" he whispered to Kera.

She shrugged, "I don't know. This is the highest I've been."

Renidos smirked. "Well, try to hold on." Her arms tightened around him, and he tapped Frostbite's side. The mountain wolf howled, rocketing off from the ground and into the sky. They soared soundlessly into the moonless night as the palace rocked awake in panic below them.

Chapter 26

Extreme Makeover Alert

Inthyl, Aenor
Asten

Asten crouched beside Erluc, concealed behind a pile of hay. "I'm sorry, I don't know what happened back there—"

"It's okay," Erluc cut him off. "We'll deal with that later." He pulled Asten, who had begun to rise, behind the haystack just as a patrolman hurried through the stables. A moment later, once the coast was clear, they both emerged.

Asten looked up to see a cloud swiftly covering the moon, then turned back to where Erluc had disappeared into a stall. "Erluc!" he hissed. "We have cloud cover."

In response, Erluc led Skyblaze out of the stall by a rope and waved Asten over. "Let's go." Once Asten had clambered onto the pegasus behind him, he quickly snapped the reins, and they ascended quickly into the protection of the clouds.

"Wait!" whispered Asten. "If we're going to the Pyre, then—"

"It's forbidden, I know," finished Erluc. "But since when have we let that stop us? And hey, if you can think of a better place where we can land a pegasus and a magically enhanced death-wolf with an istroc without someone seeing us, I'm all ears."

Asten looked down, the border of Inthyl marking a faint line far below. "It sounds risky."

"Maybe." Neither of them said anything more before Erluc brought down Skyblaze on the lush grass and creamy flowers that grew on the island. He watched the elegant blossoms with sorrow, knowing as well as Asten that they were only able to sprout in fertile ash—ash from the funeral pyres of fallen rulers.

Asten quickly slid off the pegasus and ran through the springy grass to where Renidos waited with Frostbite. Erluc dismounted and led Skyblaze up to them. Renidos, too occupied watching Elandas' statue in the renewed moonlight, didn't even notice them until Asten lightly rested a hand on his shoulder.

He whirled around. "Aaah!" Frostbite bounded to his side, growling, but he relaxed once they saw who had startled him. Erluc grinned and patted his back. "Did you make it here all right?"

Renidos nodded. "I don't *think* anyone saw us, but I didn't try hiding in the clouds. That was a good idea."

Asten stared at him incredulously. "You didn't use cloud cover? It's a miracle you weren't seen!"

"Wait," cut in Erluc. "Where's Kera?"

"Lutens Braka," explained Renidos. "She should be here soon." Asten spun around to see Kera slithering out of the water, her scepter in her hand. She wore a simple, close-fitting tunic, most likely to give her more freedom of movement. She squeezed the water out of her dark hair, asking, "So, do we have a plan?" The sight spell seemed to have worn off, but Asten wasn't too worried, especially since they wouldn't be running into anyone for at least a few days.

"I think so," said Asten cautiously. "We fly to Tirenya, then see if we can find out where the elven capital is. We might even be able to learn some local legends about the Heart if we're—"

"You don't know where the capital is?" interjected Erluc. "And I was afraid that we were going in blind."

Asten shook his head. "Urunyára *used* to be the capital, but it's abandoned."

"I've heard that story," offered Renidos. "I don't remember much, though."

Kera glided up beside him. "I do," she said quietly. "The king of the moon elves shifted the capital south long ago as a warfront. This much is certain. But there are rumors of a dark power spreading in the forest, surrounding the new capital."

Erluc looked puzzled. "Wait, exactly how many types of elves are there?"

"It's complicated," Kera explained. "They were all the same species once, but the elves that lived in the East Archanios were slowly corrupted over time and became dark elves."

An idea began to form in Asten's mind. "What if that's what's happening to the Archanios? Another blight like that… the entire forest could end up like the East."

Erluc tensed at the memory, unconsciously drumming his fingers against Skyblaze's side. "I nearly died going through there, and it looks like I was one of the more fortunate ones." His face seemed to pale as he remembered his journey. "I saw thousands of skeletons there, the skeletons of those who hadn't survived the journey. The Archanios… like that… it would be—"

"March of the undead elves?" finished Renidos, before he shook his head. "That sounded a whole lot better in my head."

Asten nodded. "We can investigate once we get there. But for now, we need to make it to Tirenya." He shook his head to clear it. "Are we ready to go?"

Kera shrugged. "I doubt there is much preparation that can be done here."

"True," acknowledged Erluc, mounting Skyblaze. "This is going to be a long trip"—he turned to Asten and Kera—"and this is your first voyage. If you need anything, you'd best be getting it now." Both of them shook their heads, and Erluc took one final look at the stars above him.

"Hold on." Renidos raised a hand. "What about Kera? The spell's worn off."

"I am not being left behind, if that is what you are suggesting," said Kera coldly.

"You two are unbelievable," sighed Asten, closing his eyes. He channeled the rune of Sight through his ring and felt a surge of energy. He opened his eyes, and Kera's hair was once again blonde. When he looked down, he saw Kera with distinctly human legs. If he concentrated, her tail flickered back into existence, but to a casual observer, she would look like an average nineteen-year-old girl in a tunic and black leggings. Asten sighed, glad that his abilities hadn't been completely altered by their previous experience.

Kera tilted her head. "I'm never going to get used to that."

Renidos raised an eyebrow. "Wait a second. If we're traveling to the Archanios, shouldn't we be disguised as elves?" he remembered. "I don't imagine that there are many humans there."

"How am I supposed to know what an elf looks like?" replied Asten. "I can give it a try after we get there, but it is quite risky, and it doesn't seem that today is exactly a good day to experiment with new spells. I don't want to end up with hair coming out of my mouth."

Erluc rolled his eyes, agitated. "Anyone want to stay for a cup of coffee, or are we finally leaving?"

Asten raised an eyebrow. "We can afford a few more minutes, calm down." He considered stalling on purpose but decided against it—the Warrior was dangerously close to impaling him.

"No, you're right. Let's just wait for them to get here." Renidos pointed to the city, where a ship was leaving the dock and sailing for the island.

Asten swore. This was why they needed cloud cover. "Time to go?"

No one complained. Without wasting another moment, he clambered onto Skyblaze behind Erluc as Kera struggled to mount Frostbite again with the dual disadvantage of a serpent tail and illusory legs. Once she had managed it with Renidos' help, both beasts took off, arcing over the lake to the northwest.

The next few days were far from easy, but the four of them together made a good team. The first two nights, they got as much rest as they could, restocking their provisions in any villages that they came across.

Although these nights were relatively uneventful, the Trinity were able to amuse themselves on the fourth night. An unfortunate gang of bandits tried to sneak into their camp and were in for a surprise when four teenagers threatened them to leave. Renidos swiped a few queltras from them, and a quick unsheathing of Telaris was more than enough to scare away the footpads.

The night in the Manos Desert, Erluc took charge of making a fire with some scrub while Kera used her scepter to summon water from the ground into the air, refilling their waterskins before letting the precious liquid drain back into the thirsty sand. By late morning the next day, the travelers had reached the outskirts of a forest that stretched north and south as far as Asten could see.

"The Archanios," he called to the others. "Tirenya is west of here, probably some way north, too."

Keeping their bearings was difficult in such a wide expanse, and twice Skyblaze went too far south before Asten saw the river below and rectified his mistake. They landed in Tirenya several hours before dusk, tying the animals to concealed but relatively easy-to-find trees on the outskirts of the city. Asten decided to wrap the weapons in a bundle and hide them in a tree, to the sound of Erluc's vehement protests. Whatever the dangers, they couldn't afford to risk being seen as a threat.

"You know," mused Renidos as they walked among the low-roofed, wooden buildings. "As strange as it is seeing an istroc in Inthyl, the elves here are probably going to be just as surprised when a group of humans shows up in one of their cities."

Erluc scratched the back of his neck. "Now that I think about it, though, why is it no one has ever actually made it into the forest? We had no trouble getting here, but nobody has ever made it into the Archanios, have they?"

"Maybe it's because we flew in," conjectured Asten. "There could be some sort of enchantment on the trees on the border." He leaned over and snatched Erluc's map out of his belt, spreading it out on the ground. "We're here," he explained, tapping Tirenya. "My guess is that the forest border goes something like this." He traced out a line in the dirt to the west, extending the border some way before drawing the western side of the forest. "Urunyára should be here." He marked a dot some way northwest of their current position.

Kera tilted her head. "How does that help us?"

"We know that the capital moved south, don't we?" Asten drew a line south from Urunyára, then marked out an area north of the border. "So, the new city should be somewhere in this part of the forest."

"What about the corruption?" reminded Erluc. "If we go in there, then we'll all be killed. If I hadn't had the Guardians' help in the East Archanios, then I definitely wouldn't have survived. I was lucky that Uldarz ordered her to keep me alive."

Renidos shrugged, even though mention of the Guardians seemed to interest him. "You only had a knife, Erluc. There are four of us now, and we all have some kind of power. And we haven't even seen the new Frostbite in action yet."

"We don't even know what he *is*," pointed out Asten. "He seems a little bit… unpredictable. We can't be sure that he'll be loyal or reliable or any of it. He was literally created by magic. He's…" He trailed off, but everyone knew the word he was thinking: abomination. He had created Frostbite by mistake, a creature that could very well upset the balance of nature. Just by looking at him, he could tell that the enhanced grmmn was capable of killing any of them easily—maybe even all of them.

"I doubt there is even a name for something like this," said Kera. "We aren't generally in the habit of bonding living creatures to runestones."

Asten rolled his eyes. *Not like I meant to.* "What if I bonded the Death rune to myself? Would I become invincible as well?"

"Let's just put in a pin in that idea for now, shall we?" Erluc looked around the group. "Does anyone have ideas for names?"

"I mean," offered Asten, "he's literally the combination of the physical embodiment of death and a wolf, so 'death-wolf' doesn't seem like too much of a stretch."

Renidos shook his head, fighting a smile. "We can definitely do better than that."

"Let me know when you have any actual ideas," Asten shot back.

"Okay." Renidos snorted. "How about… saberwolf?"

"That's actually not bad," commented Erluc. "It sounds intimidating and all."

"What does Frostbite have to do with sabers, though?" Asten reminded them. "It's not like we merged him with a sword."

"Maybe because of his fangs?" proposed Kera, pointing. "They look like they could easily be used as swords."

Despite Asten's protests, the term was quickly declared to be official by the other three, and he had no choice but to concede. "Whatever we call him, though," he went on. "he's still dangerous—not just to whatever we find ourselves up against, but maybe to us."

"It's a risk we'll have to take," said Renidos. "He's been fine so far, and let's face it—we'll need him to survive in the blight."

"Assuming it even exists," pointed out Kera. "It's a legend, not a known fact."

Erluc nodded, but he still seemed unconvinced. Asten shot Renidos a sideways glance, thinking that if he were to betray them again, this time with Frostbite on his side, then none of them would survive the encounter. He rolled up the map and handed it back to Erluc, brushing away the markings in the dirt. "So, what do we do now?"

"We use Erluc's other map to find the capital. Then we can leave tomorrow."

"You need to know the name of the place," clarified Erluc.

"Oh." Renidos seemed put out. "Then we can just ask around, find out where the capital is."

"It isn't that simple," warned Kera. "Everyone who lives here knows of the city. It will look suspicious if we aren't acquainted with its location, let alone its name."

"Exactly," agreed Asten. "We're going to need to be subtle here." He pointed at Erluc and Renidos. "That rules out both of you."

"And you," added Erluc.

Fair enough. "Kera can do the talking, then," he decided. "She must have some diplomatic experience, being a princess."

"The first time I left Lutens Braka was a division ago," stated Kera flatly. "And I was kidnapped."

"Maybe not, then," concluded Renidos. "But the question is whether you can be subtle."

Kera splayed her hands. "Maybe. But we don't have another plan, so we might as well try it out."

"Then that's settled." Erluc looked around for any dissent, and finding none, he continued, "Where to now?"

Asten shrugged, then knocked on the nearest door. At Erluc's look of irritation, he declared, "It's as good a place to start as any."

When the door opened, a tall man with long, straight, brown hair and angular features, notably his pointed ears, stood in the doorway. At the sight of the four travelers, he went pale but soon regained his composure.

"Aestalar," wished Erluc in Telmírin, and the elf's eyebrows rose up. He wouldn't have expected them to know the language, much less the elves' standard greeting.

"Aestalar," he replied smoothly. "I am Eävil. How may I help you?" He spoke in perfectly articulated Andaeric, which was a surprise to Asten as well.

452 ◆ The Promise of the Warrior

Trying his best to sound sincere, Erluc continued. "We are weary from travel and wanted to ask directions toward the nearest shelter."

"Please, allow me to help you," he offered, motioning for them to enter. "Clearly, you have traveled far to reach here."

Asten cautiously stepped over the threshold. "Thank you. I am Kosias," he glanced back at Erluc, "This is Lahen."

Erluc followed him. "It is an honor."

"I am Liliandra." Kera curtsied gracefully as she made her way inside. Privately, Asten marveled that she had managed the gesture even with a serpent body.

"My name's Diran," declared Renidos, closing the door behind him.

"I am equally honored." Eävil extended his hand and led them to a long, beautifully crafted dining table. "Come, sit. You must be exhausted."

Asten lowered himself into a corner chair next to Erluc. Leaning over, he whispered, "I think hospitality is an integral part of the elvish culture."

"And I thought he was just really happy to see us."

Eävil took the head of the table, sitting next to Asten. "So," he began. "It has been many an age since the city of Tirenya has been graced by the presence of humans. To what do we owe the honor?"

"Kosias' academic curiosity," chuckled Kera.

"Ah." Eävil nodded. "How did you get here? It seems like a long journey from Aenor."

"We—" Asten cut himself off, realizing how dangerous the conversation had become. *He wants to find out how we made it into the forest. So the borders* are *enchanted.*

Luckily, an equally tall, blonde-haired elven woman in a white dress stepped into the room at that moment. Her eyes widened, probably at the sight of four human teenagers sitting at her dining table, but a warning glance from Eävil stopped her. The two of them had a quick, intense discussion in Telmírin, before the woman nodded and sat down opposite Kera, smiling warmly. "Welcome to our home, travelers. I am Alatíra." Asten glanced at Erluc, who shook his head. At least now he knew that they weren't in any immediate danger.

"These are Lahen, Kosias, Diran, and Liliandra," explained Eävil. Each of them quickly greeted Alatíra, who then asked, "So, it was Kosias' idea to come here?"

"I've always admired the Archanios and the elves," offered Asten. "Lahen wanted to see if there was any truth to the legends of the enchantments on the borders, for starters."

"There is indeed," confirmed Eävil. "I, for one, am intrigued as to how you made it past them."

"As am I," added Alatíra.

"We…" Renidos hesitated. "We climbed the trees. We traveled through the branches until they stopped shifting." Asten raised an eyebrow—that wasn't too bad for improvisation.

Alatíra nodded, and Renidos relaxed; he'd just said whatever came into his mind.

"Ingenious," she remarked. "Excuse me." She rose and left the room while the others made conversation about Aenor and what it was like there. When she returned, she was carrying two bowls of clear broth, which she gave to Asten and Eävil. Renidos and Kera each got a bowl too, but Erluc tried his best to sound polite as he declined when the elven woman turned to get a bowl for him.

Asten took a small mouthful of the soup. It was light and crisp, sweet as the wild fruit he used to pick in Sering, but with an edge like the wind blowing through a pine forest. He couldn't even tell if the liquid was meant to be warm or cold.

He looked up in wonder. "This is amazing. What is it made of?"

"It is water from Inas Erinanth boiled with the juice of crushed dewberries," replied Alatíra with a laugh.

"What is Inas Erinanth?" asked Renidos, taking a sip himself.

"The river of… Eävil, what is it in Andaeric?" Alatíra paused, trying to remember.

"The River of Beauty," answered Erluc, surprising everyone present.

Nodding, Alatíra seemed to become more wary of him. "We call this broth *silrein*. One bowl is usually enough to last anyone a full day, but we have other foods, of course." Asten offered Erluc a sip, but when he tried it, it was all he could do not to spit it out. Some people just had no taste.

"Does it cost a lot to make?" he asked further.

"Nothing at all, actually," clarified Alatíra. "A bushel of dewberries costs one to two moonstones, depending on the rain, and that can last the two of us a week on its own."

"I see," remarked Asten. "I suppose that even for such dishes, variety can be refreshing."

The elf nodded. "Indeed. If you intend to stay on in the Archanios, I believe you would quite enjoy our cuisine."

"I must confess, I too am interested in where you have decided to go from here," added Eävil.

Asten looked directly at Kera. *This is your moment.*

Understanding, she responded, "We plan to explore the forest for another week, and then we might visit the ruins of Urunyára."

"Urunyára?" Alatíra looked apprehensive. "King Enyë outlawed travel to the ancient capital many years ago, Liliandra. Did you not know?"

Enyë. Finally, they were making progress.

Erluc looked about to add a sarcastic remark, but Asten jumped in. "I'm afraid not. But that's alright—we would learn much from going to the king's capital, too."

"You forget that no human has entered the Archanios since the days of Alydris," reminded Eävil. "If you are seen in a city as large as Neraz Valio, then there will be questions asked. You will be taken to Enyë, and I doubt your academic interest will serve as an excuse as to how and why you broke through our arcane defenses."

Erluc and Asten exchanged a look. *Neraz Valio.*

Kera seemed to get the hint as well, because she quickly steered the conversation away from travel to the capital, and within ten minutes, she and the Trinity were back on the road, their waterskins filled to the brim with *silrein.* They sprinted back to Frostbite and Skyblaze, then spread out the map Erluc had gotten from the Ancient. Erluc clearly spoke the name "Neraz Valio," and they all watched intently as the map blurred and refocused, showing a city some way south of Urunyára, in the center of the area where Asten had predicted it would be.

He eyed the Mage sourly, and Asten beamed. "I have to be right *sometimes*, you know."

Erluc crossed his arms. "Congratulations."

Renidos climbed onto Frostbite and helped Kera up, but Asten motioned for them to stop. "We can't leave yet," he warned.

"No?" Erluc finished untying Skyblaze and looked up.

Asten shook his head. "Do you remember what Eävil said? If we go to Neraz Valio looking like this, we'll be noticed right away. We were lucky here, but we can't count on being so fortunate again. We're trying to go unnoticed, and four humans strolling into an elven city—that's what they see."

"So, what do you think we should do?" questioned Renidos. In response, Asten held up his golden ring, and everyone groaned. "I thought you said that you couldn't use that here," recalled Renidos.

Sighing, Asten shook his head. "That was before I'd ever seen an elf," he explained. "Thanks to Eävil and Alatíra, I know roughly how both male and female elves look."

"So, you're going to disguise all of us as elves?" demanded Erluc.

Kera shuddered. "The blonde hair was bad enough. I don't think I could survive with those ridiculous pointed ears."

"The alternative is being captured and dragged before the king," reminded Renidos.

Asten grinned and pointed at him victoriously. "See? *He* knows what I'm talking about."

Erluc looked like he was trying to swallow an entire bowl of Alatíra's *silrein*. "Fine. But if we're stuck looking like elves forever, then…"

"Don't worry," interjected Asten hastily. Raising his hands, he closed his eyes and concentrated on Cuínwë, the rune of Sight. He saw himself, saw his friends, but several inches taller, with ears that pointed slightly at the tips. He visualized Erluc with slender, angular features, saw Renidos with lighter skin and straight, long hair, imagined all of them wearing robes just as Eävil had. His ring grew hot, and when he opened his eyes again, a soft, warm glow was swiftly fading from it.

"I think it worked," began Renidos cautiously. "But…" he trailed off.

"Did it?" Kera's hand jumped to her ears.

"You can't feel the change," reminded Asten. "Trust me, they're pointed."

Kera's expression became as grumpy as Erluc's. "Excellent."

Erluc sighed. "Can we just go now?" When nobody objected, he and Asten swung up onto Skyblaze, who reared violently before launching himself off the ground. Frostbite followed a moment later, and Erluc passed the map back to Asten.

Opening the scroll as best as he could while riding a pegasus in flight, Asten glanced over at the setting sun, squinting. The best that he could figure, they needed to fly a bit farther south. Of course, there was always some error when judging by the sun, and for whatever reason, that error had begun to increase steadily as they traveled north, to the point at which it had led them too far south twice.

He tapped Erluc's shoulder, calling, "Bear left!" Erluc shifted the reins, causing Skyblaze to turn slightly to the south. As much as he wanted to visit Urunyára, Asten knew that if there was any way to save Roxanna, it would likely be in Neraz Valio, under the watchful eye of the king. Yet still, despite that, he had a sinking feeling that traveling to the capital was a grave mistake.

On top of that, he had to set aside his sense of guilt about lying to Eävil and Alatíra, as well as coming to steal a priceless artifact. If they took it, the blame would likely fall on the dwarves, who would have to endure another full-scale invasion from King Enyë's armies.

He refocused himself by watching Erluc guide Skyblaze. Even though he was facing away from Asten, his pain and determination were evident. If nothing else, Erluc Turcaelion was easy to read—at least by someone who had known him for seventeen years. All of this was for him—for Rose. There was no room for doubt. Not now.

When he saw the trees clear in the dim light, he pointed it out, and Erluc brought Skyblaze into a sharp dive, Frostbite descending after them in a gentle spiral. Dismounting, Asten looked up and pointed frantically into the forest, and Renidos clearly got the message, landing some way into the trees in a smooth curve.

After tying Skyblaze to a tree, Erluc followed Asten in the direction in which he had last seen Frostbite, where they met Kera searching for them. "There you are!"

Asten scowled as Renidos emerged from the trees. "What were you thinking?! You could have been spotted!"

Turning to Erluc, Renidos raised an eyebrow. "Is he always like this during voyages?"

His friend nodded curtly. "It's fine. At this time of night, we would need to be terribly unlucky for anyone to have seen that."

Asten turned around unconsciously, half-expecting an elf to emerge and demand what a giant flying wolf was doing outside Neraz Valio. Given their luck, that wouldn't have been too surprising.

"We tied Frostbite to an old oak," put in Kera hastily, anxious to change the subject. "So, do we do the same thing we did before? Go to the first house we see and ask for shelter?"

"Or we could visit the palace as guests," suggested Erluc. "Head straight to the top."

"Excellent plan," shot back Asten. "We waltz into Enyë's court and ask politely if we can borrow the Heart of the

Moon, after which we are offered the option of being beheaded, hanged, or burned alive."

Kera sighed. "Subtlety, remember? We just need to find out where the Heart is and then—"

"It's as good as ours," finished Renidos.

"Hold on." Asten pressed two fingers to his forehead. "Do you remember what Alatíra said? Travel to Urunyára has been forbidden. That means that there's something there that Enyë doesn't want found."

"Like an ancient gem of unimaginable power?" offered Erluc.

"Something like that," agreed Asten. "But if you think about it, Enyë could want to keep the Heart close to him—here, in Neraz Valio."

"But we have no way of knowing which place he chose." Renidos scowled.

"We don't have time for this!" Erluc clenched his fists in frustration. "We need to go somewhere and go there quickly. Do we fly to Urunyára or not?"

Asten and Kera exchanged a look, as though they'd already discussed this. "We could split up," the istroc suggested hesitantly. "Renidos can come with me to Urunyára, and you and Asten can investigate here. If there's nothing to be found there, we'll come back and find you."

"It could work," acknowledged Renidos. "At any rate, I saw some pegasi in Tirenya, but Frostbite wouldn't go unnoticed. If we take him north, he won't attract attention. And Skyblaze in Neraz Valio—no one would give him a second thought."

"I don't like the notion of splitting up," warned Asten.

Kera raised an eyebrow. "You're the one who said that the Heart could be at either place. How else are we going to search both of them?"

"I don't know, but we're going to have to come up with something else," Asten insisted. "If there really is a corruption, we'll all need to be together to stay alive. And it's not as though we've had great experiences when we've split up." Erluc grimaced. "Both of them involved someone getting imprisoned in a dark elven fortress."

Erluc shook his head. "It's a risk that we'll need to take. We don't have any time to waste."

"So, we are separating," clarified Asten.

Honestly, Asten'd never thought that Erluc was even capable of such emotion—especially towards a girl. Ever since they were kids, Erluc hadn't once expressed or even clarified his feelings towards anyone. Not even to Asten. The issue only became worse as they matured into teenagers and had started to get more popular around town. From one promiscuous liaison to another, Erluc suppressed any and all of his feelings just because he wasn't ready to confess and commit to any one person.

Erluc would never admit it, but Asten had known him for long enough to figure it out—behind all of his pride and confidence, Erluc was scared. He was scared to invest and trust anyone else with his feelings, for fear of losing his heart. So, he would never admit his love—possibly not even to himself. And now, with everything that had happened, Asten thought, maybe Erluc was right to keep to himself.

"We are," confirmed Erluc. "But let's spend the night here. You can leave in the morning." After a quick assent from the group, Asten found Skyblaze, untied him, and led him over to Erluc, who took the reins and followed him towards the city entrance. The city's gate was forged of steel bars, twisting and coiling in the center to form an uncanny likeness of a serpent swallowing its own tail.

"You know," said Asten slowly, "of all the cities ever, I would have expected Lutens Braka to have something like this on its gate."

Kera tilted her head, confused. "Why?"

Asten shook his head in disbelief, while the others looked at Kera with exasperation. "Forget I said anything." He stepped forward. "Let's go."

Shrugging, Kera followed him as he slipped through the gates, with Erluc and Renidos discussing the Steel Trial in low voices as they headed after them. "If anyone asks," she warned, "You came here on Skyblaze. We live in Tirenya, okay?"

"Fair enough." Renidos looked around. "Wow."

"*Wow* is right," agreed Erluc.

Asten stopped studying his palms and raised his head. "Great Falcon." Tirenya, with its low-roofed wooden structures, would not have struck any of them as majestic or imposing, but the massive black stone spires of Neraz Valio commanded a whole new kind of respect. The city was beautiful, without a doubt, but it was a twisted sort of beauty, like the painting of the dragon in Inthyl's library that Asten had become so accustomed to.

Erluc shook his shoulder. "It's getting dark."

"Right," agreed Asten, thoroughly discombobulated. To break the awkward pause that followed, he added. "So, how do we talk like elves?"

"I don't know," returned Erluc. "Give me something to say."

"Um…" Asten paused, scratching his head. "I like soup?"

"Nice try," Erluc countered.

"How about, 'Your house is nice'?" offered Renidos. "You'll probably have to say it at some point."

"The divine beauty of this house is unmatched," fired back Erluc. "I think we'll be fine."

"I would say dwelling," advised Asten.

Kera hit Erluc's shoulder lightly with an air of urgency. "We should go before it gets too dark."

Erluc nodded, turning to Renidos. "Good luck, you two. Meet us here in… four days, if you don't find the Heart. If you're not here, we'll head to Urunyára to find you. If you do find it, leave us a note tied under this gate and get to Inthyl as soon as possible."

Unsure how to react to the situation, Asten nodded briskly and managed, "Good luck."

"Good luck," echoed Kera softly. "If we don't find you here, we'll take it that you've found the Heart."

"Four days," reminded Renidos. Asten watched as both he and Kera walked out of the gates and disappeared into the trees.

"Well." Erluc turned to Asten with a shrug. "This looks familiar. What do you think? Should we camp out here or explore the hidden city of the elves?"

Asten snorted, indicating the forest around them. "You want to build the fire, or should I?"

Chapter 27

A ROYAL WELCOME

NERAZ VALIO, ARCHANIOS
Asten

Yawning, Asten stood and brushed aside the bed of fallen pine needles they'd been sleeping on, then gently shook Erluc's shoulder to rouse him.

"You have that piney smell," he told his friend as he sat up, rubbing his eyes.

Erluc rose, "You know, that's strange. I always thought that people smell like *cake* after sleeping on pine needles." He rolled his eyes, stretching his arms as he straightened his tunic.

Asten snorted. "At least we'll be able to better pass off as elves." Erluc scattered the needles, and shouldered his pack, tossing Skyblaze an apple. He made sure to take Telaris with him this time—this city was too sinister for his liking.

"If you say so." He scratched the back of his head, indicating the city. "Ladies first."

Hefting his own pack, Asten handed Skyblaze's reins to Erluc, slowly walking towards the gates. "I'm well aware of your priorities, believe me." Erluc chuckled, and Asten allowed himself a little smirk as well.

For the second time, he found himself marveling at the imposing architecture that made up the foundation of Neraz Valio. From what Eävil had told him, the capital was a relatively new city, for the elves, at least; it had been constructed in his lifetime, about six centuries before. *Probably just before it became the capital.* Enyë must have had designs on the war even before he ever became the king.

"Don't forget," he warned if only to break the silence. "If there is a corruption, we'll need to be on guard."

"Judging by the houses these people live in, I'd say that it's not unlikely," responded Erluc, slipping through the gate. "Should we look for an inn and get some unsuspecting noble drunk enough to talk?"

Asten ignored this. "That'd work in Aenor," he guessed. "Not here."

"But we do need somewhere to stay," reasoned Erluc. "And that can't be someone's house. It'd raise too many questions, and personally, I'd prefer to avoid having to lapse into elfspeak every time I have a meal."

"Maybe there's some sort of rest house here." Asten pressed four fingers to his forehead.

"So, an inn," amended Erluc.

"With fewer drinks," clarified Asten with a private chuckle.

Erluc grimaced. "There goes a minute of my life I'm never getting back."

"Actually," he continued, "I've been meaning to talk to you about something." Erluc looked up, slightly intrigued. "What Renidos did… I don't think—"

"No." Erluc immediately stopped him. "I know what you're going to say, but I don't think we'll have to worry about that kind of thing again." His tone sounded like he was certain.

Asten flicked his tooth with his tongue, unsatisfied. "How can you be so sure? If he did it once, he could definitely do it again."

"Have you ever met him?" asked Erluc. "The guy is probably the most loyal person I've ever met." Asten's jaw clenched as his friend said the words, slightly offended, but he didn't interrupt. "The only reason he betrayed us was to ensure his mother's safety. Anyone in his position would do the same thing." The older boy looked like he wanted to say something, but Erluc cut him off. "We're a team now, whether we like it or not. There's no room for distrust."

"But—"

"Look." Erluc met his gaze. "If you aren't sure, then the only thing you can do is go and talk to him yourself. I'm sure that you two can figure it out." He shrugged. "And if you don't, I could always just slip into my Awakened form and beat the living daylights out of the both of you until you do."

Asten snorted. "We could take you."

Erluc almost laughed, letting out a snort of amusement. "Maybe if I was unconscious," he taunted. "No, in my Awakened form, I could easily beat the three of you."

"Three?" asked Asten, a bit too soon. "Right. I forgot about Kera. I haven't seen much of her in battle." He shrugged. "But from what you've told me, she's extremely powerful."

"You haven't seen my Awakened form either." He shrugged. "But I think that without it, a battle between Kera and me would be interesting."

"What about me?" Asten suddenly livened up. "I probably can't best the two of you yet, but I think I'm at least stronger than Renidos." His friend remained silent, and he raised an eyebrow. "Aren't I?"

"I have quite a few answers—none of which you're going to like," admitted Erluc.

Asten scowled, slowly leading the way along a wide, curving road bustling with elves. "Now what?"

"Isn't it obvious?" Erluc shook his head. "Breakfast."

"Of course." Asten shrugged. "Where do we eat, though?"

"I'd settle for anywhere right now, but we don't have any money," reminded Erluc. "Unless you know something I don't."

"Hmm." Asten produced an empty pouch from his pack and filled it with round, flat stones. "Don't look."

After sealing the drawstring, he strolled into a thick knot of elves in an intersection between two roads, then quickly walked into the congregation, knocking down a tall, light-brown-haired elf as he went, then slipped the pouch in his hand into his tunic.

Circling around back to Erluc, he opened the pouch. "How much do you reckon?"

Erluc scowled at the flat, engraved stones, glittering coldly white. "I used to hate it when you did that."

"I know." Asten smiled, replacing the pouch in his tunic. "So, these are moonstones. Another problem—my Telmírin isn't good enough for me to pass off as an elf."

Shrugging, Erluc looked around. "I guess I'm going to have to do the talking, then."

"I hope you're taking this seriously," started Asten, and an idea occurred to him. Quickly patching together what little of the language he knew from study under Alisthír, he continued, "*Or we're going to be in trouble.*"

"Ayor'a novaë, ivastarí ólastora," agreed Erluc conversationally with a shrug.

Asten's jaw dropped. "What was that?" At Erluc's perplexed expression, he quickly hissed in an undertone, "Say that again."

"*Trust me, I'm fluent.*"

Stepping back, Asten blinked twice. "Wow, that's actually pretty good. I'm jealous."

"*It comes naturally to me.*" Clearly bemused, Erluc continued, "*I wonder if pick-up lines still work the same way in this language.*"

"You're disappointing," muttered Asten, trying his best to suppress a smile. "I still don't understand why *you* got this power—as far as I know, Renidos doesn't speak Telmírin either."

Shrugging, Erluc maneuvered them away from a few passing elves. "It could be something about me being the leader," he speculated. "But, your guess is as good as mine."

Asten shook his head, but as he fiddled with the pouch in his tunic, a strong hand gripped his shoulder. The world spun for a moment before he was flat on his back, a dull pain burning in the small of his back. Once he was able to stand, he saw Erluc shouting viciously in Telmírin, as fluently as if it were his first language. The elf facing him stood to eye level with his illusory form, but Asten knew that Erluc was about a foot shorter than him in reality.

Shaking his head to clear it, Asten tried to comprehend what was happening, but they were talking too fast for him to translate. He caught only a few scattered words: thief, deserve, free and king.

King? This could get messy.

He stepped between them, facing the light-brown-haired elf, and said in a low voice, thinking fast for the words,

"*What—what troubles you?*" Any stumbling, he hoped, would be attributed to the fall.

"*You do, thief*," growled back the elf. "*And I do not take kindly to thieves.*" The ruckus that they had caused had attracted a passing troop of soldiers, who intervened almost immediately.

Luckily for Asten, Erluc shoved him out of the way and continued, "*If he is indeed what you claim, prove it.*"

"*It would be my pleasure.*" A hand shooting out, the elf reached into Asten's illusory robes and snatched out the pouch. Pulling back the drawstring to reveal the moonstones, he snapped, "*I am extremely interested to hear about where you found these.*"

He produced a pouch of his own, opening it and spilling out the small rocks inside. "*And where I found these.*" The guards looked to Asten in anticipation, their eyes narrowing when he couldn't fabricate a response.

Erluc turned to Asten, scowling. "Good job," he spat quietly in Andaeric. "He wants to take us to Enyë."

Asten grimaced, shying away from Erluc's gaze. At least their breakfast problem had been solved. Of course, they could have fought their way out of the situation—one well-placed punch from Erluc and they'd have made a break for it—but in an endeavor to stay unnoticed, knocking out a citizen wouldn't have really gone smoothly with the rest of the plan.

The guards had an intriguing array of weapons—one carried a spear twice his height, while another wielded a double-bladed battlestaff, and yet another had a sheathed sword at each hip. Asten bit his lip. *I wouldn't cross these guys.* The elf he'd pickpocketed strode confidently in front, his eyes narrowed in anger.

"You want to get out of here?" he whispered to Erluc in Andaeric.

"Let's play along for a bit," decided the Warrior. "It's just a case of theft—not as though we murdered someone." He snorted, muttering to himself. "Even if I'm coming frightfully close."

Asten frowned. "I think I have a way out of this."

"I've had more than enough of your bright ideas for one day," vetoed Erluc. Asten grimaced. Maybe pickpocketing the elf hadn't been a great decision. The light-brown-haired elf turned back, slyly smiling. Gritting his teeth, Asten hissed in reply. He couldn't say anything in front of the soldiers, so he had to keep his mouth shut.

It was going to be a long walk to the castle.

Instead of torturing himself, he decided to enjoy the twisted beauty of Neraz Valio. The narrow towers were definitely daunting, menacingly staring down upon the passersby below. Compared to Inthyl, there were surprisingly only few wanderers in the streets and fewer birds in the air.

There was an overbearing hollowness about the town as if it was all for show. In the corner of his eye, Asten saw a child look down from a balcony, watching with interest as they were escorted through the city.

He turned to look up, flashing a warm smile, and the elfling stared at him, before allowing herself a small smile. Suddenly, she ran back inside, and Asten could've sworn that one of the guards had looked up.

Erluc seemed to be lost in thought. His eyes nervously wandered the city, searching for anything out of the ordinary. But that was just it—the city was clean.

"Watch your step," directed an elf, and both of them stepped back into reality. They were at the base of a gradual staircase, at the top of which rested Enyë's palace. Asten shivered, following Erluc up.

The palace was built largely of clear, white marble, reflecting whatever light remained to the rest of the city. If Asten had considered the dwellings lining the dirt-paved streets of Neraz Valio's imposing towers, then the palace might as well have been… actually, he couldn't think of any parallel for something like that.

Compared to the rest of the city, it looked breathtakingly beautiful and surprisingly welcoming. Upon reaching the top of the flight of stairs, they passed under a great arch, stopping in front of a pair of massive wooden castle doors. The elf at the front yelled a sharp command, and there was a short, sullen silence.

Asten heard the sound of chains tightening, and gradually, the doors inched apart from each other, revealing an ornate aisle inside. Forest-green banners hung from the walls, and a grand carpet was laid out, leading into the depths of the palace.

"This way," called an elf, leading them inside. Asten turned to Erluc once more, who simply shook his head. Left with no alternative, they passed into the hall, and he turned around to witness the great wooden castle doors pulled closed behind them. Asten gritted his teeth. *Why do I feel like this isn't going to be a good day?*

They followed the carpet, continuing straight until they reached a smaller pair of doors. One elf went inside, while the others waited with Asten and Erluc.

One of the elves took a knife from the light-brown-haired elf's hand, tossing it into a basket in the corner of the room.

The same elf who had talked to them earlier turned to face them. "*Do you have any weapons?*"

"*Just a sword,*" admitted Erluc, indicating Telaris. It wasn't as if the sword was overly inconspicuous, and it probably would've been discovered soon enough. He handed the blade over, a guarded expression on his face. Fortunately, the elf seemed to be oblivious towards the unique forging of the Eclipse.

Asten sucked in his breath. Now they'd lost Telaris, too. Brushing his illusory robes aside to reveal his own sword, he snapped the fingers of his left hand, muttering, "Cuínwë." The scabbard faded from sight, and he looked up at the elf, who was turning to him, as though nothing had happened.

"*And you*," the elf said, pointing at Asten's waist.

Asten shook his head, showing him. "*I'm not much of a fighter*," he lied, trying his best to retain fluency in his speech. The elf nodded, looking him over once, and turned back to Erluc. He motioned for them to follow him, and Asten, Erluc, and the elf from the street turned to face him. There was a creaking noise, and the doors were suddenly pulled open from inside. Erluc exhaled deeply, following two elves into the hall.

As he and Erluc were escorted into the throne room, Asten allowed himself a small smile. Now he had a real weapon. The hall was incredibly well lit, brilliant white light projecting inwards from the walls of the circular chamber. At the end of the carpet started a short staircase, which led to an elevated platform. There rested Enyë, king of the elves, atop a grand, sparkling-white throne.

He was engaged in a conversation with one of his subjects, talking quickly, but in hushed tones. As soon as he noticed them, his eyes widened and then narrowed. *He saw us.* He dismissed the other elf, who bowed deeply and exited the hall. *That's it. We're dead.* Asten tensed, prepared to electrocute everyone in the hall if they tried to approach them.

The elf on the throne was taller than the others but paler, his features more angled. A single curved scar ran across his forehead and over his left eye, but somehow, the injury made him even more imposing as a ruler. Here was a survivor, Asten thought, someone who had fought his way to power. Instead of a crown, a wreath of vines rested around his brow, and across his lap lay a polished, black staff, a strange red jewel adorning the top.

The ranger leading the company knelt. "*Yóru Enyë.*" Lord Enyë.

"Nivisyos," acknowledged the king.

The ranger spoke quickly to the king in harsh Telmírin, such that Asten could understand little of the conversation, but from Erluc's expression, it seemed only to be an account of what had happened. Slightly proud of himself, Asten resisted the urge to cross his arms and did his best to stand to attention.

"*Very well.*" The king nodded crisply. His voice was low but clear, marred only by a slight rasp on the sound 'ae.' "*And where are they from? They seem no more than children.*"

Asten was unable to decipher the guard's next words, but he recognized the name 'Tirenya'. He edged to the left so as to stand closer to Erluc. "Translate for me," he breathed. Erluc nodded almost imperceptibly and began to relay what he was hearing in Andaeric under his breath.

"…is what they claim, at the very least," the elf was saying. "And they are not so young anymore."

Enyë turned to Erluc and the brown-haired elf. "*Is what he is saying the truth?*"

"*Yes, your majesty,*" admitted Erluc solemnly, looking the king in the eyes. There was no point in lying to the king—he looked too cunning to be tricked. Instead, if he tried to gain the king's sympathy, his verdict might be less harsh.

The elf he had pickpocketed looked on smugly. "*He has taken fourteen moonstones, your majesty—no small amount.*"

Enyë frowned. "*And that was all that was on your person?*"

"*It was, my lord.*"

Asten braced himself, tightening his fist. It wasn't going to be easy to fight their way out of here, but with his ring, they had a chance. He considered passing his sword to Erluc—the Warrior could have made much better use of it—but eventually decided it best to hold on to his weapon.

The king considered this, falling silent for the large portion of a minute. "*You may leave,*" he finally told the elf.

Asten raised an eyebrow, and a million thoughts started sparking around in his mind. What was Enyë trying to do? Had he figured out who they were as of yet? Was he trying to talk to them alone?

"*I beg your pardon, your majesty?*" asked the brown-haired elf, certain that he'd misheard the king.

Enyë didn't appreciate having to repeat himself. "*Consider this a lesson: Never keep so much money on your person, lest it disappear altogether. Had your culprit gotten away, you would have found yourself in a dire situation.*" He shook his head. "*You are dismissed.*"

"But—"

Enyë's eyes flashed dangerously. "*You are dismissed,*" he repeated. The elf scowled, kneeling quickly, and strode haughtily out of the hall.

Asten felt slightly guilty about causing such an uncomfortable situation, but whatever remorse he felt was overwhelmed by his elation at escaping what could have ended very, very badly. "Now," he muttered to Erluc in Andaeric, "We get out of here as fast as we can."

"Do you have a plan?"

"Do I ever?" Asten shrugged and looked up. "He'll probably just let us leave." He took a tentative step backwards, before the king's gaze fell upon them.

"*Wait,*" commanded Enyë. "*I'm not done with you two.*"

With the king focused on them, Erluc couldn't safely translate without giving up the game, but his expression clearly indicated that things were not going as planned. He hesitated, then responded tersely, his tone becoming stressed.

Enyë continued to smile and politely returned with, "Naí ráva." *I insist.*

Erluc frowned briefly at Asten before looking back up to the king. "*I am honored,*" he said simply in Telmírin. Indicating with his eyes for Asten to follow him, he knelt swiftly.

Asten hastily copied his example, managing, "*As am I.*"

"We're pardoned," Erluc muttered into his sleeve.

Asten raised an eyebrow. "We are?" he asked almost too loudly, and Erluc shot him a stern look.

"We are," he whispered in Andaeric. "He wants us to stay the night," managed Erluc. "Just be quiet and follow my lead." Asten nodded as subtly as he could, the movement of his head almost imperceptible.

"Veror'í," came Enyë's voice from above them. Erluc stood, Asten following a moment later. For a moment, Erluc quickly conversed with the king, but soon his eyes told Asten that they were free to go. The ranger from before tapped Asten's shoulder, and they followed him out of the hall, sighing in relief once they were out of sight of the king.

The elf nodded. "*It seems like our king sees something in you.*"

Erluc tensed, but he wasn't going to blow their cover just yet. "*In what sense?*"

"*Maybe he admires that youths, like yourselves, have traveled far from home upon your father's wishes,*" guessed Nivisyos. Father's wishes? That must have been a part of the lie Erluc had told. "*Or perhaps simply your bearing—for one so young, you carry yourself with inspiring confidence.*"

Both of them calmed, and Erluc smiled. "*The king is wise and merciful, and we are grateful to be his subjects.*" The sentence was painfully difficult for him to say, but he managed it. "*I'm Lahen.*"

"*Nivisyos,*" nodded the elf, leading them into a large room. "*I'll give you a few minutes to settle in, and we can journey into town.*"

Asten let his pack fall onto a bed, sitting comfortably atop its mattress. "*Thank you.*" The elf nodded, closing the door behind him as he took his leave.

Collapsing backwards, Asten sighed, covering both eyes with his palms. "What happened?" was his first question.

"He insisted that we stay in his palace as guests since we came here alone. I tried to say we'd be fine, but, you know, he wouldn't hear any of it."

Asten scoffed, removing the enchantment on his sword and dropping it onto the bed. "Lucky we didn't need this, after all."

Erluc swore, his eyes widening. "You had that the whole time?"

"Keep it." Asten smirked. "Until you get Telaris back, you're going to need a weapon." Erluc scowled at the reminder, picking up the scabbard and attaching it to his belt. "So why did he let us go?" continued Asten.

"I said we wanted to take the day to explore the city, and he let us go."

Asten laughed aloud. "No way it was that easy. What was the catch?"

"That ranger from before is going to be our escort, at least as long as we're staying in the palace," continued Erluc.

Asten considered this, still slightly bemused. "I imagine he'll be reporting everything we do back to the king."

"Well, I can't think of everything, now can I?" asked Erluc with a scowl, taking off his cloak. "But don't worry—if worst comes to worst, you'll get some practice with your ring."

"Thanks a lot," he muttered. "We're going to die here."

"I'm not the one who stole that elf's moonstones," reminded Erluc, as he walked over to the bed on the other side of the room. "Besides, it's not that bad."

"Isn't it?" challenged Asten, sitting up. "We're in the palace of the king of the Archanios, who, I might add, is acting dubiously gracious. This is the monarch who had relentlessly sent his armies to besiege the Kre'nagan, all because of a thousand-year-old incident."

Just then, they heard a knock on the door, and Nivisyos was standing ready, an elegant bow slung across his back. Erluc smiled—completely fabricated—and greeted the elf, providing him with Asten's alias as well. The Mage did his best to make sense of the conversation, but they were speaking too fast. After a brief pause, Nivisyos nodded. "*Very well.*"

"*Where?*" Asten asked Erluc quietly in Telmírin.

Erluc replied with a word he didn't recognize. At Asten's frown, he rolled his eyes and explained with the word for 'books'.

In an undertone, Asten clarified in Andaeric, "Library?" Erluc nodded and kept walking, whistling an old tune they had used to sing together, bringing back memories of late nights before a bonfire, fueled by excess wood they had worked for over a division to collect, drinking and laughing until the sun came up. Once, when the fire had refused to start, Asten had solved the problem by dousing the firewood with his bottle of ale, and Erluc, grinning, had split his own with him. There was a life gone forever. The past few divisions had cauterized whatever existed of that euphoric recklessness out of them.

Asten fingered the side of his belt, wishing he had kept his sword with him. Without a weapon of his own, he felt vulnerable, dependent on his friends. And though he would never admit it to them, he despised few things more. Being powerless was something he couldn't stand, and passively watching events unfold was never an option. Sighing, he followed Nivisyos into a large building of oak, murmuring the words to Erluc's song under his breath.

Once they were inside, Erluc quickly explained something to the elf, who nodded grudging assent, before walking outside. "I told him we would be here for a while," he clarified. "He agreed to wait outside."

"Nice." Asten nodded, but he wasn't listening anymore. *An elven library.* He smirked, running his fingers along a scroll. Even with the situation they were stuck in, he couldn't help but think that this field trip was going surprisingly well for him.

Chapter 28

The Room of Many and No Words

Neraz Valio, Archanios
Erluc

"So, what are we looking for?" questioned Asten, his eyes wandering the hundreds of scrolls and scriptures across the room.

"Old folklore, legend, anything that could point towards the Heart," returned Erluc promptly. "But looking at this, I don't think my blessing extends to elvish writing."

"Because it's elvish in origin," guessed Asten. "Telmírin was taught to the elves by Adúnareth, but this writing was their own design."

Erluc frowned. "That limits our options."

"Here." Asten took down a scroll labeled in the familiar, angular runes of Andaeric script. "I'll read this out, and you try and translate it." He peered at the title. "Eraígyon ara vanos."

"*Honor and Valor,*" Erluc responded. "Either fiction—"

"Or philosophy," completed Asten. "What about this?" The next scroll that caught his eye was labeled, "Neravír caralwë aí Arythwë-edória."

Erluc shrugged. "*Great Kings of House Arythwë.* Please. *I* could come up with a better title than that."

Asten let the scroll fall open. "Maybe there's something interesting here." He ran a finger down the scroll, reciting names. "Anahïel, Avuthor, Asturian, Arventír Laövurí…" He looked up. "Laövurí? The first?"

Erluc rolled his eyes. "Who cares? Unless Arventír the Second had a magical map leading to the Heart of the Moon, he's really the last thing we should be worrying about."

Ignoring him, Asten continued to scan the headings. "Anuveris, Andevar," he suddenly paused, "Alydris." Asten was something of his disciple, if not just a fan. Even as Erluc sighed in exasperation, he began to read the passage. Though he wasn't translating, his expression clearly signified that the content was entirely irrelevant.

Midway thought, Asten stopped reading and turned to him. "So, what's it about?"

"Some Battle of the Raging Sun. Great magical feats or whatever." Erluc scowled. "What makes this guy so special?"

"A *lot.* Have you ever heard the story of—"

"If I'd wanted to, I'd have kept listening. But we're short on time here, so I'd appreciate you *finding something relevant.*" He virtually spat the last three words, brow furrowed in impatience.

Ignoring him, Asten kept reading in the hopes that Erluc would understand enough of his recitation to find anything useful. Occasionally he would stumble over the correct inflection of a word or a character he hadn't seen but had to infer from context, but on the whole, Erluc seemed to understand what was going on.

As he read, Erluc began skimming through scriptures on the shelves, trying to decipher any illustrations that they contained. He tapped a few more scrolls, then picked out four or five that seemed relevant.

After maybe ten minutes, Erluc raised an eyebrow. "Stop. Read that again."

Frowning, Asten looked up. "The whole thing?"

"The last sentence."

Glancing back at the scroll, Asten reread the last sentence he'd seen. "Why? What does it mean?"

"The last that was heard of Alydris... was a rumor spread by his supposed murderer, the traitorous dwarven king, Horgenn, that he had discovered documents leading to an ancient jewel of some sort."

Asten's eyes widened. "No way. Alydris *found* the Heart of the Moon?"

Erluc nodded. "Keep reading."

Happy to oblige, Asten read two other sentences, but Erluc commented bitterly that they were only related to how Horgenn's treachery had sparked the Eternal War between the dwarves and elves.

"This could be important," prompted Erluc. "We need to find out more about Alydris."

"And Horgenn," offered Asten. "He would have known about the Heart. Maybe the rumors he spread had some truth to them." Opening the scroll again, he found his place and kept reading about how the war had been declared by Alydris' daughter, Araíyal, who had been assassinated in Agmern centuries later. A mysterious figure—Enyë—had taken the throne and declared war against the dwarves.

"That's not good enough," commented Erluc, agitated. They were getting close, and they could both feel it. "Look for documents from before the war started, concerning both Araíyal and Horgenn."

Asten read out the next portion, in the hopes that it would have something interesting to say, but it proved useless once again. Frustrated, he scanned the shelf to his right. "*The Twilight Council, Horgenn and Alydris, the History of the Eternal War.*"

"*What you're looking for is actually just down there,*" interrupted a soft voice, and both Erluc and Asten spun around to notice a short elf carrying two books in his hands. "*Sorry if I startled you. Arsín, at your service.*"

"*No, that's alright,*" assured Erluc in Telmírin, slightly startled. "*Do you own this place?*"

The elf cracked a smile. "*Heavens no. I'm just an assistant to old Adannir.*" He pointed at the shelves behind them. "*You see that book there, with the red spine?*" Erluc nodded, pulling it out, and Asten looked over at the book to see if there was anything interesting concerning the Heart. "*This concerns the history of our people before the beginning of the Eternal War,*" explained Arsín.

"Check this out." He spoke in mumbles so that Arsín wouldn't recognize that they were speaking Andaeric. Erluc nudged Asten, and Arsín slowly approached them. He pointed to the page, where a dark-red gem had been depicted. "*It says that the gem here can be used to store and channel energies.*"

Arsín smiled. "*That's etherinite.*" Although Erluc hadn't been present when Alisthír had used his red chalk of the same name to summon the elements, Asten had. He recognized the name immediately, even if he never knew that the chalk was originally in the form of a stone. "*It used to be* one of the most prized resources *in the Great Archanios, before the Inferno Unceasing.*"

"*The what?*" asked Erluc. "*Uh… I mean, my history always has been a little weak.*" He wasn't lying, but it would certainly be strange if an elf didn't know about the history of their own race.

Slightly suspicious, Arsín continued. "*The Inferno Unceasing was a terrible fire that broke out all across the Great Archanios, in the Anyar Thúron.*"

"*I remember this,*" recalled Asten. "*Wasn't it started by an explosion of sorts?*"

"*Many believe so, but there is no surviving record that proves such,*" responded Arsín. "*It raged for nearly a whole year before the Uruni finally managed to quench it—not a day's travel from here.*" The Uruni were the first elven empire, recalled Erluc from what Asten had been reading earlier, initiated by the very first kings of House Arythwë. "*In the East, heavy rains are believed to have calmed the fire, and when the smoke cleared, more than half of our race was gone.*"

Elven history was something Asten could talk about for ages, and he was glad that he finally had a chance to talk about it with an elf, even if he was incognito. "*They say only one-fifth of the elv— of our race remained,*" added Asten, catching himself just in time. "*And over seven million had perished.*"

Arsín nodded. "*The fire mountain Karthanos in the Far Lands was once said to be rich in etherinite, but again, there is little to no evidence to support this idea.*" He shook his head. "*No, etherinite is all but gone today, only to be found in the depths of the Arnas-i-Oredann.*"

Asten snorted. "*What about King Enyë's staff? I recall seeing a red crystal at its head.*"

"*Anirythias,*" Arsín confirmed, eliciting a small laugh from Erluc. "*You have a keen eye. The sacred staff has been passed down in the royal family for generations, before the days of Alydris himself. This stone has a cherished history as well and was a gift from the first High King of men in the Tiren Calmar—Eltar—to our own King Andevar.*" Asten nodded—Alydris' father. "*Mined thousands of years ago from the great Mount Karthanos on Andaerion, the crystal is perhaps the largest single shard of etherinite in existence. And there is no instance of the stone within three days travel of Neraz Valio, save for Anirythias.*"

Erluc grimaced. He had so many questions about the elves that were still unanswered. "*Does etherinite have any healing capabilities?*" he decided to ask.

The elf frowned. "*Not that I know of,*" he admitted. "*It mostly just stores energy.*" Arsín glanced at the books piled up in Asten's hands, and he raised an eyebrow. "*You've read 'Foes of the Survivors'?*"

Nodding, Asten hastily patched together, "*It wasn't much help.*"

"*Really?*" The elf seemed surprised. "*Out of interest, what are you two looking for, anyway?*"

Erluc stepped in, sure that Asten couldn't keep up the conversation any longer. "*We're interested in what occurred between Horgenn and Araíyal before our queen declared war on him. What was he trying to tell her?*"

Indecision flickered across Arsín's face, before understanding finally dawned upon him. "*The Heart. You seek the Heart of the Moon.*"

Evidently, Erluc had accepted that their charade had failed. He drew the dagger from the folds of his cloak, and Arsín's eyes widened. "*What do you know of it?*"

A large creaking noise escaped from behind them, and Arsín paled. "*It's not safe to talk here. Meet me behind this building in five minutes, and use the back exit.*"

Grimacing, Asten waited as Erluc explained the situation to him, before he frowned. "How do we know he won't escape?"

Erluc conveyed the question, and the elf nodded solemnly. "*You'll have to take a chance with me, or you won't have a chance of finding what you're looking for. But if King Enyë hears about this, neither of us will live another day."*

Nodding, Erluc indicated for the elf to leave, and he turned to Asten, who was still bewildered. "Well?" he questioned. "What did he say?"

"We can't have Enyë catch us talking about this. We're in enough trouble as it is," Erluc explained. "Arsín's going to help us, but he's got more reason to be cautious than we do—if any of us are caught opposing Enyë's will, this isn't going to end well."

Asten grit his teeth. "Which is why I didn't want to accept his invitation to stay in the castle in the first place." He glanced at the back door, which was already cracked open. "It's like we're being watched even when there's no one around."

Erluc nodded. "In the worst case, we'll have to trust that Renidos and Kera found something in Urunyára."

"And if they haven't?"

Erluc's jaw tightened. "That's not trusting."

"It's being realistic," returned Asten. "This elf is our best bet, but if he doesn't know anything, we'll have to leave Neraz Valio empty-handed. What if they don't find anything either? We don't have a name, a place, or anything to help us. How do *you* plan to find the Heart?"

Erluc gritted his teeth. "He'll talk." Turning around, they tentatively followed the elf's footsteps to the back of the library, into a corridor that was the furthest away from the entrance. They exited through the back door, which led to an alley. Arsín paced impatiently before he noticed them and stopped. "*Now,*" demanded Erluc. "*What do you know about the Heart?*"

"*It is only spoken of in myth and legend,*" responded Arsín, quivering behind Erluc's gaze. "*An artifact of great power, lost long ago. It radiated Void energy on a scale never seen before or since. Energy that could be used to destroy or—*"

"*To heal,*" finished Asten.

The librarian nodded, baring his teeth. "*What do you need to heal? You wish to save a loved one?*" He smiled to himself, even as Erluc clenched his fists. "*You come in vain. The relic you seek does not exist, save in the pages of song and story.*"

Erluc looked just about ready to slice him in half, but Asten put a hand on his shoulder. "*Tell us what you know of Horgenn's claim.*"

Arsín glanced at the doors, as though to call for help, but seemed to think better of it. *And a good thing, too.* If Nivisyos suspected that anything was amiss, then they were already dead. He held out his hand, and a scroll materialized inside it. "*A copy of Horgenn's proclamation to the elves, straight from the Twilight Council. All nonsense, of course, but it's not written in Telmírin, at any rate. You won't be able to read it.*"

Asten smiled grimly, taking the scroll. It was Andaeric. "*I think we'll take our chances.*" He skimmed through it, turning back to the elf within a minute. "*Now tell me honestly—do you know where the Heart of the Moon might be?*"

"*Of course not,*" fired back Arsín. "*As far as I'm concerned, it doesn't exist.* But by all means, if you do manage to find the prison and make it out alive with the Heart, and the sun by some miracle hasn't fallen out of the sky, come find me. I'd be very interested in hearing which of the legends are true.*"

Erluc looked up. "What prison?"

"The Vortex of Spirits." Arsín shook his head at their ignorance. "You don't mean to tell me that you haven't heard the legend?"

"Humor us," pressed Asten. "Where is this prison?"

"Did I not just say that it is a legend? It is thought to be west of Neraz Valio—inescapable, if memory serves me correctly. Most who go in search of it find nothing." Arsín shrugged. "The rest never come back."

"Why?" asked Erluc.

"Nobody knows for sure," continued Arsín hesitantly, "but there are rumors. Corruption infests the land, and it is said that the living and the dead walk as one at the glade. Of that, of course, there is no conclusive proof."

"*Of course.*" Asten narrowed his eyes. "*But you said that the Heart would be there, did you not?*"

Arsín's eyes widened. "*Did I?*"

He knows more than he's letting on. Asten cursed himself internally for showing his hand so carelessly. The chances of the elf making such a careless slip of the tongue again were astronomical. He turned to Erluc. "I don't think we're getting any more out of him."

Erluc shrugged. "Nor can anyone else. If he runs to Enyë now, we're finished." Asten nodded his assent. A black cloud of smoke formed around Erluc's right hand, solidifying into a gauntlet, and he brought his arm back to land a blow on Arsín, before he was interrupted by the sound of an opening door.

"*Well, what do we have here?*" questioned a voice, and Asten noticed an elderly elf, hobbling towards them with a wooden cane through the doorway. Cursing, Erluc folded his arm behind his back, willing the gauntlet to disappear. "*These folks giving you any trouble, Arsín?*"

The younger elf smiled. "*Not at all, master.*" He indicated the scroll in Erluc's hand and the books that Asten was carrying. "*I was just helping them find the way back from the latrine.*"

"*Good to hear.*" The old elf nodded. "*I was heading to the latrine myself, as it happens.*" Looking Asten over, he inquired, "*I suppose you found what you were looking for?*"

"*Yes, sir,*" answered Erluc before Asten could embarrass himself. "*We were just heading back to the castle.*" The old elf raised an eyebrow, as did Arsín. "*The great king has offered to host us as his guests for the time being.*"

Impressed, the elf nodded. "*In that case, let me escort you back to the castle,*" he offered.

"*Thank you, but that won't be necessary,*" tried Asten, rather shakily. "*Our guide is waiting for us at the entrance.*"

Arsín smiled, ushering them back into the building. "*At least let us walk you out to the door.*" Now clear that they were fighting a losing battle, Erluc and Asten hastily agreed and followed Arsín and the older elf to the exit, where Nivisyos waited.

"*Well, well. Nivisyos, it's been a long time,*" declared Adannir.

"*Adannir,*" acknowledged the other elf. "*It pleases me to see that you're still alive and well.*" Nivisyos smiled, turning to Asten. "*Were you able to find what you were looking for?*"

Glancing at Arsín, Asten gave an affirmative nod. "*Indeed, Arsín was extremely helpful.*"

Adannir nodded. "*Glad to hear it,*" he declared, patting his assistant on the back. Erluc and Asten concluded with the pleasantries and bid the librarians farewell before they started their return.

"Vor té dryln," called Arsín from behind them.

Trying his best to make it sound genuine, Erluc replied, "Vor té carast."

Nivisyos began to lead the way back to the palace, while Asten and Erluc hung back and started to converse in low voices. They followed Nivisyos up to their chamber, thanking him for his services. Erluc paused, waiting until the elf's footsteps had faded from his hearing, before he carefully shut the door behind him.

"Well, I'm absolutely exhausted," remarked Erluc, crashing down on his bed. "Listening to all that elven history was probably the most studying I've done this whole year."

Asten snorted, relaxing on the bed across from Erluc's. "You never know what might be important."

"Oh, really?" questioned Erluc, a sardonic smirk forming on his face. "I'm going to need to remember that Enyë got lonely and named his staff 'Annie'?"

Letting loose a laugh himself, Asten shook his head. "Anirythias."

"Exactly."

"And he didn't name it—Andevar did," he added. "But forget that. Can you believe we actually got a heading for the Heart?"

Erluc nodded. *The Vortex of Spirits.* "It's surprising how easily Arsín betrayed his king. I knew that the elves weren't as obedient as they let on." Turning back to Asten, he commanded, "Come on, let's get out of here."

The Mage raised both eyebrows. "Now?" He pointed to the ground. "You want to… now?"

"We have what we came here for," reminded Erluc. "And personally, I'd like to get as far away from this castle as is physically possible."

Asten scowled. "Would you calm down?" he requested. "Why are you in such a hurry?"

Erluc fastened his belt around his waist urgently. "For the first time since we set out from Inthyl, we have a real heading. Finally, we can find the Heart and take it back to Rose." He shook his head. "Besides, Renidos and Kera should be back sometime in the next day or two, and we need to be there when they return." He shoved the rest of his belongings into his bag, and Asten followed suit.

Pulling on his cloak, Erluc felt around his belt, and he suddenly froze. He turned to Asten, "Telaris. It's still hidden somewhere in the castle."

The Mage scowled. "Damn." He threw his pack around his shoulders, pushing his ring back to the base of his finger. "How're we going to find it?"

"I don't know," admitted Erluc, extremely flustered. "If we searched the castle, we'd probably just end up getting lost."

"Or captured," offered Asten.

Erluc groaned. He couldn't leave Telaris behind— especially if what Arsín had said about the glade was true. His deadliest powers were connected with the blade, and he wouldn't stand a chance against any significant opponent without it. Running a hand through his hair, he threw himself back onto the bed, staring at the ceiling. "I can't leave without it."

"Wait, I think I saw an armory closet on my way over here," remembered Asten. "It could be stored there. And even if it's not, you can take your pick from the rest of the elven blades."

Erluc tentatively ran a hand through his hair before speaking. "Well, that's better than nothing." Shouldering his pack once more, he peeped into the hallway, advancing after he made sure that it was vacant. "Lead the way," he ushered, indicating the hall with a hand.

Asten led them down the hall, trying his best to make a minimal amount of noise. Passing through two separate junctions, and forking left once, Asten stopped in front of a room with a narrow wooden door. He twisted his ring around his finger, and Erluc raised an eyebrow. "Just in case there are any guards," he explained.

Erluc shrugged, and Asten slowly pushed the door open.

On par with their assumption, the two of them instantly ran into a guard, whose first reaction was to brandish his spear in their direction.

"*Hold!*" called Asten, raising his hands in surrender. "*We're guests of King Enyë.*" He paused, gesturing at the corridor. "*Would you mind showing me the way back to my room, if it's not too much trouble?*"

The guard hesitated, ultimately lowering his weapon. One step forward and Asten smirked, clenching his fist. A moment later, the elf was sprawled across the ground, unconscious.

"What a nice guy," he added as Erluc burst into the room from behind him. Scanning the room, he saw his sword perched upon a shelf, surrounded by several other exquisite elvish blades. Both of them breathed a sigh of relief at the sight. Erluc couldn't have parted with his blade—it was a part of him. Not only that, Kovu had died fighting to help Erluc escape the Vale of Shadows. Telaris was his only legacy, and it would be an insult to his memory if the blade was abandoned in an elven city.

He unbuckled Asten's bloodsteel sword from his belt and tossed it to him. "You can have that back."

Asten returned the sword to its place at his hip, grateful for the familiar weight. He rested his hand on the hilt, looking up at Erluc. "Are we leaving?" His friend nodded, and the pair of them left the room, dragging the guard inside and closing the door.

"The exit isn't too far," he directed, leading Erluc through a pair of corridors, before he stopped in front of a pair of white double doors. Enyë's courtroom. They were close.

Passing through another hall, they arrived at the main foyer, where the main doors were already open, and two guards were waiting for them. Erluc recognized them both as two of the elves that had escorted them to the palace, three days prior.

Well, thank Adúnareth. He'd been looking forward to this.

The first elf barely had the time to open his mouth before Asten blasted him with a bolt of lightning, and was sent flying backwards, crashing into a column. The second, however, had had more time to prepare, and was charging toward them, sword-point extended. Erluc ducked under his first strike, frosting Telaris over as he prepared his own assault. Shooting a shard of ice at the elf's foot, he landed a punch to his chest, winding him.

"This way." Erluc led them away from the great doors, Asten following in hot pursuit. Just as they had passed into the town of Neraz Valio, they paused.

"Wait!" Asten called from behind, and Erluc pulled them into an alley. After catching his breath, he continued. "That was a bit too easy."

Erluc raised both eyebrows in incredulity. "Easy?" he echoed. "We just openly fought three of Enyë's guards without rousing the entire palace. If anything, we're lucky."

"And the doors?" asked Asten, still unconvinced.

"Who cares?" questioned Erluc. "Maybe someone was visiting the castle, or Enyë needed to step out for a late-night murder. It doesn't matter. If it gets us away from here and closer to the Heart, then I'll take it."

Asten considered this. "I still think it's a trap."

"By who? Who's trapping us? Why?" Erluc shook his head. "And anyway, if you haven't noticed, we have a pretty good record against malicious fiends." Even though he usually didn't allow his pride to overcome his decisions, he seemed to be allowing himself to make an exception this one time.

Asten chewed on the inside of his mouth, trying not to let his agitation show. "And what happens when our luck runs out?"

Gritting his teeth, Erluc turned, walking away from the alley. "It won't." He met Asten's gaze, a pained expression on his face. "We're too close for everything to fall apart now."

"You'd better be right," Asten muttered, looking down. The cost of failure loomed before them, weighing heavier on their consciences with every step toward the Heart. *I just hope we don't find out what that cost is.*

Chapter 29

Prison Jaw-Break

Neraz Valio, Archanios

Renidos

*F*inally.

Ducking down as they tore through the swirling fog, Renidos shifted himself slightly on Frostbite. They'd been traveling for the greater portion of the day, and it was satisfying to see that they'd finally made some progress. Heavy fog obscured most of his sight, but Renidos could hazily see the sun starting to come up on the horizon. He nudged the saberwolf's flank, motioning towards the ground.

Frostbite grunted, slowly beginning to decelerate. He spiraled down into a dense thicket of trees, the fog providing them with ample cover from Neraz Valio. Kera gripped his shoulders tightly as they descended, and he gasped in pain.

Great Adúnareth, we need to get her some gloves.

When Frostbite finally touched down, there were small tears in his tunic, leaving behind shallow, red imprints on his skin. He hastily leaped off of the beast, scratching the bottom of its icy chin as Kera did the same.

"Come on," she indicated, "I think it was this way."

Renidos shrugged, beckoning for Frostbite to follow them through the woods. The istroc led him through a mass of close-knit shrubs and vegetation, and they stopped in front of a grand pine which extended far into the skies. But that wasn't why they had stopped.

Below the grand tree, two seventeen-year-old boys were sprawled out, crawled up on gathered pine needles. Fastened around the tree, a rope led to a grand, white pegasus, who neighed in recognition.

"Well, do we wake them up?" asked Kera, turning to Renidos.

He shrugged, smiling as he relaxed against the pine. "Go for it."

She flexed her fingers, and a small sphere of water formed in the center of her palm, spinning as it passed between each of her digits. Kera repeated herself, doing the same with her other hand, and pointed towards the boys. Shooting forward, the liquid dispersed on impact, and both of them instantly jumped up, drawing their weapons.

"What the—" Erluc blurted, slowly stopping himself. "Oh, it's about time." He groaned, thoroughly shaking himself awake. "Sure took you long enough to get here."

Renidos snorted. "Tell you what," he began. "Next time, you have to travel to the abandoned ancient city, and we get to sit around and sleep under the trees."

"We missed you too." Asten groaned. "What—no 'Hello, how are you'?"

"Hello," mocked Renidos.

Kera joined in too. "How are you?"

Scowling, Asten wiped the beads of water from his face, and Erluc sheathed Telaris. "So, did you find anything useful?"

"Whoa, wait. Hold on," Renidos interrupted. "Before we start: This," he said, gesturing to himself, "No more of this. Change me back." People often say that one gets used to something unusual after a while. In Renidos' case, this was evidently not true.

"Actually, I agree. I've had enough of the elves for… well, forever." Erluc turned to Asten, who sighed, tucking his own sword into his belt. The Mage turned his ring to face upward, and his three runes met his eye.

"Cuínwë!" he barked, and the gold metal shined red before a flash blinded them all.

Renidos shook his head, blinking his eyes open. He looked around, sighing in relief. Everyone was back the way he knew them. Even Kera was once again in her true form, green scales shining in the dawn sunlight.

"Finally," she remarked gratefully, twisting her tail around in the air.

In fact, they all looked more at ease on seeing their friends as themselves. Erluc ran a hand through his hair as if he'd been long deprived of the pleasure.

Renidos emptied Asten's waterskin, tossing it back to its owner when he was done. "Good," he declared, scratching the back of his neck. "The most interesting thing we saw was this giant creature that was made of stone, who stepped on Kera's tail and almost punched my spine out of place. It almost looked like it was guarding something, but there was nothing else in the room."

"It was made of stone?" Erluc winced. "How did you get past it?"

Kera shook her head. "I blasted it to rubble, but it just reformed, so we really had no choice but to get out of there, patch up my tail, and get back here as fast as we could." She pointed at her green scales, which had been roughly wrapped in a crude, white bandage. Asten waved his hand at it, and the cloth fell away to reveal her tail, completely unblemished.

"All better." The Mage grinned. "Was there anything else?"

"Well…" Without missing a beat, Renidos launched into a vivid description of the past four days, detailing every aspect of their journey ranging from the initial search of the city to the time Frostbite accidentally froze his legs together for about half an hour. By the time he finished explaining their fight with the stone giant, Asten looked just about ready to fall asleep on the spot.

"Like Urunyára itself, our journeys to and fro were equally uneventful," he concluded. "So, unless you found anything of consequence, we've got nothing."

Asten smirked. "Well then, it's a good thing that we did."

"What!" Kera burst out. "And you just let him go on and on? Why did you even ask us what happened on our trip if you actually found something?"

Erluc shrugged, and Kera covered her eyes in disappointment. He quickly summarized what their stay in Neraz Valio had wrought, and what they had learned. "So, we naturally used the map to find the place, and—"

Renidos suddenly jumped up, and Erluc paused, startled. "You did what?"

"We used the ma—" There was a blur around the site, and a second later, Erluc's pack was open, Renidos standing above it with the scroll in his hands. "What in the world are you doing?" demanded Erluc.

Ignoring him, Renidos kept his gaze fixed upon the parchment. "Show me the Heart of the Moon." For a moment, a hesitant silence befell the camp, and not a soul moved. The scroll in his hands shimmered, revealing… a blank screen.

"I can't believe you thought that that would work." Asten shook his head. "That way, we could just find anything."

Renidos grit his teeth, setting the scroll back down into Erluc's pack. He spun Zythir in his hands, and Asten had to jump to the side to avoid losing an eye. "Then show me the place." At Erluc's request, he tossed the scroll over, and the Warrior set it out against the ground, crouching down behind it. He joined the older boy, curiously leaning against the pine. Both Kera and Asten gathered around them, anxiously anticipating what they were trying to accomplish. "Naíya quaenoros Morentyx Hrashann."

Immediately, dark lines sprouted from the center of the map, extending outwards to form tiny dots. The dots swirled around the page, multiplying exponentially, before a map of the Archanios—specifically the area around Neraz Valio—was depicted.

"Honestly, I didn't even remember that you could speak Telmírin." Renidos shook his head, turning to Erluc. "Can we trade powers?"

"I know, right?" Asten sighed. "It isn't even fair."

"Give it a rest," ordered Erluc, crouched over the map. The other two reluctantly halted their conversation, turning to look down at the map as well. "Look."

The map largely consisted of the thick forest, which was the home of the elves, extending a little further to the west as well. Neraz Valio was marked in an elegant script at the center of the map and a few hours travel to the west, a clearing marked, 'Morentyx Hrashann'.

"If I ever meet the degenerate that named that place…" Renidos shook his head in amusement. "How are you even supposed to say that?"

Erluc tossed his pack over his shoulder, "You don't have to." He climbed aboard Skyblaze, cutting the rope that was securing the pegasus to the tree. He turned to the rest of them, slightly confused. "Well, are you coming or what?"

Renidos and Kera both climbed back onto Frostbite, while Asten joined Erluc behind Skyblaze. Blasting away from the hidden city, they took to the skies, and with a tug of the reins, Erluc guided the pegasus into the setting sun.

They were traveling remarkably fast, but there was a thick layer of fog starting to form around the western side of the city, which made it nearly impossible to see their surroundings. Renidos blinked his eyes open, steering Frostbite nearer to Skyblaze. "How far?"

Erluc couldn't hear him at the speed they were traveling at, but Renidos had been asking the same question about two dozen times since they'd left, so he'd learned to simply ignore him. Looking down at the map, he saw the marker for Morentyx Hrashann get closer and closer to the center of the map, but the fog around them was too thick for them to see more than a stone's throw away.

Suddenly, Renidos heard a *swit* in the air, and beside him, Skyblaze let out a whinny and pulled into a dive.

What the-

Both Erluc and Asten were gripped with fear as the pegasus began an uncertain, turbulent descent, and for a second, Renidos spotted a faintly glowing, ethereal arrow buried in Skyblaze's flank before it dissolved into the air.

His mind raced, and he heard another *swit* whistling through the air. Luckily, Frostbite rolled sideways as a pair of similar arrows passed them.

"Down!" Renidos pointed toward the ground. "Go down to the others!" Frostbite acknowledged, twisting into a sharp dive. He couldn't see Skyblaze through all the fog, and he urged Frostbite to accelerate towards the ground. The saberwolf curved upwards just meters above the ground, landing roughly on a mossy surface.

Kera leaped towards the ground, followed by Renidos. To their right, they saw Erluc holding Skyblaze still as Asten healed the wound. The pegasus whinnied in pain as the ring glowed up, and Renidos arrived even as Erluc consoled the agitated beast. He paused, raising an eyebrow at a dark-violet light emanating from a patch on Skyblaze's hide, slowly fading as Asten sighed in fatigue. Relieved, Renidos exhaled deeply. "What in the world was that?" he questioned.

"We might have triggered the defenses of the prison," guessed Asten between breaths.

"The *what?*" Renidos' eyes widened. "Defenses?" He shook his head. "Maybe you should tell us about what we're going up against *before* we try raiding the place."

Erluc snorted. "What did you expect—a dozen elves with swords? This is supposed to be one of the most fortified places in all of the Archanios—the world, even—so keep your guard up."

"Give it a rest." Kera rolled her eyes, gesturing around them. "Does anyone want to tell me where we are?" After a moment, everyone seemed to relax, and Erluc retrieved his map from where it had fallen a few meters away from them.

Turning back-to-front, he pointed forward. "The entrance to Morentyx Hrashann should be right through there." Looking up, he groaned. The vegetation in this part of the Archanios was archaic and extensive and would be extremely hard to cut down. Blocking their way was a thick wall of vines and branches, twisted into a tight knot.

Renidos twirled Zythir in his hand, slashing at the barricade. A few branches broke away, but the mass remained largely intact. He huffed, smiling wryly. "Alright, I'm done. Anyone else wants to give it a try?"

Erluc tucked the scroll back into his pack, unsheathing Telaris. He paused, and everyone turned to look at him. "You may want to stand back," he warned.

"Try not to burn down the entire forest," Asten advised. "Once was enough."

"I didn't do it the first time, though." Erluc reminded him. "And it was thousands of years ago. They've probably gotten over it by now."

Asten sighed. "Forget I said anything—just get it over with."

"I'm kidding." Erluc shrugged, spinning Telaris in his hand. Turning to the knot of branches, he closed his eyes, and the rippled blade began to glow red hot, flames curling around it and blasting forward, slamming into the branches. His eyes snapped open, and as Asten watched in awe, he stepped forward and plunged the blade into the barricade with a yell that echoed through the forest, causing the trees to sway more insistently, whispering loudly—almost as though they were alive.

Even as the others looked on, dumbstruck, fire began to swirl around Erluc, and the branches blackened and shriveled up, and in those that remained unblemished, a bright orange glow began to creep through the veins of the wood.

Feeling sweat start to form on his brow, Asten took a step back. "Erluc…" he warned.

Ignoring him, Erluc twisted the blade, and the entire barricade erupted in a massive explosion, knocking him to the ground. Around them, trees that had caught alight began to burn even as Kera, thinking quickly, doused the flames with water drawn from the moisture in the air. He turned to Asten, breathing heavily, and the Mage knew better than to chastise him. Holding Telaris level, Erluc strode into the swirling mists on the other side of the entryway. "Let's go."

Readying his sword, Asten followed him, closely flanked by Renidos and Kera. Instantly, the chill of the prison hit him, causing him to shudder for a second, but within seconds, his body adjusted to the shock. Kera seemed more or less unaffected, but Renidos had not adapted so easily.

"Damn," he mused. "Is it just me, or do you feel like you just walked into the most depressing graveyard ever?" He shook his head, pushing Asten out of the way to get a better look around. "It's like they built a mausoleum here, and even *that* died."

It was true. Morentyx Hrashann was aptly named, and they could almost feel the sorrow and grief spread around this forsaken land. The fog around them had only made its setting that much more pensive, that much eerier. It was virtually impossible to see more than maybe fifteen meters ahead.

"I'm getting a bad feeling from this place," agreed Kera. "Maybe it wasn't such a good idea to come here."

Renidos turned to Erluc, who grit his teeth, wincing. He knew that his friend was determined as ever, but as reckless as he could be, even Lord Turcaelion couldn't deny that there was something... off about this place. He took a step forward, and immediately, a group of seven elves emerged from the mists.

"*Intruders*," spat their leader, his voice deadly silent. His skin was much paler than any of the other moon elves Renidos had met, so much so that he looked more like a dark elf. *Probably because of the corruption in this part of the forest.*

Asten instinctively stepped back along with Renidos and Kera even as he produced two shortswords and spun them threateningly.

Erluc grinned in return. "Whenever you're ready." Then he stepped in, whirling Telaris over his head before lashing out at the elf's unprotected side. His comrades closed in to aid him, and for a moment, Erluc was surrounded, fending off attacks from all sides. Then he dropped onto one hand, swinging his legs around, and two very shocked elves were knocked off of their feet. Once he'd grabbed one of their swords, he was able to make short work of the rest after throwing it at their leader.

Asten looked up at him, shaking his head. "Twenty-four seconds. Pitiful."

"I just woke up," Erluc put in hastily, yawning into the fog.

Looking around, Renidos shivered. "Although I'm beyond certain I don't want to know," he began, shaking his head, "What else did you manage to find out about this place?"

"In a nutshell?" Asten grimaced. "Nobody's ever gotten in and out of here alive."

Nodding, Renidos turned away. *Yep, definitely didn't want to know.* Rubbing his palms together, Renidos looked to Erluc. The Warrior was looking around the clearing for any incoming foes, turning back after confirming that they were alone. "So, what's our plan?"

Erluc turned back to them, motioning for them all to unsheathe their own weapons. "We have to play to our strengths." He turned to Renidos, "You're easily the fastest, and you can see the best in the dark or anywhere. Take Frostbite and search for the Heart."

No pressure, then. But Renidos simply nodded once Erluc was finished.

Looking to Kera, he warned, "The two of us can take on any defenses or opponents that we encounter and buy Renidos enough time to find the Heart and then escape. We can start by finding whoever shot that arrow."

"What about me?" asked Asten.

Erluc ran a hand through his hair, "We only have two pets, and you're not too fast on your feet." He shrugged, "You can stay on Skyblaze and fight from a distance."

Asten grimaced, muttering under his breath. "But what if—"

Ignoring him, Erluc continued. "If we run into trouble, we regroup and fight together. Strength in numb—"

"Trouble?" interrupted Renidos. "Like what?"

"It's probably nothing to worry about," offered Asten. "We should just focus on the task at hand."

"Well, I wasn't asking you, was I?" Shaking his head, Renidos turned to Erluc with a look of anticipation. "You were saying?"

"I hate to say it, but I agree with Asten," admitted Erluc. The Mage snorted smugly, and this time it was Kera who offered her opinion.

"Any information can be helpful, and if you know anything of consequence, you should share it with us," she concluded. Renidos nodded, walking over to stand next to the istroc princess. She looked up, and the fog—although still almost completely opaque—looked on the verge of dispersion. "As it is, we've wasted enough time."

"Fine," conceded Erluc. "I just think that if the Heart truly *is* here, we should be on our guard. Who knows what measures Enyë has put in place to guard it."

Asten bent down to touch the ground, the moist dirt staining his pale, white skin.

"What are you trying?" asked Kera.

"Honestly, I don't even know," replied Asten absently. "I'm trying to find a way to make sure that we don't get ambushed the second we walk into the field."

Renidos groaned. "Oh, for the love of krill." He pushed passed the others, stepping forward. Trying his best to stay light on his feet, he dashed a dozen meters forward, pausing tentatively. There was a sullen silence full of curious anticipation before he finally relaxed. "See?" He raised his arms outwards. "Nothing to worry about."

"Watch out!" called Asten, and Renidos was only just able to dive out of the way as a sword-point slithered passed his shoulder. Spinning Zythir in his hands, he shoved the tip of the weapon at the warrior who had attacked him, quickly blocking the next two strikes.

Erluc grit his teeth together, blasting a column of frost towards them. Renidos pounced out of the way, emerging with a smile behind them all.

Asten sighed. "You are *unbelievable.*" His tone had a hint of venom in it, and it confirmed that he hadn't yet forgiven Renidos for what had transpired at Ghâzash-Byrrn.

"Thanks," acknowledged the younger boy, eliciting a pained groan from Asten.

Erluc led the others to where he was standing, kneeling down to inspect the attacker. "Well," he muttered to himself. "This isn't going to end well."

Now, even more curious, Renidos turned to check what had intrigued the older boy, throwing himself backwards as soon as his gaze fell upon his attacker. Before them, sprawled across the dirt, suspended in a shard of clear, spiked ice, was a skeleton. *Mother, help me.* Renidos crawled away from the rest of the group, putting a good dozen feet between them. Asten had backed away as well, and only Erluc seemed to be handling the situation with maturity.

"Guys, you can come back," he assured. "It can't move anymore."

Renidos' eyes widened, and he shook his head in agitation. "What do you mean *anymore*?" his voice was filled with incredulity. Turning to the others, he asked, "Am

I the only one who's totally terrified of fighting undead warriors?"

"You think?" fired back Erluc. "At the very least, we know that the corruption is real." Nodding, Kera took Renidos by the hand, leading him closer to the others.

Grimacing as he laid eyes on the skeleton, he shook his head again. "That's nasty."

"Pull yourself together," ordered Kera, dragging Asten back by the sleeve. "But he does propose an important question—how are we supposed to defeat undead enemies?"

Erluc suddenly turned to Asten, Telaris extended in front of him. "Jump!" he called, blasting another beam of ice at the ground near the Mage's feet.

Asten was only barely able to comply in time, the blast just missing the toes of his shoes as he jumped away. Rising up from the dirt, he saw a pair of skeletal hands that were suspended by ice, the bony tips of the stripped fingers hungry and exposed. Now the hands were starting to appear from all around, uprooting the soil, clawing into the air.

"Kera!" called Renidos. "How long does your scepter take to recharge?"

The istroc princess growled, flicking her tail at an approaching skeleton, knocking its head clean off of its body. Unfortunately, it kept running at her. Pulling her scepter off of her back, her scales glowed white as she summoned its power, hurling the incoming beast dozens of yards backwards.

"It depends," she replied, shooting a jet of water so that a skeleton slipped on it and crashed into another.

"On what?"

She grimaced. "How much I use it."

Asten kicked off a few fingers that had got a hold of his ankle, zapping a few nearby skeletons. The lightning impacted, sending them flying backwards, but otherwise leaving them unharmed. "A little help over here!" he called, a group of skeletons forming around him.

Renidos dashed to his aid, attacking the surrounding skeletons in twos with both ends of Zythir. Grabbing the Mage's shoulder and neck with a hand each, he ran them to a safer spot. Asten seemed rather phased once they stopped, but the adrenaline in his system had yet to fade, and he continued fighting. "Thanks," he acknowledged, and Renidos nodded, dashing off towards another mass of attackers.

In the corner of his eye, he saw a flicker, bringing Zythir up in defense with no time to spare. An ugly, reverberating noise rang through the clearing, and Renidos found himself face-to-face with a stone giant.

You have got *to be kidding me.*

He struck out with Zythir, pushing the goliath back, before a blast of lightning knocked it backwards, pieces of stone cracking off and weakening the giant. Asten blasted it again, just for good measure, before pushing another skeleton backwards.

The Mage yelled, and a shockwave of energy blasted out, splitting and shattering bone. When the dust cleared, he was standing, sword aloft, in a circle of ruined skeletons, charging forward to fight at Kera's side. The istroc's stamina still hadn't recovered, and they were going to need her scepter's powers to keep them going against so many foes.

Erluc spun Telaris around in his hand, creating a wall of flame to buy her some more time. The skeletons, completely ignoring the barricade, clattered their way through, emerging completely unharmed. Swearing, the Warrior fiercely swung his fist around in an arc, knocking several skeletons to the ground.

Renidos bit his tongue. *Not even fire affects them!* He watched in anticipation as Erluc finally approached the skeletons. His experience from fighting the Ancient's undead slaves in the Vale of Shadows would undoubtedly prove to be useful in such a situation. Telaris was a blur, knocking past the feet of several skeletons in one swipe, shooting out alternating blasts of fire and ice to keep Erluc's numerous enemies at bay.

As successful as they were in the battle, Renidos soon realized that they had made next to no progress whatsoever. What's more, each of them was being slowly worn down, and it was only a matter of time before they would be overrun. Renidos didn't know what these skeletons were going to do to them, but he wasn't willing to find out.

"Asten!" he called, and the Mage looked over, blasting the surrounding skeletons backwards. "If we want to get away from these walking maggots, we have to get off the ground." He ran one end of Zythir through the foot of a stone giant, pinning a skeleton's exposed knee with the other.

The Mage swung Ulmûr's sword at an approaching skeleton, knocking its hand clean off. He nodded curtly, making his way back to where Skyblaze had hidden itself behind a tree.

Renidos turned around, looking for Frostbite, finally locating the saberwolf ripping the head off of a giant behind Kera, a wreath of bones and rubble decorating the ground around its claws.

Her scales lighting up once more, Kera sent about a dozen undead warriors flying, bending down to put her hands on her knees in exhaustion. Erluc bathed a few more skeletons in ice, allowing Kera and Renidos to cross back to Frostbite, where Asten had already mounted Skyblaze.

"Kera!" he called. "Now!"

Summoning one final blast of ice, Erluc turned and fled back to the others, leaving himself completely unguarded. Fortunately, the princess had been alert. Kera extended her arms outwards, drawing the water out from their surroundings, small droplets fusing together to form a large mass in the air.

As soon as Erluc was out of the way, she released the pressure, allowing the wave to crash forward into their enemies.

Erluc swung up onto Skyblaze, and they took to the skies, following Frostbite upwards into the fog-speckled morning.

Renidos steered Frostbite over the heads of the skeletons, deeper into the heart of Morentyx Hrashann. *If we're going to do this, we might as well not be cowards about it.* Turning back to Kera, he warned, "Watch out for those arrows."

He urged Frostbite forward, watching Skyblaze follow under them as they proceeded. The gash in the pegasus' flank was starting to steam, and it must have been impairing its ability to fly.

Suddenly, Renidos flinched. The air around him started to grow hotter, and he began to feel increasingly torrid. Within seconds, a line of sweat was dripping down his brow, and even Frostbite snarled in discomfort. The deeper they went into the fog, the worse it got. Beads of sweat started joining to form streams, and Renidos was forced to snap his eyes shut. He heard Erluc grunt from below in pain, and a moment later, a loud, hoarse cry pierced the Vortex of Spirits. Shielding his face, Renidos looked down to see Telaris outstretched in the Warrior's hand, jets of ice shooting out from its tip.

Kera suddenly gripped his shoulder tightly, and he gasped. He felt Frostbite's entire body shiver, as the saberwolf let out a harsh growl in response. Renidos turned forward once more, and his entire body stopped, paralyzed.

Adúnareth save us.

Before them, a beast the size of half the crater circled in front of them. Its sleek, muscular arms hung by its side, great black talons extending out of its hands. Sharp spikes protruded from its back and neck, continuing all the way to its winding tail. A sole rider sat on its back.

It'll be alright. It's a dragon. The dragon isn't going to kill me. Renidos couldn't bring himself to meet the beast's fiery eyes, but he seemed to have started breathing once more. *Yeah, it looks like a nice dragon.*

Unfortunately, the dragon noticed them. Unhinging its wide jaws, it revealed hundreds of perfect, white teeth. It growled, the sound reverberating across Morentyx Hrashann, a chill escaping down Renidos' spine.

Yeah, the dragon's going to kill me.

"I don't suppose that was just a playful growl," he proposed hopefully, which Kera completely ignored. The istroc seemed to be paralyzed—not by fear, but by shock. The monster was unfathomably menacing, and it radiated one thing—death.

She stuck her palm outwards, slowly bringing her fingers closer and closer together, till she formed a fist. Gradually, a long shaft of water appeared in her hand, the tip sharpening to form some kind of a spear. She grunted, hurling it at the beast. Beside them, Erluc shot a stream of fire, and Asten aimed a wave of lightning at the dragon's great wings.

The three attacks pierced the thick air, and Renidos squinted to see what would happen. As far as he knew, dragons were incredibly powerful, but not even they could hold their own against his team. He shook his head, turning to the rider.

The beams hit the beast, and it roared, the sound echoing all around the clearing. The spot where the attacks had impacted had left a small gash in the dragon's scaly exterior, but it somehow healed instantaneously.

"Renidos, look out!" he heard Kera shout directly into his ear.

The dragon had reared, and its jaw had widened, ready to dowse them in fire.

"Frostbite, dive!" he called, just as the dragon let out a burst of purple fire, obliterating everything around it. The saberwolf cut down through the fog, landing on the roof of a stone cave. Skyblaze landed beside them, and Asten tried healing the beast once more as Erluc disembarked.

Renidos shook his head, "What the heck is that?!" The dragon's form flickered, a pulse of purple darkness flowing up and down its body.

"More defenses," stated Kera, slightly irritated. The dragon roared once more and blasted another wave of fire across the prison, and Kera raised a wall of water that absorbed the inferno before it reached their side of the crater. Even as more skeletons began to claw their way out of the dirt, they were reduced to nothing more than bones after the fire passed them.

"Wh—" Renidos whimpered. "Did you see that?"

"Guys!" Erluc called. "Follow the plan. Take Frostbite and look for the Heart. Once you've found it, come back and tell us so we can make a break for it."

The Spectre grimaced. "You don't have to tell me twice." Kera swiftly hopped off of the saberwolf, joining Erluc and Asten.

"We have company," he heard Asten say from below, drawing his sword as he saw a horde of undead warriors rushing towards them from below. The Mage fired a shockwave of lightning, sending the first rank of soldiers flying backwards.

Just then, Frostbite dove forward, straight into the stampede of warriors, annihilating scores within seconds. Rejuvenated, Asten unleashed a battle cry, but he seemed little more than an ant flailing before the dragon, which reared up, unfurling its wings even as its extremities seemed to dissolve into mist. "Go!" he yelled to Renidos. "Find the Heart! I'll hold it off as long as I can!"

The Warrior, though, was two steps ahead of him, bounding forward and deflecting one ethereal arrow after another with Telaris, even as Asten repeatedly fired blasts of lightning at the dragon's head—blasts that seemed only to annoy it. Renidos wouldn't have long before they were overwhelmed.

From his right, Frostbite roared for his attention, and then he saw it—a small opening in the rock formation where he had been fighting off a stone giant. Calling on his enhanced speed, he sprinted over to the cave and slipped through the hole.

This had better be what I think it is, or we're all going to die here.

Chapter 30

Death by Dragon

Morentyx Hrashann, Archanios

Erluc

"Follow me," called Erluc, the familiar air of command entering his tone. "We need to keep the higher ground." A barrage of glowing arrows rained down from the treetops above, and Kera was only just able to blast them away in time. Erluc grunted as he kicked a skeleton back into the crater and scrambled onto the rock formation into which Renidos had vanished, firing a column of frost down the side of the terrain so that they wouldn't be able to climb up. He summoned his armor, calming slightly within its guarantee of security.

Kera grimaced as Asten helped her up. "Who's controlling these things?"

"There's a rider on that dragon," Asten recalled, leaping lightly onto the top of the formation. "He must have cast a spell that animates the bones of those who died here." He blasted another skeleton down.

Erluc chopped the legs off of a soldier, kicking it away. "We won't be able to defeat that thing in a hundred years." He closed his eyes, Telaris' blade glowing red hot, and ran it through the skull of a skeleton. "Someone's going to have to create a diversion for me to be able to fight the rider."

"You two can go," assured Kera. "I'll hold these things off."

"What? No!" Asten looked at her incredulously. "We can't leave you alone. What if you have to use your scepter?"

Kera's eyes flashed angrily as she smacked another skeleton off of the formation. "Then I use it. Now go!"

Asten hesitated, taken aback by her aggressive tone, then nodded, climbing on Skyblaze behind Erluc. The Warrior shot a final blast of ice at the attackers from above as the pegasus passed over their heads.

Finding the dragon wasn't all that difficult. For one thing, it shot purple fire every time it saw something move. Asten blasted its wings with lightning, which caused virtually no damage, but it certainly got the thing's attention.

"Fly near the dragon's wings!" suggested Asten over the sound of battle. "You should be able to get a clear shot from there." Skyblaze complied, spiraling past another blast of the purple fire as he neared the great beast.

The rider summoned another barrage of arrows, which Asten managed to knock back with his trademark electric shockwave. Erluc managed to get a shard of ice into the dragon's eye, but miraculously, it simply passed through without leaving any mark.

Suddenly, a pain broke out in Erluc's chest, causing him to clutch Skyblaze's neck with one hand. There was nothing lodged in his armor, and they weren't under fire, but the piercing pain in his chest didn't even hint at subsiding.

Asten let another blast loose. "We're nearly there, so get ready," he paused when he saw Erluc's face, contorted in pain. "You okay?"

Sure, I'm just wincing for fun. "I'll be fine," assured the Warrior, shoving the pain aside. He'd felt this once before while fighting the Ancient back in the Vale of Shadows. But that wench was dead, and her pain curse had died with her, hadn't it? Unless… unless the rider had managed to bring it back to the fore.

Erluc didn't get a chance to ponder any further, diverting an arrow aimed for his shoulder with a wide sweep of Telaris. He brought his leg over to the other side of Skyblaze's back, preparing to pounce. The pegasus tucked in his wings and dove forward, dodging yet another blast of purple fire, and Erluc felt a strange cold radiating from the flames.

"Now!" called Asten, and Erluc nodded. He closed his eyes and jumped off the pegasus.

Falling through the air, he looked down just in time to swat another pair of arrows aimed for his face with Telaris. He raised the sword into the air as he neared the dragon, digging it deep into the thick hide to slow his fall. The great beast released more fire in shock and pain, but to his astonishment, the flesh immediately became as insubstantial as the mist surrounding it, and only Asten's hand kept him from dropping all the way to the dragon's feet.

"Didn't you see?" yelled the Mage. "It has some sort of phasing ability. We can't count on it staying solid!"

Swearing, Erluc heaved himself back into Skyblaze's saddle. "So… what? How are we supposed to land a hit?"

"Take it by surprise!" Asten fired another bolt of lightning at the dragon, but the monster saw the attack coming and was easily able to let the energy pass through. Erluc rolled his eyes. *Good luck with that.*

An idea occurred to him, and he slipped sideways off of Skyblaze's back, swinging on his leg strap directly to where the rider was seated on the back of the dragon's neck. He barely heard Asten's yell of indignation as he punched the rider—who now seemed to be in the same ghostly state as the dragon—in the head, knocking him back.

Above him, Asten attacked with more lightning, but he could do little more than keep the dragon's eyes off Erluc for a few seconds at a time. Even on the opposite side of the crater, Kera seemed to be having trouble fending off the skeletons on her own.

After spotting him, the dragon immediately evaporated below his feet, but not before he leaped to another part of its back and unsheathed Telaris, summoning a column of flame that washed over the figure before him. The rider was definitely an elf, but his helm and armor made it impossible for Erluc to determine who he was. And he seemed completely unharmed and unfazed by the fire, almost amused.

Well, fire isn't going to be helpful anymore.

Erluc kept Telaris at the ready. "Do you control the skeletons?" Although he received no answer, he could see the purple swirls of darkness at the rider's fingertips, giving him the assurance he needed. "We don't have to fight," he offered, obviously lying. "Call them off, and we'll leave in peace."

Stepping forward, the rider summoned half-a-dozen arrows, and Erluc only just managed to summon a wall of flame to protect himself. Thrusting his sword forward to meet Telaris, the rider pushed hard against Erluc, his might matching even the very most of the divine strength that he could bring forth—more than he ever had. Giving up an inch of ground for a moment, he leaped back into one of the pine trees even as the dragon's back dissolved into mists, reforming just as he landed, perfectly balanced, on the branch.

Erluc slashed forward, ducking under another strike, and drove Telaris through the rider's back, flames dancing along the length of the blade. He grabbed a branch above him for balance, watching as the rider fell to his knees. Suddenly, the rider's hand twitched. The hand moved up, pushing the tip of Telaris out of his chest, and turning to face the Warrior.

Killing this one wasn't going to be easy. It might even have been impossible. Erluc looked down, watching droves of undead skeletons swarming the ground, Kera hard-pressed to defend herself. Somehow, he had to disrupt the rider's control over them.

"Alright, fine," he submitted. "We can do this your way if you want." He stretched his fingers outward, tightening his grip around Telaris' hilt. In one fluid motion, he shot a wall of flame at the rider's face, charging forward at the same time.

The rider produced a long, broad-edged sword—an elven make—blocking the blow with tremendous force. Erluc kicked the rider's legs out from underneath him, clutching the branch beside him for support. He squinted through the fog, watching the rider fall to the ground. "Huh," he remarked. "That was easier than I thought it would be."

Just then, the dragon went berserk. Swallowing everything in deadly, purple flames, it spun and reared violently, a wing slamming Erluc out of the tree and into the howling winds. The Warrior yelled out helplessly, the fog hindering his sight as he tumbled down from the skies. Suddenly, he felt the wind knocked out of his chest as he made contact with a surface, scrambling to hold on. His vision blurred, but he managed to get ahold of a leather strap, clutching it firmly with both hands. He heard noises and faintly recognized a voice, but his mind was racing too fast to be sure. Seconds passed, and then a minute before his feet finally hit the ground once more.

Erluc groaned, letting go of the strap, and falling to the soil. "Ouch!" He grimaced, looking down at himself. His armor had faded and his arms were littered with cuts and bruises from Skyblaze's saddle. "I'm starting to think that we should have stopped for coffee back in Inthyl."

Asten shook his head. "If we all survive this, it's on me," he offered grudgingly. Erluc sat up, and Kera rushed towards them.

"You did it," she acknowledged, and Erluc looked around them. There wasn't an undead soldier in sight, and he could see the last of the bones sink back into the ground.

The dragon roared, blasting the other side of the clearing with purple fire. "What's wrong with that thing?" complained Erluc, as the others helped him to his feet.

"Well, dragons aren't the most docile creatures to begin with," inferred Kera. "My guess is that the rider was controlling it too."

Asten grimaced. "It's not a real dragon," he muttered. "Nothing we've hit it with has even fazed it. It can choose to just… dissolve parts of its body, and it heals faster than anything I've ever seen." Erluc nodded, remembering the dragon's scales vanishing beneath his feet. "And its fire—" Asten paused as the beast let loose another plume of purple inferno. "It's cold. Fire can't be purple, as it is." He shivered. "Looks like it's breathing out death."

Erluc groaned, climbing back onto Skyblaze, who seemed to have recovered his stamina during the intermission. "Try not getting hit by it."

"Wish I'd thought of that," Asten snapped, but suddenly his expression froze as he turned his back on the pegasus, eyes focused far into the distant trees.

Kera raised an eyebrow. "What?"

Erluc spotted them first, a small crimson flash from a stone in their chests reflecting into the clearing. Advancing from the foliage, glinting in the meager moonlight as they growled threateningly, two stone giants approached them. He swore under his breath. *Not more of these things.* Glancing up, he twirled Telaris around once at his side, and the blade lit up in a curling plume of fire. The sight of the weapon gave the stone giants not even the slightest pause, their advance remaining horrifically rhythmic.

Then the first goliath pounced. Erluc raised Telaris to counter the strike, but before he could, a streak of lightning shot past him and blasted the beast into the dirt, stunned. That was enough for the others—in a blur of fangs, claws, and fur, they sprang forward, and Erluc lost his perception of time as he let the pure adrenaline flood his body.

Chaos was the only word for it. Gone was the elegance from his duels with Asten, Alisthír, and even the spirit rider—in its place, only the ferocity driving him forward burned its way to the fore as he lashed out at the giants with everything he had. His sword whirled around with such fluidity that as he fought, it became impossible to tell one stroke from the next. After each swing, he spun Telaris around in an arc before attacking once more. Never once did the blade of Kovu falter, never would it reverse or pause, and never once did Erluc end a strike to attack again, rather he directed his next swing as an extension of his last, never overextending, never giving up too much ground.

After a point, Erluc allowed the momentum of Telaris to take over, and the twisting patterns created by the flaming sword began to burn into his vision. Never holding back a strike, never allowing it to cut more than it needed to. Never restraining the fury, but never *quite* giving it the chance to take over. He spun the sword once more, allowing it to stop, perfectly balanced, in his hand, from which a blue light was already fading. Along with Kera and Asten, he was standing in a circle of rubble and sweat, covered in bruises that would make even the bravest men avert their eyes. Stepping forward, Erluc slashed down on the two pieces of red stone lying in the ground before him, around which rock was starting to stir. The etherinite, for that, was indeed what the stones were made of, shattered upon contact with Telaris, finally letting the stones around them settle on the ground. *So, it's a spell.* He looked to Kera, who seemed to concur.

Unfortunately, their victory was short-lived, and yet another stone giant approached from behind them, the ground cracking under its tremendous weight. "Why are they still fighting us?" asked Asten in the middle of a blow. "The rider doesn't have control over them anymore."

Kera grimaced, whipping at the giant with her tail. "The spells must be placed by someone else. Possibly someone even stronger, if they can afford enough energy to control so many of these things. Even with the etherinite, these kinds of spells take great skill to execute."

Grinning, Erluc blocked a strike to his face, slashing across the back of the giant with a glowing Telaris. "Bet you regret deciding to come with us now."

"Are you kidding?" she responded. "This is the most exciting thing that's happened over the past two weeks." She raised her scepter to the skies, lighting up, sending the stone giant flying backwards in pieces. "And you'd be dead without me."

"Pfft," he remarked, looking around. They'd been pushed farther into the clearing during the battle and had almost reached the crater at the center. Above them, the ghost dragon scavenged hungrily for prey, spitting the strange fire all around, smothering rows of trees and stone giants alike. The shadowy beast was still clearly confused, incinerating everything around it with torrents of violet flame, but to Erluc's surprise, nothing that the fire touched burned for long—after a few seconds, the blaze simply went out, leaving the target seemingly untouched. "It's distracted. Kera, you think you can manage another blast?"

Rather than the voice of the princess, another, more frightened voice called back to him. "Guys?" Asten was standing at the top of the crater, looking down. "You're going to want to see this."

Kera and Erluc looked at each other tentatively, before jogging over to where the Mage was standing. In the crater, guarded by another giant, was an elf. But unlike those that they had encountered earlier, this elf hadn't attacked them on sight. In fact, upon meeting Erluc's gaze, the corners of his mouth curved upwards in a smile.

"He must be a prisoner here," inferred Asten. "And if Enyë thinks that he's dangerous enough to have a dragon guard him, he must be someone important." Turning to the others, he spoke quickly. "We have to set him free."

As much as he hated it, Erluc couldn't allow Asten to divert his attention from the task at hand—if only to prevent him from getting himself killed. "That wasn't the mission." His jaw tightened.

"Erluc!" The Mage seemed stunned. "You made a promise, same as me. We have to honor it. The elf is an innocent, and it's our responsibility to free him."

"I know!" Erluc gritted his teeth. "But I made a promise to save Rose too, and I am *not* breaking it."

Kera didn't wait for them to settle the argument. "Go!" she urged, and Asten looked at Erluc once before charging down into the crater. The others saw him battle his way down, sending shockwaves toward the giant below.

"He'll be alright," assured Kera.

Erluc shook his head, turning about. "Come on." He climbed aboard Skyblaze, "We have a dragon to take care of."

A peculiar expression of discomfort painted across her face, Kera approached the pegasus. "Actually, I'm better off on the ground," she decided, disfiguring a giant with a high-speed ball of water for emphasis. "Flying isn't really my thing."

He raised his eyebrows but didn't question her. "Fine," he conceded. "I'll draw it out, and together we can lure it away from the crater."

Kera nodded, turning to fight the giant as Skyblaze blasted upwards.

So much for sticking together. Erluc gritted his teeth in discomfort as Skyblaze ducked under a cloud, emerging behind the ghost dragon. Unsheathing Telaris once more, he summoned his armor in preparation for the assault. Aiming for the base of the dragon's tail, he shot a barrage of ice across the dragon's spine, eliciting a howl from the great beast. But by the time that the dragon had turned around, the entire wound had healed—vanished, as if it was never there.

Well, at least I got its attention. Erluc grimaced. "Skyblaze," he started, before the pegasus understood, turning back the way it had come.

This time over, evading the dragon's attacks was exponentially more challenging. It seemed like the rider had been the one thing holding it back from going wild and destroying the entire clearing, and since Erluc had disposed of him, things just gotten a lot harder for them.

Skyblaze spun around in circles, dipping in and out of clouds to escape being mauled by the deadly, purple fire. Down below, Erluc saw Kera, a streak of water weaving around her to ward off the giant. "Down there!"

They dipped into a steep dive, momentarily losing the ghost dragon among the clouds before it too charged down from the skies. Erluc let loose a stream of flames, lighting up the giant next to Kera. The princess of the istroce looked up, nodding in acknowledgment, gripping her scepter with both hands now. If this even worked, they could only do it once. She had to make it count.

The pegasus descended sharply towards her, with the dragon getting closer and closer every second. She looked to Erluc, who nodded once. Immediately, the pegasus changed direction, leveling out at a formidable speed, rushing forward.

As the dragon barreled down at the ground, moving with far too much momentum to change its course, Kera raised her scepter to the skies. Her scales glowed a brilliant white, and a bright beam blasted from the scepter, up into the ghost dragon.

It didn't even have time to dodge. The beam crushed into the dragon, shooting past flesh and bone alike with unimaginable power. The dragon cried out, retaliating against the beam with a jet of violet flames. As the two blasts collided, a large explosion shook the clearing, sending both the dragon and Kera flying backwards.

"Kera!" called Erluc, jumping to the ground as Skyblaze skimmed near the surface. He reached down, feeling for a pulse, before he realized that istroc pulses couldn't be felt through their thick scales. *Blast.* He looked up, and the dragon had already started to recover, its mutilated exterior remaking itself.

A giant approached from the left, and Erluc didn't hesitate to smolder it in twice as many flames as he'd needed to. Another beast approached from behind, and Erluc shot a jet of flame, which it promptly swiped away with its paw, roaring ferociously.

Erluc stopped, looking up in surprise. "Frostbite?" The saberwolf growled once more, and Renidos hopped off of the beast.

"What happened?" he asked, rushing to help him support Kera.

"She's alright. She used up the last of her energy to blast the dragon." They brought her to Frostbite, setting her down against the cold giant.

He turned to Renidos, who snickered, in spite of himself. "If she was awake right now, she'd kill us."

"You're probably right," agreed Erluc, wiping grime off of his face. "Did you find anything in that cave?"

"That's why I'm here. You have to see it to believe it." Renidos shook his head. "I'm still not sure I believe it myself."

Erluc frowned. "But no crystal?"

"Not that I could see. But I wasn't in there long." Renidos motioned towards the cave. "We'd better hurry." Raising Zythir, he sprinted for the formation and smashed apart a giant that he encountered along the way so that in a split second a path had been cleared, littered with stone and bone.

Erluc moved to mount Skyblaze, charging after the younger boy towards the cave. Frostbite tore across the clearing, almost losing Skyblaze behind it twice. The beast flashed its claws across the necks of anything that obstructed them, leaving their carcasses behind for others to trip over. Not that anyone would be coming here, though. They cut across the foggy landscape, and Erluc could faintly hear the sound of fire in his surroundings. Fortunately, there was no time for him to think about it, and he braced himself as Skyblaze stopped behind Frostbite.

He jumped off of the pegasus, looking at the saberwolf in front of him. Although he wasn't completely sure about leaving Kera with the beast, he'd be next to useless if he carried her around. Looking forward, he saw a massive rock formation, with a hole wide enough for a few men to walk through. All around the opening sat dozens of shattered etherinite shards—Frostbite's victims.

"Umm," Renidos turned to the beast. "Make sure that she," he motioned to Kera, "doesn't die. I'll be right back."

The entrance was narrow, but not impossibly so. With a bit of crouching, Erluc was able to slip into the cavern after Renidos before he looked up… and his jaw dropped. "It's an illusion. It has to be."

Renidos grinned. "Is it?" Appearing in a moment some way away, he bent down, picked a moonstone off of the mountain of gold, silver, and gemstones, and flung it at Erluc, who caught it between two gloved fingers in wonder. "How much is all of this worth?"

"Could probably pay for the Twilight Legion twice over."

Renidos wasn't exaggerating. The cave was one massive chamber—tall as twenty men and wide as thirty—but the majority of the ground was covered with heaps of gold, armor, and everything from crowns to coins to swords.

"It's the dragon's hoard," proclaimed Erluc, gritting his teeth. Trudging through the loot, he flicked countless pieces aside with Telaris. "Look at all this junk."

Renidos prodded a chestplate with an end of Zythir. "What does the dragon want with all of these anyway? It's not as if it can sell them, and Enyë already has more than enough money."

Erluc suppressed a laugh, imagining the prospect. "No," he agreed, "but a dragon's loot is its pride. So, the more spoils it has, the more formidable it is."

"Well then, we're dead."

As they trudged through the thousands of spoils, Erluc allowed his armor to fade away and exhaled deeply. "Speaking of dead," he started, "Your little pet seems to have collected quite the body-count."

"The Death rune seems to have brought out some… violent tendencies in his behavior," agreed Renidos with a grimace. "Besides, it's not like it was just him who killed all of them."

Erluc raised an eyebrow, "Since when do you approve of killing?" he asked, realizing only a second too late that he knew the answer to his own question. The death of his mother had scarred Renidos permanently, and he'd become significantly more ruthless since.

"People change," replied Renidos flatly. "I guess I understand what Alisthír was saying back before the Steel Trial—sometimes, you just have to get your hands dirty to make a difference." The words left a bitter taste in Erluc's mouth, but he said nothing. Renidos had lost his mother—the sole piece of humanity in his life. Now he was just like the rest of them, completely alone and swallowed up by the crazy world that they had chosen.

Fatigued, Erluc groaned as he climbed on top of another pile of loot, rummaging through it in order to find the Heart. *Of course, nobody left this place alive. They probably died searching for this stupid thing.* Then from behind him, he heard a shrill *clink*, and he turned around immediately, drawing Telaris once more.

"Erluc…" called Renidos, pointing downwards with Zythir. "I found it."

Leaping down to the ground, Erluc rushed towards his friend. "Are you sure?" he asked, cutting himself off as the gleam of the ancient artifact washed across his eyes. "You found it," he agreed.

Finally.

Giving off a brilliant white glow, the surface of the Heart shimmered as if liquid, yet its defined edges seemed sharp enough to cut from a mere glance.

"Whoa," was all Renidos could say, but it sufficed. It was beautiful.

I can see why the dragon wants to keep this thing around. He should've been happy. Thrilled, even. But for some reason, all that he felt was… power. The same way that the sun radiated heat, every time the Heart pulsed, he felt newfound strength bubbling up in his veins.

"Man, do you feel—" he started.

"It's like I drowned in coffee," agreed Renidos. "You know, without the torture of actually drowning." He extended a hand, pausing just an inch from its surface.

Erluc raised an eyebrow. "What's wrong?"

Renidos didn't look away from it, but he exhaled deeply. "You brought us here, and this was your mission from the start; you should be the one to see it through to the end."

"But you found the Heart," reminded Erluc, with a smirk. It was relieving to know that there were still some traces of the old Renidos left—the righteous, respectful, fun-loving kid that they'd met at the Citadel all those days in the past. "Together, then," he proposed, extending his hand as well.

Renidos turned to look at his friend, nodding in respect for the older boy. *Here goes.* Erluc let out a deep breath, and they both stepped forward to touch the Heart of the Moon. He definitely didn't expect what was coming next.

As their fingers touched the rippling stone, its white glow enveloped their fingers, rapidly spreading over the rest of them.

Jumping backwards, Renidos jerked his hand away from it. The white glow had fully encompassed the Spectre and was changing, becoming darker. It faded from white, to pink, to crimson, to maroon, to a vibrant violet.

"I-I'm…" Renidos looked at himself in wonder, before turning to Erluc. "What's happening to us?"

Erluc looked down to his arms, and his eyes widened. His own glow had faded from a brilliant white to a deep blue. The same blue as his Awakened form. Yet somehow, this felt different.

When he fought Vyrnaur, he felt anger, an outburst of uncontrollable emotion. Right now, he was in total control of his actions. It was just… he felt strong. It was as if the power radiating from the Heart had flown into his body, embracing and multiplying his own.

Bending down, Erluc tentatively picked up the Heart of the Moon, weighing it in his hand. The tips of his fingers tingled, and he exhaled deeply. "Renidos," he remarked, turning to his friend. "This is it. We have to leave now."

Strangely, the younger boy was looking at the ground, and Erluc followed his line of sight to one dirt-stained golden crown.

A second passed, and suddenly, it moved. And again. And again. Another second passed, and slowly, the entire cave was shaking, rattling along to a murderous tremble of a fear-inducing rhythm.

Erluc felt his strength wane suddenly, and Renidos dropped down to one knee. *What is happening?* He looked

528 ◆ The Promise of the Warrior

down at his hands, and the blue aura had faded, just as fast as it had appeared. The cave kept shaking, and with each tremor, the vibrations only got greater. All around them, swords, crowns, and armor shivered on the ground, and the walls shook violently. Renidos groaned, standing back on his feet. He clamped a hand onto Erluc's shoulder for balance, and both of them looked to the entrance, from where the sound seemed to be multiplying.

Spinning Zythir in his free hand, Renidos watched with bated breath as the thundering rhythm continued to crescendo, and a shadow fell across the wall opposite them.

"That's impossible," Renidos remarked, brandishing Zythir fiercely.

Charging through the entrance, with acicular weapons of bone in their hands, were skeletons. Dozens of skeletons.

"Didn't you take care of the rider?" he asked. "I mean, unless—"

"Unless the unkillable ghost dragon has an unkillable ghost rider?" proposed Erluc, spinning Telaris in his hands as he crouched down into a defensive stance. "Yeah, you're right. We *are* screwed."

The first line of undead warriors charged at them, and Erluc swallowed them in a blast of white frost. It seemed like every single skeleton had been revitalized and was charging at them. And even if they could fight them all off—which Erluc severely doubted—there was not enough room for them even to stand, let alone dodge and maneuver. They had to get out of the cave.

He turned to Renidos, who was fending off about three dozen undead soldiers by himself. Dashing from one skeleton to the next, instead of the usual blur that Erluc saw, it was as if the Spectre was slipping out of being while he ran. Erluc's brow creased. Renidos had always been fast, but not this fast.

"Ren!" called the Warrior, and the younger boy kicked a skeleton square in the chest, turning to face his friend. "We have to get out of this place!"

As he spoke the words, an ethereal, massive, white, scaled foot emerged through the solid rock roof of the cavern. Then another, and then the legs. And then the wings. And the head, already rearing for a new wave of fire. Without hesitation, Erluc charged into Renidos and tackled him off of the pile even as the column of flame bathed the mountain of gold. Even as they both scrambled to get up, he handed the Heart to Renidos. "Go! Get out of here!"

Renidos hesitated for a second, then nodded, and sprinted to the cave entrance, but was forced back as the dragon painted the air before it with fire again, obscuring the opening amid a torrent of the strange, indigo blaze. Roaring, it leaped straight at Erluc but passed straight through him as it made for Renidos, who gripped the Heart with both hands, paralyzed in terror. As the ghost-like flesh occupied his own, a strange chill spread across his body, followed by a surge of pain that caused him to crumple atop the pile of valuables.

Renidos twisted aside to avoid the dragon's paw, but the swipe still hit home, slamming him against the wall of the cavern, the Heart tumbling out of his hand. Another blast of fire followed, rendering him barely able to get out of the way… but when the inferno subsided, the Heart was nowhere to be found. Erluc stood up in shock, and Renidos darted to his side. Then he was slashing and stabbing at the dragon like a demon, and Erluc raised Telaris as one would a torch, releasing a wave of fire so hot that it melted the gold it neared, straight at the dragon, which retaliated with a blast of its own.

And that explosion, where the orange and the purple met, was the most beautiful and terrible thing that Erluc had ever seen. Without breaking the wall of flame, he charged up, yelling, and sprang off the pile towards the dragon's head, and in a rush of wind, Renidos overtook him in a fevered charge to the top of the mountain of gold. Erluc spun in midair, lashing out with Telaris, and the sheer force of his blow knocked the monster's head to the side. In an instant, Renidos hurled his spear, which struck the dragon's eye an instant too late, before it passed through like it would through water. While still falling, Erluc snatched Zythir out of the air and wedged it between two scales, using it to vault up at the spirit rider.

A moment later, the two-pointed spear simply dropped through the dragon's body, forcing Renidos to slide down the pile of coins to retrieve it. Uncaring, though, Erluc swung Telaris in a wide arc overhead, bringing it down towards the rider's head. With superhuman reflexes, the spirit raised a hand to block the strike, a terrifying, jagged-edged sword materializing to meet Telaris.

Erluc narrowed his eyes. "You're not getting away this time." Beneath his feet, the dragon's scales faded out of existence, but he had long seen the strategy coming. In a single motion, he impaled the rider through the chest, hoisted himself up by the hilt of Telaris and hurled himself forward, knocking the spirit onto his back. Renidos, meanwhile, was sprinting back up to the dragon, Zythir at the ready, leaping up to assist him. Before the dragon could phase out again, Erluc tackled the rider, so that it became the only thing keeping him from falling to his death, even as Renidos charged up and buried Zythir into the dragon's eye. It roared out in pain, and the air around him flashed violet—not the sickly lavender of the dragonfire, but something darker and much more terrifying.

Unfortunately, the rider wasn't done yet. Kicking Erluc off of him, he lashed out so powerfully that just deflecting the strike caused Erluc's arms to erupt in pain. The dragon roared, swinging its head, and Renidos was thrown to the side, skidding to a halt on the side of the pile of spoils. Dislodged, Zythir landed beside him. Erluc tried to keep fighting, Telaris raised, but in a swirl of mist, the rider materialized before him, slamming him off of the dragon's back to crash into the gold at Renidos' side. The dragon stepped forward menacingly, its roar echoing around the entire chamber.

Utterly drained, Erluc gazed up one last time, watching the ghost dragon's throat glow purple in preparation for one final torrent of flame.

Just then, a bright white beam blasted the dragon in its face, forcing it to close its one good eye. Stunned, Erluc's spotted Kera behind them, ferociously raising her scepter above her head. Beside her, Frostbite was ripping through the ranks of the undead, scattering their bones as if they were blades of grass.

The dragon howled once more but had taken too much damage to fire back. The spirit rider's hands glowed a jet-black, but Renidos materialized beside him, driving Zythir through his back before he could summon any more dark energy.

Kera's beam intensified, and the ghost dragon retreated, its entire form phasing out of reality, such that her beam flew through it, into the opposite wall. Sighing, she ended the blast, leaning up against the wall. "As I said, you'd be dead without me."

Breathing heavily, Erluc crawled to his feet, fervently scavenging around the room, before he stopped. He took a dozen painful steps, reaching down to pick up the Heart of the Moon. The Warrior grimaced, marveling at the gem for a moment, before gesturing for Renidos to follow him. He walked back to Frostbite, next to whom Skyblaze was resting, and the Spectre was already there.

Erluc flinched. "Okay, how are you *doing* that?"

"Doing what?"

"How are you moving that fast?" finished Erluc. "It's like you're *blinking* in and out of existence." He tucked the Heart into one of Skyblaze's saddlebags, before mounting the pegasus himself. Renidos tilted his head in curiosity when suddenly, a great roar erupted from outside.

Kera grimaced. "That doesn't sound good."

"Wait a minute, where's Asten?" questioned Renidos, and Erluc's eyes widened, and he didn't even try to hide his shock.

Blast! Erluc clenched his jaw, and he felt his heart plunge in fear. *Asten.*

Chapter 31

Come Hell or High Fire

Morentyx Hrashann, Archanios

Asten

Asten was almost having fun.

As Kera fended off skeletons behind him, he slid down the side of the crater, blasting the giant below with a shockwave. Though he wasn't able to kill any with the power he had, the lightning was ideal for keeping his attackers at bay and giving him the time he needed to free the prisoner. Whenever the giant got too close, he would ward it off with his sword, hoping that it wasn't smart enough to realize how terrible he was at actually using it. The closer he got to the bottom, the stronger the wind around him became, until it was fast enough that he found himself struggling to keep his balance.

Once the slope began to level out, he started to run, the loose dirt slipping beneath his light boots, firing off bolts of lightning behind him to keep the goliath occupied. Now that he was closer to the center, he could clearly see the elf, curled up on the dirt in damp, emerald-green robes. Around him, an intricate array of runestones was linked by lines of a blood-red dust.

Etherinite.

Rushing forward across the base of the crater, he cautiously approached the lone prisoner. As he took another step, the elf swiftly turned to face him, yelling something rapidly in Telmírin. Asten grimaced; if he couldn't understand this elf, then how would they converse?

He shook his head. It was worth a shot. "*Uh, hello?*" he asked in shaky Telmírin. "*I'm going to get you out of there, okay?*"

"The barrier can't be broken," repeated the elf, this time in Asten's native tongue. "Not by me, and certainly not by a human."

Asten's eyes widened. "Y-you speak Andaeric?"

The elf nodded but didn't say another word. His eyes quickly flashed from Asten's ring to his mud-filled, sweat-drenched clothes, to the gemstone that lay on his chest, before he met Asten's conflicted gaze. "Which one are you?" he asked. Asten raised an eyebrow, thrown off slightly by the sudden inquiry. "You're one of the Trinity, of course. Which one?" continued the elf. His voice was strained, but he still carried an air of regal superiority.

Asten sighed. Was there anyone who didn't know about them? There was no point keeping a secret from someone who already knew it. "The Mage," responded Asten. "How do you know about the prophecy?"

"He told me you would come—that you'd come for the Heart." The elf's eyes traveled away from Asten's face. "Behind you," he warned impassively. Asten turned just in time to see the giant rushing towards him, and he swung his sword in an arc, sheathing it violently as the giant crumbled into pieces, the rocks immediately starting to stir at Asten's feet.

"Thanks for the warning," he acknowledged. "Now, who are you?"

"I had a name once—one of great power—but even that wasn't enough to save me." Smiling sadly, the elf shook his head. "Now I'm nobody."

Asten growled. "Alright, nobody, listen closely. We're a little pressed for time here, so I'd really appreciate it if you stop with the useless answers."

The elf simply nodded. "I'll leave you to it, then."

You were right, Erluc. This isn't worth the pain. Blasting the giant once again with lightning, he turned his attention to the barrier. The elf had said that it couldn't be broken.

Asten sighed, tentatively extending his hand forward. For some reason, he was moving in slow-motion, almost as if his body was afraid of advancing. He immediately discovered why. As his fingertips just barely brushed the air above the red marking, an invisible wall lit up, and Asten felt a jolt of energy surge through him.

The next thing he knew, he was sent soaring backwards into the air, landing painfully five feet away from the elf. As he clambered to his feet, breathing laboriously, Asten could make out a rune burning crimson in the air where the wall would have been, slowly fading away.

He gritted his teeth as he recognized the symbol from Alisthír's laboratory—the rune of shielding, and the sure mark of a rune seal. His task had definitely gotten much harder.

"Well, I did warn you," reminded the elf. "I imagine he'll lock you up in one of these too—if you survive long enough for him to get here, that is."

Asten scowled, opening his mouth to retaliate, when a yell pierced the air behind him. Spinning on one heel in the soft dirt, he watched in awe as a blinding white beam crushed into the ghost dragon, shoving it backwards, up into the clouds. A smile touched the corner of his mouth—that was Kera's energy. She'd managed to land a hit on the dragon, and it looked like it had worked.

536 • The Promise of the Warrior

"Not enough," remarked the elf flatly from behind him.

"It's stronger than you think," countered Asten.

"Not enough," he echoed once more, and Asten ignored him. His eyes fixed on the ghost dragon, and he saw its scales disappear as the beam shot past, only to reform themselves a moment later.

Clearly, the elf knew what he was talking about.

Dropping its great jaw, the dragon let out a burst of fire, and when the two beams, light and dark collided, it sparked a great explosion, throwing the dragon further up into the sky.

Kera!

He rushed forward, only to find himself cornered by the stone giant. Brandishing his sword, he threw the blade up into the air, attempting to distract it as he rushed past, blasting a shockwave outwards. His ruse may not have been as successful as he had hoped, but the giant was thrown backwards, colliding with the energy shield guarding the elf before dropping to the ground. The etherinite crystal was all that was left of the giant, shining brightly as it made contact with the barrier, but slowly the rocks began to assemble around it.

Asten placed both of his hands on his knees, panting as he caught his breath. You *just keep coming* back. Suddenly, a familiar growl pierced the air of the clearing, and Asten recognized it as Frostbite's. He didn't trust the beast, not after what he'd done to it. They had made a bold move, bending the laws of nature, even if it was by mistake. At the very least, he hoped it could keep his friends safe.

"Welcome back," acknowledged the elf, looking up with a blank expression.

Asten's brow creased. "What's your problem?" he questioned. "I'm only trying to help. Don't you want to be free of this prison?"

The elf's brow creased in sorrow. "I admire your righteousness, but you're wasting your time," he warned, looking up to the skies. "Go back to your friends. Quickly, or you may not go back at all."

"I made a promise," repeated Asten, determined as ever.

"I'm sure you did," was the reply. "And I suppose dying would save the lives of countless innocents elsewhere, wouldn't it?"

Asten groaned, feeling as though he was a single comment away from *actually* leaving the elf behind. He shifted his weight to the balls of his feet. "Just be quiet," he ordered. "And be ready to run once I get this thing open." The elf almost smiled but didn't continue the discussion. Instead, he relaxed out on the floor, supporting his head up with on one arm, as if watching something entertaining.

Looking down to the vermilion network of runes guarding the elf once more, Asten started trying to think of ways to somehow break the seal. Of course, if he knew who had cast it, he could just have them remove it, or could simply have Erluc kill them to end the spell.

He stepped back, aiming for the red circle, and let loose a blast. The lightning shot out of the ring, immersing itself into the energy shield, where the same rune lit up again to taunt Asten. The elf had now started to completely ignore him, tracing the dirt on the ground next to him with a long, fair finger.

"So that's it, then?" demanded Asten. "You've given up? You're satisfied with rotting here your entire life?" He shook his head. "I'm trying to get you out of here."

"Trying," the elf repeated flatly, and Asten could sense the melancholic note of solitude in his voice. "Listen, I appreciate your effort, but you have to get yourself out of here," insisted the elf.

Asten's jaw tightened. "That's not up to me." Kneeling, he examined the connections between the runes, probing for a weak spot. Though Alisthír had briefly introduced him to rune seals, he had never seen anything on this scale.

The first fallacy he noticed was cleverly disguised, but obvious once he had seen it. The seal had been set with the rune for Wind left slightly unprotected, perfectly placed for an Ice spell to knock it loose.

"Blast it," he muttered. What wouldn't he have given to have Erluc there with him—a quick touch of Telaris and the runestone would have been his.

The elf looked up, a touch more urgency in his voice. "You're wasting your time. There's no way to break a seal cast by someone stronger than you, and Enÿe is probably one of the strongest mortals alive." His brow creased. "You need to leave."

Shut up. Just then, something occurred to him—the elf had mentioned someone. Immediately, it struck him. Enÿë's staff had an etherinite gem. Asten sighed, shaking his head in disbelief. Who else would be powerful enough to conjure a barrier of pure energy?

"You must have done something pretty serious for Enÿë to lock you up in here," he started. The elf looked up, and for the first time, Asten saw life in his eyes. His face smoldered with anger, and Asten had to hold back a smile. Whoever this was, it was nice that he'd finally managed to get under his skin. "So, what'd you do?"

The elf had only just looked up, when his gaze shifted from Asten's face, his eyes widening in shock as an expanse of lavender reflected in his otherwise green eyes.

Turning back, Asten froze. The ghost dragon had re-emerged from the skies, and it didn't look amused. And it was headed straight for them. He crouched down, hiding behind his sword as he readied himself. Dashing forward, he rolled away just in time to dodge a plume of cold fire, which consumed a giant that was pursuing him.

Raising a clenched fist to the skies, he gnashed his teeth against each other as he fired a bolt of lightning at the great beast above him. The blinding white streak shot up, slashing the dragon's tail, but otherwise leaving it unscathed. If anything, it just agitated the beast further.

Firing a bolt at a giant that was charging in from the top of the crater, Asten turned to the wreckage of the dragon's previous assault. Scattered all over the ground, the scattered, violated bodies of the giants lay wasted, and he scrambled over to one. The stone had been devoured by the fire, and even the etherinite crystal had been consumed entirely.

At the opposite end of the crater, he could hear the dragon roar, the intimidating noise shaking his bones. He gritted his teeth. *Would you stop trying to kill me?* But what could he do? Lightning was proving to be ineffective, and there was only so much he could do to stay alive. Looking up to the skies, he saw the dragon dip back down out of the clouds. As it scoured the crater for him, he tried staying still in the hopes that it wouldn't notice him.

And surprisingly enough, *that* plan failed.

It breathed another dark inferno across the crater, and Asten dove out of the way, only just in time. He turned around to see the dark flames close in on the elf, who didn't even flinch. Only a few feet from his face, the flames collided with the rune seal, and for a moment, Asten thought that he saw the seal give away.

But in that moment, the ghost dragon withdrew, circling around the other side of the crater for its prey. Asten sprinted back to the where the elf stood, preparing for the dragon's next attack. Well, almost. He was halfway there when a hand burst out from the ground, its bony fingers splintering as they crashed into his ankle.

He tumbled to the floor, rolling over twice before eventually stopping. Rubbing his shoulder, and looking up, he swore. *Not again.* He brushed himself off, rising to his feet once more. *I thought we were rid of you tools.* All around him now, bony hands burst out from the ground, clawing at the air.

Asten growled, blasting everything around him. How was this possible? Erluc had dealt with the rider, hadn't he? And as far as he knew, bones didn't usually walk around of their own accord. However, as Asten soon came to realize, there was one fundamental difference with these skeletons.

They weren't fighting.

In fact, he was almost certain that they were ignoring him. As he swung his sword through their arms, piercing and chipping bone all around him, he noticed that all of the skeletons were headed away from the crater, the direction that the Trinity had originally come from while entering Morentyx Hrashann.

What are they doing? His first thought was of his friends, but they could easily hold their own against the skeletons. On the other hand, they were definitely taking their own sweet time to find the Heart. *Well, I'm not going to fight these things unless I have to.*

The dragon once again burst down from the skies. But again, instead of simply smothering everything in sight, it seemed more passive, more controlled. Its giant, black eyes glinted once it had found Asten, and it barreled towards the Mage. And Asten knew that it wouldn't miss this time. Raising his ring to the sky once more, he shot another ray of lightning, desperately hoping—in vain—that the result would be any different from before.

The dragon snorted, passing over him as he sprinted back to the center of the crater, to the elf.

"I fear that your friends are going to have company soon," remarked the elf, an undertone of worry in his voice. Asten ignored him, shooting another bolt at the ghost dragon. Although the beast was still unharmed, the blast had done its job. It swerved away from them, exiting Asten's field of vision.

Asten quickly scanned the rune seal in whatever time he had, murmuring the names of the runes that he could recognize under his breath. "Aiyar, Moren, Silrë, Ryzae, Vyrras… *Vyrras*." The aura surrounding the rune for Fire seemed a touch weaker than the others in the intricate matrix… but how could he pierce it?

He glanced briefly up at the elf, then began to draw a quick map of the connections from the Fire runestone, gauging their strength, their protection, the care with which they had been placed. It didn't help that he'd never tried to penetrate a real rune seal before, but there was a first time for everything, wasn't there?

There it was—the Rain runestone. Focusing his attention on that one stone, Asten turned his ring up, ready to shoot a bolt of lightning into the rune seal.

The elf raised an eyebrow. "There are much less painful ways of committing suicide, boy."

Asten sighed, and although he hadn't given up on his plan, he wasn't about to do something that would get him killed. "I don't plan on dying today."

"Well then, I think you had better rethink your plan, whatever it is," he stated.

Ignoring him, Asten quickly muttered "Ryzae," snapping the fingers of his left hand. The rune of Rain flared above the network of runestones, and a quick burst of energy spread from the stone, running along the lines of etherinite dust until the glow of the Fire runestone flickered and went out.

Smirking triumphantly, Asten lightly picked up the runestone and tapped it to his ring, watching as it dissolved into light and entered the circle of gold. Raising an eyebrow at the elf, he challenged, "You were saying?"

The elf huffed. "I'll give you credit for courage." His eyes traveled to Asten's right. "Duck."

Not waiting to question him, Asten dove into the dirt as a giant's stone claws tore through the space that he had just occupied. With a blast of lightning, the goliath was thrown backward, parts of its arm detaching as it impacted the ground. Asten coughed, pushing himself up to his knees. "Thanks."

"Don't waste it," warned the elf. "For starters, I suggest that you regain as much stamina as you can before the beast returns, and refrain from using your ring unless absolutely necessary."

"I think I'll be fine." Asten snorted. "Besides, what do you know about fighting?"

"Not nearly as much as I'd once hoped," agreed the elf with a shrug. "However, I am relatively well versed when it comes to magic." He raised his hand hesitantly, indicating a ring with a red jewel set into it.

Etherinite. This elf was definitely more than he appeared to be. "How did you get that?" questioned Asten, taking deep breaths in between words.

The elf's face hardened, and Asten got the sense that he wasn't going to answer the question. "Enough—you need to leave, now."

"I can't just leave you here," Asten insisted.

The elf was opening his mouth to respond when a thunderous roar echoed far behind. His heart leaping into his mouth, Asten spun around on his heel to see Erluc, Kera, and Renidos struggling to hold their own against the massive dragon.

Frowning, Asten noticed that one of its eyes was closed and parts of its wings had been injured severely. *Looks like the others have made some progress.* Unfortunately, the rider had somehow reclaimed his place on the dragon's back. At the very least, that explained what had happened with all the skeletons.

In the distance, Renidos sprinted behind the dragon faster than Asten had thought possible, even for him, and taking a running leap, stabbed behind its knee with a yell. Kera raised her scepter, but even she was unable to conjure more than a weak bolt of energy before the weapon fizzled out.

They wouldn't last long.

Asten raised his arms, drawing on every last reserve of strength he had, and brought them together. Almost instantly, a spark appeared between his fingers, wavering suspended in the air, and as he began to pour energy into it, began to stabilize, to expand. He could almost feel the vitality leaving him as the spark developed into a sphere of pure power that he was sure would kill anyone who touched it.

"Wait," advised the elf. "On my mark."

Over by the other side of the clearing, Erluc mounted Skyblaze to try and reach the rider once more, but the air before him rippled, and two spectral arrows materialized out of it. He was able to dodge the first, but the second drove deep into his arm, causing him to scream and lose control of the pegasus. As he flailed wildly, trying to regain his balance, a third arrow struck him in the right side of his chest. Though the wound wasn't deep, the pain seemed to keep Erluc from focusing long enough to maneuver Skyblaze safely. Yelling loudly enough for even Asten to hear him clearly, he froze the dragon's foot to the ground and sliced at its legs, quickly landing his pegasus before he fell off and suffered a more permanent injury.

The elf's long, slender fingers curled into fists. "Now."

Almost too tired to take another step, Asten briefly contemplated the swirling ball of energy between his hands, and with a final effort of resolve, he willed it to erupt in the most powerful shockwave he had ever created. When the surge of energy struck the seal, the runes all flared up again, and as it washed over the forces of the undead, bones splintered and shattered from the sheer power of the lightning wave.

Although Erluc, Renidos, Kera, and the dragon seemed unharmed by the shockwave, it clearly got their attention, and the dragon roared so powerfully that the hair on the back of Asten's neck stood on end.

The elf raised an eyebrow. "Your fight is not yet over," he warned. "But as it is, I've had the most fun in almost a decade watching you fight, so know that you'll be sorely missed."

Asten groaned. "Please stop talking."

As if to emphasize his point, the dragon fixed its soulless gaze on Asten, completely ignoring the other three as if they weren't worth its time. Erluc looked up at it lethargically as though considering attacking, but even Asten could see that he'd exhausted every last scrap of energy he could muster.

Planting its feet, the dragon reared and blasted another torrent of fire at Asten, which he rolled to avoid. As it touched the force field around the elf, the runes flickered even more intensely than before, but once the strange, purple flames were gone, the shield stabilized and began to glow defiantly once again.

Dragonfire—the only thing that could cause this rune seal to falter.

Holding a hand out towards the ground burning violet before him, he murmured, "Vyrras," and a wisp of flame leaped from the long grass into his hand. Right there in his palm, suspended barely an inch from touching him, a small globe of the dragon's purple fire was swirling before his eyes. The Fire rune glowed on the rim of his ring.

Lightly, he blew on the flames, and the wisp swelled into a fireball about the size of a large rock. Now that it was big enough, he could clearly feel it tapping into his strength, draining his life force itself. His eyes traveled to the elf, who finally seemed intrigued enough to look up in wonder.

High-kicking into a windup, Asten focused on the dragon's chest, and with a yell, he released every ounce of his pent-up energy, hurling the fireball at the creature. In response, it fixed its eyes on him, almost as though it were laughing at him, and the upper half of its body dissolved into mist. As the swirling flames enveloped the dragon, though, they still seemed to hurt it, causing it to roar in pain until the rider evaporated them with an almost imperceptible wave of his hand.

For the first time, a smile tugged at the corners of his lips. He'd finally found a way to fight back. When the next column of dragonfire came, he was already prepared for it. Moments before it washed over him, he thrust his hands out before him and yelled, "Vyrras!"

Mere feet away from him, the inferno stopped in midair, coalescing into a violet ball of energy just between his palms, only a few inches wide. The dragon's blast intensified, and beads of sweat appeared on Asten's forehead, but his refusal to give in far outstripped the power he was now forced to contain. As more dragonfire condensed into the sphere, it began to shine so brightly that Asten's eyes hurt just looking at it.

The elf's eyes widened when he realized what Asten's plan was, and he gave him a nod of respect. "Perhaps I judged you too soon, young mage."

Asten grimaced, but his eyes glinted in pride. "What?" he called over the roar of the dragon's blast. "I'm sorry, could you say that again? I couldn't hear you—this dragon is really loud." The elf shook his head, trying to mask a wry smile.

You made an elf laugh. Not bad, Asten. He shook his head, spitting into the dirt in disgust as a bead of salty sweat trickled into his mouth.

"My name's Asten," he offered, and the elf grimaced.

Finally, the torrent of fire subsided, leaving Asten struggling to contain the six-inch-wide ball of energy, blazing purple, between his hands. One slip-up, one lapse in his concentration, and the explosion would consume everything up to a mile away. He couldn't afford to let that happen.

His arms shook with the effort, the lavender sphere beginning to glow out even more brightly. Although the dragon's roar seemed to drown out everything else, he could just barely catch a voice—Erluc's voice—yelling his name amid the thunderous howl of the wind tearing across the crater.

When he looked up, his friend was astride his pegasus at the edge of the prison, his sword extended as though to threaten the spectral beast. Telaris began to blaze blue, blasting a column of fire at the dragon, but it simply phased through without leaving a mark. Scowling in pain, Asten yelled up, "*Go!* What are you still doing here?" His knees were beginning to tremble, and black tendrils were a hair's breadth from completely taking over his vision. Between his hands, a red glow started to suffuse the surface of the purple ball of energy.

Asten shook his head, just about ready to pass out, when a surge of newfound strength spread through his veins, stabilizing the tremendous power he was forced to contain, and restoring his will to stand up just a little taller. To fight just a little harder. To hold on just a little more tightly to consciousness.

He looked up and was met with the image of Erluc sprinting down the side of the crater to him, yelling.

"No!" Asten yelled back, hoping to Adúnareth that the words could be heard amid the howling winds. "Stay back!" His throat was raw from the force with which he was screaming, but as a response echoed across the crater, he sighed in relief.

Erluc's voice sounded as though it came from a million miles away. "I'm not leaving you! There's got to be another way!"

"There's not!" Tears began to well up in Asten's eyes at his friend's stubbornness. Why, why couldn't he see that he had to run? That there was nothing he could do to help, except possibly die in vain? "Erluc, you have to trust me!" The crimson globe of power between his hands began to shake violently, strange, red flares erupting from its surface. "Go! I promise—I'll be okay!"

After what seemed like an eternity, Erluc nodded, turning around and breaking into a run. It killed Asten to have to lie to his friend, to say everything would be fine even when he knew it wouldn't, and a single tear began to roll down the side of his face.

He felt his feet slip against the soil below, and he gritted his teeth. Red sparks began to jump between his fingers.

"Asten!" He heard Erluc's voice echoing from afar, but he was far away. Safe.

Gathering up the very last of his strength, Asten twisted and blasted the energy between his hands into the rune seal. Once again, the runestones flickered violently against the power of the dragonfire, and as Asten intensified the beam of red light, the connections between the runes began to fizzle and burn out. The darkness started at the edges, but even as Asten kept the dragonfire focused on the seal, the damage spread between the links until it finally reached the Shield runestone at the center. In that one instant, time seemed to slow to an infinitesimal crawl, just long enough for him to smile.

Then the world returned to normal, the runestones flared painfully bright, and the seal erupted in a colossal explosion that ripped the crater apart.

Chapter 32

Aftershocks

Morentyx Hrashann, Archanios
Erluc

"*I'll be okay!*"

Asten's words echoed in Erluc's skull as Skyblaze galloped to safety, and his heart pounded like a hammer on an anvil with each step of the pegasus' hoof. It would be alright. Asten was safe. He'd promised that he'd be safe. The farther Erluc got from the dragon, from Asten, the heavier the feeling in his chest grew.

Two yards from the opening in the branches that marked his escape, his fists clenched of their own accord, Skyblaze's hooves skidding to a halt in the soft dirt. Without even pausing to think, Erluc reversed direction and began to ride towards the red light illuminating the entire crater. What had he been thinking? He couldn't leave Asten there by himself. Erluc drove his heels into Skyblaze's side, and his eyes flashed dangerously. The pegasus cried out, accelerating through the dense fog, towards the crater.

Erluc felt Skyblaze slow down, and the pegasus slid down to the ground, hooves uprooting dozens of rocks. "No!" commanded Erluc. "Keep going. We have to get to him!"

But the pegasus couldn't continue. Toppling over, it fell to its side, and Erluc jumped off as it rolled across the murky dirt of Morentyx Hrashann. Spitting in disgust, he drove his feet into the ground even harder to gain every precious second he had to help his friend.

"Asten!" A pain like a fist closing around his heart erupted in his chest as he continued to run, faster than he thought he could.

Just halfway to the edge of the crater, Erluc could see the light flare up so brightly that he was sure it would be burned into his vision, and the ground itself was ripped up so violently that the force of it swept Erluc off his feet and hurled him back the way he had come, through the entrance to the prison. For a moment, he could feel his body suspended in the air, almost as though he were flying. And then the instant was over, and he had crashed into the dirt, skidding five feet and rolling ten more.

Several seconds passed with him on the ground, dazed, before he pushed himself back to his feet and began to move again. "Asten," he croaked, eyes fixed on the blur of red in what was left of his vision. As the scene focused, the shaking of his legs slowed, and he managed an erratic stagger towards the blast.

A whinny echoed faintly in his ringing ears, Skyblaze cantering up beside him. Too exhausted to say anything, Erluc hazily mounted the pegasus and snapped the reins. Skyblaze whinnied fearfully, banking through the dense fog and diving into the tearing winds—towards the crater, through the smoke, to Asten.

Leaving him there alone had been a mistake.

Beside him, Frostbite's bat-like wings extended to their full reach, slowing the saberwolf enough that both Renidos and Kera could be seen covering their faces with their arms to protect their eyes from the piercing heat of the blast before them. They'd stayed back on his command before, but conventional plans tended to fall apart when things exploded.

Erluc felt Skyblaze slow down, and the pegasus slid down to the ground, hooves uprooting dozens of rocks. "No!" ordered Erluc. "Keep going, we have to get to him!" His eyes burned as he kept his gaze fixed upon the fading light from the center of the crater, the pale-purple dragonfire devouring the land around him.

"Asten!" he called once more, the sound rendered almost completely inaudible by the furious whirlwind. Fiery dots spread across his field of vision, but he didn't care.

He had to save his friend.

Charging forward with Telaris outstretched, he battled the screaming winds whipping across his face, each step labored as he struggled to keep his balance. Fueled by the gale, the dragonfire blazed ever higher, and yet he refused to relent. He was close enough now to see Asten, he was sure of it, but the smoke rendered him almost completely blind. If only the blasted whirlwind trapping it in the crater would subside, then maybe he would know for certain if his friend was okay or not.

"Erluc?" Renidos' voice, little more than a murmur over the howling wind, just barely reached his ears. "Erluc, we need to go!" Erluc turned on his heel, and Renidos materialized next to him, an unpleasant-looking bruise on his jaw. "What are you doing?"

Shivering as he moved, Erluc clenched his fist, his teeth smashed against each other. "This can't be the end—there has to be a way for us to save him." He turned back to the center of the clearing. "We have to go back for him."

"We can't go back for him if we're dead," supplied Renidos with an undertone of urgency.

A blaze of purple light began to filter through the fog, and he just had enough time to pull Erluc to the ground before a blast of dragonfire tore through the air where they had been standing.

Renidos took a step back, and Erluc's eyes widened in horror. "No…"

Then a massive translucent wing emerged from the smoke, and then the other, and a thunderous roar erupted with a force that made Erluc instinctively brace a foot behind him. From within the fading smoke, the vortex of the dragon's remaining nightmare eye opened once more.

Asten's sacrifice had failed.

Erluc turned to Renidos, and the Spectre could see it in his eyes. He knew. He knew that Asten was gone. But he wasn't going to let himself believe it. He tore Telaris out of its sheath and roared a battle cry at the dragon, the familiar brown of his eyes turning to a furious blue.

Instantly, the sword was wreathed in blue fire, and as he began to run towards the center of the crater, the flames engulfed him, his vision tinting cobalt as they covered his eyes. Once more, the same surge of power that he had experienced back at Ghâzash-Byrrn suffused his limbs, but even as he lifted his sword to bathe the dragon in fire, the blue aura dissolved, and the last of his strength with it. His right knee buckled with the next step, and he crashed into the mud.

"Erluc!" shouted Renidos, and Erluc heard his footsteps splashing in the mud next to his head. He groaned, trying to speak, but couldn't manage anything intelligible as his friend lifted up his torso with unnatural strength and draped one of his lifeless arms around his shoulder. He looked up to Renidos, his eyes glazed brown with pain, before slumping to the ground. "You need to get him," he croaked, his throat too raw to keep shouting. He gripped Renidos' shoulder with his right hand, a helpless look in his eyes. "Please."

Renidos grimaced, as if he was trying not to meet Erluc's eyes. "Hang on, Erluc." As he began to run, a bitter cold gripped Erluc, and what seemed like seconds later, the chill subsided. "Kera! Help me get him onto Frostbite!" She threw his other arm around her shoulder, and they dragged him to Frostbite. Slinging him over the saberwolf's saddle, Kera climbed upon the beast.

Renidos nodded. "Go!"

"What about you?"

"I have to get Skyblaze." He shook his head. "This dragon isn't going to hurt anyone else—not while I'm still here. Now go!" *Thank you,* Erluc thought, even though he was too drained to open his mouth, let alone form words.

Everything after that was a blur, and as Frostbite finally launched himself into the air, Erluc felt himself slip into unconsciousness.

The force of the landing jolted Erluc awake, but though he could think perfectly, even the effort to raise his head from the saberwolf's cold fur was far beyond what his shell of a body was capable of. All around them, he could sense the cold stench of death radiating from the dragonfire. As he forced his eyes open, even the blurry shapes of the trees around them were clearly decayed, once-grand trunks now riddled with chipped bark. He hadn't experienced a feeling so perverse, so *wrong*, not since his encounter with the Ancient a year before.

Where's Telaris? The fingers of his left hand moved slightly, lightly brushing his belt, but the scabbard was missing from its familiar place at his hip. He could hear a faint flapping noise, and with a *thump,* the familiar sound of Skyblaze's hooves behind him calmed him somewhat. Even as his vision gradually cleared, he could make out the sounds of Renidos and Kera dismounting, the former stepping briskly to his side. "What happened to him?"

"I'm not sure. It might have just been the strain of trying to summon his Awakened form when he was already so tired. Remember what happened at Ghâzash-Byrrn?" Kera looked up, and her eyes met Erluc's. "Still, it's not him I'm worried about." Her gaze continued past Renidos, and he averted his eyes, his jaw tightening.

Looking over to Erluc's helpless body, Renidos quivered in shame. Erluc himself closed his eyes, wanting more than anything to tell him not to blame himself. He'd put his life on the line on Erluc's orders, and almost lost it trying to save their friend. And now... they'd failed.

They were supposed to be a team. How could they have let something like this happen?

Erluc tried again to speak, but only a groan escaped him. At the very least, he thought, the pain from the curse had finally abated.

Renidos crouched before his face. "Erluc? Can you hear me?"

Erluc barely managed the faintest of nods, burying his face in Frostbite's cold fur. With each passing moment, a trickle of strength invigorated his limbs just a little more.

Kera walked past him, peeking past the cover of the thicket of trees. The princess cut aside a fallen branch with her tail, whipping it out in frustration, before tentatively looking out to the clearing.

The dust had only just started to clear, joining the fog to form a crude, opaque mixture of brown and gray. The clouds were polluted with a black ash, and the ground in front of them was torn out in several places. Kera grimaced as she saw the undead giants and skeletons caught in the explosion, parts of their remains simply vanished, eaten away by the dragonfire, leaving behind an incomplete maze of bones.

"See anything?" Renidos asked Kera, who was scanning their surroundings. His tone was hopeful, but Erluc could tell that it was little more than a mask.

Then a roar split the air, and Kera's eyes widened. "Move. *Move!*"

Renidos didn't hesitate, sprinting to Skyblaze and mounting him. Kera climbed up behind Erluc, and as Frostbite took off, he could feel the familiar sensation of his stomach dropping through his body. *Please don't throw up.*

The hair on the back of his neck stood on end, and sure enough, Kera was forced to raise her scepter, and four thin streaks of light arced through the air. When each one collided, Erluc could see a spectral arrow drop from the sky. His gut clenched in dread.

"How do you fly this thing?" Renidos' terrified yell was almost drowned out by the dragon's howling roar.

This time, when Erluc rose, he was able to sit up without too much trouble. The moon was on its way down, and Renidos and Kera were resting side by side against the trunk of a broad pine tree. Though Renidos was likely asleep, Erluc knew the istroc was wide awake—whatever the reason for her closed eyes, she physically couldn't sleep. Either way, their voyage must have taken a lot out of them.

Steadying himself against the tree, Erluc slowly got to his feet, but at the first step he took, Renidos' eyes snapped open.

"You're up." Though his voice was quiet, it was no trouble for Erluc to hear.

Erluc nodded. "Was I that loud?"

Standing up carefully so as to not disturb Kera, Renidos tapped his left ear. "Not really. I'm just a light sleeper." He lightly made his way over to Erluc. "You okay?"

He was just opening his mouth to speak when he remembered Asten. A wave of despair washed over him. "Not really, but I'll live."

Renidos seemed unsure what to say to that.

"What happened?" he continued.

"You…" Renidos trailed off before trying again. "How much do you remember?"

"I remember the dragon survived." Erluc felt at his hip for Telaris again, but the sword was missing.

Apparently having perceived his motion, Renidos gestured at Skyblaze and Frostbite, who were sleeping some distance away. "Don't worry. Telaris is over there." He sighed. "The dragon came at us a second time, and we barely made it away. I don't know how long we have until it finds us."

"It's still hunting us?" clarified Erluc, and Renidos nodded. "So, we were walking into a trap the whole time."

"I guess so," agreed Renidos dismally.

"And the Heart?"

Renidos nodded again. "It's in Skyblaze's sa—" He stopped, and in that moment, Erluc felt a pressure like a fist closing around his chest, squeezing the life out of him. The pegasus was unhurt, but it had lost all of its saddlebags—all the runestones, the enchanted map, and all of Erluc's other belongings were gone.

"They're gone. The saddlebags are gone," said Renidos hollowly, a hint of venom hidden in his words. "Skyblaze must have lost them while we were escaping... we lost it."

Erluc wanted to collapse, but he couldn't quite bring himself to let go. Instead, he turned to Renidos. "While we were escaping?"

Renidos lifted his left legging, revealing several thin cuts across the side of his leg. "I tried a maneuver while flying over the clearing, but between the fog and my inexperience with flying, we didn't really stand a chance. We dodged most of the arrows. One of them must have cut the saddlebags loose."

The Heart of the Moon was lost.

Shaking his head, Erluc sighed. The news should have depressed him even more, but his entire body seemed to be numb—he didn't know whether it was from exertion or sheer hopelessness. The runestones, the map—all gone.

Just then, a glowing, translucent arrow materialized in front of Erluc, racing for his chest, before the Spectre's lightning reflexes caught the shaft an inch away from his tunic. At the inevitable roar of the dragon moments later, Kera's eyes opened, and only now did Erluc realize that she had been returned to her natural serpentine form. "They've found us," he said quietly. "Kera?"

"Let's go," she agreed. Turning to Renidos, who seemed frozen in place, she added, "Get to Frostbite." Renidos turned to face her, wearing a bemused expression. Looking up at him, Kera sighed. "The crystal has been lying in this prison for a thousand years. It's not going anywhere."

"But... we failed." Renidos shook his head.

"And we can succeed tomorrow, if we live to see it," put in Kera, and to Renidos' surprise, Erluc nodded. "We can't fight like this."

"And *him?*" Renidos didn't turn to meet her gaze. "What about Asten?"

Kera, grabbing her scepter to shoot another blast of white energy, her scales lighting up the same color. "He wouldn't have wanted us to die in vain. As long as we're still alive, we can avenge him." The Spectre nodded his head solemnly, tucking Zythir into his belt. From across the clearing, he saw that the dragon had recovered from Kera's blast and was even more vicious than before.

From its back, the rider raised his hand, and the air before Renidos rippled, and two spectral arrows like the one that had hit Frostbite materialized, aimed directly at his head. His reflexes had never served him so well as when he twisted and caught one of the arrows, allowing the other to sail past to Kera, who shot it down with a blast of water.

The dragon roared once more and blasted another wave of fire across the prison, and Kera raised a wall of water that absorbed the inferno before it reached the trees sheltering them.

Erluc tried to get up, but his knees buckled before he could reach full height, the edges of his vision blurring. His head fell back to the ground with a thump, and he could feel his consciousness slipping away.

"Do you have any Prima Brilexa for him?" asked Kera worriedly, indicating Erluc.

"If we *did*, it was in the saddlebags." Renidos dodged another arrow, while Kera pushed another wave forward. "We can't hold that thing off alone," judged the Spectre grimly. "We have neither the energy to keep fighting nor the power to overcome that beast."

If Erluc could stand, he'd be fighting alongside them. Instead, he was a liability that they had to protect while they fought the ghost dragon. *Blasted curse.*

"Help me with Erluc," called Kera, shooting a spray of water out at the dragon. Erluc could feel Renidos lift his legs, while Kera fastened them into Skyblaze's saddle. The pegasus was still wounded and would fly faster with one passenger. Pushing Erluc so that he lay slumped against the grand, white stallion's back, they made sure that no movement would cause Erluc to fall.

Kera whispered something to Skyblaze, and the Skyblaze grunted. Erluc felt the pegasus' muscles moving underneath him, and he finally lost consciousness as Skyblaze took off in the cover of the fog. *I'm sorry, Asten.*

Chapter 33

Hounds of the Void

Morentyx Hrashann, Archanios
Renidos

Renidos sighed, giving Skyblaze one last look as it took off towards the south. At least Erluc would live tomorrow.

Kera shot an arrow out of the air, pulling him up onto Frostbite beside her. The ghost dragon roared fiercely, shooting up into the sky. "We have to lose this dragon if we hope to leave this place alive." Its remaining eye glinted, and it lashed out with its muscular forelegs as it landed once more, sinking its jet-black talons into the dirt.

Renidos' heart suddenly jumped. "It won't follow us out of here, will it?" After all, they didn't have the crystal.

"I pray it won't," admitted Kera, glancing worriedly at the rider, whose arrows Renidos had diligently been slashing down. "But there's only one way to find out."

I thought you would say that. Renidos gripped Zythir tightly, silently wishing for someone to come to their aid. But who could? This was their responsibility—this was why they'd gotten the blessing. If they couldn't do this, then how could they expect help from someone else?

Exhaling deeply, Renidos looked up again to see Kera maneuver Frostbite around the clearing, hiding in whatever fog remained, while the dragon soared above the crater, searching for them. *We can do this. I can do this.*

Slowly, Kera steered Frostbite into the Archanios, and suddenly they were zipping over the dense, green treetops of the forest, Morentyx Hrashann left behind far behind them. Tentatively looking over his shoulder, Renidos squinted. *It's not following us.* He sighed, turning to Kera. "We're clear—it didn't follow us out of there."

Kera relaxed slightly, urging Frostbite to reduce its speed slightly. The saberwolf complied, and even then, they flew at a faster pace than he himself could run.

"Why don't we slow down a little more?" he questioned, hiding behind her to block himself from the harsh winds. After all, they'd been fighting non-stop for the greater portion of a day. And Asten was… gone. Erluc was hurt. The one and only thing that Renidos wanted to do was sleep. Sleep and never wake up.

Kera grimaced. "I'd breathe easier once we get as far away from that place as possible."

Nodding, Renidos rested his head against her back. He silently agreed. Kera had lived her entire life under Comet Lake—the life of a princess. And in the past four weeks or so since they'd met her, she'd seen and done things far too foul to be experienced by *anyone*. The fact that she was still in control and by their side was worth more respect than he was capable of giving her.

He wasn't far from being overwhelmed himself. What they were doing… they couldn't keep doing it, not without consequences. *Asten.* Renidos shook his head, recalling how he'd reacted when they'd discovered their powers for the first time. He'd been scared but in a way of excitement. They'd been given these powers, but what he hadn't understood was that they'd been given an obligation, a responsibility, to use the powers that they'd received to fulfill their promise.

But this much responsibility was a burden, just as great power breeds grave danger. And although Asten had been consumed by this treacherous promise, he had held true to it until the very end.

"There," he heard Kera call, and he lifted his head up. Soaring diligently through the clouds, he could faintly make out the shape of a pegasus against the setting sun. *Skyblaze.* Squinting, he sighed, recognizing Erluc's misshapen silhouette pressed against the pegasus' neck.

Thank Adúnareth. Kera guided Frostbite closer to the Skyblaze, the saberwolf ferociously cutting through the wind. The pegasus was fast, no doubt about it, but Frostbite was on a spectrum of its own. It caught up in no time, and Skyblaze immediately slowed its pace once it saw the others.

Frostbite similarly slowed down, before the two creatures were cruising beside one another. Erluc was still unconscious, and Skyblaze was exhausted from the continuous exertion.

"We should land," postulated Kera, turning back to Renidos. Her face was similarly worn out, and in all probability, so was his own. He opened his mouth to answer, before she pushed him backwards, swinging her scepter where his head would've been.

Gasping, Renidos clutched ahold of Frostbite's cold side, and the saberwolf growled ferociously, rattling his bones. *What in the world?*

Out of the corner of his eye, he saw a glowing, purple arrow fall down into the trees below them, and he gritted his teeth. *You've got to be kidding me.* Kera helped him up, just in time too, as another barrage of nearly a dozen arrows attacked them once more. This time, Renidos was ready, spinning Zythir in a circle, and swatting the arrows out of the air.

He turned around, his mouth twisted into a snarl, and there it was. The ghost dragon flashed into existence, the spirit rider standing motionlessly atop its back. *Bloody dragon.* The beast could disappear at will—no wonder Kera was so apprehensive about getting away from Morentyx Hrashann.

Renidos spat out in frustration, turning to her. He was generally useful in a fight, but not against a dragon. "Switch places with me," he proposed, and she nodded. Standing on Frostbite's wing, he watched carefully while she shuffled closer. He rushed past her, and the next thing he knew, she was behind him.

Maybe Erluc was right. He *had* gotten faster.

The dragon growled, inching closer and closer to them, while Renidos urged Frostbite to accelerate. And while the saberwolf could probably outrun the beast, Skyblaze was minutes away from dropping from the sky. The spirit rider shot another barrage of arrows, Kera easily blocking them with her scepter.

"We can't lose it," conveyed Renidos. "Do you think you can—"

"Maybe." Kera sniffed, shooting a blast of water at the dragon, who countered with dragonfire. "But, I suppose I'll have to try, won't I?" She snarled, raising the scepter above her head. Curling each finger around the silver shaft, she clenched her fist. Her green scales flared up, flashing a brilliant white, and the scepter emitted a concentrated beam, shooting out with unimaginable speed.

Renidos saw the spirit rider flinch as the white light surrounded him, and the dragon screeched in pain. It tried phasing out of its form, but the beam had impacted too fast, shoving it back with tremendous force.

Take that. Just then, Kera leaned back onto him, panting, her scepter steaming in her lap. "Ugh," she groaned, and Renidos squeezed her hand. She was alright. And thank goodness—he couldn't survive this journey alone.

"You did great," he assured her, looking back up behind her. They'd left the ghost dragon far behind, and it was nowhere in sight. *For now.* If they were caught again, they wouldn't have enough strength to repel the assault. They needed to recover.

Off to his side, Renidos heard Skyblaze neigh loudly, and he turned to the pegasus.

Skyblaze was looking down in fear, and Renidos gasped. In the distance, he saw the sea of green treetops bleed out. They'd reached the southern tip of the Archanios.

Helping Kera sit up, she grimaced as she saw the last of the trees near them. "Now what?" she asked, her voice still sore and filled with fatigue.

"I don't know," admitted Renidos. "This was *your* plan, wasn't it?"

"Well, south was the only way we could've gone without being put in even worse danger. There was no sense in going north or west, and Neraz Valio was directly east of Morentyx Hrashann," she explained. "And it's not as if I had much time to decide."

"Alright, alright," conceded Renidos. "But we still don't know what we're going to do now."

Kera shifted in her seat. "We could go back to Inthyl."

Renidos snorted. "I don't think Erluc would be too thrilled with that plan," he warned. "Especially not after what happened during our last stay there. Besides, the Council would have his head if he returned without Roxanna's attacker… or something better."

"And we lost the Heart." She shook her head, opening her mouth to continue, before her gaze shifted from Renidos, and her brow furrowed. Swiftly turning around to see what had gotten her attention, the Spectre turned around, and he gasped.

Frostbite zipped over the tip of the last tree, and the Archanios was finally behind them. They'd reached the southern plains.

What in the world?

The plains beyond the great forest were lined with barracks and tents, torch fires burning brightly around each separate structure. Without another breath, Renidos immediately turned to Frostbite, "High! Fly as high as you can!"

The saberwolf growled, spreading its wings and cutting upwards through the clouds. Skyblaze followed hastily, its own climb much more labored and hesitant.

In turned out that his command was just in time, because hundreds of arrows whizzed towards them from below, all of them only missing by a hair's breadth.

Hissing once more, Kera jabbed Renidos' shoulder. "What's happening? Who's firing at us?"

Renidos grimaced. How could they have been so neglectful? There was only one thing that was south of the Archanios: the Kre'nag Mountains. And the elves and the dwarves had been at war for nearly thirty years. They must've set up forward staging posts for their attacks here in the southern plains. "It's the elves," he decided.

"I've just about had it with these elves," Kera gritted her teeth, clenching her scepter in her hand.

"No!" Renidos held out a hand. "Don't fire back. This way, we can lose them in the clouds, and you can save your energy." She relaxed, and he sighed. "And anyway, they're probably just archers looking out for any threats. Just because their king is a cunning bastard, it doesn't mean all of them are."

Sadly, he wasn't entirely right. As soon as he'd finished, the archers launched another volley of arrows, and Skyblaze cried out, a brown shaft protruding from one of his legs, neighing in pain.

Damn!

The pegasus flailed wildly, rapidly losing altitude. Renidos looked down below them, searching for a safe place for them to land. Finally, he spotted a deep fissure in the distance. Its origin and end stretched both east and west beyond sight. There were several damaged bridges, none of which actually transversed the great abyss, all of them broken by one side or the other.

Skyblaze faltered once more, and Frostbite growled vehemently as an arrow punctured one of his wings. Kera gritted her teeth, and Renidos turned back to the crevice. *At the very least, the elves won't follow us down there.* Placing a hand on the saberwolf's side to calm it down, he pointed down towards the gargantuan gorge. "Down there!" he directed. "We can take cover in that chasm."

Frostbite was only too willing to comply, shooting down from the clouds, flanked by a wounded Skyblaze. Kera jabbed his shoulder, her eyebrows furrowed. "Are we actually doing this?"

"If you have a better idea, now's the time," replied Renidos, and the princess of the istroce grimaced. He gripped Frostbite's cold fur tightly as they left, screaming towards the ground, pelted by another volley of arrows.

Grunting, Kera swatted an arrow off the air with her scepter, her other hand firmly clasped on Renidos' shoulder. Just as they neared the ground, Renidos heard a bewildered cry from Skyblaze's back, and he turned to witness Erluc's arms flailing above him as he fell backwards, the restraints on his feet acting as his sole anchor to Skyblaze.

They finally dipped down into the crevice, and Frostbite immediately slowed for fear of colliding with any of the acuminate rocks protruding from the sides of the rock face. A menacing orange light emanated from below them, and Renidos didn't dare to look down at it.

How deep does this thing go?

Skyblaze found it easier to decelerate, spreading its wings to their full breadth, hovering just out of sight of the archers on the surface above them. The pegasus followed Frostbite down to a hollow inside a wall of the crevice, Erluc still hanging from his feet.

"Someone get me off this!" he yelled indignantly, and Renidos flashed a wry smile. Just as Frostbite touched down onto the ground, he jumped off the saberwolf, racing to where Skyblaze was heading. He lifted his spear, taking a moment to aim. Eyes narrowed, he hurled it with deadly precision, and it whistled through the air, slicing through the harnesses on Erluc's feet.

The Warrior fell about two meters straight downwards, holding his hands out to shield the rest of his body. As he impacted the ground, his palms crushed into the bottom of the hollow, creating several cracks in the stone. Groaning, Erluc allowed himself to fall onto his back.

Kera leaped off Frostbite, landing considerably more gracefully than Erluc had, and rushed to the boys. "You alright?" she asked him, just as Renidos helped him to his feet.

Grimacing, Erluc nodded slowly. "I've endured much worse than pain curses," he assured. Looking around, he saw Skyblaze weakly trotting towards them, and he approached the pegasus. Its side was swollen purple now, and the life was slowly fading from that part of Skyblaze's skin.

"Easy, boy," comforted Erluc, stroking its snout. "You'll be alright." As he said the words, he turned to his friends, his dark eyes flickering from Renidos to Kera and back. "Asten?"

"Erluc, there was nothing we could do," stated Kera hesitantly, and the Warrior's jaw clenched. "Any of us."

Turning away in one jerking motion, he clenched his fist. "That's not true, and you know it." Kera's grip tightened on her scepter, but when she turned to Renidos, he simply shook his head. "I could've saved him. I could've—"

"He wouldn't have wanted anyone's help," provided Renidos softly.

"Spit on what he wanted!" barked Erluc, his voice wavering dangerously. "The fool was in over his head, trying to take the dragon on alone."

Kera exhaled slowly. "He was honoring his promise. Your promise."

"And that *honor* made a lot of difference, didn't it?" His fingers reached for Telaris, only to stop, inches from the blade's hilt. He sighed, and he felt a tear brim up on the edge of his eye, gently rolling off the side of his face. "I broke the promise… and Asten…" he trailed off.

Kera placed a hand on his shoulder, calming the trembling tension that threatened to take over. "What happened to Asten was not your fault," she assured. "He made the same promise as you did, and he fulfilled it as he saw fit."

There was an eerie silence, where their poisonous emotions washed around inside them, until Erluc spoke once more. "If—" Erluc paused, wiping another tear away from his face. "If I ever see that dragon again…" He trailed off, and Renidos sighed.

"Unlikely," completed the younger boy, looking around them. "The worst we have to worry about here is probably just the cold."

Erluc took a moment to recover before turning around. "And where exactly is *here?*" he asked, glancing at their surroundings for the first time since they'd landed. The bottom of the canyon was sparsely lit, with only the clouded rays of light from the rising sun allowing them to see what they could.

"If I'm not wrong," he began, his brow furrowed. Now that he thought about it, he remembered studying about this place years ago—the canyon between the Kre'nag mountains and the Archanios. "I think we're somewhere *inside* the Arnas-i-Oredann."

Renidos explained what he'd seen, and what had transpired while Erluc had been unconscious, and the Warrior nodded. "Good call," agreed Erluc, "We should be relatively safe down here."

"What I don't understand is, why would the dragon follow us once we lost the Heart?"

"Enyë." Erluc nodded. "The weasel probably set us up, with the hope that his pet dragon would take care of us."

Renidos raised an eyebrow. He hadn't met the king of the moon elves as of yet, but the logic that Erluc put forward made sense. Aenor was an ally of the dwarves, who were his enemies. And a troop of elves had attacked them earlier, when they'd first entered Morentyx Hrashann—they must have been there by the king's assent.

Kera grimaced, settling on the floor and picking up two stones. The stones sparked once in her hands, before she sighed, throwing them into the abyss in frustration. "Would you mind?" she asked him, indicating Telaris.

He drew the blade with a hesitant moue, planting it into a narrow crevice between Kera and Renidos. "Using Telaris as a bonfire," he shook his head. "Never thought that it would come to this." As he stepped back, the blade lit up, flames racing up from the flowing silver blade up to its ornate hilt, and their camp lit up brightly.

"Well, we have nothing," concluded Erluc, burying his face in his hands. "We failed to get the Heart and lost our only resources. I betrayed my vow to the Falcon, and that prisoner is dead because of it. The dragon is completely unharmed, Rose is still on the cusp of death, Therglas will most likely have me executed if we go back to Inthyl empty-handed, we're utterly and completely alone, and Asten is… gone."

Kera gritted her teeth, splashing Erluc's face with water. "That doesn't mean that you should just roll over and die." Wiping his face on his cloak, he sneered, shoving her lightly. Taking his arm, she continued. "You of all people should know it doesn't matter if you fall, as long as you remember to stand up and fight."

"She's right," agreed Renidos, rising up to full height. "And we're not completely alone." He sat down next to Erluc, putting an arm around the older boy's neck. "We have each other, and we have Adúnareth watching over us."

Letting out a breath, Erluc looked up, the fires of Telaris dancing in his eyes. "Not all of us." He sat incredibly still, never removing his gaze from the flames that burned up the blade of his sword. "He didn't deserve this."

There was an unpleasant silence, the rumble of the fire and the faint noise of the battle above them forestalling silence. *No, he didn't.* Renidos felt a tear brim in the corner of his eye, but he didn't bother brushing it away.

Erluc stood slowly, pulling Telaris out of the ground. The flaming blade was probably unimaginably hot so close to him, but he didn't seem to care. Walking up to the cave wall, he slashed four times, leaving a gash shaped like an arrow pointing upward in the stone—the letter 'A'.

Renidos saw the older boy close his eyes for a moment to pay his respects and followed his example. The tear finally fell as he closed his eyes, and he couldn't bring himself to open them again. Supporting his head with his arms, he collapsed onto the cold, hard stone floor, sleep only too welcome to save him from the cruel world.

The skies thundered, and he immediately jerked his head up in annoyance. "Is that—" Then he recognized the sound, and his eyes widened.

"Hide!" yelled Kera, already moving. Erluc grabbed Telaris, which was embedded in the floor, running into the great shadow of the canyon's wall. Renidos pulled Frostbite behind him, concealing the towering beast in the shadow, just as they heard another roar.

What the hell is that thing doing here? Skyblaze limped behind them, and they all flattened themselves against the rock face. If the dragon cornered them here, they would be finished. Frostbite couldn't fight it alone, and the rest of them were far too drained to survive another encounter.

Erluc growled, spinning Telaris in his hand, before Kera held out a hand.

"Not now," she whispered harshly. "We'll get vengeance for Asten soon, but we're just not strong enough right now." As she spoke the words, a massive shadow crept over them, bringing darkness on everything below. Renidos bit his tongue, mustering all the courage he had remaining, to look up. The dragon's wings were spread out fully, spanning almost half the width of the crevice.

Fortunately, the rider—whose sword was still drawn—seemed to be distracted searching only the plains, completely overlooking the depths of the chasm. Renidos found himself to be holding his breath, slowly exhaling as the dragon passed overhead, crossing to the other side of the ravine. Hastily relaxing, he tucked Zythir back into his belt, turning to the others.

Although he'd not broken their cover, Erluc's gaze was fixed on the southern end of the gorge, where the dragon had passed. He glowered for a moment, before returning Telaris to its sheath. "We have to go after it," he decided.

Renidos scowled. "In the state that you're in now, you couldn't kill a housecat." He knew that agitating Erluc likely wouldn't prove to be an advisable approach, but he meant it. They needed to rest.

"It doesn't matter," he declared. "The dragon is here because of us, and if it kills anyone here, it's because we failed."

"If we fight it like this, we'll fail again," countered Renidos.

"Maybe." Erluc's eyes glinted. "But I don't plan on dying today." He turned to Skyblaze, who seemed to have recovered its stamina if nothing more.

Kera put out a hand, finally entering the conversation. "The only things south of the Arnas-i-Oredann are the Kre'nag Mountains, which are only a day's flight away. At the very least, the dwarves should give us a couple of nights' lodging and a good meal."

Both of them considered this, but it was Renidos who spoke. "What about you?" he started. "Without the Sight rune, the dwarves are going to find out about the istroce."

She grimaced. "Well, it's either this or I go back to Lutens Braka," replied Kera, her voice wavering slightly. "And I'm not leaving you here."

"But—" Erluc opened his mouth to protest, but his stomach growled instead, and both Renidos and Kera turned to look at him awkwardly. "Oztarr made us promise."

"It had to happen sooner or later, and we'll die out here in the state we're in." Shaking her head, her mind was seemingly made up. "Trust me, the dwarves are our best bet."

Chapter 34

THREE TICKETS TO A WAR

SOUTHERN PLAINS

Erluc

Erluc looked out to the horizon, the afternoon sun peering down on him from above. Placing a hand on Skyblaze's wing to balance himself, he ran his other hand through his hair, adjusting the sweat-infested locks.

They'd taken cover in the clouds as they flew over the remainder of the southern plains for fear of triggering an attack from the dwarven encampments. Renidos had even spotted a few abandoned fortresses, as well as a forward staging post of the elves.

Now that he'd seen the situation with his own eyes, Erluc realized why Elandas had agreed to resurrect the Twilight Legion—without the aid of men, the dwarves wouldn't have stood a chance against the elves.

In the distance, he could see the Kre'nagan getting closer every second, the tops of the looming mountain range hiding above the clouds. The site was absolutely breathtaking. Erluc shook his head, evidently impressed, before his smile immediately faded away. Asten had always dreamed of visiting the dwarven halls, visiting their smiths, reading their texts. He'd never even gotten the chance.

Grimacing, Erluc looked over to where Frostbite was cruising, a little ahead of Skyblaze. Both Renidos and Kera had regained some of their stamina over the course of the journey so far, but they weren't at fighting condition. Not even close. Renidos was right—if they *did* manage to find the dragon, things could get messy.

Skyblaze snorted, suddenly slowing its pace. "What's wrong?" questioned Erluc, his brow furrowed as he consoled the beast. Looking up, he saw the problem. Several trails of smoke were streaming up from the mountains, gathering into dark clouds in the sky.

What in the world? Erluc called for Skyblaze to accelerate forward, just as Renidos did the same for Frostbite. If there was one thing that Erluc knew, it was that wherever there was smoke, there was danger. Without exception.

He squinted, trying to get a closer look at the source of the fumes. Although the clouds and sheer distance marginally barred his vision, he was able to make out multiple fires all across the face of the first mountain, with other mountains guaranteed to have sustained additional damage.

Frostbite arrived at the scene first, lingering in a spot on Renidos' command. "I think they're under attack," he explained hurriedly to Kera, who frowned.

"By the elves?" she postulated, just as Skyblaze pulled over beside them. Erluc surveyed the damage from above, his eyes scanning the horizon. The dwarven encampments across the southern plains had been utterly demolished, less than a dozen left standing. The fortresses had been reduced to rubble, and he could see fires broken out all across the Kre'nagan.

There was no way that the elves could've done all this.

"No," decided Erluc, finally turning to his friends. "It was the dragon. It has to be."

Kera hissed, scanning the mountains around them for the beast. "Well then, where is it?

"It could be anywhere," muttered Renidos. "And the dwarves, with all their might, wouldn't even have been able to put a scratch on it."

Erluc shook his head, finally gesturing to a valley a little way south. Although there was still a trace of the smoke rising from the lowlands, the fire itself had been put out. "Down there," he directed. "There might still be a dwarf or two alive." There was no way that the dwarves could battle the dragon, but a few might've gotten to safety while the others fought the beast.

Renidos grimaced. It was certainly a long shot, but his fingers were crossed.

They descended to the ground, warily taking cover behind a thicket of trees as they disembarked. Erluc drew Telaris cautiously, as Renidos did with Zythir. Kera brandished her scepter, leading Frostbite behind the boys.

Erluc even considered summoning his armor but decided against it. They needed to be as quiet as possible, and even if they were spotted, gleaming, black plates didn't exactly radiate hospitality.

They trekked to the base of a mountain, easily the largest of the surrounding hills. All around them, they saw trees, stones, and all kinds of vegetation, the color completely drained from their tarnished, decayed shrubbery. Built onto the side of the mountain was a fortress, now in complete ruin. Columns, rocks, and all kinds of debris were scattered across the ground, the remains of the attack.

Renidos stepped over a branch, scowling as he looked down at it. It was thoroughly blackened as if it had been burned and coated with ash. "You might be right about the dragon," he admitted, turning to Erluc, who had stumbled upon something even more interesting.

He beckoned for them to follow him as he advanced, and Renidos raised an eyebrow. Running up next to him, Renidos finally got a glance at what had captivated the older boy.

On the side of the mountain, a wide cavern spilled out into the valley where they were standing. "The dwarves?" asked Kera from behind them.

Leaning into the mouth of the cavern, Renidos slowly opened his mouth. "Hello?" he shouted, and the sound echoed once, twice, four times before fading out. He smiled, content with himself, before Erluc clutched his shoulder.

"Are you out of your mind?" he whispered harshly, just as the leaves rustled from all around them. Dozens of dwarves burst out of their surroundings in an instant, holding shortswords and battleaxes at the ready. Sighing, Erluc let go of Renidos' arm.

A dwarf barked out a command, and there was a short silence. *Well, do you expect an answer?* He didn't speak the language of the dwarves and he very much doubted that these dwarves spoke Andaeric. He turned to Renidos, who was looking at him with an identically bewildered expression.

Kera suddenly raised her hands in surrender, cautiously lowering her scepter to the ground. "Mae tacshir." *We surrender.* A murmur broke out from among the dwarves, and they hesitated, momentarily lowering their weapons.

Erluc raised an eyebrow, reluctantly following her example. "How can you—"

"Istroce are fluent in nearly every language spoken in the Mortal Realms," recalled Renidos.

Kera nodded. "My Larranti was never exemplary, but it should do." Reluctantly lowering Zythir to the ground, Renidos' gaze darted from one dwarf to the next. They stood nearly a foot shorter than he did, which made it that much harder to fear them. Yet somehow, hiding behind their axes and hammers, the dwarves stood fiercer still than any men he'd met to date.

"Nasoi Kera, haress'a Oztarr, jiraisha'a istroce ra," declared the princess with a calm, regal composure. "Aisir mae whaewa." *We come in peace.*

Another dwarf barked something else at Kera, and she replied calmly. Erluc shook his head, tired of simply standing around helplessly. He stepped forward, addressing the dwarves directly. "We're not here to fight, so just put down your weapons, and we can talk this through."

Just then, about four of the dwarves immediately dropped their weapons, leaving everyone in shock. *Didn't expect that to happen.* The rest of the dwarves growled, brandishing their weapons, and Kera shot him a warning look. Just then, three more dwarves burst out of the cavern, decorated in now-tarnished golden robes. As they arrived, the other dwarves immediately lowered their weapons, standing at attention.

Erluc narrowed his eyes. Now that he looked more carefully, the other dwarves all had on the same colors, hidden behind mangled remnants of armor. *Soldiers.* He turned to the dwarves who had just arrived and met the gaze of the one standing in the middle. *They must be higher-ranking officers.*

The commanding dwarf kept his gaze fixed on Erluc, shouting a directive to the other soldiers. The Warrior watched suspiciously as the dwarves tentatively approached him, and he bent down to reach for Telaris, just as Kera turned back to him.

"Don't," she whispered softly. "From what I gather, they aren't going to hurt us. And if we want their help, we're going to have to trust them." Erluc grimaced, turning to Renidos, who gave an affirmative nod.

Erluc sighed, leaving his blade on the ground. *I hope you know what you're doing.* He turned back up to the leader of the dwarves, who was showering him with a scrutinous gaze. He grimaced, holding his arms out in surrender. He didn't want to bend the knee in front of these stature-less soldiers, but they had nowhere else to go. And if worst came to worst, they could always escape.

Another command boomed out of the dwarf's mouth, and the dwarves sheathed their weapons, approaching what was left of the Trinity. A rather obese dwarf advanced from behind them, producing three black hoods.

Watching the dwarf cover both Renidos' and Kera's heads, Erluc grimaced as the rough cloth was pulled down over his own eyes, covering the world in darkness.

Gah. Erluc groaned as the hood was finally lifted from his head, blinking his eyes open. He was in some kind of chamber, walls made of smooth, polished stone, with torches arranged in specific intervals.

Behind him, the same overweight dwarf exited through a doorway behind him, and Erluc silently cursed under his breath. *You better hope that you're wearing that hood the next time I see you, or I'm going to strangle you with it.* Rubbing his eyes, he slowly ran his hands through his hair, adjusting the dark, wavy locks. It might've helped to have a mirror of some sorts, but he'd been doing it long enough that his hands simply knew what to do.

"I hope I'm not interrupting anything," spoke a voice, and Erluc looked behind him, to see a dwarf enter the chamber. The same dwarf who had ordered for him to be brought up here.

Erluc raised an eyebrow. "You speak Andaeric?" he postulated aloud, but it was obviously not a question. "If you hadn't covered my head with a hood for the past half-hour, I might've been relieved."

The commander snorted. "You can never be too careful."

"No, but you can tell your underlings to be a little less harsh," offered Erluc. "I was painfully close to giving them a piece of my mind."

"I shall keep that in mind." The dwarf nodded, taking a seat on a stone step across from Erluc. "But it doesn't change the fact that we know far too little about you. Your companions did tell us a fair deal, but I'd like to see if the information matches up."

"It's almost as if you don't trust us." But upon mention of his friends, Erluc finally gave up the game. "Where are they?"

"Safe," assured the dwarf. "Although the one with the green skin—the one who can speak Larranti as well as one of us—she certainly isn't a human. The people want me to throw her into the dungeons, along with the rest of you."

"What's stopping you?"

The dwarf grimaced. "At the start of the second division, the Twilight Legion marched to our aid. Your armies interceded the elves' attack, driving them back to their side of the Arnas-i-Oredann. If it weren't for them, we probably would've been overwhelmed. As it stands, my people are in debt to yours."

"Your people?" questioned Erluc. "So, you're the king?"

The dwarf's face immediately hardened, and he stood. "My name is Damzar, son of Barduen. I am the commander of the dwarven army and chief advisor to the king."

"I'm—"

"Your friends told me exactly who you are," continued the dwarf. "Lord Erluc Turcaelion, son of Neran, champion of the Steel Trial, slayer of Ulmûr, and leader of Adúnareth's Trinity—the legendary Warrior."

For a moment, Erluc froze up. *How could they have revealed his secret to this dwarf?* They'd tried their best to keep their identity concealed for as long as possible, and they'd just told someone who'd kidnapped them, and who they didn't know—someone who they probably couldn't trust. He looked up at the dwarf, who smiled grimly.

"Don't worry, Warrior," assured Damzar. "Your secret is safe with me. I knew of the prophecy before you were born. I've been waiting for this moment for centuries."

Erluc's hand clasped around Telaris' hilt, which—to his great surprise—had been returned to his belt. "How do I know that I can trust you?"

"I trusted you," reminded the commander, nodding towards a loaf of bread that was placed on a platter next to Erluc's feet. "Enough to give you back your blade, and enough to face you alone. Trust is something that is earned." He adjusted his golden robes, turning to Erluc. "You needn't fear me. As long as I am around, you can rest assured that you will be treated with nothing but hospitality among my kind. Inthyl and Agmern have remained friends and allies for centuries in the past. Why should we be any less today?"

There was a short sullen, silence, and Erluc considered the dwarf's words. He was evidently well-spoken, and as far as Erluc could tell, everything he said was the truth. He nodded, grabbing the loaf of bread. "So," he began. "This place is Agmern?"

"Aye," confirmed Damzar with a nod. "Your High King was one of the last humans to set foot in our halls—it is a great honor."

"The *late* king," whispered Erluc softly.

The dwarf grimaced. "I heard. He was a good man, Elandas. Still, my condolences." He turned back to the walls, caressing the embedded stone tiles. "I would give you a tour of the city, but in light of recent events, I'm afraid we'll have to abandon the pleasantries. We have much to discuss."

Erluc raised an eyebrow, ripping a chunk out of the loaf. "What about?"

Damzar winced as if he was pained just to think about it. "Come." He stood, beckoning for Erluc to follow him. Hesitantly jogging behind the commander, Erluc stepped into the corridor, bumping his head against the doorway as he left the chamber. He swore aloud, catching himself a second too late.

The dwarf turned back to him with a smile, "Careful—these tunnels weren't built for men." Hunching his back, Erluc snorted as he followed Damzar down the hall.

His brogans made no sound as he stepped over the hard surface, and they walked in silence for the majority of the walk. Damzar did once stop, however, to change course. "We'll have to take another route," explained the dwarf. "Several of our tunnels are collapsed, and some are still unstable." By the time they'd reached their destination, Erluc had already wolfed down the remainder of the loaf, wiping the crumbs from his face.

Damzar led him through another doorway, and Erluc made sure to duck down as he passed under it. His face immediately brightened as he saw Renidos and Kera, who sighed in relief when they saw him. They'd both seemed a little more relaxed, and their weapons were propped up against the wall.

"Did they get you anything to eat?" asked Kera.

Erluc nodded wryly. "Still exhausted, unfortunately."

Damzar barked an order, and the guards near the entrance exited the chamber without another word. Erluc turned to face the dwarf, and he noticed someone else—a dwarf sitting on a grand throne of polished rock. The dwarf's combed beard was mostly white, and he too was dressed in golden robes, and an ornate crown, decorated with a rainbow of gemstones.

"Jiraja han, lasoi Triome ra," he proclaimed in Larranti, and Kera whispered the translation to Erluc, who nodded gratefully. *My king, I present the Trinity.* Turning to the group, Damzar continued. "May I present King Horgenn Vilmanarth, son of Húrnen, ruler of the Kre'nag Mountains."

Erluc knelt, the others following his example. "It is an honor, your majesty."

"Oh, is the king here?" asked the dwarf immediately, an elated smile on his face. He clutched Damzar's arm, before turning to Renidos, his eyes wide in reverence. "Excuse me, your majesty," he declared, bowing down on one knee before the Spectre.

Renidos raised an eyebrow, hastily rising to his feet. "Am I missing something here? Who is this?"

"I'm Horgenn, your majesty," interrupted the king stubbornly. "But my friends call me Horgs." Renidos broke out into laughter, and even Kera flashed a reluctant grin. Frowning, Erluc looked up to Damzar, who was watching the older dwarf with a worried gaze.

"What happened to him?" inquired Erluc softly.

Horgenn shrugged. "I feel fine."

Erluc nodded sarcastically. "I'm sure you are, *Horgs*."

Damzar shot him a warning look. "Horgenn is our king, and it is by his grace that you are alive. You would be wise to remember that." Erluc nodded an apology, and the dwarf sighed. "As the sun set yesterday, we held a conference in the fortress beside this great mountain."

"The one that was destroyed?" asked Renidos.

Nodding, the dwarf continued. "The meeting was halted, and we rushed outside to witness a great beast, white as the clouds, breathing purple fire, laying waste to everything around it. The Ras'horra."

"White demon," translated Kera, turning to Erluc, who flashed her a worried look. He was right. The ghost dragon had indeed followed them south, with the hope to finish them once and for all. He cursed Enyë under his breath.

"Wait, did you say *this* mountain?" interrupted Renidos. "So right now, we're inside the mountain?"

Damzar didn't appreciate the digression, but he nodded slowly. Renidos grinned, turning to Erluc, who shook his head with a sigh. "The beast laid waste to our camps in the southern plains, and only a handful of people made it out of the fortress," continued Damzar. "We lost a great many soldiers to the dragon, but that wasn't even the worst part."

Kera flinched but kept her thoughts to herself. Evidently, they were all still on edge about the battle. "Continue," she prompted.

"Its rider," finished Damzar. "The master of the beast was some kind of alchemist, conjuring and firing arrows without the use of a bow or quiver." He shook his head. "It was madness."

Renidos raised an eyebrow. "So, what happened to King Horgenn?"

"As commander of the dwarven forces, I was charged with keeping the king and his family out of harm's way during the attack." Damzar paused, closing his eyes. "But when Prince Halthar perished in the blast of the dragonfire, Horgenn went after the Ras'horra himself."

"And?" prompted Erluc hopefully.

Damzar snorted. "Our king was mighty, maybe even the strongest of all dwarves, but *nothing* could overpower that monster." Sighing, he turned to look at Horgenn, who was fiddling around with his throne, picking his teeth with his left hand. "One of the rider's arrows struck him in the back of the head, and he collapsed. I managed to bring him back here, to Agmern, and our healers did everything they could to salvage his life. He *did* wake up, but… he's been like this since yesterday."

"Are the princes coming too?" inquired Horgenn, a spark in his eyes. Damzar whispered something quickly in Larranti, and the once-great king of the dwarves stood. Looking Erluc up and down, he frowned. "You're awfully tall."

Erluc grimaced, watching as the dwarf left the chamber. "How did your forces manage to defeat the dragon in the end, without your king?"

The dwarf's expression grew even more pained. "We didn't," he responded. "From what I can tell, the rider was looking for something. He must not have found it, so he left on his own."

Turning to the others, he sighed. *He deserves to know.* Both Renidos and Kera nodded, and he turned back to Damzar. "We know what it was looking for," he started, "because it was looking for us."

"What?" The dwarf's raised an eyebrow, evidently confused. "I'm not sure I understand."

Erluc sighed. "You may want to sit down for this." And so, they took turns telling the commander of how they had come to find themselves in the Kre'nagan, how Vyrnaur attacked Roxanna, and how they had traveled to the Archanios and met Enyë. They even told him of the Heart of the Moon, and Erluc could see the dwarf flinch, hastily covering up his reaction.

He knows something. He knows something about the Heart.

Still, Erluc didn't interrupt Renidos, and he completed the tale. When they were finally finished, Damzar exhaled deeply, shaking his head. "So, you led the Ras'horra down to the Kre'nagan? All this is because of you?"

"I'm sorry," acknowledged Erluc, turning to his friends. "It's true. The dragon attacked the dwarves because Enyë sent it to kill us." Erluc shook his head, shifting his gaze back to the dwarves. "I promise you that we'll make up for what happened to Agmern, and we'll find a way to cure your king."

"How?" challenged Damzar. "From everything you have told me, you're a fighter, not a healer. What can you do to save Horgenn that nobody else has already tried?"

"You already know of what all I've done," countered Erluc. "After all, you recited my entire title for me." He looked down directly at the dwarf, "I made you a promise, and I never break my promises." He grimaced as he said the words, and both Renidos and Kera averted their eyes. Now he was a liar and an oath-breaker.

Damzar turned to Renidos, who looked too tired to pay attention. "You have my condolences upon the loss of your friend." Renidos winced, and Kera shook her head. "He died fighting the Ras'horra, did he not?"

Running a hand through his hair, Erluc nodded. "He was trying to save a prisoner, and the dragon attacked him while he was alone."

The dwarf slowly nodded. "I *am* impressed that you got away alive. As psychotic as Enyë is, he's no fool. Surviving a trap laid by the elf king is no small feat." His eyes betrayed a sense of melancholic memories, long in the past. "I have learned a great deal about Enyë in the years of the Great War, but I still can't believe that he is Queen Araíyal's son."

"Why not?" questioned Kera.

The dwarf continued, nodding tentatively. "I didn't know Queen Araíyal well, but I did meet her on occasion. When she was assassinated, it was certainly an extremely dark day for the Mortal Realms." He paced back and forth, speaking faster and faster as he continued. "Then, when the Twilight Council received Enyë's proclamation of war on Horgenn, the elf accused our king of murdering the queen."

Renidos snorted, shaking his head. "That's how succession works. And it makes sense that he'd be enraged upon the assassination of his own mother."

"I learned long ago never to underestimate the elves of House Arythwë, however psychotic they might be. Skilled magicians, the lot of them. I've no doubt that Alydris himself could have defeated the Ras'horra." Renidos thought to question the significance of the information he was receiving, but he didn't want to interrupt the dwarf. Luckily, Erluc had the same feeling.

"Well then, it's too bad he's not here," muttered Erluc, just as Horgenn wandered back into the chamber, humming a cheerful tune. "And besides, I think you have more pressing issues at hand."

Holding the dwarf in place, Kera led him back to his throne. As he took a seat, Horgenn groaned, repeatedly poking his thumb into his cheek as if he were bored. "I'll say," she agreed in frustration.

588 ♦ The Promise of the Warrior

"I don't mean any offense," started Renidos hesitantly, "but surely the king cannot rule in the state he's in." To emphasize, Horgenn lifted up one of the loose strands of Kera's dark hair, before she slapped his hand away.

Erluc nodded in agreement. "He must have appointed a successor or named an heir."

"He did," remarked the dwarf wryly. "Prince Halthar was the king's heir, and he was one of the first casualties we faced during the attack." Erluc groaned, and Renidos buried his head in his hands. Damzar found himself a chair, sighing as he eased into it.

"Wait a minute." Kera raised an eyebrow, turning to Horgenn, who seemed to be rather put off by the fact that she had not let him touch her hair. "He just said 'princes', didn't he?"

Damzar nodded. "Prince Huvar is currently in Varthagos with Queen Hirella. I've sent word to them about the attack, and they should be back here within the fortnight." Even as he said the words, he remained deep in thought, and the others looked at one another in surprise.

"So, then the problem's solved, isn't it?" asked Renidos tentatively. "Huvar ascends to the throne, at least until we fix Horgenn."

"If only it were that easy," replied Damzar, shaking his head. "The prince is far too young and far too inexperienced to govern our kind, especially in times of war. Maybe with another hundred years of training and the counsel of a dozen seasoned advisors, he could succeed his father, but he simply does not know enough to rule as king."

"A hundred years?" Renidos eyes widened, but the dwarf retained his solemn expression. "Well, how old is he?"

"Prince Huvar turned forty-seven this year," informed the dwarves. "When Horgenn succeeded his father, he was one hundred and sixty-two, and even he was met with the elders' disapproval."

Erluc shook his head in bewilderment. "What about the queen?"

Damzar looked up, the pain clearly visible on his face. "Aye, Queen Hirella is knowledgeable, and would even make a good queen. Unfortunately, as per our tradition, only those with the blood of the royal family in their veins can sit on the throne. And since both Horgenn and Huvar are still alive, the people would never accept Hirella as a ruling queen."

"What does that leave you with?" asked Kera weakly.

"Well, until we manage to find a way to make him remember who he is, Horgenn won't be much help in this situation," concluded Damzar. "But he is still king and has been for a millennium. If we tell the people that he has fallen now, there will be utter chaos. Better yet, if the elves manage to catch the drift of what happened here, they will push harder than ever before, capitalizing on our weakness."

Renidos raised an eyebrow. "How are you going to keep his condition a secret from your own people? They'd be able to recognize something is wrong with their king when he starts bowing down in front of the first person he sees."

"I can try to keep him in isolation for as long as possible, using Prince Halthar's passing as an excuse," tried the dwarf. "Between Queen Hirella and myself, we should be able to govern my kind relatively effectively."

Erluc ran a hand through his hair. "That could work, but it won't be long before people start to suspect something is wrong."

"Which is why you should start forming a plan to cure Horgenn," agreed Damzar. "But first, I suppose all of you should get some sleep. You're no use to anyone like this."

Rolling his eyes, Erluc rose, turning to his friends. "Well, someone had to say it," agreed Renidos. "He's right. We've been fighting an undead dragon for the past two days—I think that merits a few hours of rest." Erluc turned to Kera, who nodded, tucking her hair behind her ear.

"I could use a bath," she finished. "A nice, warm bath."

Erluc sighed. Here they were, talking about relaxing, while their friends suffered. Rose was comatose, Horgenn had lost his mind, and Asten was gone. Hundreds of dwarves were dead. He'd failed them. He'd failed them all.

Damzar barked a command, and the two guards re-entered the room, standing at attention for the commander. "If you would follow them, they'll show you back to your rooms," he informed. "We'll speak again tomorrow morning, when you've regained your strength."

"And how exactly are we supposed to know when it's morning?" inquired Kera. "I don't see any windows, and we're inside a mountain."

The dwarf took a moment to consider this. "I'll have someone wake you," he decided finally. Renidos nodded, and both he and Kera started following the dwarves out of the chamber, just as they looked back to see that Erluc was lost in thought.

"Erluc?" called Kera, and he turned to them, nodding.

Turning to Damzar, he extended a hand. "Commander." The dwarf met his hand, and they shook once, before Erluc followed the guards out the door.

"Oh, one more thing," added the dwarf, and they turned back to glance at him. "I just recently fought alongside the General of the Twilight Legion during the Battle of Karnas Alegon—stout man, extremely loud. Do you know of him?"

Looking to Renidos, Erluc gritted his teeth. "Therglas. Yes, we've met a few times; I'm not exactly a fan."

"No, I wouldn't think so," agreed Damzar with a grim smile. "When news of Elandas' passing reached us, some of my men did overhear talk of him being Elandas' successor."

Erluc grimaced, shaking his head. "You can rest assured that the highest rank the general will achieve is the one that he currently possesses. Our kingdom is a lot like your own in that respect—only children of House Laethon may sit on the throne of Inthyl."

"That's good to hear." The dwarf nodded. "He's a fair swordsman, but a little quick to anger. The last thing Eärnendor needs right now is another impulsive king."

Of all the people in Aenor, Erluc would probably be the most enraged if Therglas was chosen to rule. "Don't worry. We'll make sure that Horgenn is his former self again. We'll restore all the rightful kings and queens to their thrones, as we promised."

And he would. Even if it was the last thing that he did.

Chapter 35

THE PROMISE

AGMERN, KRE'NAG MOUNTAINS
Erluc

Yawning, Erluc cleared his hair from his face as he sat up on his bed. *Why did I have to wake up?* Over on his right, Renidos was putting on a new tunic, his hair still wet from his bath.

"Gold really is your color."

Smiling, Renidos turned around to face the older boy. "Look who's finally up," he noticed. "I bet you're glad that you got some rest now, aren't you?"

Ignoring the question, Erluc rubbed his eyes, trying to make the world come back into focus. "What time did you wake?" he asked, and Renidos shrugged.

"I actually don't know," he admitted. "But a dwarf woke me up not too long ago. He tried waking you too, but it obviously didn't go too well."

"Mmm." Erluc nodded, groggily stepping off of the bed. "Kera?"

Renidos' head became a blur as he shook it vigorously, spraying droplets of water in every direction. "I haven't seen her yet, but she's still in her room. Probably getting dressed." Erluc tugged on his tunic lightly, before a cloud of dust was kicked up around him, and he reappeared a few feet away.

"So, what do you think about him?" questioned Erluc. "Damzar, I mean. New clothes, private chambers, total freedom—he's definitely got this hospitality thing down." He scratched his forehead, glancing up at his friend. "Do you think it's for real?"

Taking a moment to consider, Renidos nodded. "He seems like a pretty nice guy to me. And unless he gives us sufficient reason to think otherwise, I think we should trust him."

"Even after what happened with Enyë?"

Renidos shrugged. "The dwarves are allies of Aenor. The elves aren't." He paused, the corners of his mouth curving upwards. "And hey, if I'm wrong and they *are* planning to betray us, you can feel free to kill him."

"Seems fair," agreed Erluc, finally getting out of bed. "Where'd you get the clothes?"

Renidos indicated a smaller wooden door leading out of the main chamber, which was left half-open. "They're folded in the corner by the bath." Wiping the rest of the water out of his hair, he set the soaking towel over a stone chair. "You can just leave your old clothes in there. The dwarf said that he'd have them cleaned."

Erluc nodded, lazily ducking down as he entered the adjoined room, pulling the door closed behind him. The majority of the room was taken up by the bath, which was definitely still hot. In the corner of the room, fresh tunic and slacks were folded neatly, just as Renidos said they would be. Next to them, his belt and sword were hung up on the wall.

He took his time, relishing the feel of the warm water against his skin. Almost twenty minutes later, Renidos knocked on the door. "We'll have to meet Damzar again soon, so you need to finish up soon." Erluc shrugged; he wouldn't be too much longer. "You didn't go back to sleep in there, did you?"

"If only," muttered Erluc. "Actually, I think I'm going to try that."

Renidos snorted. "Very funny." There was a short silence, and Erluc sighed. He drowsily got out of the bath, reaching out for the dry towel on the ground.

Before he grasped the fabric, though, Telaris' hilt shot into his hand, causing him to stumble back in shock. His ankle caught against the side of the bath, and he tumbled into the water, sending waves cascading around the chamber. As he regained his footing, Erluc frowned. *What in the world?* He tossed the blade to the side, slowly reaching for the towel again. That had never happened before. *Weird.*

Wiping himself dry, he quickly put on the golden tunic, slacks, and cloak. He strapped his belt on too, hesitantly picking up Telaris, sheathing the blade with utmost caution.

As he exited the room, he saw Renidos sitting on the bed, turning over a polished rock in his hand. "What happened in there?" he asked. "Did you jump into the bath?"

"Not exactly," said Erluc, and he explained what had happened with Telaris.

Renidos shrugged. "That's pretty strange," he agreed, inspecting the ornate sheath. He handed it back to Erluc with a sigh. "I tried to check on Kera, but she's still in her room." Buckling Telaris to his belt, Erluc followed him out of their room, to the door at the opposite end of the hall.

"Is it locked?" questioned Erluc.

"No, but you don't just go into people's rooms without their consent—especially if they're super-powerful princesses."

Erluc rolled his eyes. "Come on," he said, pushing the door open and revealing the room behind. It looked a lot like their own, except there were dozens of books and scriptures littered all over the unused bed. He swept his eyes around the room, and in the corner, Kera had seated herself atop her coiled tail. She had a book in her hand, her eyes scanning the pages with difficulty. Erluc grinned. "Well, it looks like you've had an eventful night."

Looking up from the book, her face brightened, and she uncoiled her tail as she landed back on the ground. "I figured I'd brush up on my Larranti while I had the chance." She'd also worn the fresh clothes that they were wearing, and her hair was still wet from what Erluc suspected was an extremely long bath.

"And how's that going?" questioned Renidos.

She shrugged, making a face. "It's as hard as I remember, and I'm a little out of touch. But the structure is fairly similar to that of Kyesti, so I'm not completely clueless." She indicated the bathroom. "Anyway, it was nice to get to breathe without having to rely on my scepter for a while."

Just then, a female dwarf tentatively entered the room, stopping in her tracks when she saw them. She seemed relieved that they were all there, and immediately began to speak hurriedly in Larranti. Erluc and Renidos looked at each other with the same expression, in complete ignorance to what the dwarf was saying. She spoke quickly with Kera, before the princess replied in short, turning to the others. "Damzar's summoned us."

Grimacing, Erluc uncomfortably ran a hand through his hair. "And then there's that too," he muttered. "I *did* promise him that we'd find a way to cure Horgenn."

"I think you actually may have a serious problem." Renidos rolled his eyes. "It's as though with every person you meet, you promise to do something for them."

"What?" Erluc frowned. "Come on," he chided. "He seems like a good person, and it was our fault that all those dwarves died fighting the ghost dragon."

Grinning, Kera nodded. "Hold on, Renidos might have a point," she agreed. "Rose, my father, Alisthír, Damzar, and even Adúnareth himself." She shook her head, amused. "You've promised everyone something or the other at some point." Erluc took a moment to go through the list, his face falling once he realized that she was absolutely right.

Joining in, Renidos could barely hold back a chuckle. "And each time, your promise has somehow gotten us into trouble," he declared. "Maybe you ought to stop making promises from now on." Though they were clearly just pulling his leg, none of them could help but recognize a grain of truth in everything they said.

Erluc scowled, obviously not enjoying his friends' observation. "*Maybe* we should focus on the task at hand," he proposed. Just then, the same dwarf reappeared, calling for them to follow her once more. "And it's not every person."

Without ceasing his grumbling, he led them out of the chamber, following the dwarf through the same series of tunnels that they'd passed through the previous day. But this time they passed Horgenn's chambers, which were sealed by a thick, stone door and patrolled by two armed guards.

Erluc nodded at one of them, and they grunted in unison. *Not too friendly, then.* The dwarf finally turned into a large, thicker tunnel, and Renidos squinted to see where they were being led. They could see a faint, white light in the distance, widening with every step they took.

Finally, they walked up a short staircase, before the dwarf stopped. In front of them, there was a thick wooden door, and one more bearded dwarf stood guard outside.

"Rheva," said the dwarf, looking up to meet Erluc's eyes. "Tacshir shi zefren wa."

"He wants you to leave Telaris outside," Kera explained. As Erluc unbuckled the sheath and set it against the wall, the dwarf nodded.

"Leifa," he proclaimed, directing them inside through the doors. Kera nodded, and the boys reluctantly followed her through.

The doors led to a balcony of sorts, and Erluc winced as he was faced with sunlight once more, blinking his eyes open. As he finally regained his sight, he gasped.

From where they were standing, they could see the icecaps of the neighboring mountains above them, the fresh winds blowing the morning breeze across their faces. They could only just see the sun peeking over the mountainous curtain in front of them, but the heat energized Erluc. "It's beautiful," he breathed.

"Yes, I thought you might appreciate stepping outside or a while," declared Damzar, and they turned to look at the dwarf. He was seated at a small, stone table, sipping a dark-brown liquid from a goblet. "Elandas, too, enjoyed the view from here, as did his father before him." He dismissed the female dwarf who had led them here, and she bowed before him before scurrying out of the door.

Kera wished Damzar a good morning, and he invited them to sit beside him. "This is one of the only parts of Agmern that was kept untarnished from the Ras'horra, which makes it all the more precious to us now."

"Will Horgenn not be joining us today?" questioned Renidos.

"At least until the queen and prince arrive, I've decided that it would be better to keep the king away from the public." Damzar raised a hand, and a young dwarf whom Erluc hadn't noticed earlier advanced towards the table with a pitcher in his hand.

The dwarfling filled Damzar's chalice to the brim before he turned to Erluc. "I actually don't partake," decided Erluc, and Renidos almost laughed. *This whole situation is my fault, isn't it? If I hadn't gotten so carried away that day, I might've been able to save Rose from the dart.* He wouldn't be making another mistake—not until he'd made up for his last one.

"Are you sure? Our ale is renowned all around Eärnendor," reminded Damzar. "Or it was before everyone started warring with one another."

Erluc grimaced. "Perhaps under happier circumstances, then."

"I'll hold you to it." Damzar nodded before turning to the steward. He spoke quickly, and the boy nodded curtly, filling both Renidos' and Kera's goblets to the brim. Renidos looked like he wanted to protest, uncomfortable with drinking while he was still not of age, and he shot Erluc a pained look.

Taking a moment to consider, Erluc looked down at the goblet. His own father hadn't exactly been strict about the consumption of alcohol, as was the custom in Sering, and both Asten and Erluc had started drinking as adolescents.

The princess took a sip of the ale, turning to the commander. "Don't take this the wrong way, but after what happened with the ghost dragon, your people are going to need a leader. Someone to rally them together and explain the situation."

"Aye," agreed Erluc. "And after all the casualties you've suffered, you'll have to fight doubly hard against the elves, who must have, no doubt, heard of what happened here."

Damzar calmly took a deep sip from his goblet. "I've sent out a message to all the lords of our cities across the Kre'nagan, complete with Horgenn's signature and seal. They will supply at least a hundred warriors each, which should more than make up for the lives we lost in the attack." He turned to Erluc. "The only thing that remains is the matter of Horgenn—the king was a formidable warrior and inspired our soldiers like no other. Without his presence out in the field, our chances of surviving the next year of this war are minimal."

Erluc grimaced, wishing he hadn't denied the drink. "We're working on a way to get him back."

"I've trusted you with my plan," reminded Damzar. "I'm rather keen to hear yours." He surveyed the three of them, who were trying their best to improvise a solution to the situation. "If you have indeed found a cure for the king's condition, then I will help you in any way that I can to retrieve it."

"Well, we could always just use the Heart," offered Kera. "If we can use it to cure Roxanna, why not Horgenn?" As she said the words, Erluc saw Damzar flinch again. This time, he wasn't going to let it go unnoticed.

"What?" Erluc raised an eyebrow. "Do you know something about the Heart?"

Damzar looked from Erluc, to Renidos, to Kera, and he sighed. "Nothing that will prove any help to any of us." He took another sip from his glass. "Besides, I'm not the right person to say anything about such a topic."

"What do you mean?" questioned Renidos. "Who *is* the right person?"

"Let me guess… Horgs?" interrupted Erluc, rolling his eyes when Damzar nodded curtly. "Fabulous."

Renidos shook his head. "Anyway, we haven't lost anything. This just means that we have to return to Morentyx Hrashann for the Heart."

"And how will you retrieve it?" challenged Damzar. "As far as I recall, your powers—those of the Trinity—were insufficient to fight the Ras'horra," he concluded firmly, turning away. "Not to mention that you've lost one of your companions."

"It doesn't matter," whispered Erluc, looking up to meet their gazes. "We set out to do this, and I won't stop until it's done." He ran a hand through his hair. "Besides, we're not the same as when we walked into the Vortex of Spirits for the first time. Something happened to us when we touched the Heart of the Moon. I felt it." He turned to Renidos, who nodded.

"He's right," agreed the Spectre. "I didn't think much of it at first, but something *did* happen. I'm much, much faster than I was before we went to the Archanios. When I run, it's as though the world around me is sort of… warping. And down in the canyon, I could see clearly even without the fire."

Damzar shook his head and drained his goblet in one long draft. "Forgive me for saying so, but I don't think that the Ras'horra will be defeated by heightened eyesight."

"No, I suppose not," concurred Erluc, standing up. "But I *did* have something else in mind." He extended an arm out towards the door, focusing. Damzar watched him intently, setting his empty glass down, and a shout of fear came from just outside the balcony.

A moment later, the doors burst open, Telaris shooting out and into Erluc's hand, flames instantly running along the length of its blade as he grasped the hilt.

Marveling in wonder, a small spark appeared in Damzar's eyes. Finally, Erluc stopped the torrent of fire, slowly sheathing the sword as he took his seat.

"That—" Damzar set his goblet down on the table, talking nervously. "That would certainly help." He shook his head. "And the Heart is responsible for this?"

Renidos shrugged, brushed his shirt. "We don't know why it happened, really. But when I touched the Heart, I felt an unnatural surge of power. It's possible that our strength may have been multiplied, and our abilities seem to have enhanced."

"This is promising news, indeed." Damzar nodded. "But do you think you'll be able to survive another fight with the Ras'horra, even with these new powers?"

Erluc shook his head. "There's only one way to find out," he declared. "And besides, I've sworn too many oaths to back out of this now."

Nodding, Kera took another sip from her goblet. "And we're with you till the end."

"All of us," put in Renidos, and Erluc uncomfortably ran a hand through his hair. Part of him wished that the Heart of the Moon could save Asten, but the other half of him dismissed the idea completely. *He's gone.* And they couldn't bring him back, but they could complete his mission, and uphold his legacy. They could avenge him.

Erluc nodded. "We will fly for Morentyx Hrashann, and we will retrieve the Heart of the Moon, come what may," he declared. "By the time the queen and prince arrive, Horgenn will be cured."

"Well, then I suppose a toast is in order," declared Damzar. He barked another command, and his steward scurried out to them, hastily approaching the table. He carefully skirted around Kera, and the princess did her best to hide her annoyance.

Filling everyone's goblets to the brim, the steward quickly exited the room, and Damzar raised his glass to the clear, beautiful day. "In such times of loss and hardship, I take it as a sign that the Falcon brought us face-to-face. And although the difficulties that lie ahead are sure to be more perilous than those we have ever faced before, we will keep fighting for what we believe in, with the promise of peace for tomorrow."

"And even here, far from home, whatever we have lost is made up for by our united strength," continued Kera. "By the strength of each other's swords, may we be triumphant against the ultimate enemy."

Renidos nodded. "For our friends and family, who gave their lives so that we could be here today, and those who have protected and guided us to this point. Let us honor their memories and fulfill their goals, as well as our own."

They all turned to Erluc, but he couldn't bring himself to say anything. He'd lost everything—Rose, Asten, the Heart, his pride, and his will to continue living the parasitic dream that his life had become. Slowly closing his eyes, he stepped away from the table without another word, unsheathing Telaris calmly. Kera and Renidos looked at each other uncertainly, before indicating for Damzar to continue.

The dwarf nodded grimly. "For your success and the well-being of those who cannot protect themselves." Everyone brought their cups together, and Erluc extended Telaris' tip above them, careful not to impale any of them. "For the Trinity—may your swords never dull, and may your spears pierce even the skin of a dragon."

"For our friends," adapted Renidos, which both Damzar and Kera echoed. Their goblets touched together, and three of them drank, while Erluc stared absently into the distance.

He turned, looking out to the tranquil expanse of hills surrounding them. The mountains above them were pure and sun-kissed, both heat and cold perfectly matching one another. There wasn't a cloud in the sky, and the light blue stretched to the corners of his sight. From here, the world looked different, so clear, so straightforward. He'd been running for so long, not bothering to look around even once.

This is what the sky should look like.

He closed his eyes, trying to savor the sight. One day, when all this was done, they would return here. Rose and him. It would take a lot of convincing, but he always knew what to say to her. And when she would finally agree, she probably wouldn't fancy the cold too much, but then she could always bring her jacket. They'd bring lots of beer and whiskey, and that would keep them warm for a while. When they ran out of those, he could light a fire with Telaris. And they could stay there all through the day before night finally came. He could play the strings, and she could laugh every time he'd make a mistake.

He felt a tear starting to gather in the corner of his eye. He'd made a promise to save Rose, and he'd dedicated himself to it completely. But in his haste to claim the Heart of the Moon, he'd allowed his best friend to face a dragon alone. And Asten had paid the price for *his* mistake.

Blinking the tear away, he shook his head. After he'd cured Rose, he'd go back to the Vortex of Spirits, and he'd drive his sword through the ghost dragon's good eye. Then he'd do the same to Enyë and Vyrnaur and anyone else who'd ever dared to hurt anyone he cared about.

He sighed, and he could feel his face burning against the cold weather. His dream was just that—a dream. Nothing more, nothing less. It could never come true, not anymore.

Erluc felt a hand on his shoulder, and he turned to see Kera beside him. "You'll get her back," she assured softly, handing him a goblet. He tried to refuse it, but she cut him off. "It's water. I thought you could use some."

Thanking her with a nod, he took the goblet from her, sipping it lightly. "Sometimes, I wonder what would have happened if we'd never met." He didn't mention her name, but Kera knew that he was talking about Rose. "She would be alive and well, and Elandas might not even have been killed. We would never have set foot in that foul prison, and Asten would have been with us right now."

"You know that's not what he would have wanted," remarked Renidos, hastily sipping from the goblet in his other hand as he approached. "You can't just erase her from your life—not after this. He would have sacrificed his life if it meant you could be with Rose."

"I know," admitted Erluc. "And I'd have switched places with him without a second thought."

Nodding, Renidos kept his eyes fixed on the mountains. "I know the feeling," was all he said, and Erluc knew that he was referring to his mother. He'd failed to protect her, just as they'd failed to protect Asten. Erluc could only imagine how Renidos must have been feeling.

Just then, a dwarf burst out of the castle towards them, and a loud horn blasted once above them, causing the mountains to cry out with it.

"What's happening?" questioned Renidos, as Damzar listened to the messenger dwarf.

Gritting his teeth, he turned back to them. "We're under attack," he informed them. "The elves have started to rally near Karnas Brekkis—they must have heard about the rampage of the Ras'horra."

Erluc grimaced. "We can fight," he offered.

Nodding his head, Renidos whistled a shrill note, the sound echoing all around them. A second passed, and a fierce growl sounded from down below. Frostbite landed on the balcony with a *thump*, and the dwarves still on the terrace retreated slowly.

"No," decided Damzar immediately. "No, our fortresses in the Kre'nagan are almost impregnable. We'll be able to repel anything short of—well, a dragon." He shook his head. "Unless Enyë himself is leading the charge, we can withstand it." With a flick of his hand, he barked a command, and all the soldiers on the balcony rushed inside, including the messenger. "My forces need me on the battlefield," he informed. "I know this is a sensitive time for us all, but we mustn't act hastily. The three of you are going to need all of the rest you can get if you are to survive your next encounter with the Ras'horra."

"Very well." Erluc turned to the dwarf, understanding. "Good luck, Commander." Skyblaze landed behind him soundlessly, and he stroked the pegasus' mane softly. "And if this is goodbye, then you should know that it was an honor to meet you."

"Likewise, Erluc Turcaelion." Damzar nodded before wishing Kera and Renidos farewell and taking his leave.

"I know what you're thinking," said Renidos. "I'm dying to help too, but we're not going to be saving anyone unless we have time to heal." He paused, shifting uncomfortably. "And grieve."

Erluc grimaced, unable to meet the eyes of the younger boy. Instead, he looked to the skies that stretched northbound to the forest of the elves. To his left, Kera traced her finger against the stone in front of her. "And then what?" she wondered aloud, her voice wavering. "What do we do after that?"

The Spectre's eyes glinted in the morning sun, filled with fiery defiance. "We go back, and we fight."

"And if it isn't enough?"

A strong breeze pushed Erluc's hair back, howling in his ears as it passed by. "Then it's not enough," he delivered, his voice worryingly stable. "And we die." He smirked, running a hand through his hair. "After everything, it's not too hard to imagine." His voice was heavy and flat, lacking any recognizable flicker of life.

"What about Adúnareth? What about the prophecy?" asked Renidos, distraught.

"I don't know," responded Erluc blankly. "I don't think it matters. The only thing that does matter is the choice: whether or not to keep going. And as long as there's something for us to live for, we can't stop trying."

He clenched his fist, and his gemstone pulsed at his chest, a calm, harmonic energy flowing through his veins. They wouldn't fail this time—he could feel it. They would get the Heart and heal Horgenn. He would cure Rose, and he would avenge Asten. Even if he had to go into the Void and rip the Heart from Atanûkhor's claws, he'd do it.

I'll keep fighting and I'll leave everything behind if that's what it takes. His vision started to clear, and the steady, painful throbbing of his bruised muscles stopped for a moment. *But I won't ever give up. I promise.*

Looking up, Erluc could see the last star in the sky start to vanish, giving way for the day. With a deep breath, he watched patiently as the small, white light slowly dimmed out of existence, and he closed his eyes. *I'll do it for you, Asten.*